the mistake you crave

PIPER HALE

For Kyndal. I hope you find comfort in these pages and hear whispers of Dave's love for you in these words.

And also for Refe, who inspired Maddox's protectiveness in chapter 43. Thanks for being the best brother ever when my world was falling apart.

foreword

While I have tried to stay as true to the rules and realities of professional hockey as I can, I may change or adapt some things to better serve the story. Please also note that while the story takes place in actual towns and cities, the vast majority of the places and businesses described are fictional. My hope with doing this is that you won't be pulled out of the story if you read it five years from now. If the places and businesses are fictional, they can't change or disappear.

Ultimately, this is a work of fiction, and I hope it will provide a temporary escape from the real world. And a new book boyfriend to swoon over.

Happy reading!

one

MIRA

I HATE MOVING SO MUCH THAT I'D DO ALMOST anything to avoid reliving this torture. Bargain away my first-born child to some creepy faerie creature? Probably worth it. Sell my soul to the Devil himself? Eh, why not? It's all such a soul-sucking ordeal, I'm not sure I've got much of one left, anyway.

If you'd told past me that my boyfriend and I would only cohabitate for a few months before breaking up, I would have scoffed. If you'd gone on to tell me I'd be moving in with my older brother's best friend and team-mate, I'd have called you crazy.

But that's the funny thing about life, isn't it? It never works out the way we plan.

"You ever going to tell me exactly why you and Jared broke up?" My big brother Maddox asks as we load all my earthly belongings into a small moving truck. His dark brown hair is wet with sweat, dripping into his brown eyes and making him grimace. It's the first time he's helped me move, but my third time busting my back hauling boxes in as many months, and I'm over it already. That's why I'm grumpy. He's grumpy because he broke up with his sweet girlfriend, Isla, a few days ago.

"Gonna tell me why you and Isla broke up?"

He grunts. "Touché."

That's one of the nice things about my big brother. He cares, but he doesn't push. He's got his own complicated dating history. Though, I really thought he'd found *the one* in Isla.

I guess both of our pickers are broken. Not that I'm surprised. It seems to run in the family. My mom picked a real shithead too. He left us when I was only five years old. I barely remember him. Maddox was seven, so he has a few more memories of the guy than me.

When one of your parents leaves and you have to watch the other struggle to do everything alone, it leaves a mark. On how you view family, whether you want kids, and how you view love. My big brother never really wanted to fall in love.

Me? I'm a sucker for happily-ever-afters. I've always dreamed of finding a love that eclipses everything else in your life. The kind that romance writers go on and on about. The *I'll burn the world for you* stuff. Soulmates and fate and being fully seen and fully loved shit.

I hoped I'd found that with Jared, but after a few months of living together, it became clear he was *not* my soulmate. I was looking for a knight in shining armor. He was looking for a maid/mommy/living sex doll.

I'm sure as hell not telling any of that to my grumpy older brother. The last thing I need is for him to hunt Jared down and kick his ass. Maddox is having enough image problems right now. I don't need him getting kicked off the pro-hockey team he plays for because of a basement-dweller like my ex.

"That everything?" my brother asks as he follows me inside Jared's cute little house. A house I thought would be *my* cute little house for a lot longer than three measly months.

I survey the living room, making sure I haven't forgotten to pack any little knick-knacks or my favorite throws. The sad part is, I hadn't even fully unpacked by the time I realized Jared had duped me into thinking he could be marriage material. "Pretty sure, yeah."

A heavy arm lands on my shoulder, and I let myself lean into my brother for comfort. I left Minneapolis for Chicago because I wanted to create a life for myself outside of his shadow.

It's not easy growing up with a hockey god for an older brother. Especially when you don't have any particularly special skills of your own to make you stand out. It was nice living seven hours away for a while, but I've missed being in the same city as him. I suppose if one good thing has come out of all this, it's that we'll get to spend more time together now. And he'll get me free tickets to watch the Rogues play whenever I ask.

I grew up watching Maddox play hockey. It's just as much a part of my blood as it is his. Plus, the guys on his team are solid human beings. They're the kind of people who have your back no matter what.

Which is why I'll be living with one of them for the foreseeable future. At least, until I get situated and my website and branding business becomes more profitable. A couple of weeks ago, when I was visiting Maddy, I asked him and the guys if they knew of anyone looking for a roommate or who had a room to rent. I shouldn't have been surprised when Griffin Wright—Maddy's best friend and the Rogues' star left winger—offered to let me stay with him. Rent free.

"You sure you want to live with Wright? I love the guy, but I'm worried he'll drive you crazy. I did warn him to keep his hands to himself, though, so you shouldn't have to deal with that. He knows you're off-limits and that if he ever tries anything with you, I'll disown him in a second." Maddox rubs the back of his neck, and I resist the urge to roll my eyes at the protective older brother schtick. "You know you can always stay with me."

"I know," I reply sweetly. "But this will be fun." Plus, I'm still holding on to hope that Maddox will pull his grumpy head out of his ass and fix whatever went wrong with Isla. I don't want to have a shared wall with my brother if that happens.

There are some things siblings just shouldn't share.

"Fine. But you always have a place with me if you need it."

Feeling kinda squishy inside, I wrap my other arm around my brother's middle and give him a big hug. He may be only two years older than me, but when our dad left, he became extra protective. Our mom never made him feel like he had to step up and become a little parent or anything, but I believe some part of him still feels like it's his job to protect us both, since he's the only man in the family. "Thanks, Maddy-poo."

"Please don't call me that in front of my team," he says with a groan.

"I make no promises."

"You're a little shit sometimes, you know that, right, Mi-Mi?" Maddox rubs his knuckles over the top of my head, messing up my braid.

I squeal and shove him away. "Not the hair!"

He chuckles, enjoying the mess he's made of my long, brown tresses. The bastard's not even remotely threatened when I narrow my green eyes at him and purse the full lips I inherited from our sperm donor.

"All right. If this is everything, are you ready to head out?"

I nod, giving the place one last good look. It's not lost on me that I'm more annoyed than I am sad about things ending with Jared. Guess that tells me everything. Blowing out a breath, I say a silent goodbye before turning to Maddy. "I'm ready."

"Jared's not even going to see you off?" Maddox looks affronted by the fact, but I wouldn't be surprised if Maddy's just mad he won't get a chance to intimidate the guy. He loved doing that to my boyfriends. Especially since he's always been so much taller and broader than any of the guys I knew.

Hockey players are just built differently.

"Nope. And I'm glad. Really." I am glad that Jared hasn't shown his face. I said some things when I broke up with him that were pretty harsh. Even though it's taken me a bit to move out since then, Jared and I have done a solid job of avoiding one another. There's really nothing left to say to the guy I thought I loved, but who, as it turned out, only loved being taken care of.

"Okay, then. Let's hit the road. I want to get to Wright's place before dark." Maddox walks out of the house, and I follow, locking up one final time before tucking the keys under the welcome mat.

I give my brother another hug before he climbs into the U-Haul. We're driving separately so I can take my little old silver Toyota. I'm well prepared with iced coffee and water in the cupholders, and plenty of snacks on the passenger seat. It's only a seven-hour drive from the Chicago suburbs to Minneapolis, but boredom hunger is real.

When I turn the key in the ignition, my car sputters and whines. "Oh, come on. Seriously? Not today, Artax. Not. To. Day." I glare at the ignition while turning it again, and it finally sputters and starts. It probably wasn't the smartest idea to name my car after the horse that gets sucked into the Swamp of Sadness, but some movies stick with you. I don't know any kid who wasn't emotionally damaged by *The Neverending Story*. My mom must have been feeling particularly sadistic when she made us watch it.

Whatever. As long as Artax doesn't succumb to the sadness today, it'll be fine.

"You good?" Maddox rolls down the moving truck window and asks with a raised brow.

"Yep. Let's go." The last thing I need is for this stupid car to break down at the same time everything else in my life is crumbling.

As the miles accumulate, my mind wanders to my new roommate, Griffin. He's Maddox's best friend and the Rogues' first-line left winger. The guy is crazy talented and so much fun. He always makes me laugh, and he's never made me feel like I'm just Maddox's little sister. Griffin treats me like a friend, and I enjoy his company.

But living with him could be interesting. Because,

while Griffin is one of the nicest men I know, he's not the steadiest. As far as I can tell, hockey is the only thing he takes seriously. He loves to go out, drink, and have a good time. Then there's his reputation with women. If Maddy and the gossip blogs are to be believed, there's a steady stream of puck bunnies flowing through Griffin's bedroom. And almost no repeats.

Which could be awkward.

Who wants to be drinking their morning coffee, only to be greeted with some random chick's ass when they do their walk of shame?

I know it's Griff's place, but we're going to have to lay down some ground rules.

On the plus side, if I decide I need some rebound sex, I know he won't judge me for it.

My phone buzzes, and an incoming text pops up on my screen, momentarily obscuring my GPS directions.

GRIFFIN

Madds says you're on the road. I hope you like Chinese, because that's what I'm ordering for dinner. All the guys will be here to help unload your stuff. Drive safe, Little Gravesy. Or should I say, ROOMIE?

Grinning, I stop worrying about silly things like how I'll deal with Griffin's hookups. It'll be fine.

Besides, this is just temporary. Two friends sharing a space.

What's the worst that could happen?

two

GRIFFIN

Sex is the best way to unwind when you're stressed.

"Damn, girl." I flop onto my back, sweat beading along my body. My new friend, Bethany, giggles as she lies down beside me. Her perky little breasts bounce when her back hits the mattress. "I don't even need to work out after all that."

Bethany and I met at a bar last night when my teammate Logan and I hit the town. After a less-than-stellar start to the hockey season, dealing with Maddox's relationship problems—which involved some sleuthing on my part and minor threats against his girl's ex—I desperately needed a release.

Plus, Mira is moving in today, and I promised Madds I wouldn't bring an endless procession of bunnies home while she's staying here. If I had to curb my socializing for anyone but Mira, I'd be pissed. But my best friend's little sister is cool as hell, so I'll deal with it.

Doesn't mean I can't go out with a bang, though.

Or at least six bangs. But who's keeping count?

"Wanna order some food, and then we can go again?" Bethany asks. Her pretty, hooded brown eyes sparkle as she pushes the thick black fringe of her bangs off her forehead.

"Nah," I say. "We just had breakfast. We can order lunch later."

Bethany giggles. "It's almost dinnertime, silly."

What? No, it's not. Turning toward my alarm clock, I jolt out of bed, all traces of my previous exhaustion gone. The clock reads three-thirty.

Mira will be here by five.

"Ah, shit, Bethy-baby. We're going to have to call it quits. I lost track of time between your thighs."

An adorable blush colors Bethany's golden cheeks.

I love making women blush. There's something intoxicating about making a beautiful woman feel pretty or special or desired. I may be cursed when it comes to finding real love, but that doesn't mean I don't love appreciating the women I spend a night or two with. If they don't leave our encounter feeling better about themselves than they did before we started, I've fucked up. I figure it's the least I can offer, since they're soothing an ache in me. Both of us know this won't go anywhere, but that doesn't mean we can't connect on a cosmic level for the short time we have together.

"Are you sure?" Bethany rolls onto her side. She draws her thin lower lip between her teeth. "I don't have anything to do tonight."

"Sorry, but I do. My new roommate is moving in." I lean over and press a kiss to her abused lips. "Let me clean you up. I'll be right back."

Bethany hums, her eyes taking on a mischievous glint. "Is your new roommate as good-looking as you? Maybe he could join us."

A momentary image of me, Bethany the bunny, and Mira all tangled and naked in bed flashes in my mind's eye, and I have to remind my dick that Mira may be beautiful, but she's off-limits. Like, my best friend would chop off my dick, asphyxiate me with it, then bury my body in the woods kind of off-limits.

I shudder at the thought of losing my dick, but then I'm laughing. "Sorry, hot stuff, but I don't think *she* would be interested."

Bethany's lips pull into a pout. "Oh, I see. I've never done it with a woman, but it could be fun."

Nope, I remind my dick as I stride into my attached bathroom to wet a washcloth for Bethany. I'd offer to let her shower, but the little minx would probably try to turn it into sexy times, and I really need to get dressed before Mira and Maddox arrive. Plus, the guys are waiting for a text so they can come help unload the moving truck, and I need to put in a huge order of Chinese for delivery.

Sadly, I don't have time for a shower-blowie.

"As hot as that sounds, this is where our sexual journey comes to an end."

She pouts but doesn't protest. The women I sleep with know what they're getting. A night of mind-blowing sex with an attentive partner who will always make them come first, some laughs, and some conversation. It's well known that I don't do relationships. I'll make any woman feel like a goddess for a night, but that's as far as it goes. One night. Maybe two. I'm not as hardcore about time limits as my buddy and teammate Logan Byrne is. The dude is cynical as fuck and hates love. I don't.

I'm just cursed. Cursed to never find the real thing. Cursed to fall hard and fast, only to be left depressed, rejected, and alone before we can even celebrate our six-month anniversary. Then those women? The ones I'm madly in love with? They always find Mr. Right as soon as they dump me. Good for them, I guess? Crappy for me.

Relationships with me have an expiration date. So I might as well make sure they expire before I get my heart broken once again.

"I'd say to call me if you want," Bethany says as she climbs into the driver's seat of her little sports car, "but you won't, will you?"

"Sorry, gorgeous." I lean down and press a kiss to her cheek. "You're amazing and stunning and so much fun. And if a relationship was in the cards for me, I'd program your number into my phone in a heartbeat. But it's not."

She offers me a sad smile. "I understand. I hope that changes for you someday."

I'm silent as she closes her door and drives away. I've spent too many years hoping to find the woman who completes me. Hell, I've read a few hundred romance novels all about finding *the one,* so at least I can live vicariously through stories of others finding their match.

That's not meant for me, though. And no amount of hoping will change things.

"HEY, ROOMIE," I SAY AS I OPEN MIRA'S DOOR. I offer her my palm and tug her out of the car when she places her hand in mine. She looks exhausted. There are dark circles under her pretty moss-colored eyes, her long brown hair is falling out of her braid, and her full lips take a moment to curve into a smile.

"Hey, Griff." She doesn't pull back when I wrap her fit body in a hug. Just loops her arms around my middle and leans her cheek on my shoulder. Hugging her is nice. She's the perfect height.

Giving her a grin, I pull back and boop her on the nose because my dick is apparently still in sexy mode from earlier today, and that will *not* fly with Mira. Can't get a hard-on while hugging my best friend's little sister and my new roomie. Pretty sure that goes against the best friend code *and* the roommate code. "How was the drive, Lil' Gravesy?"

"Ugh." Her shoulders slump. "Long. Fine, though."

"How's Madds? Did you two leave at the same time?" I don't see the moving truck yet, but he can't be too far behind.

Mira rolls her big green eyes. "He's grumpy as hell. I tried to get him to tell me what happened with Isla, but he wouldn't talk."

Describing my best friend as *grumpy as hell* may be an understatement. The guy broke up with the love of his life not even a week ago, and he's wrecked. And he may not have told Mira what happened, but the doofus doesn't even know the full story himself. I do, though. Because unlike the big, dumb idiot, I actually talked to his lady love after he overheard her talking to her ex-fiancé.

It blows my mind. The guy found real love, and he just

walked away from it without fighting. But those two are meant to be. I know it, Mira knows it, and our best friends on the team, Logan Byrne and Sebastian Navarro, know it. I may have resigned myself to a life of shallow relationships, but I refuse to let Maddox do the same.

"Come on," I say to Mira, giving her wrist a tug. "Let's go on up so I can show you around, and I'll tell you what I found out when I went to talk to Isla myself."

Mira gapes at me. "You did what?"

"Your brother's my best friend. I hate seeing him miserable." I shrug, because it doesn't seem like a big deal. I did what any good friend would do. "You can help me figure out what to do about it. He's going to want to win her back. But for now, let's get you situated so you can rest."

I text the guys, telling them they can head over, as we walk into my building. It's a nice place in the heart of Minneapolis. There are restaurants and bars nearby, plenty of things to do and places to meet people. I have a sweet spot with lounge chairs and a grill on the roof—I call it *the backyard*—and the building has solid security. Which means I can relax and not worry about paparazzi or crazed fans showing up at my door. Not that I think it's likely, but people are weird about professional athletes.

And as much as I hate hurting anyone, there's always the possibility that a bunny will get it into her head that we're meant to be. If that happens, I have Ed as a first line of defense.

Mira and I stride across the dark marble floors of the lobby toward the security desk, where I introduce Mira to Ed. I make sure he and the other security guys know she's living here now and to look out for her.

"Welcome to the building, Miss Mira," Ed says with a wide smile. He's a cool guy. In his early fifties, retired military, and a huge Rogues fan. He and the other guards take extra care looking out for me because I make sure they get jerseys and a few tickets to our games each season. "Let us know if you ever need anything, okay?"

Mira returns Ed's smile and thanks him. Then we get in the elevator and I push the button for the top floor.

"Oooh, top floor," she teases. "Fancy."

"It's no fancier than your brother's," I say. But it is pretty posh. I'm the first-line left winger on a successful NHL team. And I've been playing long enough to have a cushy contract and plenty of endorsement deals. I don't blow my money on dumb stuff, so yeah, I own a nice apartment in a safe building. There's no point in buying a big old house in the suburbs when it's just me.

Mira whistles when I let her in. I try to look at my apartment through her eyes. Gleaming hardwood floors, huge walls of windows, and a large, open-plan living room that flows into a modern, tricked-out kitchen. I keep things tidy, and I had the place professionally decorated, so it doesn't look like some college bachelor pad.

"Wow, Griff. Do you ever use that kitchen?" Her eyes sparkle as she looks over her shoulder at me.

I shrug. "I dabble."

I actually love to cook. Since it's just me, I don't do it as often as I'd like, but I'm decent at it. Maybe with Mira here, I'll have an excuse to cook more often.

"Come on, let me show you your room."

Mira follows me down the hall. There are two doors across from each other. The door on the left is my bedroom, so I push the one on the right open and usher

her in with a flourish of my arm. She makes a little gasping sound when she takes it all in.

Madds told me she'd gotten rid of her bed when she moved in with her stupid ex-boyfriend, so I had my interior designer purchase bedroom furniture for her and paint the room a rich teal. It's got a modern bohemian vibe that I thought suited Mira perfectly. Besides the queen-sized bed and end tables, there's a desk in the corner where she can work on her business, a mustard-yellow velvet armchair, and an upholstered ottoman at the foot of the bed. A door on the far wall leads to her en-suite bathroom.

I may have gone a little overboard with the decorator because I'm not sure Mira's planning to live here long, but the room's been sitting empty and undecorated since I bought the place. Might as well make it into a room Mira's comfortable in.

"Holy shit, Griffin. Did you do all this?" She spins around, her mouth open as her attention darts from detail to detail.

"Nah. I paid someone to do it. I'm great on the ice but shit with decorating." I give her a wink when she focuses her attention on me.

"I don't even know what to say." Her voice comes out breathy and filled with emotion, and I have to tell my rogue dick to chill the fuck out because this is Maddox's sister and my friend. We can't be thinking about how she'd sound gasping my name at the height of an orgasm.

"Just say you like it, and I'll be happy," I reply honestly.

"I love it." Mira closes the distance between us and throws her arms around me in an enthusiastic hug. "Thanks, Wright."

"Don't mention it, Lil' Gravesy." I give her a squeeze, then pull away. "Let's go back down and start getting things out of your car. The guys should be here soon, and I doubt Maddox is too far away by now."

"You going to tell him about Isla?" Mira asks.

I nod. "Yep. Gotta set him straight."

"Good." Mira shoots me a dazzling smile, then saunters out of the room. My eyes go to her luscious ass as she walks away.

I adjust my dick in my jeans.

Apparently, I'm going to have to set my dick straight too.

three

MIRA

A KNOCK ON MY OPEN DOOR PULLS ME OUT OF MY head as I hang clothes in my closet. Turning, I see Griffin leaning against the frame in nothing but low-slung gray sweatpants with a mug in his hands.

"Hey. Thought you could use a break. And maybe some tea. It's mint."

Even though I'm so, *so* tired, a genuine smile curves my lips. "My favorite."

"I know." Griffin hands me the mug and watches as I blow on the steaming liquid before taking a tentative sip. "You've had a long day. D'you want to watch a movie or something?"

My phone shows the time is nine. I don't have everything unpacked, but I'm almost ready to drop. Still, my brain is too loud for sleep. Everything with Jared swirls around and around in my head, and I keep replaying things. Did I miss a parade of red flags, or was this truly out of the blue? People can be great actors, but it feels like I should have seen his behavior coming. "A movie sounds good."

"Come on then, Lil' Gravesy. I'll make some popcorn."

I follow Griffin down the hall and into his large, open living space. When he points at the couch, I don't protest, just sit my tired butt down. He can handle making popcorn by himself. "Have any chocolate?"

Griffin hums low in his throat. I track him as he moves around the kitchen. His defined athlete's muscles ripple and flex as he works. "Sorry, but no chocolate. Gotta keep to my meal plan, especially during the season."

I try to eat well. I run and do yoga regularly. But I'm not super careful about every last calorie I put into my mouth. Not the way Griffin and Maddox are. But I suppose they're professional athletes, so staying in shape is literally part of their job. "I'll keep my junk food stash in my room so you're not tempted."

He laughs at that, the rich tenor of the sound bouncing around the open space.

I've always found Griffin attractive. Who wouldn't admire a guy with shaggy golden hair that looks effortlessly messy, multi-hued hazel eyes that appear to change color, depending on the light, and full lips that are perpetually smiling? Add in tan skin, a strong, angular jaw, a straight nose that has somehow never been broken, and a six-foot-four frame honed into muscular perfection over years of strength training and hockey, and he's basically a walking wet dream. He looks just as ready to catch some waves as fly across the ice.

It's a good thing Griffin and I have such wildly different outlooks on love and relationships, or I'd have found myself in trouble a dozen times over since he and Maddox met. But Griffin doesn't do serious. And I don't do casual. So I'm free to admire him with no fear it will go further than that.

Though, living with him may test my restraint. Especially if he makes a habit of walking around shirtless. Because even if our goals in life aren't compatible and he's off-limits because he's my brother's best friend, I'm not dead. I have eyes. And Griffin Wright is objectively gorgeous.

"How're you holding up?" he asks, turning to face me once he's started the microwave. The soft sizzle of oil as it heats provides a dull background noise. Hazel eyes sweep over my features, and whatever he sees has a little line forming between his eyebrows.

"I'm fine." And I am. Mostly. Living in the same house with Jared for a few weeks after we'd broken up did a pretty good job of curing my heartache. It helps that I concluded I'd never really loved Jared. He just seemed to tick all the boxes.

Responsible? *Check.*

Good job? *Check.*

Reliable? *Check.*

Similar goals for the future? *Check.*

I suppose it should have rung some alarm bells that my friends were never Jared's biggest fans. And sure, he was more affectionate when we were alone than when his friends were around. But that's normal, right? I could overlook all of that if he met the real requirements.

He had to be the kind of man who wouldn't abandon me. Someone steady, serious, and reliable. Someone completely the opposite of my sperm donor.

Unfortunately, he ended up being a serious ass with a steadily decreasing desire to pretend he was some great guy.

You can only maintain a mask for so long when you live with someone.

Once the interval between popping kernels slows, Griffin takes the now-inflated bag out while I shake myself from my thoughts. I go back to watching him as he moves around the kitchen. He grabs a large bowl from a cabinet, pours the popcorn out of the bag, and lightly salts it. Then he palms two water bottles and makes his way over.

"What do your friends think about you moving here?" The couch dips as Griffin sits beside me, leaving just enough space to set the bowl of popcorn between us.

My friends. I shake my head. "Honestly, we sort of drifted apart. I'm not sure any of them care all that much."

Drifting apart is probably the wrong way to describe what happened. It's more like I threw myself into a relationship I thought would be long term and let Jared take up all my time outside of work. I put too much stock in his opinions. Acquiesced when he whined about spending time with my friends instead of his.

Tale as old as time. Girl meets boy. Girl loses all sense of self. Boy takes advantage. Girl ends up alone.

Again.

I paste a tight smile on my face when I notice Griffin studying me. Like he can see through all my bullshit and straight down to my soul.

But then his serious expression morphs into a blinding smile and he boops my nose. Again. "Well, you've got us, now."

"Yeah," I say with a chuckle. "I've got a bunch of big, sweaty hockey players."

"And Isla."

"Hopefully. What if they don't get back together?" I hate even voicing it out loud. My brother's girlfriend is amazing. Sweet, fun, and she totally puts Maddox in his place. Part of me expected him to propose and for Isla to become my sister. A built-in best friend guaranteed to stick around.

Griffin waves a dismissive hand in the air. "They will. I have a plan."

That piques my curiosity. Griffin is way more invested in Maddox and Isla getting back together than I thought he'd be. "Do I get to hear this plan?"

"Not yet." He flashes me another of his disarming smiles. "Still working out the kinks. But you'll be a part of it, don't worry."

"Oh, yeah?"

He nods. His shaggy golden hair flops around atop his head. "Someone will have to sit with her at the hockey game so she doesn't run away."

"Right." I laugh. "Well, of course, you can count me in."

"Good. Now what movie should we watch? A rom-com?"

"No." I may not be all that cut up about things ending with Jared, but I'm still disappointed that my dreams of finding love came tumbling down once more. "Horror movie?"

"Slasher or suspense?"

Easy question. "Suspense. I hate all the gore of slasher flicks."

"Fair enough." Griffin turns on the TV and begins searching. We land on one neither of us has seen and snuggle in to watch. It's good—and plenty scary—but I'm tired enough that my eyes grow heavy and little shivers make me tremble.

"Do you want me to turn this off so you can go to bed?" Griffin murmurs.

I force myself to sit up a bit and blink owlishly at him. "No, I'm good." I dig into the popcorn bowl and bring a few salty kernels to my lips.

Griffin chuckles. "If you say so." He doesn't try to convince me to go to bed, but he does grab a throw blanket from a basket in the corner, which he drapes over my chilly form. "Let's at least make sure you're warm."

I catch maybe another fifteen minutes of the movie before I lose the fight with my eyelids. The TV is dark when Griffin gives me a gentle shake. He must have finished it.

"Come on, Lil' Gravesy. This couch is great, but it's not as comfortable as your bed." He laughs when I groan. "Need me to carry you?"

"No," I grumble. He lets me struggle with the blanket for a few minutes, his chest shaking with silent laughter, before strong, calloused hands engulf mine and pull me to my feet.

"Never thought I'd see the day when Mira Graves was as grumpy as her brother."

"Shut up," I say as he leads me toward my bedroom. There's no heat behind the words, and he knows it, which makes him laugh out loud this time.

"So grumpy." Griffin pauses at my bedroom door,

watching me. Probably to make sure I don't trip on a box and face-plant on the floor.

If that were to happen, I'd just stay there, I'm so tired.

"Good night, Griffy."

His smile blooms into something way too radiant for this time of night. I make a mental note to use the nickname again.

"Night, Gravesy." His hazel eyes meet mine and linger for a few seconds before he shakes his head, turns around, and softly pulls the door closed. I'm shuffling toward the attached bathroom when I hear him shout, "Sure hope you don't snore!"

I giggle.

Moving in with my brother's best friend may have been one of my more impulsive decisions, but I think it'll work out just fine. Maybe it'll be fun to live with a guy when there are no romantic feelings involved.

As long as he doesn't leave the toilet seat up.

four

GRIFFIN

"There he is!" Maddox slaps my back hard, his face lit up with a smile. My best friend has been in a much better mood since winning his girl back a few days ago. We're out at a club, celebrating them.

"Hey, man." I pull him into a hug and grin at Isla. She watches us with a soft, affectionate expression. I reach out a hand and motion for her to get in on the lovefest. "Get in here, Teach. We need a group hug."

Isla chuckles, but jumps right in. Maddox and I smoosh her between us, and her chuckles turn into full-blown laughter. "You guys are suffocating me!"

"All right, all right." Mira grabs my arm and tugs me back. "Don't suffocate my friend. I just got her back." My roomie sticks her tongue out at me. Little shit.

"First round's on me," Sebastian says to the cheers of our group. A smiling server follows behind him with a full tray of beers balanced on her palm. Her blue eyes find me and do a slow inspection of my body.

"Looks like someone's checking you out." Mira waggles her dark eyebrows. She looks beautiful tonight. I may be her roommate, but I'm not dead. Even if I can't act on anything with her, I will always notice a beautiful woman. Her dark hair is curled and sleek, smoky shadow and pink blush accentuating her green eyes. And the dress Mira's wearing?

Fuck. Me. The skintight, slinky black number hugs every single one of her perfect curves. Objectively speaking. Her curves are objectively perfect. Anyone would agree.

My dick has been straining at my zipper since the moment she sauntered out of her room in that little getup. Which is inconvenient, because Madds will kick my ass if he notices I have a stiffy for his little sister.

"Huh?"

Mira giggles. "The waitress, Griffy. She's checking you out. She's pretty."

"Is she?" I shrug. "Didn't notice." And I didn't. Which is weird.

Logan slaps me on the back. "How the hell didn't you notice? That woman is stunning." His gray eyes make a sweep of her body as he smooths his dark-blond hair away from his face.

"You should talk to her, then." It's not like I called *dibs* or anything. Besides, you can't *dibs* a human being.

"You sure?" Logan squints, his attention pinging between me and Mira. Whatever he's thinking, he needs to stop. There's nothing going on with the two of us. Nothing at all. And nothing ever will happen. Because she's my roommate. And my best friend's little sister. And I don't want to die or have my balls chopped off.

I'm kinda attached to them.

"Yeah, man. I just want to hang out with everyone. I'm not looking to hook up tonight."

"Suit yourself." Logan shrugs. And when the blonde server walks away, he follows her. I have no doubt he'll take her home when her shift is over.

"Who wants to dance?" Mira grabs hold of Isla's hand and drags her onto the floor. The guys and I share a look before following them. There's no way Maddox is letting Isla out of his sight tonight. Not after everything he went through to get her back. And when some scrawny guy with a patchy beard starts making his way over to dance with the ladies, Madds levels him with an impressive glare.

We dance as a group—even Byrne, after he gets the server's number—drinking and laughing together. I haven't had this much fun in a while. Between my guys and Mira and Isla, I'm completely at ease. I don't have to pretend or be on my game or do anything other than be myself.

Maybe there's something to be said for going out and not trying to pick up women. Because I don't care if I'm dancing like an idiot, and neither do any of the people I'm with. I'm not trying to woo anyone or charm them into my bed. It's freeing. And when women do approach our group and try to dance with me or Bash or Byrne, I choose to ignore them.

"I'm having so much fun," Mira shouts in my ear as we all jump up and down to an energetic song with a driving beat. The dark hair around her temples is slick with sweat, and her cheeks are flushed. She glances at her brother and Isla, who have their arms wrapped around each other as they sway and grind to the beat. "It's so good to see them back together."

"It is," I agree. I have to lean in close to be heard, and the scent of her jasmine perfume hits me square in the chest. Why does she have to smell so good? "They belong together."

"Totally," she shouts with a huge smile. Mira fans herself with her hands. "I need a drink. I'm so hot."

"I can go with you."

She pats my chest and grins. "You don't have to do that. I'm a big girl, Griffy. I'll be right back."

And before I can protest, she slips through the crowd and heads for the bar. I watch her the whole way. Just to make sure no assholes try to grope her ass or anything. Because I look out for all of my female friends when we're out. Especially at places like this.

"You good?" Sebastian asks. His head cocks to the side as he studies me.

"Yeah, man. I'm good."

"How's living with Mira going?"

Does he really want to have this conversation in the middle of a club? It's a little loud for a heart-to-heart. "It's good. She's cool. Honestly, it's been fun having a room-mate again."

Bash nods, but he doesn't say anything. Just kinda stares at me.

"What?" I ask him.

"You sure you can handle this?" His attention goes to Mira. She's at the bar now, and some suit with a five o'clock shadow has his hand on the small of her back as he leans in to say something. Mira throws her head back and laughs.

My stomach flips, and I scowl. "Handle what?" I ask Bash with a little more bite than I intend.

"Living with a beautiful woman you've always been attracted to."

I tear my eyes away from Mira and the suit so I can glare at my friend. "I'm not attracted to Mira."

Navarro's lips twitch as he raises one dark eyebrow. "Oh, no?"

"No."

"Then why do you look like you want to punch the guy talking to her?"

I *do* want to punch the guy. It's unnerving. And stupid. Mira's my friend, and she is definitely not interested in me that way. She's always been fun and a bit flirty, but she's done nothing to make me believe she sees me as anything other than her brother's best friend. I have no claim on her, and no right to judge who she flirts with or hooks up with.

God, the thought of her hooking up with the asshole in the suit makes my stomach turn. What the hell? If I didn't know any better, I'd think I was jealous. Which I'm not. At all.

"Just looking out for my friend," I tell Sebastian. "Her ex was a dipshit, and business bro over there looks like a dipshit too. I don't want her getting hurt again, that's all."

"Is it?" Sebastian watches me. "Or are you afraid to admit to yourself that you like her?"

"I don't."

He lifts one shoulder. "Wouldn't blame you if you did. She's a cool chick. Not to mention, beautiful."

"She's Maddox's sister," I say, stating the obvious. He knows what I mean. She's off-limits.

"I know. But if you really liked her and weren't only trying to get in her pants, I don't think Madds would be as pissed as you assume."

Sebastian has always been the levelheaded one of our group. He's like a big brother, or maybe even the team dad. Lots of guys go to him for advice, and normally, he's spot on. But not with this. Because Madds *would* be pissed. And even if I did like her that way, I'm cursed. All I'd do is ruin our friendship and pave the way for Mr. Right to sweep Mira off her feet when things between us fizzled out. And for some reason, that thought fills me with all sorts of rage.

"I'm not trying to get in her pants, and I don't like her beyond friendship." I clap Bash on the shoulder. "You're way off base on this one."

The suit still has his hand on Mira's lower back. She's facing him now, and they're smiling and flirting with each other. My grip on Sebastian's shoulder tightens.

"Sure." His shoulders shake as he chuckles. "Sorry for saying anything. I'm obviously wrong. You don't feel anything for Mira. Nothing at all."

"I don't." Dropping my hand from his shoulders, I try to sound casual when I say, "I'm thirsty. Want another beer?"

"Why not?" His eyes dance with mirth. The fucker's laughter follows me all the way to the bar.

I push through the crowd, so I end up right next to Mira and the suit, and drape my arm around her shoulder. "Hey Lil' Gravesy. Thought you got lost." I motion to the bartender and call out my order.

Mira rolls her eyes and shrugs off my arm. "I told you, Griffy. I'm a big girl."

That, she is. And I'm being an ass, I know I am. Doesn't stop me from sticking out my hand and staring suit guy down, though. "Hey, man. I'm Griffin."

Although the suit looks confused, he's been socially conditioned to return a shake when offered, so he clasps my hand. He squeezes harder than he needs to, probably thinking I'll do the same, but I don't need a strength contest to know who has the bigger dick.

Obviously, it's me.

Turning back to Mira, I grin brightly. "Everyone was worried you got lost or something. Come back and dance with us."

She narrows her eyes at me. "Right. I'm sure they were so worried." But she must not be that into the suit, because she sighs and turns her attention his way. "It was nice to meet you, but I'm here with my friends, so I'm going to head back there."

Suit guy's brow furrows, even as he plasters on a smile. "No worries. Can I get your number?"

I'm about to drag her away before she can offer it, but Mira surprises me. "I don't think so. You seem nice and all, but I just moved back to town and got out of a relationship. I'm not really looking to hook up with anyone right now."

The guy's smile slips. "Oh, uh, sure. Maybe if we run into each other again."

That won't happen.

"Right. Sure. Maybe then." Mira lifts her beer in a little salute, then I grab her hand and lead her back across the dance floor toward our friends. She rolls her eyes but doesn't protest. "You're a clit block, you know that, right?"

"Me? No way. Just helping you find your way back to the group." Luckily, she's behind me enough that she doesn't see my lips twitching.

"Sure. Whatever you say, Griffin. You're just lucky I wasn't really interested in that guy."

I knew she wasn't. "What was his name, anyway?"

She laughs at that. "You know what? I wasn't even paying attention when he said it. I was calling him Mr. Fancy in my head because of his suit."

I throw my head back and laugh as we dodge dancing couples and spilling drinks. "I was calling him The Suit in mine. Seriously, who wears a suit to a club like this?"

All her feigned annoyance forgotten Mira wrinkles her nose. "Right? Totally weird."

We start dancing again, and I completely ignore the knowing look Navarro throws my way.

five

MIRA

Griffin and I slip into an easy routine, and three months fly by in a blink. Although he's gone a lot with practice and games, when he's home, we spend a lot of time hanging out. Part of me thought we'd sort of coexist, but he's gone out of his way to make me feel welcome and included. I no longer think of him as my brother's friend. I think of him as mine.

Which is one reason I'm so excited for tonight. Because I love cheering on my friends. That, and we're in Las Vegas. And compared to the sub-zero temperatures of Minneapolis at the end of January, the almost sixty-degree evening here feels utterly balmy.

"I love going to away games," Isla says with a bright smile. Her long, red hair shines under the bright lights that are so quintessentially Vegas. Her blue eyes scan the crowd of fans, most of them decked out in the gold and brown of the Scorpions. We occasionally catch a flash of gold and gray jerseys with Rogues' logos on them, but they're few and far between. "No one recognizes me here."

A few months ago, Griffin helped my brother put together a plan to win Isla back. It was the most romantic thing, but it was very public, and between the team's social media manager and fans with phones, Maddox and Isla have become something of a local spectacle. But they're back together, so that's all that matters. My brother has the love of his life back, and I have my friend.

Hopefully, soon to be my sister. Isla doesn't know it yet, but Maddox has plans for her after tonight's game. The kind of plans that involve sparkly diamond rings. It's a struggle to keep my face in check because if I beam at her like an idiot, she'll know something is up.

I only wish Ryder Hanson's girlfriend could have come with us. Lexi Cross is awesome, and the three of us have become fast friends. It still blows my mind that her dad was the head coach for the Rogues. Until he got sacked for being a deeply disgusting misogynist who called his daughter all sorts of vile names at a game where the whole thing was caught on camera. It was super traumatic for her, but the rookie won us all over when he stood up for Lexi without caring about what happened to his career.

Talk about romantic.

We make our way to our seats three rows up from the boards, both of us in our Graves jerseys. It's convenient to share a name with one of the star players. And I grin like an idiot when I realize Isla may share that name soon too.

Shortly after we find our seats, the announcer introduces both teams as they hit the ice for warm-ups. The crowd *boos* the Rogues, but the guys don't even notice. It's just the nature of the beast. Hockey fans are rabid and vocal, and shit-talking is part of the game for both players and fans. The guys all wave when they notice us. Maddox does that cute thing where he puts his hand over his heart when he sees Isla, and Griffin gives us both a wink.

Isla and I have become a regular fixture at their games since she and Maddox got back together. At least, the home games. This is my first time traveling to an away series. But it's Vegas and a special occasion.

Honestly, though? I love to travel. I could get used to jet-setting for games.

We watch the guys warm up, both of us snickering at the giggles and wide-eyed stares of the women around us as they watch the players stretch their hip flexors. I can't really blame them—it does look a bit scandalous.

"Holy crap," a young woman a few seats over says, fanning her rosy cheeks. "It looks like they're fucking the ice."

Isla and I share a look, then burst out laughing. Some-how, Griffin hears it, and when he catches my gaze, he lifts one dark blond eyebrow in question. I roll my eyes and shrug.

Isla studies me curiously. "How's living with him going?"

"Good. He's actually a great roommate. He doesn't leave messes everywhere, he likes to cook, and we have a lot of fun." Ironic, that the man I thought might behave like an overgrown child has proven to be a million times more self-sufficient than Jared ever was.

Isla hums. "It must be annoying when he brings a new conquest home every night."

"He hasn't brought a single woman home," I tell her. "At least, not that I've seen."

My friend's blue eyes widen. "Seriously? Not one?"

"Nope. I know everyone loves to talk about how easy Griffin is, but that hasn't been my experience. Are you sure that's not the guys over-exaggerating? He can't be that much of a manwhore." I grin. "And I mean that in the most affectionate way."

Isa shakes her head. "Um, no. They're not exaggerating. At one point, he genuinely considered screwing a sixty-year-old teacher at my school because she's some kinky dominatrix."

"Oh." That has my nose crinkling. "I thought that was just the guys being dicks. Whenever he doesn't have a game, he's usually hanging out with me. We watch movies or play board games or get coffee."

The way Isla studies me, I feel like a specimen under a microscope. Her hair falls in a curtain over her shoulder when she turns to look at Griffin, who's completely oblivious to being the subject of our conversation. He's too busy running drills with the rest of the Rogues. "Hmm."

"Hmm what?"

"Nothing, it's just…" Isla narrows her eyes at Griffin, as if she can see through him with X-ray vision or something. "It's just unexpected."

GRIFFIN

"You want to go out and pick up some lovely ladies with me after we celebrate tonight?" Logan Byrne, the right wing to my left and my good friend, asks with a waggle of his eyebrows. Our goalie, Sebastian Navarro, shakes his head, but if Logan notices, he doesn't acknowledge it.

Bash has never been one for our promiscuous ways. I used to think he was a stick in the mud, but now I'm not so sure. Maybe he's on to something. Maybe there's something to be said for watching and waiting for something real. I know Mira and I aren't together or anything—and we can't be, or Madds will kick my ass—but it's been nice sharing my space with her. Really nice. We've become great friends, and I feel lighter when she's around. I don't have to put on a show for Mira like I do the women I hook up with. It's refreshing. And it's taken some of the shine out of sleeping my way around the U.S.

"I don't think so, man. Why don't we all go out and hit a club together? It's been a while since we did something as a group." I slap a puck into the net, then another, and another from the pile in front of us. "Besides, we'll want to celebrate Madds and Isla's engagement."

"Don't jinx it," my best friend says.

Bash chuckles. "There's no way she'll say no. She's just as in love with you as you are with her."

"I'm excited for you, man, I really am," Logan says. "But it feels like the end of an era. One of us is getting engaged." He shudders like death breathed down his neck. Theatrical bastard. He turns to me before firing off a shot. "At least I'll still have my wingman."

"Right." I don't bother voicing my growing discontent with the shallow way Logan and I connect with women. I know a real relationship isn't in the cards for me and Mira won't be staying at my place forever, so there's no use working him up. Besides, this is the longest I've gone without enjoying a woman's body, and I'm not sure how long my hand will cut it.

As soon as warm-ups end, we cut the bullshit and play like beasts. Not only are we at the top of the leaderboard in the Central division and determined to stay there, but we need to give Maddox a reason to suggest we all go out and celebrate. For the proposal, he rented out an entire pod of the High Roller, which is a mix between a Ferris wheel and an observation wheel. But instead of cars, they're big spherical rooms with bench seating.

It's an intense game. The Scorpions are determined to eke out a win after their loss last night. But we're more determined. The arena fills with *boos* every time we score, but even over the roar of Scorpion fans, I can make out the cheers of Mira and Isla. Maddox isn't the only one whose gaze is drawn their way throughout the game. Mira rolls her eyes when the refs make a bad call, screams at the Scorpions when they slam one of us against the boards, and cheers her heart out when we score a goal. She also makes goofy faces at me whenever she catches me looking their way.

Logan shouts at me to get my head in the game more than once, but whatever. Mira has become one of my closest friends in the last few months, and I like seeing her happy like this. It's not that deep.

As the game ends with a Rogues win, we're all flying high. Another win closer to the cup, and we've ensured Maddox has an excuse to suggest we celebrate on the Strip tonight.

My best friend is getting engaged.

It makes me feel old as hell.

I may also be just the tiniest bit jealous. But that's crazy, right?

Right.

six

GRIFFIN

"To the future Mr. and Mrs. Graves," I shout over the din of the club, drink raised.

"To Maddox and Isla," our friends agree. The clink of glasses punctuates a night none of us will forget.

My best friend is engaged to the redheaded teacher who stole his heart.

I totally called it the first time I saw them together.

Mira pulls Isla in for yet another hug and squeals, "I can't wait until we're sisters!"

The women do a happy dance and start talking at hyper-speed about wedding dresses, venues, and what kind of cake is best. I'm thrilled for my friends. They deserve every happiness, and I'm so glad they found each other. I'm sure whatever wedding they plan will be beautiful. Though I still think my earlier suggestion of eloping—because we're in Vegas and there are 24-hour chapels everywhere—was solid. They could be married right now. But hey, it's their lives.

Our drinks are gone in record time, and we order a second round for the table. I'm feeling loose and happy, and I'm not the only one.

"Let's get out on the floor and dance," Mira shouts.

Her brother scowls. "Can't we just relax with a drink for now, Mi-Mi?"

"Oh, come on," she says, unperturbed. "Are you really going to sit here like a bump on a log, instead of getting out there and dancing with your future wife?"

Isla peers up at Maddox with a hopeful expression and bats her eyelashes at him a few times. And that's all it takes.

"Fine," he grumbles. "But if anyone grinds against you, I'm kicking their ass."

That earns a giggle from Isla, and I grin when he leads her onto the dance floor. A pretty little brunette with dark golden skin catches Logan's eye. She nibbles at her bottom lip, offers him a smile, and I know that is the last we'll see of Byrne for the night. The woman whispers something to her equally beautiful blonde friend, who eyes Bash up like he's her next meal.

"Come on, Navarro." Logan tugs Bash to his feet. "None of that priest shit tonight. We're in Vegas. And you know what they say about Vegas."

Sebastian sighs, resigned to his fate. "Don't waste your money on the slot machines?"

Logan laughs as he drags Bash toward the women.

"And then there were two." Mira levels me with one of those smiles I've grown to look forward to. The kind that lights up the whole room. She stands and extends her hand, palm up. "Wanna dance, Griffy?"

"Hell, yeah."

Mira leads me onto the floor with swaying hips and a bounce in her step. She doesn't even notice the appreciative stares from just about every guy we pass. Not that she ever seems to. I've watched guys on the team try—and fail—to flirt with Mira. But she rarely catches on to the fact that they want her. I can't tell if it's because she's oblivious, she's just not interested in dating, or she doesn't understand how beautiful she is. She's made a few comments about her ex in the months we've been living together, but I still don't know the entire story. It's possible he messed with her head enough that she has given up on men. At least temporarily.

I hope I never meet the guy, because I'd rather not get arrested for assault. It doesn't matter if he didn't do anything terrible, like raise a hand to Mira or break her down emotionally like Isla's ex did to her. The simple fact of the matter is that Mira's ex was a douche, and that's all I need to know.

Only once we're in the middle of the dance floor does Mira stop. She turns to me with an effervescent smile and begins to move her body. She's sexy as hell as she sways her hips and undulates to the driving house beats blaring through the club's speakers.

Shit. I cannot be thinking things like that about my best friend's little sister.

I've held myself pretty well in check in the months she's been living with me. Of course, I've acknowledged that my roommate is beautiful. And sure, I've had to fight a few stiffies when she does yoga in the living room in nothing but tight little shorts and a sports bra. I'm not dead. But even watching Mira practice yoga has nothing on feeling her tight little body grinding against me in a skimpy black dress.

Pure. Fucking. Torture.

Still, I keep my hands from blurring the lines between friends and fuck buddies. The last thing I want to do is screw up the friendship we're building.

"You're a good dancer," Mira shouts over the music. Her skin glows with the finest sheen of sweat.

"And you're surprised?" I let my palms rest lightly on her hips as we move in sync with one another.

She shakes out her sweaty, dark hair and grins. "Maybe a little."

"Baby," I tease, "I've got moves you've never seen before."

"Show me!"

I do. I don't care who sees or who may take a video of my ridiculousness. I bust out moves from the lawnmower to the shopping cart to make Mira laugh. And laugh, she does. When I add some hip thrusts to the shopping cart, she nearly loses it.

"Oh my god. You're terrible." Mira shakes with laughter as she fans her face. "Truly awful."

"What? I'm amazing." When Mira keeps fanning her face, I lean in and shout, "Do you need another drink? Maybe a water?"

"Water is for the weak. I want a mojito." She waggles her eyebrows at me and licks her lips. She's ridiculous. And she probably does need some water, but I'll make sure she has some after our next round of drinks.

"Stay right here. I'll be back in a minute." I notice

Maddox and Isla dancing a few feet away and signal Madds to look out for his sister. He gives me a nod, then I push through the crowd toward the bar. I lose sight of Mira while I wait for our drinks, but I can see Maddox's giant head over most of the crowd, so I head back in that direction. It's difficult not to spill the drinks in the sea of writhing bodies, but I somehow make it back to where I left Mira with two full glasses. Except, Mira is no longer alone.

"What the fuck?" I growl under my breath. Two guys have their hands all over her as they dance way too close to my roommate. Close enough that I'm sure she can feel the outline of at least one of their dicks, if not both.

I catch Maddox's eye, and his expression darkens when he sees the dudes grinding on his sister. At least I'm not the only one pissed by this. Madds is looking out for his sister, and I'm looking out for my friend. That's all this is.

Pushing through the people dancing between us, I use my hockey skills and hip-check one douchebag away from Mira. He glowers at me, but when he realizes I have a solid six inches of height and at least fifty pounds of muscle on him, he backs away.

Good choice, I mouth. He narrows his eyes but keeps his mouth shut.

Douche number two is harder to shake, so I press against Mira's back and shout that I'm back with her drink. She spins around with a smile, and just like that, douche number two is forgotten. He tries to grind against Mira a few more times, but when I shoot him a dirty look and she continues to ignore him, he finally gives up.

"This is so good," Mira shouts as she gulps her drink. I

warn her to slow down, but she either doesn't hear me or chooses to ignore my words.

Screw it. When in Vegas.

I toss back my drink and set our empty glasses on a passing server's tray.

A new song comes on, and Mira squeals. "I love this one!" She throws her arms around my neck, and her body sways against mine. As she dances, she gets closer and closer until one of my knees is between her thighs and my hands grip her hips to keep her from losing her balance and toppling over.

Isla and Maddox move closer to us, and we all dance together. And if Maddox notices how little space there is between his sister's body and mine, he doesn't say. He's too lost in his fiancée.

We get another round of drinks, then Logan flags us down. He's got the little brunette under his arm. Sebastian stands near the blonde, but they don't look as cozy. No doubt, the poor guy is trying to figure out how he can get out of sleeping with her.

"We're getting out of here. See you guys at the hotel tomorrow morning."

"Be safe," Isla calls after them. Logan just waves a dismissive hand in the air. She rolls her glassy eyes and then turns to us. "Another round?"

Maddox hums. "I don't know, Short-Stack. You sure you're not done for the night?"

"One more," Isla says with a pout. Of course, Maddox caves. He's a sucker for a pouty lower lip and the woman he loves. Maybe it's the alcohol, or maybe it's my secret romantic heart, but watching them makes me feel all gooey inside. A sweet kind of gooey. Not the sex kind of gooey. They're perfect together, and I couldn't be happier that Maddox pulled his head out of his ass and begged his woman for a second chance.

If I was in Maddox's shoes, I'd never let a woman like Isla slip away in the first place.

But all's well that ends well, I suppose.

The four of us down another round of drinks. What is that? Three? Four? Whatever it is, I'm feeling good. And if I'm feeling good, I know Isla and Mira have got to be well on their way to being totally drunk, if they're not already there. When Isla stumbles for the tenth time, Maddox pulls her into his arms and tells her it's time to call it a night.

"You two heading back now?" he asks Mira and me. I'm set to say yes, but Mira has other plans.

"No way. I'm having too much fun. Stay out with me, Griffy?" She flutters her eyelashes at me in a move that's probably meant to be sexy, but she's a little too drunk to pull it off. It ends up looking like she's got something stuck in her eye.

It's cute as hell.

"Okay, well, don't stay out too late," Maddox tells his sister. Then he turns to me. "I'm trusting you to keep her safe and not do anything stupid."

I roll my eyes because, duh. Of course, I'll keep her safe. Yeah, she's his sister, but she's my roommate, and more importantly, she's my friend. I'd never let anything happen to her. "You don't have to worry. We'll be good."

Madds gives us a nod and then carries a sleepy-looking Isla out of the club. It's kind of hilarious watching the crowd part for the big grump.

"Let's get one more round before we get back on the

floor," Mira says. Her eyes are glassy, and she's got this perpetual goofy grin on her face. She's definitely drunk, and I'm damn close. I should probably cool my jets.

"I don't know, Lil' Gravesy. Don't you think you've had enough?"

Mira gasps in faux outrage. "Excuse me, mister, but I am on vacation in Vegas. I haven't had enough until I'm seeing double."

Oh boy. Nope. We're not getting that drunk. That idea has *disaster* written all over it.

"One more round," I relent.

Her smile grows. "Then, I get to pick the drinks."

"Fine." I'll probably regret it, but she's having so much fun, I'm loath to tell her no.

"Yay!" Mira claps her hands and goes to the bar. When she returns, she's got a fruity drink in one hand and a double shot of something that smells like lighter fluid in the other. She holds the double shot out to me with a wicked grin. "Bottom's up, Griffin."

The alcohol burns going down, and I have a fleeting thought that I've made a mistake.

We dance for another twenty minutes, but Mira's covered in sweat and I'm getting sick and tired of the limp-dick dude-bros trying to invade her space. "Want to walk around the Strip?" I shout.

Her green eyes light up at the suggestion. "Hell, yeah! Let's go see that big fountain that squirts along with music."

I have to close my eyes for a minute at her drunken word choice and tell my dick that she's not asking us to make her squirt. "Not sure that's the right term, Mir."

"Eh. Potato, potahto." And with that, she grabs my hand and tugs me out of the club.

As soon as the cool night air hits my overheated skin, I sigh deeply. I hadn't realized how sweltering it was in there. I'm glad we're here in January rather than the height of summer. Spending so much time on the ice throughout my life has made me a huge baby when it comes to the heat. I don't know how people live in places like this year-round.

"Come on, I think the fountain's this way." I don't realize Mira is still holding my hand until she uses it to tug me down the sidewalk. We dodge tourists and street performers, stopping a few times to take selfies with them. Mira is particularly excited to see a somewhat convincing Lady GaGa impersonator, and I buckle over with laughter, holding my stomach, when Mira belts out an insanely out of tune rendition of "Bad Romance."

By the time we make it to the fountain, we're both giggling and swaying slightly. We may have had a few too many rounds at the club, but we're not the only inebriated people out tonight. I'm pretty sure the couple next to us is drunk off their asses. How do I know?

The guy nearly topples over onto his butt when he tries to get down on one knee to propose to his girl, and she hiccups through her rambling acceptance.

"Look at them," Mira says, her head cocked to the side and her eyes all glassy. "They're so in love. Everybody's in love." Her pretty face scrunches up in a frown.

"What's wrong?" I slur. The world spins a little as she turns and peers up at me.

"I thought I was gonna marry Jared."

Huh. I don't know why I hate those words so much, but I do. "Really?"

She nods her head emphatically. "Mmm-hmm. Thought he ticked all the boxes, and I'm not getting any younger and he was okay in bed, so that was good, you know?"

He was okay in bed? Glowing praise.

"I wanna get married." Mira blinks those big jade eyes at me. "I don't want to end up alone, like my mom."

Mira end up alone? The idea is ludicrous. She's smart, driven, and sexy as hell. A bunch of my teammates drool after her every time she comes to a game. The only reason none of them have gone past subtle flirting is because she ignores them—and because Maddox has promised a broken hand to anyone stupid enough to lay a finger on his little sister.

And a broken dick if they're dumb enough to go there.

"You won't end up alone," I reassure her. Since she's no longer paying attention to the fountain, I lace our fingers together, so we don't get separated in the crowd, and lead her down the Strip. We don't have a destination in mind. We simply wander. She *oohs* and *ahhs* over the lights and architecture, but it's a little white chapel with a neon sign that has her stopping in her tracks.

"Ohmygod, it's so cute," she gushes, holding a hand to her heart. "I wonder if this is one of the chapels where you can have an Elvis marry you?" A giggle slips out of her parted lips.

"I tried to convince Maddox and Isla to get married at one of these tonight," I tell her.

She giggles again. "I know, silly. I was there."

"Oh. Right." We both stare at the white chapel, swaying slightly. "Wanna see if they do tours?"

"Tours?" Mira scrunches up her nose. "That place is tiny. What would we tour?"

I shrug. "Wanna see if they have an Elvis?"

"Yes," she says, clapping her hands. That idea has her excited.

"Do you think he'll be a young Elvis or an old Elvis?" Young Elvis really knew how to make the ladies go crazy for him. Old Elvis liked weird-ass sandwiches that give me heartburn just thinking about them. I hope it's a young Elvis.

"I don't know." Mira leans forward a bit, narrowing her eyes like she might develop X-ray vision if she tries hard enough. It's adorable.

I tug her toward the chapel's front door. "Let's find out."

We only stumble twice on our walk up to the little white building, but it has us giggling like idiots.

Mira shushes me as I open the door. "Shhh. People might be getting *married* in there." She smashes her finger against my lips.

I shut my mouth because she appears super serious, and I don't want to piss Mira off. The Graves siblings have a *temper* if you rub them the wrong way. She seems mollified when I nod, even though I almost burst out laughing again when her finger ends up in my left nostril because of the motion. We stagger inside, and a Dolly Parton lookalike gives us a megawatt smile.

"Well hey there, sugar dumplins. You two looking to get married tonight?"

Mira and I look at each other and break out into more giggles. Us? Get married? That would be crazy.

"Tell me," Mira says. "Does Elvis himself do the marrying?"

Dolly smiles. "Why, of course. There's nothing quite like being married by the King himself."

Maddox is such an idiot for passing this up.

"Is he an old Elvis or a young Elvis?" I ask.

Dolly throws back her head and laughs. "Young Elvis tonight, darlin'."

I turn wide eyes on Mira and bounce on the balls of my feet, because Young Elvis? Hell, yeah! That's what I'm talking about. "It's young Elvis, Mir. *Young Elvis!*"

"So, is that a yes?" Dolly asks. "We've got a few different packages I'd be happy to tell you about. But a beautiful couple like you? I'd recommend the Enchanted Graceland package."

"Enchanted Graceland? That sounds pretty," Mira says.

"Oh, honey, it is." Dolly waves us over to her little reception desk and flips open a brochure. "Let me tell you all about it."

seven

MIRA

Why is it so hot? And why can't I move? Where am I? Everything hurts and my mouth tastes like ass.

What the hell did I do last night?

My head is throbbing, so I obviously had too many drinks when we all went out. That much, at least, is clear. I vaguely remember Maddox carrying Isla out of the club when she started to fall asleep, but everything after that is hazy. Kind of like my mind right now.

Opening my eyes is harder than it should be. Number one, it hurts. Number two, my eyes feel like they're full of sand and grit. I blink a few times at the unfamiliar ceiling. The weight pressing against my stomach shifts, and every cell in my body freezes.

No wonder I'm hot. I'm not alone in this bed.

Don't panic, I tell myself. Except, now that my brain is coming online, I'm pretty sure I'm naked, and that is *definitely* a semi-hard dick pressed against my hip.

Oh god. *Oh god.* I have no memory of meeting a guy last night, which means I could look over and find myself sleeping next to some man who looks like the Crypt Keeper or believes the earth is flat. I don't get drunk often, because drunk Mira makes bad choices. Drunk Mira is not to be trusted.

A soft groan has my heart rate spiking, and even though I *really* don't want to look at the naked man snuggling against my equally naked body in his sleep, there's no way to avoid it.

"Don't be eighty years old," I whisper. Then I turn my head—and my heart stops beating.

Oh no. Oh, fucking shitballs. Curse you, drunk Mira. This is bad.

The naked body and the semi-hard dick pressing against me don't belong to a decrepit old man. They don't belong to some idiot who believes the earth is flat—at least, he better not. No, the golden skin, muscular thighs, washboard abs, and broad shoulders of the man beside me belong to someone I know very well.

Someone whose dick I should never feel pressed against my right thigh.

Someone whose dick will be ripped off by a very angry older brother if said older brother ever finds out about this.

Griffin's golden hair is an adorable mess. He looks peaceful and young with his features relaxed in sleep. And his dick. His dick feels huge.

Oh god. Nope. I cannot think about Griffin Wright's penis or how it feels pressed against me. And I definitely can't acknowledge the way heat is pooling low in my belly.

I need to get out of here. To extricate myself from his arms, find my clothes, and go back to my room before anyone realizes I'm missing. Except, it's not just Griffin's arm that's wrapped around my waist; he's also got one leg hooked around mine.

So stupid, Mira.

I slap my forehead and wince when something hard connects with my skin. What now? Bringing my left hand in front of my face, the world seems to slow as it tilts on its axis. My brain stutters, threatening to go offline.

This must be a dream. A really weird, alcohol-induced dream. I'll wake up any second now. And to help that along, I grab my cheek and pinch.

Motherfucker, that hurt. So, not a dream. Oh shit.

Oh. Shit.

This can't be happening. This can't be real. Because there's no way the plain gold band on my ring finger means what I think it means. Right?

My breathing picks up, and it becomes harder and harder to suck in a lungful of air. Panic is a maelstrom inside of me, swirling, tumultuous, and wild. I'm naked, in bed, *wearing an ugly wedding band*, with Griffin Wright. When his left hand twitches against my stomach, it takes every ounce of my resolve to lower my eyes to said hand. Maybe if he's not wearing a matching band, I just did some drunken jewelry shopping? Totally plausible. I'm sure that's it.

Except, when I look down at Griffin's long fingers splayed across my belly, that idea becomes much less likely. He's wearing a matching gold band. It's thicker than mine, but just as plain and ugly. So, either we both did some drunken jewelry shopping and both have absolutely garbage taste, or we...

Slamming my eyes shut, I try to deepen my breathing.

I'm getting lightheaded, and the nausea churning in my gut is no longer simply alcohol related.

What happened last night?

I try to recall anything, but all I get are little flashes of moments. Griffin and I walking hand-in-hand down the Strip. Going to the fountain. Dolly Parton?

Griffin shifts beside me, a soft, nonsensical murmur puffing out from between his full lips. Lips which, as he curls farther into me, end up pressed against my neck. Heat flares low in my belly, and when his hand slips down my stomach, the heat turns into a flame. As his fingers glide against my lower belly, which hollows out, I can't hold back a gasp.

"Mmm." Griffin's dick hardens against my hip and his face nuzzles my neck. It's like his body is waking up before his head. Well, his big head. The little one is wide awake and more than ready to start the day. His lips brush against my neck and his fingers flex, getting dangerously close to my pussy. If they slide a little farther down, he'll feel how wet I am right now.

Bad Mira. Now is not the time to be turned on. This is not a sexy situation. This is a disaster of epic proportions.

Kinda like Griffin's dick. The epic proportions, I mean. Because holy crap, that thing just keeps growing.

And then his long fingers do start to slip lower, and I let out a strangled squeak.

Griffin's body goes still. His muscles tense against me and his wandering hand halts its journey. When he pulls his face away from my neck, I feel an idiotic stab of loss.

"Mira?" His voice is gravelly and rough with sleep. Confusion laces his tone. I suck in a deep breath and turn to meet bleary hazel eyes struggling to focus on my face. "What are you doing in my bed?"

I squirm against him, acutely aware of my exposed breasts and the fact that the sheet covering our lower halves sits so low on my hips you can almost see my mound. The movement draws Griffin's attention from my face down to my body, and the multi-hued hazel of his eyes turns molten. I feel his perusal as if it was a physical caress. His eyes make hungry sweeps of my body, lingering on my peaked nipples and the rapid rise and fall of my chest, which makes my breasts bounce slightly. When they dip lower to find his hand flexed, half-covered by the sheet, inches away from my pussy, he lets out a strangled sound. As if he's finally registered the position we're in.

"Mira." His gaze jumps to mine. "Shit. I don't... I don't remember what happened last night. Did I... Did we...?"

"Have sex?" I try to smile, but it must come off as more of a grimace because Griffin takes his hand off my stomach like he's worried he's hurt me. He drags the sheet up my body to cover my breasts. Worry creases his brow, and I want to reach out and smooth my fingers over the lines. "Um, I'm not sure. I don't... I don't think so?"

He winces at that, studying my face, for what? "But we're naked. Are you sure? Oh god, Mira, I'm so fucking sorry, I—"

"Hey, I was involved in this situation too," I say quickly, needing to interrupt his panic. Whatever happened last night, it's not all on him. One thing I distinctly remember is talking him into drinking more alcohol when he was ready to call it quits. So really, if anyone's to blame for our current predicament, it's probably me. "But I'm pretty sure we did more than get naked."

Griffin's frown deepens. "What do you mean?"

"I mean..." I swallow and try to keep the maelstrom of nerves in my gut from making me puke all over my... husband.

Oh. God.

I take one deep breath, then another. My left hand shakes as I lift it in the air for him to see. "I think we..." I clear my throat when the words come out as a croak. "I think we got married."

GRIFFIN

I think we got married.

  I think we got married.

  I think we got married.

The words echo through my foggy, pounding skull again and again, but I can't seem to make sense of them. Nor can I make sense of the plain gold band clinging to Mira's ring finger. In what feels like an out-of-body experience, I lift my own left hand to find a wider matching gold band.

My ears ring.

"Griffin?" Mira's voice slices through the haze. She sounds panicked. Like she's ten seconds away from freaking the fuck out. I mean, join the club, but I hate the idea of Mira spiraling. It makes my chest ache.

"It's okay," I say, propping myself up on one elbow so I can look down at her. Mira stares up at me with wide, glassy green eyes. Like I have all the answers. She stares at me like I can fix this.

I have no fucking clue how to fix this. Not only have I potentially messed up my friendship with this woman who has become such an integral part of my life in three short months, but I also may have ruined my relationship with the best friend I've ever had. Because if Maddox finds out I married his little sister during a drunken bender in Vegas, he will kick my ass, then never speak to me again. Not to mention the fact that, even if we didn't have sex, I spent the night spooning her naked body with mine. A fact my dick seems pretty excited about, but he's a goddamn idiot.

Mira's not the only one panicking, though I do my best to keep the terror zinging through my body from showing on my face. Pressure isn't anything new. Every day on the ice, I'm faced with impossible shots and potentially dangerous hits.

I can figure this out. I can help her calm down.

"How is any of this okay?" she asks, clutching the sheet to her chest as she sits up. I sit up too and try not to focus on the naked expanse of her back and the swell of her perfect ass. "We're naked and wearing wedding rings, Griffin. *Wedding rings!*" Mira's voice pitches higher. "Can you remember getting married last night? Because I can't."

Rubbing my forehead, I try to recall the night before. I remember dancing with Mira, drinking a double shot of something that burned like hell going down, and then watching some guy drunkenly propose to his girl at the fountain. Then, somehow, we got to talking about Elvis? Everything else is a blur.

"I don't remember much from last night, if I'm honest," I tell her with a wince. Even that small movement makes my head pound and my stomach churn.

"Maddox is going to kill me." Her green eyes are full of

panic. "And I don't want to be the reason your friendship ends. How could I have been so reckless?" Mira's chest starts to heave and her breath comes out in shallow little puffs. The color drains from her pretty face as she grips her messy dark hair with her left hand and holds the sheet to her body with her right. "What do we do?"

Something cracks inside me at the sight of confident, fiery Mira looking so lost and scared. I hate it. I want to wipe the fear from her eyes.

"Hey." I angle my body toward hers and gently cup her cheeks. "Look at me, Mir. Look at me." She does as I say, though her chest still rises and falls too quickly. Her breathing is still too shallow. "Everything is going to be all right. We'll figure this out."

"Right." She nods her head, but I don't drop my hands. The rhythmic slide of my thumbs across her cheekbones seems to be calming. She sucks in a breath. "We can figure this out. This doesn't have to be the end of the world. People get drunkenly married in Vegas all the time, right? We just need to talk to a lawyer and get an annulment."

"Um, I'm not sure it'll be quite that simple," I say, glancing down at our naked bodies. "Doesn't, uh, consummating the marriage sorta make it legally binding? We can't be sure we didn't have sex."

It's the wrong thing to say. A deep red flush blooms along Mira's chest, up her neck, and across her cheeks. "Oh, my god. So we get a divorce, Wright. We pretend like this never happened, we tell *no one*, and we get a divorce. No one ever has to know that we were married for all of a week. We can pretend this epic fuckup never happened."

Something about Mira's words makes my chest squeeze painfully, and I drop one hand from her face to rub at my chest. Sure, neither of us made the decision to get married with a sound mind, but the way she says that no one has to know hurts. That this was an *epic fuckup*. I get that I'm not many people's idea of husband material. And I know that a large part of that is a problem of my own making. But I thought Mira saw through my bullshit. At least enough that she wouldn't be completely embarrassed to call me hers. No matter how temporarily. A memory of my college girlfriend, Carissa, assaults me.

"This can't be a surprise, Griffin. We've been having fun, but did you really think we'd get married? You're hot and sweet, but come on. You think you're going to play hockey for a living. I can't bring a guy like you home to my parents. They're doctors."

"Right," I say, my voice tight as I scan her face. "No one has to know."

Her expression shifts at my tone. "Griffin... Come on. It's not like you want to be married to me, either. This was a drunken mistake. We never would have done anything this stupid if we were sober."

Yeah, we were drunk, but hearing Mira call this a mistake rubs me wrong. Because what she's really saying is that *I'm* a mistake.

I'm always a mistake. Here for a good time and a great fuck, and nothing else. I'm not the guy you bring home to your parents. Not the guy you tell your brother about. Not the guy you risk anything for. I'm just a mistake. And that has my ire rising.

Which is why I open my mouth and say something truly unhinged.

"It wasn't a mistake."

Mira goes still, blinking slowly at me. "What?"

This is dumb. I know it's dumb. But the words have been said, I'm feeling hurt, and I dig in my heels without consciously deciding to.

"I'm not divorcing you, Mira. I want to stay married."

"Come again?" she squeaks.

I swallow the lump in my throat. In for a penny, in for a pound.

"I won't divorce you, wife."

eight

MIRA

I MUST HAVE HEARD GRIFFIN WRONG BECAUSE there's no way he just said what I think he said.

"I'm sorry. I could have sworn you said you won't divorce me, but that's sheer fucking insanity, Griffin." My voice rises in both pitch and volume with each new word. "Because we're not in a relationship. We have never been in a relationship. We're roommates and friends, and that's it."

I know my eyes look crazy right now, but whatever. I feel crazy. Might as well look it too. My body feels like it's buzzing. Like a swarm of angry bees has built a hive inside my chest.

"You don't even *do* relationships. Why in the hell would you want to stay married to me?"

At this point, I'm so filled with anxiety and confusion that I can't physically sit still. So I yank the sheet off Griffin and the bed, wrap it around myself like a toga, and begin to pace the room. Until I realize his dick is out there for the world to see. And it's big. A little longer than average, but thick as hell.

Oh my god. We definitely didn't have sex last night, then, because I'd be feeling it this morning if that monster had been inside of me.

At least there's that.

I'm still staring at Griff's dick a few seconds later, snapping out of my trance only when he clears his throat.

"Like what you see, wife?" He leans back against the headboard with his arms crossed behind his head. His one-eyed monster points to the ceiling.

"Wh-what? Shut up. And don't call me *wife*." I tear my eyes away from his dick and find him grinning at me. It's the same smile he gives me when he's goofing off and trying to make me laugh, but this time, there's an unfamiliar heat layered over it that makes my belly swoop.

"Why not?" His smile widens. "That's what you are."

"Please be serious," I growl. "And put your dick away. I can't talk to you with that thing staring at me."

He throws back his head and laughs. And damn him, but it's quite the sight. I want to lick the column of his throat and run my hands over every inch of his golden skin. And fine. Maybe I want to know what it would feel like to be stretched by him. Because Jared was *not* packing that kind of heat.

"The thing is, Mira, I am being serious."

I watch, entranced, as his muscles flex and stretch when he stands. There's a brutal sort of beauty to a man like Griffin. One who's honed his body to lean, muscular perfection. He crosses the room in three long strides, and a pathetic squeak escapes my lips when he stops close enough that our chests brush with each ragged inhalation. Gulping, I peer up at him. His palms cradle my face. "What are you doing?"

"The way I see it, we're screwed no matter what. At some point, this will come out. Whether we annul this marriage now, divorce six months from now, or make this work, your brother is going to find out, and he'll probably want to castrate me." A flash of worry darkens his eyes for only a second before he forces the emotion away and slips back into his mask of unflappable mirth. "And yeah, this wasn't the plan, and we were drunk, but would it be so bad to be married to me? I've never felt as comfortable around any woman as I've felt living with you for the last three months. We have fun together. I get you, and I think you get me."

"I do, Griffin. And I love living with you. But that means we make great friends. Not that we should be married."

He lowers his face so his mouth hovers mere centimeters away from mine as his hazel eyes search me. After a moment, the corner of his lips twitch, as if he's come to some kind of decision. "We are great friends. But are you sure that's all we are? Do you think I haven't noticed how you look at me when you believe I'm not paying attention?" He drags his nose along mine, and the scruff on his jaw scrapes against my cheek. "Do you think I've never caught you checking out my body when I walk around in sweats and nothing else?" His nose skims along my cheekbone, lips feathering across my heated skin.

It's all I can do to keep my knees from buckling, because having Griffin's naked body pressed against mine with nothing but a sheet toga between us is intense enough. Feeling his hands on my face and his nose and lips teasing my flushed skin is almost too much. There's no denying that I'm attracted to Griffin, but he's always been off-limits. I could look but not touch. But this? Having him touch me like I'm precious and beautiful and wanted?

My resolve is fracturing at an alarming rate.

"Griffin," I murmur as my eyes fall closed. I don't know if it's a plea or a protest, but it doesn't seem to matter, because my body leans into him. It doesn't care that this is a bad idea. Isn't worried about the consequences. All my body cares about is that Griffin is beautiful, warm, and hard in all the right places. And my body wants him. His lips twitch against the corner of mine like he's smiling.

"Mira." His hands shift and move, so one cups the back of my head and the other charts a sensual path across my collarbone, down my arm, and over my hip before he grips me and pulls me tighter against his body. Shivers and heat spread over my flesh, and when he grinds his hard dick against my belly, I gasp, which earns me a chuckle. "Are you telling me that if I pulled this sheet off your body and dipped my fingers into your hot little pussy, they wouldn't be coated in your arousal?"

My core clenches at his dirty words and the feel of him as his hips gently buck against my stomach. The cracks in my resolve grow larger. "N-no."

Griffin chuckles. "No, they wouldn't be coated in your arousal, or no, you're not telling me that?" His grip loosens on my hip, and I gasp when his fingers skim across my pubic bone. "Because there's a simple way to find out if you're lying."

"I... I..." I'm short-circuiting because Griffin's lips press against my neck.

"Should we find out just how wet you are, beautiful wife?" His fingers tug on the sheet I'm clutching to my body. "See if your pretty thighs are messy?" Another gentle tug. He doesn't pull on the fabric hard enough to rip it from my body. Not unless I let him. And I am more tempted to let go of my grip with every passing moment.

"If you're messy, I'd be happy to clean you up." He nips at my jaw. "I do love eating dessert for breakfast."

Fuuuuuck me.

Being the object of Griffin's focus when he's like this is heady. No wonder he has women falling at his feet on the regular. Between his golden-boy good looks, his hard body, and his filthy mouth, I'm ready to combust.

I need to stay strong.

"This is crazy," I say. The words come out breathy, and raspier than I'd like. So much for staying strong.

"Is it? Or does it make perfect sense?" Griffin kisses down my neck and my back arches, giving him easier access. His low chuckle sends tingles shooting across my skin like tiny fireworks. When his lips feather across the swell of my breasts, I gasp.

"God, Griffin." Tangling my fingers in his messy hair, I let my eyes fall closed. He hasn't touched my nipples or my pussy, and already I'm damn near ready to come.

"Do you want me to stop?"

I should say yes. It would be smart to say yes. This is dangerous territory, even without the issue of our drunken elopement. Add in the fact that I want to undo what we've done and Griffin—for some inexplicable reason—wants to give this a shot, and this thing between us is fraught with so many landmines, we'll be lucky if both of us don't end up maimed and broken beyond repair.

My mind recognizes this.

My body doesn't give a single flying fuck.

I mumble out something incoherent.

"I need your words, wife." Griffin chuckles against my chest. "Do you want me to stop?"

Yes.

"No."

Dammit, Mira.

Another chuckle sends goose bumps skittering across my arms. Then Griffin gives the sheet another soft tug, I release it from my grip, and my whole body erupts in goose bumps when I'm exposed to the cool air and Griffin's warm body.

Then his mouth descends on my breasts and I'm a goner.

"So fucking beautiful," he murmurs between nips and kisses. "God, Mira. You're absolutely stunning."

The reverence in his tone causes warmth to spread in my chest. Boyfriends have called me beautiful before. It's not a particularly original compliment. But no one has said it with the weight and gravity Griffin just used. I'm scared to open my eyes. Scared that whatever I see will make me give in to his ridiculous demand.

He wants us to stay secretly married? It's insanity. It's a terrible idea. No one in their right mind would agree to such a thing.

Griffin's calloused hands join his very talented mouth. He kneads and pinches one breast while he laves my other nipple with his tongue, sucks on it, and makes my core flood with arousal when he tortures me with playful bites. In between kisses, he turns me so my back is to the bed and begins to herd me toward it. His large hands go to my bare hips and push. I land on the king-size mattress with a gasp and a giggle.

"Look at you," Griffin nearly purrs. His hazel eyes are hooded, his pupils blown wide as he lazily peruses my body. His right hand fists his hard cock, pumping it indolently a few times and making the slit weep pre-cum.

I want to taste him.

When I try to sit up, desperate to wrap my lips around his thick length, he shakes his head and plants a palm on my sternum, keeping me from moving. "We'll have all the time in the world for you to wrap that pretty mouth around my cock, baby. But right now, I'm hungry." He flashes me a devilish smile before leaning over me and taking my mouth in a searing kiss. It's possessive and wild and it makes my core flood and my legs open for him. When he pulls away, I'm dazed and so needy, I whine. Which seems to please Griffin greatly.

"Does my wife need relief?" He hooks his arms around my thighs and tugs me to the edge of the bed so my ass nearly hangs off. He rests my knees over his shoulders and hisses when he sees the state of me. "Oh, baby girl, you do need relief, don't you? Look at you, so wet and swollen. And I haven't even touched this perfect pussy yet."

Jesus Christ.

Griffin's eyes don't leave mine as he leans down and drags the flat of his tongue from my slit to my clit. He laps up my juices like a cat gorging itself on a bowl of cream. "Shit, baby girl. You taste like heaven." He uses his hands to spread my lips before spearing his tongue inside my pussy, using it to fuck me and take his fill of my essence. His nose bumps my clit again and again, and the sounds that come out of me are breathless and needy.

I've never made sounds like this during sex. And this is only Griffin's tongue. Something tells me he's even better with his dick.

When my cries grow louder, his tongue moves to my clit while two thick fingers press into my body so slowly and deliberately that I thrash and whine. I need more. I need him to fill me.

"Griffin." My fingers grip his hair tightly, but he doesn't even flinch.

"Call me *husband*," he demands, his lips still against my pussy. The vibration of his low words has everything tightening inside of me.

"Griffin, please." I can't do it. I can't bring myself to call him husband. This is just sex. Really fantastic oral sex. But that doesn't mean we're staying married. Because no. Just no.

"Say it," he says, his fingers pushing in all the way with punishing force before he drags them out and fucks me hard with them again.

"No."

"No?" His tongue lashes at my clit while his fingers thrust and curl inside of me. My back arches off the bed and my stomach hollows out. I'm so close.

"No," I gasp.

He sucks my clit between his lips, and every nerve in my body lights up. My pussy tightens around his fingers. Pleasure coils tight in my belly. As he nips my clit with his teeth, I go off like fireworks on the Fourth of July. A strangled scream tears from my throat, my back bows off the bed, and my pussy ripples and squeezes Griffin's fingers. His tongue lashes at my clit, drawing the orgasm out until I'm a shuddering, shaking mess.

No one has ever made me come like that. Ever.

I want more.

It takes a minute to focus my thoughts and my eyes. When I do, I'm met with the most erotic thing I've ever seen.

Griffin's hair is wild from where my fingers tugged at it. His body glistens with sweat. His eyes are dark with lust, and his cock is rock hard. But it's the shine of my arousal coating his lips and chin that does me in. His face is covered in my cum from his nose to his chin. He licks as much of it off as he can before swiping his fingers over his chin and licking those clean too.

Holy. Shit.

I want him inside of me. Now.

"Damn, baby. You taste better than I could have imagined." He sucks his fingers with a wet *pop*. "I think I'd like to eat dessert for breakfast every day."

I just came harder than I have in my life, and I'm already so turned on, I know I could come again. And with the way Griffin's cock drips pre-cum, I know he needs release too.

"Griffin." I spread my thighs even wider. "Fuck me. Please, fuck me."

A predatory gleam makes Griffin's eyes sparkle. Gently, he nudges my thighs off his shoulders so they hang off the bed before he stands.

Yes. I'm so ready for this.

Fisting his dick, Griffin catalogs the state of me. He takes in my disheveled hair, my glassy eyes, parted lips, heaving chest, and swollen pussy. There isn't an inch of my body his eyes don't caress. He pumps his cock a few times, using his thumb to spread the bead of pre-cum over his head. "You want me to fuck you?"

"Please," I beg.

His wicked grin grows wider. "Call me husband."

I shake my head. "No."

He shrugs, stroking his length a few more times while he considers something. Then he silently turns and walks away.

"Griffin?" I sit up, confused. "Where are you going?"

"To take care of this in the shower."

"What?" I screech. "You're not going to fuck me?"

"Nope."

"Why the hell not?"

"Because." Griffin pauses when he makes it to the bathroom door, turning to look at me over his shoulder. "From now on, this cock is only for my wife. Until you decide that's what you want to be, you'll get my mouth and my fingers only."

Spluttering, I try to form words, but nothing comes. I'm too full of indignation to form a coherent sentence. When I finally open my mouth, it's to shout, "That's bullshit!"

Griffin's smooth laughter reverberates through the luxurious bathroom. "Maybe. But if you want my cock, you know what has to happen."

Disappointment melds with rage. I let out an animalistic shriek that is *so* not sexy. "Fuck you, Wright. It's never going to happen."

His laughter continues, even after he's shut the bathroom door and locked it.

I can't believe he's trying to use sex to get me to agree to this marriage!

And I can't believe that, for a split second, I actually consider it.

nine

GRIFFIN

What the hell did I just do?

My mind races as I fist my dick in the shower. I'm so fucking turned on from the sight and taste of Mira that I won't last more than a minute or two. Hell, I was about ready to come from eating her out, none of Mira's hands, lips, or tongue on my dick necessary.

But crazier than that? I married my best friend's little sister in Las Vegas, while drunk, slept naked with her, then ate her out while he's a few rooms away. Am I trying to get myself murdered? Because that's a distinct possibility.

Focus, Wright.

What am I going to do? And why the hell did I tell Mira I won't divorce her? What's the plan here? After Carissa all but laughed in my face when I proposed to her in college, I resigned myself to the fact that marriage wasn't in the cards for me. She was the third woman I'd dated since freshman year who had her fun with the hockey player, dumped my ass mercilessly by the six-month mark, and then got engaged to some other dude less than six months later.

They all made it perfectly clear that I was last-fling material, not forever material. A message that I took to heart after my high school and college experiences.

So why did waking up married to Mira feel like a second chance at breaking my curse? Yeah, I've been attracted to her since day one. And yeah, living with her has been the most exquisite torture, since she's off-limits. She's beautiful, sexy as hell, and so damn smart. Being around her is simultaneously like drinking four shots of espresso and taking a pot gummy. She makes me feel energized and alive, but she also mellows me out in a way no one else ever has. Waking up married is like a gift from the gods. An excuse to hold on to her and see if we could be more than good friends who are not-so-secretly attracted to each other.

I pump my dick a little harder.

Yeah, I know Mira's always been attracted to me. I've seen the way she looks at me when she thinks I'm oblivious. And maybe it was having Maddox as a cock-blocking buffer between us, but even though she's always wanted my body, she's never treated me like I'm some himbo piece of ass. She actually sees me. She's taken the time to get to know me.

It's probably batshit crazy, but I truly think we could work together. I just have to convince her to give this a real shot.

A plan comes together in my head as I stroke my cock faster and faster. I'll make a deal with her. Six months. Six full months where we stay married and give this relationship a real chance. I'll ask her for six months to prove that not only are we perfect for each other, but that I can also check off all her boxes. Mira wants a husband who meets a certain set of criteria. So I'll give it to her. I'll be boring and responsible. I'll wear button-down shirts every day and read the newspaper in the morning instead of sports sites. Mira wants someone dependable and straightlaced. I can be that guy. Although the straightlaced part will be rough, I can do it. For her.

If, at the end of six months, she still wants a divorce, I'll give it to her. I'll pay for everything and sign the papers without a fuss. It will suck if that happens, but I want a shot with her, not to trap her. And if we're married, I'll have an excuse to pay for everything and take care of her. Give her a real chance to invest her time and money into her business. Hell, I can be one of her first big clients. I've seen the work she's been doing and the mockups she's created for smaller athletes and brands. She's a whiz at creating websites and branding, and she understands the needs of pro athletes because she grew up with one.

Six months. If I contested the divorce, things could be tied up in court much longer than that. And I'd never do that, but Mira doesn't need to know. If I make it seem like I would, it may be enough to get her to agree.

My stomach tightens and tingles start at the base of my spine and in my balls. I picture Mira a few months from now. She writhes beneath me, happy and glowing, as she calls me her husband and tells me she's in love with me.

My balls tighten as pleasure whips through my body in a tsunami. Grunting, I pump my cock furiously as cum erupts from me and paints the shower wall. Breathing heavily, I barely register that it's the thought of Mira loving me that pushed me over the edge. Not her sexy, toned body, not lust in her eyes, not the image of her breasts bouncing as I fuck her hard. If I give it too much thought, I may rethink this batshit scheme because it's obvious that this has the real potential to hurt me if it doesn't work.

"Fuck." I shudder as the last waves of my orgasm wash over me.

Mira is worth the risk.

I finish my shower and dry off before striding back out into my room with nothing but a towel wrapped around my hips. For a second, I worry she won't be waiting for me. That she'll run back to her room and pretend none of this ever happened.

But she's sitting on the bed in last night's clothes, her cheeks pink, wringing her hands in her lap. I don't miss the way her eyes darken with lust when she sees me, or the way her gaze lingers on the vee of my hips where it disappears beneath my low-slung towel. She's not unaffected by me. Which means I have a chance.

"Wife." I grin when she rolls her eyes and purses her pretty lips. "Do you want to take a shower? You can wear some of my clothes, so you don't have to walk around in last night's outfit."

Her cheeks flare a brighter shade of pink. "I... Maybe. But first, we need to be serious for a minute." She tracks me as I move toward my suitcase and pull out a clean pair of boxer briefs, jeans, and a simple white tee. She lets out a strangled sound when I let the towel drop and step into my briefs.

"Sure. I agree. We do need to have a serious discussion."

"Exactly," she says. Her voice is strained, and I smirk,

knowing I'm having this kind of effect on her. "Now that we've both had a few minutes to cool down, I think we can agree that the only way forward is an annulment. Or divorce. Whatever you want to call it, our only option is to undo what we did."

"I don't agree, actually." I pull the tee over my head, and my smirk grows into a full-fledged smile when she makes a frustrated little growl. "I'd like to propose an alternate plan."

"Alternate plan?" She rises from the bed and stalks toward me. Her pretty green eyes spit fire, and damn, do I love seeing her like this. Full of life and passion. "Quit fucking around, Griffin. This isn't funny anymore."

I cross my arms. "I can assure you, Mrs. Wright, I'm not fucking around. I wish I was, but you haven't agreed to be my wife yet. Unless you're changing your mind?" I raise an eyebrow at her. It takes all my self-restraint not to laugh when she splutters out some unintelligible, indignant sounds and shoves my chest.

"I'm not your wife, and I'm not *going* to be your wife. We were drunk, Griffin. We did what lots of drunk people do in Vegas. We got married in a stupid chapel and woke up with a hangover and regrets."

"I don't regret it," I tell her honestly. She gapes at me like I've lost my mind, but I ignore it, brushing a lock of her dark brown hair from her face. "And I'd argue that sometimes the things you do when you're drunk are things you really want but are too scared to admit to wanting when you're sober."

Mira rolls her lips between her teeth as she stares up at me. Encouraged by her silence, I continue.

"So I propose we give this a real chance." When she opens her mouth to argue, I forge ahead. "Six months, Mira. I'm proposing that we give this marriage a real chance for six months. We go on dates, explore our feelings for each other, sleep in the same bed, have meals together. We stop fighting this pull between us and give in to it. And if, at the end of the six months, you still don't want to be married, I'll sign the divorce papers without a single protest."

Mira scoffs. "And you think Maddox is going to be okay with this?"

"No." I scrub my hand over the back of my neck. "I think he's going to kick my ass, but it's a risk I'm willing to take."

"Well, I'm not! Why would I do this when I can just file divorce paperwork, Wright?"

I shrug. "You could do that. But going through the courts when both parties aren't in agreement can take a hell of a lot longer than six months, wife. And if you do it that way, everyone will find out."

The color drains from her face at that, and I try to ignore the guilt that twists my stomach. "Six months. I'm only asking for six months."

"Why?"

"Maybe it's crazy, but I really believe we could have something special." I shrug like I'm not laying my heart on the line with that admission. Like I'm not ready to vomit, and it's not because of the alcohol sloshing around in my gut.

Mira studies me for a long, agonizing moment. She weighs her options and runs through scenarios. I watch the thoughts play out across her features like a silent film.

Finally, her shoulders sag. "If we do this, no one can know, Wright. I mean it. *No one.*"

Hiding my disappointment at her stipulation, I nod. "Of course. We'll keep it a secret. When we're out with Maddox and our friends, we'll act like we're just roommates until you're ready to tell them otherwise."

She shakes her head. "Griffin, that's not going to happen. We're too different. We want different things in life."

Do we, though? She believes that, but I suspect our secret hopes aren't that dissimilar. Saying that to her now won't do any good, though, so I keep my mouth shut and lift one shoulder. "Guess we'll find out."

"This is crazy," she whispers, more to herself than me. "I must be losing my mind to agree to this."

"Is that a yes, then, wife?"

"Stop calling me *wife,*" she grumbles. "But yes. It's a yes. Let the record show that it's a yes under duress."

I chuckle. "Noted."

"You know this is a terrible idea, right?"

Probably. The thing is, I'm the one likely to end up hurt, not Mira. Which makes this a terrible idea I'm willing to risk it all on. "Terrible or genius?"

"Terrible." She sighs, suddenly looking exhausted. "Look, I need to get back to my room before someone realizes I'm gone and they find me here. We can talk about this more at home."

Home. It sounds different coming out of her mouth now that we're married. And it also sparks a fantastic idea. I'll have to give my housekeeper a call.

I take a step toward my gorgeous wife and nudge her chin up with the side of my finger. Her pupils expand, and

I don't miss the way her breath hitches. "Okay, beautiful wife. We can talk more about this at home. Are you sure you don't want a pair of my sweats and a tee?"

She shakes her head, tongue tied.

"Okay, then. Go shower. We're supposed to meet everyone for lunch before our flights home." I lean down to press a tender kiss to Mira's lips, pleased when they part on an inhalation and she kisses me back. It's difficult, but I pull away before the kiss deepens. Slow and steady. I'll have to take this slow and steady if I want to win her over. To prove I'm not just some fuckboy who's only good for one thing.

This may not have been a part of my plan, but it feels right, and I won't screw this up.

"See you soon, wife."

Mira shakes her head slightly, looking up at me with wide eyes. "Don't call me that."

She turns on her heel and leaves, my laughter trailing after her.

ten

MIRA

I THINK I MAY THROW UP.

After stashing my wedding band in my toiletries bag, a long, extra hot shower, a first-class freak out, and a pep talk in the mirror, I make my way down to the hotel restaurant where we've all agreed to meet for lunch. Luckily, I didn't run into anyone when I fled from Griffin's room, and no one knows that Griffin and I are—*gulp*—married.

But I feel like they'll all know as soon as they see me. Like there's a neon sign blinking above my head that reads *this dumbass drunkenly married the left winger last night,* and that'll be that. Maddox will flip out, the guys will look at us like we've lost our minds, and Isla will try to tell me everything will be all right while my brother murders my accidental husband in public, then gets locked up for the rest of his life.

Oh my god. *My husband.*

The hostess points me toward a table in the corner when I arrive. I'm the last one here, which is unfortunate, because that means I don't get to choose where I sit. There's only one chair left, and it's beside Griffin.

"You can do this," I mutter under my breath before pasting a fake-ass smile on my face. One I hope is convincing enough. If anything, they'll probably assume I'm hungover. Which I am.

"Mira! I was just about to come knock on your door to make sure you weren't still sleeping." Isla stands, wrapping me in a tight hug. "How late did you and Griffin stay out last night?"

I refuse to look Griffin's way. "Uh, not too much later than you guys, I think."

Lie number one. Something tells me I'll have racked up quite the collection of lies by the time this meal is over. And I hate that. I hate that I'm lying to the woman who is going to be my sister-in-law, my brother, and the rest of our friends. I hate that Griffin has put me in this position. But mostly, I hate myself for getting drunk and doing something so epically stupid in the first place.

"What did you end up doing?" Maddox brings a glass of water to his lips and takes a sip as he studies me. Does he know something's off?

"We went and saw the Bellagio fountains," Griffin answers for me. "And an Elvis impersonator."

Oh no.

I shoot him a quick look that screams *shut the hell up, you idiot!* He just smirks.

"Old Elvis or young Elvis?" Logan asks. What is it with these guys and that question?

"Young," Griffin says with a grin. "Obviously." He looks between Logan and Sebastian. "How was your night?"

Logan chuckles. "Mine was better than Navarro's. He didn't feel like company, so I entertained both ladies."

Ew. Entertained means he banged them both. Honestly, who does that? Sure, Logan is good looking, but what self-respecting woman goes along with a threesome just because the guy is hot?

What self-respecting woman drunkenly marries their roommate because they're hot? my inner bitch taunts.

Touché, self. Touché.

Griffin shakes his head but mostly ignores what Logan said. Instead, he turns to Sebastian with a look of brotherly concern that does funny things to my insides. "You okay, man? You've been more withdrawn than usual lately."

"I'm fine," Bash says. "Just wasn't in the mood to hook up with some random woman, you know? I know it never gets old for you and Byrne, but it does for me."

"I get it." Griffin nods his head in understanding. "I've been feeling that way for a while, too."

That draws the attention of my brother and Isla. While Maddox looks at Griffin with his brow at his hairline, Isla cocks her head to the side and studies Griffin like he's a specimen under a microscope. Her eyes narrow slightly, then flick my way for half a second.

Crap.

"Really?" My brother stares at Griffin. "When did that happen?"

Griffin lifts one shoulder. "You made me promise not to bring random chicks home while your sister lives with me, and I've realized I don't miss it. I'm done with that life."

I *knew* my brother must have said something to Griffin about that.

The table goes silent until Logan scoffs. "Bullshit. There's no way you're done enjoying a beautiful woman's company."

"Nah, man, not *done* done. I'm just ready to be a one-woman man."

Isla's eyebrows arch, but instead of giving Griffin a hard time the way Logan and Maddox do, she reaches across the table and squeezes his hand. "That's great, Griffin. I'm sure you'll find the right woman for you."

My for-now husband smiles brightly, squeezing her hand back. "I'm sure I will too. Now, tell me how it felt to wake up this morning an engaged woman with a giant rock on your finger?"

Conversation turns to Isla and Maddox, but I remain mostly quiet. Stuck in my head with the words Griffin said, trying to figure a way out of this mess.

"GRIFFIN?" I STEP INSIDE OUR APARTMENT WITH MY stomach a mess of nerves. Since the team flies on their own plane, they made it home a solid two hours before Isla and me. It's almost seven, and I'm exhausted. All I want is to eat a late dinner, take a shower to wash away the travel grime, then go to bed.

"Welcome home, wifey," Griffin calls from deeper in the apartment. Probably his bedroom. "You hungry?"

I roll my carry-on farther into the place and notice a vase full of fresh roses on the kitchen island, along with a bottle of champagne chilling in a bucket of ice and two crystal flutes. What the heck?

"Uh, yeah. I was going to order some pizza or something."

"No need." Griffin strolls down the hallway in nothing but a pair of those damnable gray sweatpants guaranteed to make me horny. "Dinner should be delivered in about..." He checks his smart watch just as someone knocks on the door. That has him smiling brightly. "Now."

Griffin heads for the door, and before I can make my way to my room to drop off my suitcase, he asks me to set some plates and silverware out on the table. I'm starving and grateful that he ordered dinner, so even though I want to complain and make a beeline for my room, I don't. I set the table while he tips the delivery driver and carries a large paper bag to the island. The smells coming out of it are absolutely divine, and my stomach rumbles in anticipation.

"Hungry?" Griffin asks, amusement lacing his tone.

"Starved," I reply as he takes my plate and fills it with steak, roasted vegetables, and fresh bread. Since he seems to have things under control and I'm exhausted, I sink into my chair and watch him. "You went all out."

The twitching of his lips shouldn't be as sexy as it is. "Of course, I did. We're celebrating."

"We are, huh? And what are we celebrating? Lying to my brother and our friends?"

That makes him scowl. "No. That was your idea, not mine. We're celebrating our first dinner in our home as Mr. and Mrs. Wright." He fills a plate for himself, then pops open the bottle of champagne and fills the flutes.

"I'm not Mrs. Wright," I tell him. I'm already tired of this fight.

But Griffin simply smiles at me as he places the plate and champagne in front of me. "You don't have to change your name if you don't want to. I could change mine."

I almost choke on the sip of bubbly I just took. Coughing and sputtering, I stare at Griffin as he sets his own plate down. "I'm sorry, what?"

"I'm a modern man and a feminist. It's not fair that women are always expected to give up their names. But I do want to share a name with my wife, so if you'd prefer not to be Mrs. Wright, I'm happy to become Mr. Graves." He cocks his head to the side and narrows his eyes. "Though that may get a little confusing on the ice. But we'll figure it out."

"I don't... You can't... No one is changing their name!"

"We can wait if you want time to consider it. That's completely reasonable." He nods, like he didn't say something so utterly ridiculous I don't have words for it, and cuts his steak. "Oh man. This is so good."

Still at a loss, I take a few bites of my own dinner, and we eat in silence. Only the sound of our silverware clanking against the ceramic dishes fills the apartment.

"How was your flight?" Griffin finally asks. He's making small talk. He conned me into staying married for six months, and he's making small talk. Exhaustion presses down on my shoulders.

"Cramped," I say, shrugging one shoulder. "Isla and I got stuck next to this businessman with long legs, and he manspread into my space the whole flight. It was annoying as hell, and I wanted to stab him with my keys."

"Sorry, baby. That sucks. Next time, buy first-class tickets." Griffin sips his champagne as I stare at him.

"I can't afford first-class tickets, Griffin," I say, exasperated. "I'm still getting my business off the ground."

"You can totally afford first-class tickets." He looks at me like I'm silly.

I want to scream.

"We're married, so what's mine is yours. And my wife will never have to fly in coach again."

What? No way in hell am I spending Griffin's money like some gold-digging jersey chaser. Absolutely not. Never going to happen.

"No."

Griffin fights a smile. "You seem to love that word today. But this isn't a battle you can win, wifey. Even if you buy tickets in coach, I'll call and pay to upgrade them. Why waste my time and yours when you can book them first class from the get-go?"

"You can't do that," I say, sounding very much like a petulant toddler, before shoving the last bite of food into my mouth.

"I can and will. Resistance is futile."

Steam may be coming out of my ears. "We're not on an episode of *Star Trek*, Wright. This is real life. *My* life."

"Is that where that quote is from?" Griffin tilts his head and considers it. Then he simply goes back to finishing his dinner without addressing the rest of my statement. It's infuriating. He's infuriating. How dare he think he can go over my head like that?

Yes, my inner bitch drawls, *how dare he offer to fly you across the country in the lap of luxury?*

Gah!

Pushing away from the table, I level Griffin with a glare. "Thank you for dinner, but I'm tired. I'm going to go to bed." Grabbing my carry-on, I roll it down the hallway without another glance at Griffin's smug, stupidly handsome face. I'm grumbling nonsensical insults as I go to my room, slam the door, and let out a huff.

I can't believe this is my life right now.

Too tired to unpack, I shed my clothes and open my dresser drawer to grab clean pajamas.

Except, it's empty.

What the hell?

I open another drawer. Empty. And another. Empty.

Someone stole all of my things! Rushing to the closet, I fling the doors open and instead of my clothes, I find an empty space. Not even a single solitary hanger to be found.

What. The. Hell?

Pissed and panicking, I rush to my bathroom and find all my towels, toiletries, and makeup gone. I know I have decent taste, but I'm broke, so it's not like anything I own has any real value. Why would someone steal my stuff?

"Griffin!" I shout from the bathroom. My hands press against the vanity as I lean forward and drag air into my lungs. The weight of everything is pressing down on me—the marriage, the lies, the feeling of control slipping through my wedding band-clad fingers—and I'm dangerously close to losing my cool.

The door to my room opens and Griffin's footsteps grow closer. "Yes, my wife?"

"Someone stole my stuff!" I shout, turning to face him. And completely forgetting that I'm wearing nothing but a simple cotton bra and panty set. Griffin's eyes take me in hungrily, and I try not to notice his thick cock as it rises to greet me, but I'm only human, and he's clearly free-balling it.

Damn him. Damn gray sweatpants.

"No one stole your stuff," he says, chuckling.

I'm going to punch him in the dick. Throwing my hands out to the sides, I say, "Obviously they did, because everything's missing!"

"It's not missing. It's in our room."

Our room.

Our. Room.

"Excuse me?" I'm two seconds away from exploding. From epically losing my shit. He better not have done what I think he did.

"I didn't want you to have to move everything when we got home. I knew you'd be tired, so I asked the house-keeper to move everything for you." He says it all so matter-of-factly. Like it's not crazy and invasive to ask the woman who deep cleans his apartment twice a month to move my goddamn underwear. He turns, walks out of the bathroom, and makes his way to his room. I silently follow because I'm too pissed for words.

Ignoring the calming dark green walls and the massive bed in the center of the room, I trail Griffin to a walk-in closet that's twice the size of mine. He waves his hand toward the right wall where I find all my clothes hanging neatly, my shoes in individual cubbies, and my intimates folded in a small dresser.

My breathing grows shallow and comes in quick bursts as I stare at my clothes hanging across from his. I don't know why this is the thing that's going to push me over the edge, but it is.

"This is too far, Griffin." I turn to face him. His eyes

twinkle with mirth. The smug bastard. "Why would you do this?"

"Because you agreed to give us a chance, remember? For the next six months, you agreed to give this marriage a real chance. Which means, this"—he sweeps his arms out to indicate the closet and the bedroom—"is your bedroom too."

No, no, no. I didn't think he'd actually try to enforce sharing a bedroom. It's crazy. And a recipe for disaster. Because as much as I can deny my attraction to Griffin until I'm blue in the face, I know my damn body will betray me at every turn.

"I'll let you get ready for bed." He presses a kiss to my forehead while my mouth flaps open and shut like one of those stupid, singing fish people hang on their walls, then walks out of the closest. "I've got a few things to do to get ready for practice tomorrow. I'll be in soon."

Ha. Joke's on him. I'm still going to sleep in my own bed.

"Oh, and Mira?" Griffin turns and levels me with a dangerous smirk. "Don't even bother trying to sleep in your old bed. I'll just carry you back to ours."

He would, too, the jerk. It's becoming all too clear that Griffin Wright was completely serious about giving this marriage a go for six months.

I'll think of a way out of it tomorrow. For tonight, I'm far too exhausted to play these games.

I take a shower, get ready, and crawl into his unfamiliar bed. Right in the middle. And then I starfish my arms and legs.

If I won't be comfortable tonight, neither will he.

eleven

MIRA

I WAKE UP WITH MY BACK PLASTERED TO GRIFFIN'S chest, his hand cupping my breast, and his hard-on pressing against my ass. I don't remember snuggling up to him, but apparently my plan to make him uncomfortable failed miserably. Instead, I'm the one who's uncomfortable because I'm sweaty and horny from being pressed against his naked body all night. Seriously, how can you wake up horny?

As quietly as I can, I slip out of Griffin's hold, grab some clean clothes, and tiptoe into his bathroom. I lock the door and stare at myself in the mirror before starting the shower.

I feel like I should look different. After everything that's happened the last two days, shouldn't I have some outward manifestation of the ridiculous changes in my life?

But I don't. My long, dark hair is tangled from sleep,

there's a crease on my cheek from the pillowcase, and my green eyes are still bleary. Nothing about my appearance screams *I'm an accidentally married woman now*, which is good. Because no one can know about this. Especially not Maddox. Griffin is his best friend, but I'm his little sister, and that protectiveness he feels for me will override any bonds of friendship he and Griffin share.

I don't want to be the thing that comes between them. Not only that, but I've been working so hard to get people to take me seriously—my brother included—and admitting to a drunken marriage doesn't scream *serious*.

Shaking my head, I take a quick shower and blow-dry my hair. I swipe a quick coat of mascara over my lashes, get dressed, and psych myself up to leave the bathroom. Living with Griffin for the past three months has been easy and comfortable. Fun. But everything has changed now, and I don't know what to expect. I'm pissed at myself for getting drunk and doing something so stupid and reckless, and pissed at Griffin for this whole six-month scheme of his.

I feel off balance. Like my safe space is gone. Because that's what he and this apartment had become. My safe space.

When my stomach growls and my head pounds, I know I can't hide out in the bathroom any longer. I need food and caffeine, then I need to get to work. I've been building a website for this baseball team in Georgia that combines baseball with comedy and dancing. They're hilarious and fun, and the project has been one of my favorites to date. Who wouldn't love designing a website for a group of guys who intersperse musical numbers in between innings? It's also one of the biggest jobs I've had yet. Until this point, I've built websites and branding mostly for individuals. It feels like this could be a stepping stone to something bigger, and after a weekend in Vegas, I'm ready to get back to work.

Griffin is no longer sleeping in his bed when I peek my head out. As the scent of bacon tickles my nose, I follow it into the kitchen, where he's working in front of the stove in nothing but a pair of boxer briefs, humming. Since he hasn't noticed me, I give myself a moment to take in the scene.

A bowl of chopped fruit sits on the dining room table, coffee percolates in the machine, and Griffin is flipping a fluffy omelet while bacon sizzles in another pan. Remnants of chopped ham and peppers are sprinkled across a cutting board. He's made us breakfast a few times since I moved in, but something about this seems so much more domestic, and I don't know how to feel about that.

When my stomach rumbles, Griffin turns to me with a bright smile that makes my heart flip-flop.

"Morning, wifey. Sleep well?"

Ignoring the nickname, I pad toward him. "Would have slept better if I was in my own bed," I lie. Because I *did* sleep well last night, dammit. "Can I help with anything?"

Griffin ignores my lie and gestures toward the coffeemaker. "You could get a couple mugs out for us and pour the coffee. Breakfast should be ready in a minute."

"It smells good." I offer him a slightly-more-awkward-than-normal smile before turning to open the cabinet behind me and grabbing two mugs. I still when Griffin's chest presses against my back and his hands cage me in against the counter.

"You smell good," he murmurs as he skims his nose along my cheek before pressing a kiss to my temple. "Good enough to eat."

Heat floods my body as his words cause a memory of his tongue on my pussy to flash through my mind. An embarrassing little whimper sneaks through my lips as they part. Griffin chuckles, and I swear I feel it down to my core. "The eggs are going to burn," I say, desperate to get him away from me.

If I'm going to make it through the next six months without making any more stupid decisions, I need to keep my wits about me. And when Griffin touches me like this? That's difficult to do.

I sag against the counter when he goes back to the stove, though some sadistic part of me misses his solidness and warmth. That part of me can shut the hell up, though, because solidness and warmth are not a good enough foundation for a marriage.

By the time I'm done pouring two mugs of coffee, Griffin has finished the food, and soon we're eating in companionable silence. It's good. Really good. He's a solid cook, which is nice, since the extent of Jared's competency in the kitchen was reheating takeout.

"I have practice today, then a meeting about a potential sponsorship deal. I probably won't be home until late." Hazel eyes meet mine from across the table.

"Okay." I shrug.

Griffin's lips twitch. "I know you're working on that big project. Do you want me to arrange dinner to be delivered so you don't have to worry about it?"

Why does he have to be so sweet? It's infuriating. "I'll be fine. You don't have to do that."

"Okay," he says, plate clean. He rises from the table and carries it to the sink, where he washes the plate and the cookware he used to make breakfast. I'm totally not mesmerized by the flex of his thick thighs, the curve of his peachy ass, or the ripple of his back as he works. Nope. Not mesmerized at all. Completely, one-hundred-percent unaffected. "Do you want a refill on your coffee before I go get ready?"

"Hmm?"

Griffin laughs, his eyes sparkling. Dammit. He totally caught me checking him out.

Flustered and blushing, I shake my head. "Nope. Thanks. I'm good."

Mercifully, he doesn't give me a hard time before heading to the shower.

I'm getting the desk in my room prepped and ready to start work when Griffin appears in the doorway. "I'm heading out. Text me if you need anything today, okay?"

I nod. When he walks away, I pull out my phone.

ME

I need a divorce.

"Not happening, wifey," Griffin calls from inside the apartment.

Well, it was worth a shot.

THE DAY HAS FLOWN BY, AS IT ALWAYS DOES WHEN I'm enjoying my work. The site I'm building is coming along nicely. I'm quite proud of it.

A glance at my phone tells me it's six, which means I

need to be done for the day. Sitting hunched over a computer without coming up for air or taking breaks is hell on my back, and it pops a few times when I stand and stretch.

A knock on the door has me frowning. I'm not expecting anyone.

Padding through the apartment, I look through the peephole in time to see a guy walking away from the door. I wait a few moments to make sure he's actually gone, then open the door and stick my head out. The hallway is empty, but there's a bag of takeout at my feet.

They must have delivered it to the wrong apartment. Grabbing it, I'm about to run after the delivery guy when I notice the name on the receipt.

Mrs. Wright.

I can't help the smile that blooms on my face, despite my annoyance at the name. Griffin ordered me dinner, even though I told him he didn't have to. And from the smell of it, he ordered from my favorite Indian place.

I'm full and sleepy when he gets home around eight. He flops down next to me on the couch where I'm watching the first season of *New Girl.* It's my comfort show, and I've seen every episode at least three times.

"How was your day?" I ask, noting the exhaustion on Griffin's face.

He slumps down onto the couch and offers me a smile. "Good. Long. But I landed that sponsorship deal. The one with the sports gear company."

"That's great." And I mean it. He and his agent have been working toward this deal for months. Sponsorships are important for pro athletes in a sport like hockey, where the risk of injury is so high. When players could suffer a career-ending hit at any moment, it's wise for them to make sure the game isn't their only source of income. "Are you hungry? There are plenty of leftovers."

"Nah, I grabbed some dinner with my agent."

"Okay. Thanks for that, by the way. You didn't need to."

My stomach is a puddle of goo when Griffin turns his head and offers me a blinding smile. "That's what husbands do, Mira. They take care of their wives." He reaches across the space between us and runs a finger up the outside of my thigh. "I like taking care of you."

All I can do is stare at him. His words affect me more than I'd like to admit, and it makes swallowing past the lump in my throat difficult. Because I like having someone look out for me. I've spent so many years taking care of myself and trying to prove that I can do it without any help. I can't deny how nice it is *not* to for once.

Griffin turns back to the TV. "I love this show. Winston's my favorite."

I chuckle. "Mine too. Especially in the later seasons when he gets weirder."

"Totally."

We sit like that through four more episodes, and it's nice. It feels like it did before Vegas, before our drunken marriage, and before things became complicated. It's almost more dangerous than when he touches me with those expert fingers or wicked tongue. Because when we're quiet like this, comfortable and completely artless, I find myself wondering if maybe we could be good for each other.

But that's crazy. Griffin and I are too different. We want very different things in life. And I'd be wise not to forget it.

twelve

GRIFFIN

Is there anything better than a game night? The anticipation, the cheering fans, the adrenaline pumping through my veins. All of it makes me feel so *alive*. It's always been my favorite feeling.

"The girls are here," Ryder says with a nod to the first row of seats beside our bench. His girlfriend, Lexi—our former coach's daughter—waves to him. She's got a huge smile on her face, and I love that they're doing so well. They had a rocky start to their relationship with all the shit Coach Cross put them through. It's good to see the rookie so happy. I know having Lexi here to cheer Ryder on when he doesn't have any family is everything to him.

When they notice Lexi waving, Isla and Mira look our way. And I realize that the anticipation of a game night is no longer my favorite feeling. No, my new favorite feeling is the sense of pride I get seeing my wife in the seats, excited to watch me play.

My wife. Fuck, it's still surreal. I'm married to the most stunning, intelligent, hilarious woman on the planet.

The only downer? She's not wearing my name. *Her* name if she wants it.

We'll get there.

The guys and I skate up to the glass and shout hello, wave, and generally act like besotted idiots. Because that's what we are. Not that Maddox or Ryder can know I've joined their ranks. Hell, I've managed to *out*rank them. Because I'm married, while Madds is just engaged and Handsome is only dating his girl.

"The fuck has you grinning like an idiot?" Logan asks as he skates up beside me, gives the women a wave, then turns his attention my way. "You have gas or something? You know you shouldn't eat ice cream before a game."

"What?" Frowning, I shake my head at him. "You're a moron."

I'm grinning like an idiot because I'm married to the prettiest woman in the arena, I want to say. But I can't. We're keeping this a secret. For now. Which I hate, but baby steps and all that.

"I was thinking about setting my sister up," Maddox says as he gives Mira a little nod.

It's all I can do to keep my jaw off the ice as I turn slowly to gape at my best friend. "I'm sorry, what?" I glance at my wife as she waves *hi* to Sebastian when he comes to drag our asses away from the boards to warm up.

"I've just been so happy with Isla, and I know Mi-Mi has always wanted that, you know? She's not like me. She's never given up on the idea of finding love, and I think it would be good for her." Maddox shrugs like he didn't just punch me in the metaphorical nuts.

Sebastian shakes his head. "You really think that's a good idea? I know you two are close, but setting up your little sister seems like a bad idea."

Our goalie has no clue how bad an idea it truly is.

"You didn't see her when I went to help her move." Maddox's grumpy face comes out to play. "She thought that douche was the one, and he couldn't even be bothered to be there to say goodbye when she left." He turns to me. "Has she ever told you what happened with him?"

A little, actually. There were a few times we both got a little tipsy while sitting around watching movies. The wine would flow, and so would Mira's words. She's only told me bits and pieces, but it's obvious that her ex-boyfriend was an idiot. One of those guys who thinks that just because he has a penis, the world should revolve around him. He treated her like a queen until she moved in. Then he started treating her like a maid. Or a mommy he could fuck.

I'll never understand dudes like that. If you want a maid, hire one. Don't treat your woman like that.

Graves clears his throat. *Right.* Got a little lost in my head there. "He took her for granted," is all I tell him. "But if you want to know, you'll have to talk to her about it yourself. I'm not going to betray her confidence."

Bash pats me on the shoulder and nods approvingly.

Graves scowls and narrows his eyes. "It's not betraying her confidence. I just want to make sure that dickhead didn't do anything that warrants an ass-kicking."

"Nah, man. Nothing like that. You know I'd be right there with you if he had." Hell, I'd be ten steps ahead of Maddox if Jared had done anything insidious. Well, more insidious than acting like he didn't know how to wash his own clothes.

Glancing behind me, I find Mira's eyes tracking my movements. I want to blow her a kiss or something equally cheesy, but I can't. So I settle for a wink and fight my inner caveman when her cheeks flush that pretty pink I love so much. Although it's almost impossible to tear my gaze away, I manage. Turning to her older brother, I say, "She doesn't need you to set her up."

"I know she doesn't," Madds says with a roll of his eyes. "But my agent's got a nephew in marketing, and it seems like they'd have a lot in common. He's smart, serious, and responsible. Exactly the kind of guy Mira needs. Maybe he could even help her get her business off the ground."

"She doesn't need some random marketing bro to help her," I snap. "She's perfectly capable of doing it herself. You should see the stuff she's been working on." It doesn't escape my notice that Sebastian is studying me. Hell, I swear the guy can see right through me. He's too perceptive by half, and I'm going to need to watch myself around him. "Let her live her life the way she wants to. She's smart and strong and capable. She doesn't need her big brother setting her up. Or *helping* with her business."

Maddox opens his mouth, no doubt to tell me I don't get a say, when Coach Fry signals that it's time to leave the ice so the crew can get it ready for the start of the game. I hustle across the rink before Madds can say anything else, and I swear I can feel Mira's and Sebastian's eyes on my back the entire way while Maddox's words swirl around in my mind, picking up speed until they feel like a whirlwind.

He's smart, serious, and responsible. Exactly the kind of guy Mira needs.

Smart.

Serious.

Responsible.

The kind of guy Mira needs.

In other words, not me. Because I'm just the goofy idiot who makes people laugh and who doesn't do relationships. I'm the comedic relief. The dumb jock who's never good enough to bring home to Mom and Dad.

Never mind that Mira is happy living with me. I'm sure the thought of setting me up with his sister never crossed Maddox's mind.

***

EVERYONE CHEERS AND PATS ME ON THE BACK after I've washed the stink off and make my way to the family room where the women wait for us.

"Those were some serious hits tonight, Wright," one of the security guards says with a huge grin. "Who pissed you off out there?"

My best friend.

"No one," I say as nonchalantly as I can, even though my insides buzz with anxiety. "Just had to show their agitators what happens when you run your mouth against the Rogues."

"I know that's right," the guy says, clapping. He nods his head, and I return the gesture before continuing to the room where my wife waits for me.

My wife.

At least, for now.

That thought sends a fresh wave of nausea rolling through my gut. I need to get myself in check. Acting like a petulant child won't win Mira over or prove that I can be the man she needs. The other guys join me in the hall, laughing and chattering away. We've got plans to go out for drinks. Ryder and Lexi want to celebrate Maddox and Isla's engagement, since they weren't there when it happened.

"Great game, everyone," Lexi says when we walk into the room. She high-fives the guys as they pass before throwing herself in Hanson's arms. "Hey, Handsome."

All around me, couples embrace. Maddox and Isla, Ryder and Lexi, and the other guys with wives and girl-friends waiting for them. When my eyes find Mira, she's shuffling uncomfortably from one foot to the other as she takes in the scene. Then those gorgeous green eyes of hers meet mine, and some of that roiling storm in me calms.

"Hey," she says softly as she closes the distance between us. She looks more unsure than she ever has when meeting us after a game. Which makes sense, I suppose. Every game before this, she was merely Maddox's little sister and my roommate. Now? Now, Mira is my secret wife, and she's lost her equilibrium. "You okay?"

Fuck it.

As I pull her into a hug, a deep sigh gusts from my lips, making her hair move. "I'm fine," I lie. And I let her go. I don't want to, but I let her go. Because she asked me to keep this a secret, and if there's one thing I'm determined to do, it's keeping my word with Mira. Always. I want to be dependable. I want to be the person she leans on because she knows I'll never waver or crumble. So, as much as I want to continue holding my wife, I drop my arms and take a slight step back. "Did you have fun tonight?"

Mira is studying me, cataloging every twitch of my muscles and tic of my jaw. She's not buying my lie, but she lets me keep it. Blowing out a breath, she fists the hem of her jersey—the one with her brother's name on the back— and nods. "I did. You killed it tonight." Her lips twist as she tugs the pillowy lower half between her teeth. "I don't think I've ever seen you throw so many hits."

All I can do is shrug. Because the alternative is admitting that her brother made me feel like I'm not good enough for her. His words recalled all the breakup speeches given by ex-girlfriends through college. The alternative is admitting that I've never longed for anything as much as I want Mira to choose this marriage and to choose me. And as much as this woman lights my soul on fire, I know we're not there yet.

"Got tired of listening to their d-men chirp insults every few minutes."

Mira continues to abuse her lower lip, but she doesn't call me on my bullshit. Instead, she nods. "Understandable."

"Everyone ready?" Maddox asks the group.

He's smiling like a damn lovesick fool, and I love that for him. I need to get my shit under control. Tonight isn't about me or my feelings. Tonight, we're celebrating Madds and Isla on our home turf. Letting my hand rest lightly on the small of my wife's back, I suck in a slow, deep breath to calm my racing heart and gently lead her out of the family room and toward my car.

thirteen

MIRA

Something's up with Griffin. He's quiet on the ride to the restaurant, and I don't miss the frown lines marring his brow. I want to ask him what's wrong, but I don't quite know how to *be* in our relationship since we got drunk and married. Since he told me he wants to *stay* married.

Squirming in my seat, I steal glances at him, my stomach twisting. Griffin played an aggressive game tonight. I've never seen him throw so many hits, and even though fights and getting slammed into the boards are a part of the game I grew up watching, I'm surprised by how much it bothered me when it was Griffin taking the hit.

Griffin is my friend. It's natural to be worried about him. But this went beyond a friendly worry. Which is completely illogical because this marriage is a sham. I agreed to Griffin's six-month stipulation because the alternative was unthinkable, but that doesn't make this a real marriage. Neither do a few mind-blowing orgasms or waking up in his arms each morning, despite falling asleep as far away from him as I can get on his king-size mattress.

So why am I so worried?

I'm lost in my thoughts when Griffin pulls up to the valet and helps me out of his car.

"You look beautiful tonight," Griffin murmurs lowly, his hand lingering on mine. "I should have told you sooner. I'm sorry."

My gaze shifts to meet his, my cheeks heating. "I'm just wearing jeans and a jersey."

His eyes smolder, and so do my panties. "You always look beautiful, wifey. But next time, I want you wearing my name on your back."

"Griffin," I hiss, scanning the surrounding area to make sure no one overheard him.

My temporary husband sighs deeply, and for a moment, he looks so *tired*. Tired or frustrated? Whatever it is, he takes a step back, and I immediately miss his warmth. Which is stupid. "No one heard me, Mir. Don't worry. You won't be forced to claim me."

Fuck. The way he says those words has my stomach twisting. "I didn't mean—"

"Let's head inside," he says gruffly, cutting me off. His palm hovers over the small of my back. "It's cold and you're not dressed very warmly."

"I'm fine." I try not to shiver.

"Just humor me, Mira. For once, don't fight me on every little thing."

That makes my hackles rise. "I don't fight you on every little thing."

Griffin cocks one eyebrow.

Okay. Maybe I've been fighting him on every little thing since Vegas, but can he really blame me? He has backed me into a corner, turned my life upside down, and I feel like I have a bad case of emotional vertigo.

"Whatever," I mumble, letting him lead me into the restaurant. He tells the hostess who we're meeting, and I'm hyper aware of his palm against my spine. At least, until the hostess ushers us into a private room where we see Isla, Lexi, and the guys, and then Griffin drops his hand.

It's what I want. I've asked him to keep this *agreement* between us a secret, but my insides still lurch when he takes a step away from me.

Get your shit together, Mira.

Luckily, I don't have long to dwell on my roller-coaster emotions, because we're soon enveloped in hugs and easy conversation. Isla's best friends, Jess and Nevaeh, join us a few minutes later, and our server produces several bottles of expensive champagne.

When we're all halfway through the appetizers and everyone is on their second glass of bubbly, Isla's best friends are regaling everyone with the story of how they bid on my brother at the Rogues' online date auction. I crack up when Isla describes the truly awful dinner she shared with Maddox and scold my brother for almost running off my future sister-in-law.

I love hearing their stories. I wish I'd been around for more of them, but I'm here now. No more missing important moments in my big brother's life. I'm back in the Twin Cities, I've made amazing new friends, and a year from now, when we're all sitting around reminiscing, I'll have been present for all of those stories.

"Oh my god," Jess says, grabbing Isla's wrist with wide, amused eyes. "Do you remember at the silent auction dinner when that girl was telling Griffin about all the kinky shit she was into?"

My back stiffens, my heart lurches, and Griffin's attention swings to me.

"Ew." Isla's freckle-covered nose crinkles. "I do. What was her name? Some weird food."

Griffin shifts uncomfortably in his seat beside me. "We don't need to talk about thi—"

"Quinoa," Nevaeh nearly shouts. She shakes her dark curls. "I'll never forget that name. Who the hell names their kid after a grain?"

Everyone at the table laughs. Everyone except for Griffin and me.

Isla's blue eyes glitter with amusement. "That's right. As I recall, she went into great detail about her favorite butt plug." She turns her attention to Griffin. "You were so bummed that she left without giving you her number. You two had *plans*."

Isla's laughter sounds muddy and far away as something ugly and uncomfortable bubbles up inside of me and my ears ring.

Griffin clears his throat. "I was drunk. I don't remember anything about that. Can we please change the subject?"

"Oh, come on," Jess teases. "You looked like someone kicked your puppy. I wonder what would have happened if you'd gotten her number. Maybe she was your soulmate. You could have been celebrating your own engagement tonight and picking your future baby names. There'd be little Barley and baby Farro…"

Jess trails off in a fit of giggles and everyone else joins in. Griffin shifts in his seat. He's got a fake smile plastered on his face and he won't meet my eyes.

"Ha-ha," he forces out. "But like I said, I don't remember her, and she certainly wasn't my soulmate. Let's talk about something else."

Sebastian eyes Griffin thoughtfully for a moment before changing the subject.

Thank god.

"Have you two made any wedding plans yet?" Sebastian asks Isla and Maddox, glancing back at Griffin and frowning when he sees his friend glaring at the table in front of him.

Despite the acidic taste of bile in my mouth from Jess's story about Griffin and the confusing cocktail of jealousy, disgust, and the knowledge that I shouldn't actually care, because Griffin is my husband in name only, I still want to reach over and grab his hand. And if we were alone, I would. But there are too many sets of eyes at this table, including my brother's, who's regarding his best friend with a frown.

So I do the next best thing. I press the side of my foot against Griffin's beneath the table.

He sucks in a breath and peeks at me cautiously, pressing his full lips into a thin line as pink stains his cheeks. Under any other circumstances, I'd find it adorable, but this isn't the flush of happiness or pleasure. This is embarrassment. And despite my annoyance with Griffin Wright and his half-baked plan to get me to stay married to him, he's still become one of my best friends in the months I've lived with him, and I hate seeing him embarrassed. I'm about to ask him if he's okay when Isla answers Sebastian's question about their wedding plans.

"Actually," my future sister-in-law drawls, her blue eyes glowing with happiness,"we have made some plans." She's completely oblivious to Griffin's emotional state and my inner turmoil. As it should be. This night is about them.

She reaches for Maddox's hand, almost bouncing in her chair. "I was really hoping that the four of you ladies would be my bridesmaids." Isla's cheeks must ache from how broadly she's smiling. "Jess and Nev, you two have been my besties for so long, and I never would have met Maddox if not for your meddling."

Her two best friends chuckle as tears flood their eyes. They both give Isla emphatic *yeses*. She turns to me. "Mira, you're the sister I've always wanted. You have been since that first day we met. Now we get to make it official."

Now I'm tearing up, too. I love my brother and always have, but I can't deny spending lots of time wishing for a sister when we were kids and Maddy was always away at hockey practice or some game. "I can't wait," I tell her honestly.

"And Lexi," Isla says, turning to the newest woman in our group. "Even though we haven't known each other very long, I am so glad we've become friends, and I just know we'll be in each other's lives for a long, long time."

"I'd be honored." Lexi gives Isla's hand a squeeze, then beams at her boyfriend.

Maddox clears his throat. "You guys are brothers to me, you know that. You've always been there for me, and"—he turns to Griffin with nothing but gratitude written all over his features—"I wouldn't have gotten my girl back if not for you."

When I glance over at Griffin, moisture fills his eyes. He nods at my brother and smiles softly at Isla. He's always been their biggest champion, and Maddy is right. If Griffin hadn't gone to speak with Isla and confronted her ex, my stupid brother would have believed a lie and never would have tried to win her back.

"Anyway," Maddox says gruffly, "would you assholes be my groomsmen?"

Logan, Sebastian, and Ryder hoot and shout their agreement, but Griffin is silent for a beat. Only when my brother looks his way does Griffin's expression clear and a huge smile splits his face.

"I'm the best man, right?"

Maddox rolls his eyes. "Obviously."

"Then, hell yeah, brother. You know I wouldn't miss it for the world."

Griffin puts on a pretty convincing show for the rest of the evening, but I've lived with him long enough to know that he hasn't let go of whatever was bothering him before the game. Nor has he brushed off the story of his almost fling, Quinoa. Even as he smiles and laughs and joins in with the conversations that flow around us, there's a tension in his shoulders and jaw that won't seem to fade. And despite my happiness for Maddox and Isla and how much I enjoy the company of the people around me, I'm always hyper aware of my temporary husband. As the night wears on, my thoughts are consumed with going home and figuring out what's bothering him.

Not because I'm his wife. Because I'm his friend.

And I'm definitely not looking forward to curling up together in his big old bed.

Not even a little bit.

fourteen

MIRA

By the time Griffin and I make it home, I can't take the silence any longer.

"Okay, what's up with you?" I ask the minute we walk through the door. "You've been quiet and weird all night."

He's silent as he puts his duffel bag in the front closet. He still doesn't say anything as he shrugs out of his suit jacket and tosses it over the back of the couch. And he won't meet my eyes when his shoulders curl inward in a posture of defeat I've never seen before on Griffin Wright.

I don't like it. Rubbing my sternum, I wait.

Ten seconds tick by, then twenty, then thirty. I'm starting to wonder if he'll say anything at all when he sighs deeply and runs a hand through his shaggy, blond hair.

"I'm tired of being the punchline of everyone's jokes." He pauses. "I get that it's my fault because I'm the one who acts like nothing ever bothers me and I'm always happy, but fuck, Mir. I'm an actual person, not some two-dimensional caricature of one."

My heart lurches and I unconsciously take two steps toward him. My words are soft but firm. "You're not a joke."

A humorless laugh tears its way out of Griffin's throat. "Sure, I am. I was a joke to my highschool girlfriend, I was a joke to my college girlfriend, who I stupidly almost proposed to, and I'm a joke to my friends. I'm the guy you call for a good time. Not the one you reach out to when shit hits the fan. I'm the guy you fuck, but not the guy you settle down with."

That statement has my stomach dropping all the way down to my toes.

Griffin sighs. "I'm the idiot people tell stories about because they think I never take anything seriously, and I play right into the stereotype. Again and again and again." He tilts his head toward the ceiling for a beat before blowing out a stuttered breath. "You know what? Ignore me. I'm just tired. I'm gonna go to bed."

God, I feel like shit. Because how many times have I thought that Griffin doesn't take much seriously? How many times have I brushed off things he's said or done as him being ridiculous?

I'm no better than everyone else, and I hate it.

"Griffin, wait," I say, crossing the space between us and grabbing his hand before he can head down the hall. He doesn't turn to look at me, so I move to stand in front of him. And what I see makes me suck in a sharp breath.

Griffin's usually sparkling hazel eyes are dull and dark, his lips boast no hint of a smile, and his brow is creased and heavy. He looks so fucking *lost*.

Reaching up, I gently smooth the furrow between his eyebrows with the pad of my thumb before running my knuckles across his forehead. It takes a moment, but eventually, Griffin leans into my touch. His eyes flutter but don't close. They never leave my face.

"You're not a joke," I whisper as my heart thuds. My fingers trail down the side of Griffin's face and drag along the stubble lining his jaw. "You're not a punchline."

He still doesn't speak. Just watches me so intently. Like I possess the secrets of the universe, and he's waiting for them to tumble off my lips. It's heavy, the way he's looking at me. Waiting to see what I'll do next.

"You're one of the most supportive, selfless men I know," I tell him, taking a step closer so our chests almost touch as I look up at him. My fingers still scratch at the stubble of his jaw. "You lift up the people around you effortlessly. You see the best in people, Griffin. Sometimes, I think you see them more clearly than they see themselves."

Griffin's Adam's apple bobs and his breathing speeds up. One of his hands finds my hip and squeezes, which has my breath catching in my throat.

"I mean, you offered to let me move in without a second's hesitation and never asked anything in return. You figured out what really happened with Isla and Maddox and made sure they worked their shit out. The guys on your team depend on you, and not just on the ice." My left hand splays over Griffin's heart while my right cups his jaw. His heart is beating so fast. "I'm sorry Isla's friends made you feel like a joke, Griffin, but I promise you, that's not how they actually see you. No one who really knows you could ever think that."

"My college girlfriend thought that," he whispers.

I don't know this story, but I'll get it out of him one day. And then I'll look this chick up, find her, and punch her in the tit. "Yeah, well, she sounds like a stupid bitch."

Griffin's eyes widen before he barks out a shocked laugh. "Oh, yeah?"

"Mm-hmm." I nod, my gaze captured by this giant, sweet man's hazel eyes, which have regained some of their sparkle.

His strong chin dips and his head tilts ever so slightly to the side. "You don't think I'm a joke, sunshine?" His gravelly voice scrapes along my spine and pebbles my nipples.

I shake my head. "I think you're amazing, Griffin. And if anyone is sunshine around here, it's you. I wish you could see yourself more clearly."

Smoldering hazel eyes hold me captive for a single beat, then Griffin's lips crash against mine, hungry and desperate. My own lips part with a gasp, and he wastes no time sweeping his tongue inside and absolutely owning me. His hand still grips my hip while the other wraps around my back and drags me firmly against his very broad, very firm chest. And when he lets out a rumbly sound that is reminiscent of a growl, I swear my knees almost buckle.

Griffin walks me backward to the wall and pushes my spine against it, bracketing me with his body. His lips never leave mine, and the hand that was wrapped around my back skims up my side beneath my jersey. When his calloused fingers tug on the cup of my bra and push inside to play with my peaked nipple, I almost buckle.

"Easy there, sunshine," Griffin murmurs against my

swollen lips as his grip on my hip tightens and his knee wedges between my thighs to hold me up. I moan when his muscular thigh presses against my heated core. "I won't let you fall."

Without giving it a conscious thought, I reach for the buttons of Griffin's dress shirt and fumble to undo them as quickly as possible. When the cotton gapes wide enough, I run my palms along his smooth, golden skin.

"Fuck, babe," Griffin moans against my lips. His fingers leave my breast, and I whine at the loss of them until they tangle in my dark hair so Griffin can tug my head back, angling me to better plunder my mouth.

I hate that he's been questioning himself. Hate that I ever thought any of those things about him. I want to make Griffin forget his self-doubt and the stupid stories Isla's friends told at dinner. I want to show Griffin Wright that I don't see him as a joke or a caricature. I want to make him feel good about himself.

I want to make him feel *good.*

With a little shove, I flip our positions so Griffin is the one with his back to the wall. My belly swoops when he looks down at me with lust-clouded eyes. "What are you doing?"

Smirking, I palm his very hard dick through his dress pants and drop to my knees. "Showing you how seriously I take you." The sounds of his zipper and our heavy breathing fill the apartment.

"Mira, you don't have to do tha—*fuuuck.*" Griffin's head falls back against the wall as I free his cock and suck it down without preamble. I moan as the salty taste of him floods my mouth and take him as deep as I can. I don't have much of a gag reflex, so I can take him all the way to the back of my throat before my body starts to protest. Still, I ignore my discomfort and hold him there for a few beats before pulling off and sucking in a few deep breaths. When my lungs are once again full of air, I lick along the side of his shaft before taking the thick tip back into my mouth and swirling my tongue around the ridge.

"Goddamn it, sunshine." Griffin's hips buck as I suck hard on his cock, my head bobbing up and down his length enthusiastically. And when his fingers tangle in my hair and he presses me to take him deeper, my panties flood.

Making him unravel is one of the sexiest things I've ever done. And when his eyes stare at me, so full of awe and affection, my arousal spikes even higher. I may not know how to deal with our marriage, but this? This feels right. Right now, this is exactly what we both need. Connection. Release.

"You're so beautiful, Mira. God, look at you, taking me so deep." His hips press forward, making me gag. "Choke on my cock, wifey. I want to see tears streaming down those pretty cheeks of yours."

God. Damn. I squeeze my thighs together, and I do. I take Griffin so deep my nose bumps against his pelvis. Tears stream down my face as I fight against my gag reflex, and my fingers snake down my belly beneath the waistband of my jeans. I moan around his dick when I swipe two fingers through my dripping folds before playing with my clit.

"Fuck, that's hot," Griffin murmurs, his hips bucking more erratically as he gets closer to his release. "Wanna see more of you. That damn jersey is blocking my view."

I let out a whine of protest when Griffin takes his hard

dick away, but the whine turns into a squeak when he rips my jersey off, followed by my thermal, then my bra.

"Take off your pants and underwear," he rasps, stroking his hard shaft.

It's not graceful, but I hurry to comply, and soon I'm kneeling, completely naked, at Griffin's feet while he stands above me, fully clothed, save for his pants and boxer briefs which pool at his ankles. He strokes his cock faster.

"Spread your knees and touch your pussy, wife."

I'm so turned on, I'm aching for release, so he doesn't need to tell me twice. I widen my knees so he can see my fingers as they circle my clit. This won't take long. My body is already tightening in anticipation of my orgasm.

"Damn, baby. That's so fucking hot." Griffin groans, stroking himself harder, faster. His head falls back with a moan and his hips buck. The sight of him spurs me on, and I move my fingers faster. Little gasps and mewls spill from my lips. "Yes, Mira. Just like that."

"Griffin," I whine, looking up at him, desperate to come but unsure what I'm asking for.

"I know, babe. You want this cock."

I nod. I do. I really want his cock.

His hand moves faster now, his hips thrusting. "Are you close?"

All I can do is nod.

"Good." He grunts. "Fucking come, Mira. Come while I paint those perfect tits."

I'm already teetering on the edge, and Griffin's words push me over, my orgasm screaming through my body. I cry out his name, gasping for air as he grips his dick hard, and, murmuring curses and praise, does exactly as he said he would. He paints my breasts with ropes of hot cum.

We're both breathing hard as we come down from our orgasms, Griffin staring at the way he's marked me. His eyes flare when I run a finger through his release, pop it into my mouth, and suck it clean.

"Perfect," he says, almost reverently. "Absolutely perfect."

He swipes some of his cum off my nipple with his thumb before pressing it into my mouth. I suck hard, reveling in how different his demeanor is now compared to when we got home.

I did that. I had that effect on him.

"Come on, Mrs. Wright. Let's get you cleaned up. It's been a long day, and I just want to hold you." Before I can rise to my feet, Griffin bends down and scoops me up, pressing me to his chest. He kisses the side of my head and whispers, "Thank you."

The thing is? I'd do just about anything for this man, but if I tell him that, he'll run with it and demand we announce our marriage to the world or something. And while I'd do *almost* anything for Griffin Wright, I'm not ready to do that. So I keep quiet, snuggle closer to him, and press a kiss to the scruff of his chin.

I try not to think about how right it feels to be held in his arms.

fifteen

GRIFFIN

The other night was a wake-up call. I thought the people who loved me really *got* me, but maybe they don't. Despite Mira's reassuring words, there was no hiding the look on her face when she tried to convince me I'm not a joke.

Some part of her has never fully taken me seriously. I can't say I'm surprised, but it sure as hell burns. The worst part is that I don't have anyone to blame but myself. I'm the one who donned the good-time persona back in high school to differentiate myself. My grades were just okay, and while hockey was my life, I grew up in a football town where my classmates and neighbors bled Wildcat navy and white. I spent so much time playing and training that it was difficult to make real friends at my school. I didn't give a shit about football, and I was at the rink too often to join any clubs. So I became the guy you wanted to invite to parties. The guy who'd make you laugh. The guy who could charm his way into almost any girl's panties with flirtatious banter and a few well-timed flashes of washboard abs.

Girls love washboard abs.

It made friendships easier, even if they were shallow, and I kept the act going through college. The guys on my college team—including Maddox—became true friends, but the good-time persona was a hit with the ladies, so it stuck. Which was probably part of the reason my college girlfriend never took our relationship as seriously as I did.

Maybe it's time for a change. Time to be *serious* and *responsible*. The kind of man Madds is so convinced his sister needs.

The real shit part? I am responsible. I own my home and car and I'm not in any debt. I save more than I spend, and I don't take my salary for granted. Hockey is a brutal mistress, and no one plays forever. One day, the money will stop flowing in, and when that happens, I won't be taken by surprise. Plenty of guys act like they'll always be rolling in cash, spending it as quickly as they make it. Those guys are irresponsible.

And serious? I'm one of the best wingers in the league for a reason, and it's not because I treat my career like a joke.

But I don't wear polos and loafers and walk around with my ass cheeks clenched like I'm trying to use them to squeeze juice out of a lemon. There's a certain mental picture people have when they hear the word *serious*, and I don't fit it. It's narrow-minded, but it's undeniable. If you stood me next to a stuck-up looking asshole in a chambray button-down, khakis, and boat shoes, you'd assume that guy has his life together. It doesn't matter that he could be living in his mom's basement, snorting coke at clubs, and walking around calling women *females*. He'd look the part.

I can wear polos and khakis. I can look the part too.

The thought makes my stomach twist uncomfortably because I hate the idea that Mira may only give me a real chance if I change who I am, but she's worth it. So I Google *where can I find preppy rich guy clothes*, grab my keys, and head out to buy a new wardrobe.

Maddox thinks Mira needs someone *serious*? Fine. I can be serious.

I *MAY* HAVE GONE A LITTLE OVERBOARD. BUT IN MY defense, I didn't realize monograms were so important to preppy rich people.

Straightening the new bath towels I bought, I grin. Maybe it's lame, but I like them. I also like the monogrammed bathrobes that look like they came straight out of some fancy spa.

My phone buzzes with an incoming text.

WIFEY

Do you want me to pick up dinner? The
girls and I are almost done hanging out.

Mira may act like she doesn't feel this thing between us, but I know better. She thinks about me when she's out, she comes to my games, and the other night... *Fuck*, the other night was everything. The sight of my wife on her knees, sucking my cock as she tried to cheer me up, will live rent free in my mind until I'm a shriveled husk of a man rotting away in a nursing home somewhere. She can't only see me as a friend if she's willing to do something like that, right?

Time to enact my plan to get Mira to see me as more than a friend or a fuck buddy. Time to get my wifey to see me as a husband, and that means no more takeout. I'm going to take care of my woman and show her I'm not like her shitty ex-boyfriend, Jared. I won't ever expect her to do everything while I sit around with my thumb stuck up my ass.

ME

No need. I'm cooking dinner. What time will you be home so I can have it ready?

I grin when the ellipses that tells me she's typing flashes on the screen right away.

WIFEY

Oh! Um, I should be home in an hour. Can I pick anything up?

ME

Nah. I've got everything under control. Have fun with the girls and tell them I say hi.

Okay. Thanks, Griffy.

Griffy. It's the first time she's called me that since we got married. Who would have thought a silly nickname would make me feel so warm and fuzzy inside? Shit, it may be better than the blow job she gave me the other night. Grinning like a fool, I throw on an apron—a new, non-perverted one because I'm *serious* now. RIP, *Eat My Meat* apron—and gather everything I'll need to make my wife a healthy, delicious meal. I'd rather be wearing my gray sweats than these starched and stuffy khakis, but it's a small sacrifice to make in the effort to win over my wife.

When the door opens just over an hour later, I have the table set—with cloth napkins and everything—and I'm setting the roasted chicken and veggies on trivets.

Mira wanders into our home and stops dead in her tracks when she sees me. "Oh, wow." Her stunning moss-colored eyes ping between the food, the fancy place settings, the candles at the center of the table, and me. They widen when she takes in my outfit. "Is there some special occasion I forgot about tonight?"

Chuckling, I pull out a chair for her as she washes her hands. "Just wanted to make sure you had a healthy, home-cooked meal."

She eyes me speculatively as she sits down, her pretty cheeks growing pink as I push her chair in for her.

"I know I'm not around often to do stuff like this, so I want to prioritize it when I am."

"Griffin," she starts, chewing on her lower lip, "you don't have to do that."

I shrug. "You're my wife. I want to." I don't break eye contact with Mira, even when she shifts in her seat, unsure how to read me or what to say.

"Griff…"

"Nuh-uh, sunshine. Save your protests. I know you have your reservations about all of this, but I'm perfect for you, and I'm going to prove it. Now, eat your chicken before it gets cold."

She has one eyebrow cocked like she's about to say something sarcastic. Instead, she says, "Why are you suddenly calling me sunshine?"

Warmth spreads through my chest. And that's why.

"Because you shine so damn bright, baby. You make me feel warm and happy. You're walking, talking, sexy-as-fuck sunshine."

Mira's cheeks turn an even deeper shade of pink as she tilts her head down and drops my gaze. "You're such a flirt."

That won't do. I don't want this woman who consumes my thoughts to believe this is just some flirtation. Hell fucking no. This is the real deal. "Nah, Mir. I'm not flirting, I'm being completely serious. Ever since you moved in, it's like my world is brighter. I want to be around you every second of the day to soak you up. When I'm on the road with the guys, I miss the hell out of you. This isn't flirting. This is me telling you I don't want to live without you."

My wife opens her mouth to say something, sucks in a breath, then stares at me. No words escape her lips. I think I've broken her. As she blinks those pretty eyes at me, a grin tugs at the corner of my lips, growing wider with every second she sits there, at a loss for words. I scoop some veggies onto her plate and slice up some chicken. When I'm satisfied she'll have enough, I say, "Eat, beautiful."

Mira holds my gaze for a few beats before shaking her head and spearing a piece of roasted asparagus. The hum she makes when she chews fills my chest with a proud warmth.

"This is really good, Griffin. I knew you liked to cook, but this is fancy."

"It's easier than it looks," I tell her. "The trick is cooking the chicken in the air fryer so the skin gets extra crispy and using the right ratio of balsamic glaze on the veggies."

She blinks at me, chewing her food. With another grin, I focus on my plate and dig in. It really is good, and I can't help the pleased groan that slips from my lips.

Mira shifts in her seat, her cheeks flushing slightly.

"So, sunshine, tell me about what you're working on right now? I want to hear all about it."

Those stunning green eyes of hers rise to meet mine, and she smiles. "I'm almost done with this website for the most fun baseball team ever. You'd love them. They do choreographed musical numbers throughout their games, and they're so funny."

I hang on every word she speaks, just like always. I'm obsessed with this woman, after all. And no matter what it takes, I'll prove I'm exactly what she wants and needs.

sixteen

MIRA

WHAT IN THE HECK IS WITH ALL THIS NEW monogrammed crap? Was it here last night, and I was too tired to notice, or did some snooty, rich-person fairy drop them off while we were sleeping? Like the tooth fairy, but in reverse—and if the tooth fairy had a weird obsession with embroidery.

Eyeing the fluffy white towel with *M.W.* emblazoned on the lower corner in a loopy, black script, like it may bite me on the ass, I take in the damp towel Griffin must have used this morning that says *G.W.* in the same spot. Then my eyes catch on the hand towels emblazoned with *Mr.* and *Mrs.*

What. The. Fuck?

I'm tempted to text Griffin to demand answers, but he's at the arena, and I can't risk my brother seeing any of our exchange. Shaking my head, I dry off, wrap the towel around my damp body, and pad over to the linen closet inside the bathroom to see if I can find a towel that doesn't have my initials monogrammed on it. The *wrong* initials.

Stacked neatly in crisp lines are more white bath towels, and I groan because I just know they're all the same. I pull a few out anyway and can't help laughing at what I find. Because, yes, all these ridiculous towels are monogrammed with our initials, but half have a *W* as the last initial and half of them have a *G*. When Griffin said before that he would change his last name to Graves if I wanted, I thought he was joking.

Maybe he wasn't.

Warmth floods my chest, and my cheeks hurt from smiling.

This idiot.

I can't stop smiling the entire time I get ready for the day, and my lips are still curved when I sit down to finish the website I've been working on. And four hours later, when my phone buzzes with an incoming text message, I'm still grinning.

Sitting up straight and twisting my back to give it a crack, I open my messages to find one from Lexi.

LEXI

Hey, girl! Want to get lunch today? I need a break from these online classes. I swear, I'm going stir crazy.

My stomach chooses that moment to growl, making my answer an easy one. My eyes are blurry and dry from staring at the computer screen, and I could use some fresh air. Plus, it's been so long since I've had girlfriends to hang out with, I'll always jump at the opportunity to spend time with Lexi or Isla.

ME

> Yes! That sounds great. I can leave right now if you want. Where should we meet?

LEXI

> Halle-frickin-lujah. Meet at that little ramen place on Eat Street?

Eat Street has some of the best restaurants in downtown Minneapolis, and I'm obsessed with The Ramen Bowl. Honestly, you can't go wrong at any of the restaurants on Nicollet Avenue.

ME

> Yes! I'm in. I'll leave in five.

LEXI

> Yay! See you soon.

Humming, I put my computer to sleep, run a brush through my hair, throw on some mascara, slip into my Converse, then head down to the parking garage. Artax, my old silver Toyota, looks sad and clunky compared to the sleek, expensive vehicles parked in the surrounding spots. I feel a momentary pang of self-consciousness but brush it off. Who cares what kind of car I drive, as long as it gets me from one place to another? I give the hood a little pat before unlocking the door, sliding in, and putting the key in the ignition.

"Don't let these fancy cars make you feel bad, boy. It's what's inside that counts."

I turn the key, and Artax splutters.

"Come on," I growl, turning the key again. The engine tries to turn over, makes an ominous clunking sound, then sputters before dying. Because of course. Of *course* this would happen. "Apparently, what's inside you is crap, huh?"

Groaning, I bang my head on the steering wheel lightly before pulling my phone out and texting Lexi.

ME

My stupid car just died. Gonna call a rideshare, so I'll be a little late. Sorry, girl.

Her response is almost instant.

LEXI

Don't do that! You know I'm not that far away. I'll come pick you up. Meet you out front of your building?

ME

You sure?

Duh. Don't be ridiculous.

Okay. Thanks, Lexi. See you soon.

With a dirty look in Artax's direction and a kick to the front tire, I don't even bother locking the stupid thing before heading toward the front of the building. If I'm lucky, someone will steal it so I can get at least a few hundred dollars from my insurance.

But I won't be that lucky.

My fingers itch to text Griffin so I can tell him what happened, but I restrain myself. I don't need to involve him in every little thing. I can't deny that I want to, though. Which is something I try not to look at too closely, because I'm scared of what it means that he's the first person I think about going to with my problems.

I'm still mulling that over a few minutes later when Lexi pulls up. I don't know why I'm relieved to see that she doesn't have some fancy car either, but I am. Despite my annoyance at my stupid Toyota, I give my friend a big smile as I slide into the passenger seat.

"Hey, Lexi. Thanks for picking me up."

My blonde friend smiles brightly, her green eyes sparkling in the noonday sun. "Anytime. I seriously don't mind at all. Sorry about your car, though. Did you call a tow?"

"No." I shake my head. "I'll deal with it when I get back. It's an old car, and I know it won't last much longer, but I can't afford to replace it, you know?"

Lexi hums a sound of understanding as she pulls out into traffic and starts making her way to the restaurant. "Totally. I plan to drive this thing until it dies too."

She gets me. It's so nice having friends who get me.

"So," she says, drawing the word out in a sing-song tone, "how's living with Griffin?"

Side-eyeing her, I try not to act suspicious. It's an inno-cent question. She doesn't know we got drunkenly married. No one does. She's making conversation because that's what friends do. "It's good."

Eloquent, Mira.

Lexi chuckles. "Just good? You two seem to get along well. Is he as sweet to live with as he is to hang out with? I know he's kind of a goofball sometimes, but I've always really liked Griffin. He's good people."

A smile quirks the corner of my lips because he *is* good people. He offered me a place to live without hesitating, then had my room beautifully decorated. He makes sure I eat, makes me laugh, listens with his whole body when I talk, and he's always genuinely interested in what I'm doing. Not to mention, he's supportive. And unlike my shitty ex, I don't think Griffin is feigning interest in me just to get me to sleep with him.

Or stay married to him, as the case may be.

"He's a great guy," I agree. "Honestly, I've had more fun living with him than I've ever had living with anyone else."

Lexi nods. "I could see that. How long do you plan to live with him? I know you're working on getting your business off the ground."

"Um, at least for the next six months," I say, my belly twisting strangely. Wanting to get us away from this particular line of conversation, I turn it around on Lexi. "How's living with Ryder? Is it weird or great?"

Lexi and Ryder moved in together not too long ago after their relationship became something of a local, and even national, spectacle. Lexi's dad was the head coach of the Rogues for quite some time until he was caught on film at a game starting a fight with Ryder and saying some truly vile things about his daughter when he found out she and Ryder were secretly dating.

It was a huge scandal for a while, and people rallied behind Lexi and Ryder, which was great, but it also meant that Lexi lost her ability to go to school on campus because people were always going up to her, taking photos, and generally making her feel unsafe. That's when Ryder insisted Lexi move in with him. They hadn't been dating all that long, but clearly, the two of them are meant to be, so Lexi jumped right in and said yes.

My blonde friend sighs, hearts in her eyes and a dreamy look on her face. "It's so great, Mira. At first, I was worried it was too fast, you know? But then I thought about how amazing it was to spend that week alone together at the cabin over Christmas, and he was a total stranger at the start of it." She smiles dreamily. "I love him so freaking much."

"I'm so happy for you," I tell her honestly.

"Thanks, girl. I'm really happy too. Now we just need to find someone for you so we can triple date. Me and Ryder, Isla and your brother, and you and some dreamy hunk."

Forcing out a laugh, I rub the back of my neck. "Uh, no, you guys don't need to find anyone for me. I'm good."

"Oh, come on, Mira. There's gotta be someone on the team you think is hot." She glances my way. "You're gorgeous and smart. Any of those men would be lucky to date you."

"Right," I say. "Except they'd all probably be too scared my brother would kick their asses to ask me out." The city goes by in a blur, and before I know it, Lexi pulls into a spot on the street.

"You might be surprised," Lexi says as she opens her door and climbs out. She smiles brightly at me over the roof of her car. "Isla told me Maddox has been talking about wanting to set you up with someone too."

What? I gape at my friend. My brother wants to set me up with someone? Why would he want to do that? "I'm sorry, what?"

Lexi chuckles. "I guess he has someone in mind for you."

"Someone on his team?" I ask as we walk into the restaurant. I'm so distracted by the whole conversation, I almost walk into a post.

"I don't think so. Some guy his agent knows or something? I'm not totally sure. Isla only mentioned it in passing. It's sweet that your brother wants to set you up with someone."

"Right. Sweet." The effort it takes not to roll my eyes cannot be overstated. But I manage to keep my face in check as the host greets us and leads us to a table.

Maddox wants to set me up. That's...not great. I'll have to figure out some good excuses to put him off, because I sure as shit can't tell him the truth. Because telling my brother I accidentally married his best friend, and said best friend is practically blackmailing me into staying married for six months, would be a death sentence for Griffin. And as much as I may have wanted to kick Griffin's ass when all of this went down, now the thought makes my chest ache.

How is this even my life?

seventeen

GRIFFIN

Coach Fry calls us over to the bench. We've been running drills and perfecting new plays all morning, and I'm exhausted, but our upcoming series in Toronto against the Icons will be a brutal matchup. Their team is on fire this season, so Coach Fry has been pulling out all the stops to get us ready.

Having Fry take over for Coach Cross has been an adjustment, but the guy is a solid offensive strategist. Not to mention a way better human being than Coach Cross ever was.

"Huddle up, men." Coach Fry's dark brown eyes scan each one of us, his rich sienna skin tinged slightly with pink from the cold nipping at his cheeks. "Good work out there today. I know I've thrown a lot of new stuff at you, but I think you've got it. How do you all feel about the new plays?"

A chorus of *Good, Coach* and *We're ready* fills the air.

All of us are eager to prove ourselves against Toronto and silence any of our remaining critics who don't believe we have what it takes to get to the playoffs after everything that happened with Coach Cross.

"Good. Now I want all of you to go home, get some rest, then be at the airport at seven sharp tomorrow morning. Be ready to play your asses off, because Toronto's going to come at us hard and fast. Their goalie's been on a hot streak, and we're going to be the one to break it. But that means no sloppy plays and pointless penalties, you got me? We don't want any penalty kills against this team." Coach Fry scans each of our faces. "Clean hits, be aggressive but not sloppy, and I want to see immaculate puck handling out there, gentlemen. If we can do all that, we'll kick their asses."

The guys and I all cheer. We're determined to take this team as far as we can go this season.

"Go hit the showers. You all stink."

Laughter bounces off the boards as Coach flashes us a smile, then we all race off the ice. I'm anxious to get home, and I'm not the only one. We leave tomorrow morning for three consecutive away games, which means we'll be on the road for almost a week. A week without falling asleep with Mira wrapped in my arms or waking up to her soft body pressed against mine. A week where I won't get to see or talk to her much, if at all.

Will Mira want to talk to me while I'm gone? Can I convince her to FaceTime me, or will she be relieved to have me out of her hair for an entire week? I'm not delusional. Just because she went down on me doesn't mean our marriage is real to her.

Shit. I'm in way over my head.

"Hey, Graves," Ryder says after we're all showered and getting dressed. "Sounds like your sister's car broke down."

My ears perk up, and I turn to face the rookie. "What do you mean, her car broke down?"

Ryder stares at his phone as it buzzes with an incoming text. "She and Lexi got lunch and Lex had to pick her up. Said she couldn't get the car to start."

Maddox rubs the back of his neck. "She's been driving that hunk of junk since she was in high school. I've tried to get her to let me buy her a car so many times, but she's stubborn." Though my best friend rolls his eyes, there's no real irritation behind it. He's proud that Mira is stubborn and independent. I know, because he's told me on more than one occasion. "I'll call a tow."

Nope. Like hell am I letting Maddox swoop in and save the day. That's what husbands are for. "Don't worry about it, Madds. I'll take care of it."

Maddox's eyebrows rise. "Why would you take care of it?"

"Because she's my roommate and my friend, and it'll be easier for me to meet them in the parking garage than you."

He doesn't look convinced, so I aim my next argument toward his soft spot. "Besides, I know you want to spend as much time as possible with Isla before we leave."

My best friend winces at that, studying me for a beat before sighing. "You sure?"

"Yep. I've got this. Go spend time with your future wife. I'll take care of Mira."

I can feel Sebastian's eyes on me, but I ignore him. It's like when toddlers play hide-and-seek. If I pretend I can't see him, maybe he'll go away. I seriously need Bash to be a hell of a lot less perceptive, because if anyone is going to figure out what's going on between me and Mira, it'll be that insightful bastard.

Maddox sighs. "All right. Thanks, man. I owe you."

"No, you really don't. Now get the hell out of here. I'll see you tomorrow." I turn to Ryder. "Thanks for the heads-up, Handsome. Does Hot Cross Buns need me to pick Mira up?"

Ryder chuckles, shaking his head at the codename we gave his girlfriend so our ex-coach wouldn't know we were talking about his daughter earlier this year before he got sacked for being an unwashed asshole. "No, she said they're watching a movie, then she'll bring her home."

Good. That will give me time to get Mira's car towed to my mechanic, have him look it over, and let me pre-pay for any repairs. It'll also give me time to fill my car up with gas. I can't leave my wife without transportation for a week, and what's mine is hers. She'll just have to drive my G-Wagon while I'm gone.

"Cool. Thanks, man. Shoot me a text if you need me to pick her up."

Ryder agrees, and we all say our goodbyes, but I'm distracted, too busy plotting how I can get my wife into a safer car without too much of a fight. Although I want to buy her something pretty and new, I have no doubt she'd give me hell for that. I guess I could have her car completely rebuilt, but the thing is a hunk of rusted junk. It seems silly to spend so much to rebuild a car that's probably worth five hundred bucks.

I'll have to do some brainstorming. Once I convince my wife to stay married to me, I'll buy her a brand-new car. For now, I'll have to settle for fixing her Toyota.

By the time I pull into my building's parking garage, I've called a tow and spoken to my mechanic, who assures me he'll give Mira's car a thorough inspection, then fix every last issue with the damn thing, down to replacing the windshield wipers. The tow truck arrives less than half an hour later, and by the time Mira walks through our door, I'm packed and ready to leave in the morning. I don't want to waste a single minute I could be spending with my wife.

"Hi," she says, a pretty blush staining her cheeks.

"Hi." I cross the space between us and pull Mira into a tight hug. She's stiff for half a second, and then she melts into my embrace, her arms wrapping around my middle. "God, I missed you."

She giggles, the sound muffled against my chest. "You saw me this morning before you left for practice."

"I know. It's been too long." The thing is, I'm not even making a joke. With every passing day, I fall harder for this woman, and being apart from her makes me feel anxious and empty. She's quickly becoming the most important person in my life.

Mira laughs again, and it's followed by a sigh. "I kinda missed you too."

"You did?" I can't hide my surprise. Although she's softening to me, she's also still fighting this thing between us. Pulling away from her just enough to see her face, I search for the lie but don't spot any evidence of one.

She nods, pulling her bottom lip between her teeth. "I did."

The smile that breaks out over my face is so wide, my cheeks hurt. *She missed me.*

Needing to hold her, I bend at the knees, wrap my arms

around her waist, and lift her feet off the ground. Mira's giggle vibrates through me as I spin us around, only stopping when I'm dizzy. Then I let her body slide down mine before palming the back of her head and kissing the shit out of her. The little sighs she releases against my lips have me rock hard and desperate for her. I want nothing more than to sink inside her and make love to her all night long, but I told her I wouldn't fuck her until she was on board with being my wife. And while I may cave at some point in the future, it feels important not to cave now.

Lips still fused with hers, I walk Mira over to the couch and pull her onto my lap so she's straddling me. Her denim-covered core settles over my slacks-covered dick, and she grinds against me as our lips and tongues clash.

"Fuck, wife," I grunt as she undulates against me. My fingers dig into her hips—as much to tether her to me as to keep myself from doing what I really want to do—and she mewls softly. I swallow the sound like it's a drug, because I'm desperate to be high on her.

"Griffin." She moans my name, her eyes heavy lidded and full of need. Her lips are already puffy from kissing me, and god, if that doesn't turn me on even more.

"What do you need, Mira? Hmm? Let me take care of you."

Mira bites her lower lip as she meets my gaze. Her eyes are so full of need, but there's uncertainty too. Why is she still fighting this? Doesn't she feel how *right* this is? Doesn't she understand I would do anything to make her happy? That we fit perfectly in all the ways that matter?

Kissing along her jaw and neck, I let go of her hips and allow my fingers to wander. They skim up her sides, slip under her shirt, and trace a path along the satiny skin of her rib cage before my thumbs brush the undersides of her breasts. When Mira's breath hitches, I grin against her neck. I want her to be as needy as I am right now. Every cell in my body vibrates with desire for this woman, and my cock is painfully hard. "What do you need, wife?"

"You," she says with a sigh. "I need you, Griffin."

It's what I want to hear. At least, partially. Gripping the hem of Mira's shirt, I gently tug it up as she lifts her arms in the air to help me get it off. Her perfect breasts heave in a simple black cotton bra, and I'm struck speechless for a moment. But only for a moment. "You're so beautiful. So fucking perfect. Look at you, sunshine. You're every fantasy I've ever had come to life, only better."

Mira's cheeks flush, and she looks at me from beneath the fringe of her lashes, suddenly shy. That won't do.

"I want you every second of every day. Do you know how hard it is to keep my hands to myself, hmm?" I reach around her back and unhook the bra before sliding the straps off her shoulders. She shrugs out of it, and I toss the garment to the floor. Her dusky pink nipples tighten in the cool air, demanding I lean down and take them into my mouth.

Mira gasps. "Oh, fuck."

I suck and play with her, nipping at the sensitive little buds, laving my tongue over one tight nub while squeezing and kneading her other breast with my hand. Mira's hips rock more urgently against my rock-hard dick, making me groan.

"You want my cock, baby?"

She nods. "Yes. Please. I want your cock."

Grinning, I nip at her breast. "You want me to stuff your wet, needy pussy with my big, thick cock?"

She nods again, eyes glassy with need.

"I bet you feel so empty right now, don't you, sunshine? Are you desperate to feel my head dragging along your G-spot? For me to pound into your tight cunt and rut into you until you're screaming my name?" Grabbing handfuls of her jeans-covered ass, I buck up against her hot little center, earning a gasp and a moan from my needy wife.

"Yes. Fuck, yes. Fill me with your cock." Mira rocks against me, throwing her head back and closing her eyes as her need takes over.

"Wanna take you bare," I growl against her breast. "Want to paint your insides with my cum, then watch it drip out of your pretty pussy."

"Oh, god."

Fuck. My need for her is goddamn painful. But if I'm going to do all the things I'm saying to her, I need her to admit that she wants this. That she wants me. Not just my body, not just sex, but *me*.

"You want that, baby?"

All she can do is nod her head vigorously.

"Then tell me you're mine. Tell me you're my wife. That you want this as much as I do. That you want me to be your husband." Every word of my plea is laced with need and raw truth. Can she hear it? *Feel* how much I want her?

"Griffin..." She still rocks against me, but her eyes are sharper now, less hazy with lust than they were a moment ago.

"Why are you fighting this?" I grind my cock against her core, and she moans. "Why won't you give this a real chance? You promised you'd try."

"This will never work." She gasps as I pinch her nipples. "We want different things."

Letting go of her breasts, I unbutton her jeans. She shimmies out of them, then goes back to rocking her soaking wet center against my lap. A damp spot forms on my slacks, and I'm tempted to never dry clean these pants again. Dipping my fingers beneath the waistband of her panties, I drag them through her soaking slit, coating them instantly in her slippery wetness. "Are you sure about that? It sure as hell feels like we want the same thing right now."

Mira lifts her hips enough for me to push two fingers inside her hot little pussy, and she whines with pleasure at the intrusion. "Of course I want you. I'm not dead. But wanting to fuck you isn't enough to base a marriage on."

I pump my fingers in and out of her faster, fighting my irritation at her words. "You don't only want to fuck me, sunshine. You like spending time with me. You like living with me. I make you feel safe and special."

"Y-you do," she stammers, confusion flickering across her features. "But that's because we're friends."

"Is it?" I ask, adding a third finger and enjoying the way her eyes roll back in her head. I want to make her fall apart. To scream my name. So I pull my fingers out of her and flip us so she's lying with her back on the couch. Desperate to taste her, I rip Mira's panties off and throw them onto the floor. Using my shoulders, I push my wife's thighs apart before spreading her pussy open with my fingers. She's swollen and wet, and I want her sweet musk to invade my senses. "We're just friends?"

"Y-yes."

I look up at her from between the juncture of her thighs and grin wickedly. "Really? If we were just friends, would your pussy be dripping with need for me?" Maintaining eye contact, I flick my tongue out and lap at her slit, her clit, and then I spear her fluttering pussy with it. Mira moans, her back arching. I fuck her with my tongue before suckling her clit.

"If we were just friends, would you let me eat your juicy cunt? Would you moan like a pretty little slut desperate for more?"

"Griffin…" She's conflicted. I watch it play out across her features. She wants me, but she's not ready to admit it to herself. Even though it's not what I hoped would happen, I can be patient. I'm playing the long game, and I'm playing to win.

"Fight this all you want, wife, but you know we're inevitable. We fit perfectly, and one of these days, you won't be too scared to admit it."

"I'm not scared," she says breathlessly.

"You are." I'm scared too. How can I not be? But waking up married to this woman was a gift of fate, and I won't waste this chance, scared or not. "That's okay. You can be scared, but I'm not going anywhere. I'll be right here, worshipping at your altar, until you can admit to yourself what I already know."

"And what's that?" She mewls as I circle her clit with my tongue.

"That I was made for you. That I can make you happy." I push two fingers inside of her while I continue to lap at her clit, grinning when her back bows off the couch. "But most importantly, Mira? That I'm all in, and I will *never* walk away from you. For as long as you'll allow me to be in your life, I will *never* leave. Not ever."

Her breath hitches and her lower lip trembles, but she

doesn't say a word. That's okay. Words are overrated. It's actions that matter. So I lower my mouth to her pussy and show her with every flick of my tongue how much I want her. I show her again and again until tears stream down her face and her body convulses with pleasure. Then I carry her to the bathroom, draw her a bath, and show her I care in yet another way.

I'll prove she can trust me. I'll prove that I can take care of her.

Whatever it takes.

eighteen

MIRA

"Shit." Water splashes around me as I sit up in the massive jacuzzi tub.

Griffin smooths my hair away from my neck and presses a lingering kiss there. "What's wrong?"

You steal all my sense every time we're together and it's only getting worse the closer we grow.

"My stupid car broke down, and I forgot all about it with all the"—I wave my hands around haphazardly—"distractions when I got home."

Griffin's body vibrates against my bare skin as he laughs, pulling my back against his chest where I've been snuggled since he washed my hair.

He washed my hair.

No guy has ever done that for me, and I can confidently say it was one of the most erotic, intimate moments of my life. Between the orgasms and the bath, is it any wonder I got distracted?

"Distractions, huh? Is that what we're calling multiple orgasms these days?"

He sounds so self-satisfied. I want to be annoyed, but I can't be. Because yeah, Griffin gave me multiple orgasms. Multiple *powerful* orgasms without asking for anything in return or letting me wrap my lips around his cock. Only an idiot would truly complain about something like that. Though I did want his dick, and he only gave me his mouth.

Stupid rule. I know he wants me to give in and agree to be his wife forever. He wants me to call him my husband and tell our families and friends that we're married and in love.

In love.

It's crazy. Isn't it?

"Well, those multiple orgasms distracted me from my piece of crap car, and now it's probably too late to call a tow without paying extra. That's how that works, right?" Hell if I know.

Griffin chuckles. "I don't know, sunshine, but you don't have to worry about your car." His long fingers skim my sides and thighs, creating ripples in the hot water.

"What do you mean?" I ask, turning my head to look at him. He looks so peaceful and happy. Like this is the only place in the world he wants to be. Here, naked, and cuddled up with me.

"I mean, I was with Ryder when Lexi let him know you couldn't get your car to start, so I had it towed to my mechanic's shop." Griffin says all of that with the easy nonchalance of someone with money to burn. I guarantee his mechanic charges way more than I can afford, and even though my savings account has rebounded some since moving in with Griffin and not needing to pay rent, it's still depleted more than I'd like from moving twice in three months.

Moving isn't cheap.

"And what did you tell your mechanic?" I ask, afraid to hear the answer. I was so relaxed, but now my stomach flips, filling with acid.

Those long fingers still, then Griffin wraps me in his muscular arms. His lips are centimeters away from my ear when he answers. "I told him to fix your car. You can't drive around in something unsafe, Mira."

"What if it's more than I can afford?" I ask, my voice rising in pitch. "Is he going to call to get approval and give me a quote before he does anything?"

"No, baby, he's not. Because you don't need to worry about any of that."

"Griffin," I say, looking at him with wide eyes that probably look as panicked as I feel, "you can't just tell me not to worry about something like that. I'm not... I don't have a bank account full of disposable income like you and Maddy."

"You do, actually," the infuriating man says with a shrug.

Breaking out of Griffin's arms, I spin to face him fully. I take a few deep breaths in an effort not to lose my absolute shit and pinch the bridge of my nose. "What?"

The man has the audacity to roll his eyes at me.

He rolls his eyes.

Hockey gods help him.

"You're my wife, Mira. What's mine is yours. So yeah, you do have a bank account full of disposable income." His head cants to the side and his eyes narrow. "Actually, now that I think about it, I should add your name to my checking account and get you your own credit card."

Breathe, Mira, breathe. Do not scream. Do not flip out. Do not murder the sweet idiot with the massive dick sitting in front of you.

"I don't want your money, Wright."

His straight nose wrinkles as he frowns. "It's not just my money, Mrs. Wright."

Narrowing my eyes at the use of his last name in place of mine, I nearly growl. "Swear to god, Griffin..."

"You can fight with me all you want, wifey, but I'm fixing your car. It's already there, and I've already given them my authorization to fix everything, then charge my card. I don't see what the big deal is. I'm your husband. I care about you, and it's my job to make sure you're safe." He pauses, those multi-hued hazel eyes of his burrowing through me. "I *want* to make sure you're safe. And like you said, I have an account full of disposable income, so what's the problem?"

The problem? The problem is that if he keeps this shit up, I'm going to fall for him. Then I'll have to explain to my brother and my mom how we ended up married in Vegas after a drunken night of dancing, where I pressured Griffin into drinking too much. I'll have to look my brother in the eyes—my brother, who has always had his shit together—and tell him that, not only did I do something stupid and irresponsible, but that I basically instigated it. All the work I've done to prove myself will disintegrate in a moment.

"I don't need you to take care of me." It's the only thing I can think to say, and it sounds weak, even to my own ears.

Griffin's handsome face softens as he reaches for me and tugs me into his lap, my knees straddling his thighs. "Of course you don't. You're perfectly capable of taking care of yourself. I know that. But I like taking care of you." He studies my expression, brushing a strand of dark hair behind my ear. "It makes me happy that I can take some things off your plate, baby. Will you let me do that?"

I should say no. I almost do, but the look on his face kills me. He's so damn earnest and hopeful that I'll let him pay for my car or make me dinner. Griffin truly means it when he says that taking care of me makes him happy, and even if that didn't pluck at some deep, secret desire in me, I'm not sure I could deny him.

Because I care about Griffin Wright. I want to make him happy.

But it scares the hell out of me that the thing that makes him happiest is taking care of me and making me happy. Because this is something I've always wanted, right? For a man to stick around and care about me enough to put in the effort. I just never thought that man would be my brother's best friend and that we'd end up together because of a drunken mistake.

I don't know how to let go of that.

"Let me take care of you," Griffin asks again, his voice barely above a whisper. "Please, sunshine."

I'm weak, that's all there is to it. Because, instead of telling Griffin no, I sigh and bury my face in the crook of his neck so I don't have to face him when I say, "Okay, Griffy. If it will make you happy."

Those strong, safe arms wrap around me again, pulling me flush against his naked body. It simultaneously makes me feel protected and needy, and I have to force myself not to grind against the hard length of him that's just out of reach.

"It would make me so happy, Mira." He kisses the top of my head. "You make me happy."

"You make me happy too," I whisper, as though speaking it softly will somehow make the words carry less weight. Because I'm not all in—I still think this marriage was a mistake—but I can no longer deny that there *is* something here. And maybe, in a different life, Griffin and I could have been soulmates. A life where he wasn't my brother's best friend. The best friend he made promise not to touch me. The best friend he'd beat the shit out of if Griffin hurt me. The best friend I know it would kill Maddox to lose.

This isn't that life, though. Griffin and I both have so much to lose if—when—this ends badly. The problem is, I'm no longer sure that's enough of a deterrent to keep me from doing something even dumber than marrying my brother's best friend one drunken night in Vegas.

And that's falling for my accidental husband.

nineteen

GRIFFIN

"I GOTTA GO, SUNSHINE." LEANING DOWN, I PRESS A kiss to my wife's forehead. It's early—five in the morning —and the sun isn't even out yet. Though I hate to wake her, I hate the idea of leaving without saying goodbye more.

Mira stirs, does this cute little groan, and then her beautiful green eyes blink slowly at me as she fights to open them. "Griffin? What time is it?"

"It's five, baby. Bash is picking me up to take us to the airfield, so I need to meet him downstairs." Brushing my fingers through the hair tangled around Mira's face, I wish I could stay home with her. Every game, it grows harder and harder to say goodbye.

"Why aren't you taking your car?" she asks as she stretches.

Grinning, I press another kiss to her forehead, then one to the tip of her nose, enjoying the way she smiles up at me. As though maybe, just maybe, she's starting to accept what I already know. "It's your car this week. The tank's full, and the keys are on the kitchen island."

That has her sitting up, the comforter slipping down her naked body, revealing her perfect breasts and peaked nipples. I groan, because now, not only is it going to be hard to leave Mira, but my dick is hard as steel, and I'll have to get it to chill out before I head down to the lobby.

"I can't use your car."

"Why not? I won't need it." Unable to help myself, I let one of my hands skim over my wife's naked form, grinning when she sucks in a ragged breath as my thumb grazes her nipple. "And your car is in the shop. I won't leave you stranded here for almost a week."

"Your car costs more than I make in a year. By a lot." Mira's eyes are wide and a bit panicked.

"So?" I don't see what the problem is. She needs a car; I have one I won't need.

"What if I get in an accident?" Her voice rises in pitch with each word.

Eyebrows drawing together, I shrug. "Then we get it fixed. It's just a car. All I care about is you being safe."

"Griffin." Mira shakes her head before pushing her wild hair away from her face. "Seriously, I can't take your car. I don't even have full coverage on my insurance."

"That's what you're worried about?" Silly wife. Like I haven't already taken care of all that. "I added you to my insurance yesterday."

It's cute the way her mouth drops open in surprise. Mira is rarely speechless, but this is one of those moments, and it feels like a win. In fact, I think leaving my wife speechless may be one of my new favorite things, and I decide then and there that I'll do what I can to get this reaction out of her whenever possible.

"You added me to your insurance." She doesn't say it like a question, even though I know it is.

I grin. "Yep. Any more objections?"

"I... You... This is..." She's so flustered, it's impossible not to laugh. And when Mira levels me with a glare that could shrivel a lesser man's balls, I laugh harder.

"Just drive the car, wife. Now, as much as I wish I could stay here and keep arguing about silly things, I really need to go. Bash should be here any minute." Reaching out for Mira, I tangle my fingers in the hair at her nape and pull her in for a kiss. She's hesitant at first, but when I sweep my tongue over the seam of her lips, the tension melts out of her beautiful, naked body, and she kisses me back just as eagerly.

I don't pull away until my phone buzzes with a text in the pocket of my suit pants, and even then, it takes every ounce of my self-control. To my great pleasure, Mira looks as reluctant to end this as I feel, a quiet whimper leaving her lips. Pressing my forehead to hers, I breathe her in for a moment.

"Fuck, sunshine. I don't want to leave you. I'm going to miss you so damn much." Pulling back, I meet Mira's eyes. "Can we talk while I'm gone? It would mean a lot to me if we could FaceTime after games."

With her lower lip rolled between her teeth, Mira nods.

"Can I text you?"

She nods again.

Grinning, I gently grab her face with both of my hands and pull her in for another kiss. "Good. That's good. If you need anything—anything at all—just let me know, okay? I asked Ed to keep an eye out for you, too, while I'm gone. He'll be working security at the door most of the week."

Mira leans forward, stealing another kiss, before she looks up at me with bright eyes and pink cheeks. She's a fucking vision, naked and beautiful, open and eager, with a hint of shyness. She's everything. "Thanks, Griffy. I'll be fine."

"I know you will be," I tell her honestly. "Doesn't mean I won't worry. I—" Fuck. I have to stop myself from saying *I love you.* It's too soon, and I know it, but I'm shaken by the realization that I *want* to say it. "I'll miss you."

The pink in her cheeks deepens. "I'll miss you too. Be safe, okay?"

I kiss her one last time as my phone buzzes again. "I will. You too, baby."

"Tell Sebastian I say hi." Mira offers me a soft smile, shivering slightly as I step away. She grabs the comforter and wraps it around herself. I've never been so jealous of an inanimate object.

"I will. Call you tonight, okay? Text me whenever." I take a reluctant step away.

"I will. Now get out of here before Bash gets frustrated."

That makes me chuckle. Sebastian Navarro is one of the most patient men I know. Even if he got frustrated with me, he'd never admit it. She's right, though, I need to go. With one last, lingering look at my beautiful wife, I finally turn and head to the door. I grab my duffel bag and suitcase, forcing myself to get into the elevator and head down to the lobby. I say goodbye to Ed and thank him for looking out for Mira before bracing myself for the late-winter temperatures.

Sebastian pops the tailgate of his SUV when he sees me. I toss my stuff in the back next to his, then climb into the passenger seat.

"Hey, man, sorry about that."

He shrugs. "No worries. Wake up late?"

"Nah, just running a little behind." My mind is still filled with my naked wife as my teammate pulls onto the road and heads toward the airstrip the team's plane will leave from. "Thanks for picking me up."

"Sure thing," Bash says. "Mira's car still in the shop?" I filled Sebastian in on the situation with Mira's car when I asked him for a ride. Obviously, I didn't tell him I was the one paying for the repairs, but I did tell him I wanted to leave her my car for the week.

"Yeah. Not sure when it'll be done. That thing is old as hell. I worry about her driving it."

Bash glances at me from the corner of his eye, one brow rising. "She's a big girl, Griffin. And if she needs help, she can always ask her brother. I don't think you need to worry about her."

His words make me bristle, and even though I know he doesn't realize he's poking at a sore spot, he is. Because I want to tell him I have every reason to worry about Mira. That she's my goddamn wife, and it's my *job* to worry about her. No, not my job, my *privilege* to worry about her. But I can't say any of that. Not without obliterating the tentative trust I'm building with her.

"She's my roommate," I say instead. "And my friend. I'd be an asshole if I didn't worry about her at least a little bit." I'm going for nonchalant with my tone, but if the way Bash looks at me is any indication, I don't quite achieve it.

"Right. She's your friend." The way he says the word

friend has me shifting uncomfortably in my seat. Does he suspect something? The guy is way too perceptive, but he's also a genuinely good guy, so he won't make accusations without proof. Still, it gets my hackles up.

"You trying to say something, Navarro?"

Sebastian runs a hand through his dark hair. Light from streetlamps and the headlights of oncoming traffic bounce across his face as he drives. "Just that you and Mira are both adults. And you've been different since she moved in with you. More focused, settled. Like you're finally comfortable in your own skin in a way I've never seen in all the years we've known each other. And Mira? She seems happy. It was obvious that things ending with her ex shook her confidence a bit. But since she started living with you, she's got her light back." He glances at me. "And don't think I haven't noticed that you don't even spare a glance at any woman that isn't her."

Shifting uncomfortably in my seat, I shrug. "She's Maddox's little sister. And she's my friend."

"Is that all she is, though?"

"He'd kill me," I respond, unwilling to answer the question. Bash will see right through me if I lie.

My friend and our goalie hums. "Maybe. But if you were serious about her and she was serious about you? He'd get over it. He only wants what's best for her. And you."

"He wants to set her up with his agent's nephew," I say, some of the bitterness I feel about that leaking into my tone. "Because he's serious and responsible and the kind of guy Maddox thinks Mira needs."

Sebastian's eyebrows rise. "And you're not serious and responsible?"

"Am I?" I bark out a bitter laugh. "Or am I just the fuckboy comedic relief?"

I know that's how people see me, and I'll do whatever I can to start changing those perceptions, but it won't happen overnight. And Maddox has known me since college. He's seen me through my most unserious fuckboy moments. There's no way he'll see me as someone worthy of his sister.

"No one sees you that way, Wright."

"They do." I shake my head. "And I know it's my fault."

Sebastian is silent for a moment, and my stomach twists. "Who is the first person on the team to hype everyone else up? Who shows up, day in and day out, and does whatever it takes to make sure morale is high?" He glances at me, but when I don't respond, he continues. "Who has stuck his neck out for his teammates and their women when shit hits the fan? Who refused to accept that things were over between Isla and Maddox and stepped in to make sure Maddox didn't ruin his own life with his stubborn pride?"

Warmth fills my chest, and the back of my eyes begin to burn, but I still can't speak. Although I appreciate what Sebastian is saying, none of that means Madds would ever support my relationship with his sister.

"You're never late to practice, you show up even when you're sick or injured. You square up for every single man on our team if some asshole starts shit on the ice. While some guys blow through their salaries, you found someone to help manage your money, then made sure we all did the same. You may not be the captain of the Rogues, but we depend on you because we know you care, and you care deeply. If that doesn't make you the kind of guy worthy of

Mira, then Madds doesn't really want his sister with anyone."

Sebastian's words wrap around me like a warm bro-hug. I want to believe him; I do. But even if I wanted to sit Madds down and have a heart-to-heart with him, I can't. Mira has sworn me to secrecy about this marriage, and until she's all in, I can't do anything to jeopardize this.

"Thanks, man. I appreciate that, I really do. But there's nothing to say about me and Mira, okay? Please don't mention anything to him."

Sebastian steals a few glances at me as he pulls up to the airstrip's security gate. "Okay, Griffin. But you can talk to me about anything. You know that, right?"

I nod as he rolls his window down and shows his ID to the guard, who opens the gate and waves us through.

"Yeah, I know. Thanks, brother."

"You're a good man, Wright," Sebastian says as he parks. "I'm sorry we've turned you into the butt of our jokes. I'll get the guys to knock it off."

"It's fine," I tell him. Because whether they give voice to their jokes or not, that's exactly how they see me. A joke.

Bash shakes his head. "It's not. And if there *was* something going on with Mira, she'd be lucky to have you. I hope you know that."

It doesn't matter if I know that or not, only that Mira does. And as of right now, I haven't done enough to convince her. I will, though. Whatever it takes, I will prove that she can rely on me. That I'm it for her and she's it for me.

twenty

MIRA

I know I'm in trouble when, halfway through the week, I've yet to sleep straight through the night. Not a single time. The only time I come close is when Griffin FaceTimes me before bed, so I can't even lie to myself and claim it's not at least partially because I've grown so used to feeling him beside me.

Never before have I needed another human being in bed with me in order to fall asleep or stay asleep, and, not for the first time since I woke up married to my brother's best friend, I wish I hadn't pushed all my girlfriends away for stupid Jared. I could really use someone to talk to about all of this with. Someone who doesn't know my brother or isn't engaged to him. I consider calling my mom, but Camila Graves wants me to find Mr. Right as much as I do, so I have a feeling she'd deafen me with an excited scream, then demand to know when we're giving her grandbabies.

Probably not the most helpful or productive conversation.

Isla has asked me, Lexi, and her two best friends to go wedding dress shopping with her today, so I could try to find a roundabout way of bringing all of this up, but after some of the looks Isla has given Griffin and me, it seems likely she would figure it out.

Suffering in silence, it is.

Parking the G-Wagon isn't as easy as parking my little Toyota, but I love her heated seats, top-notch sound system, and smooth ride. What I *don't* love is the curious look it earns from Isla when I pull into the spot beside her car just as she's climbing out.

"Hey, Mir. Is that Griffin's car?" My future sister-in-law stands on the sidewalk with an unreadable expression on her face as I climb out of Gertie. Which is what I've named the car. Because, obviously, all cars should have names.

"Hey." I wrap the redhead in a hug before we head into the bridal shop. "Yeah. Artax died, so Griffin's letting me use his car while they're on the road. I'm hoping to hear some news about my car from the mechanic soon."

"Really? Huh." Isla smiles and waves at her best friends, Jess and Nevaeh, who are already enjoying mimosas and laughing about something in some plush white leather chairs toward the back of the shop. "That's *nice* of him."

Not loving the emphasis she puts on the word *nice*, I shrug, playing it off. "Yep. Pretty sure Griffin would give anyone the shirt off his back if they needed it. He's a good guy like that."

"He is. But he also loves that car. Maddox has tried to get Griffin to let him drive it a few times, and Griff always says no. That he doesn't trust Maddox's giant feet not to press down on the wrong pedal and crash his baby into a wall or something."

That has me snorting out a laugh because I'm sure that pisses my brother right off, but it's also a hilarious mental image. "Well, I suppose he's letting me drive it because I don't have oversized ogre feet."

Isla chuckles at my use of her nickname for my brother and shakes her head as we join her friends. The little bell on the door jingles a few seconds later, and Lexi steps in. "Right. I'm sure that's it."

"Babes!" Nevaeh rises from her seat and drags Isla into a crushing hug, which Jess joins. "You're getting married!" They hop a few times, holding on to each other and doing one of those excited, high-pitched screams. It sends another pang of regret through my chest that I torpedoed my friendships in Chicago before moving back to Minneapolis.

"How many mimosas do you think they've had already?" Lexi asks as she comes to a stop beside me. We've been texting more and more, and I think she and I could end up being close, which is soothing.

"At least two," I answer. "Should we grab one so we're not left behind?"

She nods, grinning. "Absolutely."

***

"Eh, I like it, but I don't think it's *The One*," Jess says as Isla flounces out of the dressing room in a frothy, tulle wedding gown.

Lexi's eyes narrow as she studies it. "It's kind of a lot."

Isla glances my way, and I shrug, going for sisterly honesty. "You look like a cupcake. Or one of those cakes where they shove a Barbie into the top, so it looks like she's wearing a frosting-covered gown."

My future sister-in-law giggles, checking herself out in the mirror. "Yeah, I do kinda look like that, don't I?"

"Next," Nev proclaims, and Isla nods. We all chuckle as she struggles to make her way back to the dressing room, weighed down with far too much tulle.

We've been here for an hour already, and Isla has tried on at least a dozen gowns. She has liked a few, and a couple received enthusiastic reactions from the peanut gallery, but none of them have brought tears to Isla's eyes —or ours—so the search continues.

As she changes, my eyes wander around the bridal shop, lingering on beautiful beaded gowns and fairy tale dresses with flowers and vines embroidered down lace sleeves and full skirts. My mind keeps recalling the photo I found in my suitcase when we got home from Las Vegas of Griffin and me, smiling and drunk, at the little twenty-four-hour chapel where we got married. My dress is far too sexy for a wedding, my hair is a bit disheveled, and the veil I rented as part of the Enchanted Graceland package is slightly askew. Griffin isn't wearing a tux or even a suit jacket. The sleeves of his dress shirt are rolled up nearly to his elbows, and the top two buttons are undone.

I can't help imagining what we would look like if I had been wearing a beautiful dress, and he had been wearing a fancy suit or a formal tux. A little pang of something that feels an awful lot like want spears through my chest, and I rub absently at my sternum.

None of that is how I pictured my first—and hopefully

only—wedding to go. I always imagined myself in a gown like this, with my family and friends surrounding me. I imagined dating for a year or two before he'd get down on one knee with a stunning diamond in a little velvet box, and the look on my mom's face when I'd show her the ring. She'd cry and hug me before dragging my fiancé into the embrace. Then we'd go shopping at a pretty shop like this one, where I'd spend hours trying on dresses before finding the perfect one.

"This one is so pretty, isn't it?" Isla's question pulls me from my thoughts as she walks out in a gorgeous gown. It's covered in beaded lace, has delicate straps that plunge into a deep neckline that somehow appears elegant rather than scandalous, and a skirt that flares out just enough to provide some drama without being overwhelming. The train is modest and rustles as she walks. It's... exactly the kind of dress I would have chosen. For myself, that is.

My future sister-in-law looks absolutely stunning in it.

"I feel like I'm too short for it, though, don't you think?" She does a little spin, and the beaded skirt twists around her. It restricts her movements just enough that she stumbles.

"You're right," Lexi agrees. "I love the shape of the top half, but I'm not sure the bottom half is quite right."

Isla nods, then looks at me. "You know who would look absolutely stunning in this dress? Mira."

"Ooooh, yes," Jess says, appraising me. "She's got the legs for it."

"You should try it on," Isla says. "It's fun."

Laughing them off, I wave a hand dismissively. "I don't want to waste the salesgirl's time."

The woman who's been helping us grins. "You

wouldn't be wasting my time. Besides, I get to help women play dress up all day. My job rocks. Come on, I'll put you in the dressing room next to the bride."

I hem and haw and try to get out of it, but everyone insists, so with a deep sigh, I strip down to my undies and step into the heavy dress. I don't look in the mirror until the salesgirl zips me up before going back to Isla's dressing room and helping her with her next gown.

Lifting my eyes, I gasp at my reflection. Even though I'm wearing minimal makeup and my hair is braided to the side in one thick plait, I look...ethereal. The dress hugs my curves in all the right ways, flaring out at my hips and plunging between my breasts. The ivory color is soft and elegant against my more golden skin tone.

I look like a bride. A real one. Not a bride who rolled up to a little Vegas chapel after too many drinks with her friend and got married so they could see young Elvis. The woman in the mirror is one I've dreamed of seeing for years, and something twists in my chest. Because I can't help imagining myself walking down the aisle in this dress. Can't help imagining a flower-covered archway in an outdoor location somewhere with a petal-strewn aisle and a beaming groom waiting for me at the end.

And fuck me, because in the fantasy that takes hold of my mind, the groom isn't some faceless future possibility. He's not Jared, not Mr. Fancy from the club all those weeks ago, when we celebrated Maddox and Isla getting back together. No, the man waiting for me in my fantasy has shaggy golden hair, sparkling hazel eyes that catalog every ivory-covered inch of my body, and full lips that have kissed me senseless time and time again since we got home from Vegas.

Wearing this stunning dress and imagining the perfect wedding calls Griffin Wright to mind, and that scares the shit out of me for so many reasons.

"Come out, Mira," the girls call. "You've been in there staring at yourself for ages. Is it bad?"

Clearing my throat, I open the door of the dressing room and walk out. Lexi's eyes go wide as she takes me in, and Isla's friends fall silent.

"So, no. Not bad. The opposite of bad," Nev says to herself. Her beautiful umber eyes meet mine. "Mira, you look amazing."

I open my mouth to protest when Isla walks out and everyone falls silent once again, my little moment of dress-up forgotten as the real star of the show floats onto the platform in front of the three-way mirror. She's a vision in ivory silk and minimalist beading.

"Oh, Isla," Lexi says on an exhalation. "You look absolutely stunning."

Tears glitter in Isla's blue eyes, and I feel them pooling in mine too. "I think... I think this is the one." She looks my way, and her eyes widen as she takes me in, but I nod. This moment is about her, not me.

"I think you're right. That dress was made for you." My words come out choked and full of emotion.

Isla's lips curve in a tremulous but vibrant smile. "I'm going to marry your brother in this dress."

She looks so happy. After everything she's been through, Isla Harding deserves all the happiness in the world. And even though I'd love to punch her ex-fiancé in the dick for breaking up with her two weeks before their wedding, I'd also like to send him flowers and thank him for freeing this woman from what would undoubtedly have been a miserable marriage, and allowing her to meet my brother. Because she's everything he's ever needed, and I couldn't ask for a better sister.

"He's going to cry like a baby," I tell her, pulling her into a crushing hug. "He won't be able to take his eyes off you."

The same way I keep imagining Griffin wouldn't be able to take his eyes off me.

twenty-one

MIRA

AFTER THE ROGUES WIN THEIR SECOND GAME OF the series, I'm lying in bed, waiting for Griffin to call. Our bed, not the one in my old room. The room I should want to retreat to when Griffin isn't here, but I don't. I love spending my workday there, but I've started thinking of it as my office, rather than my bedroom.

Is that crazy?

Who am I kidding? This whole damn situation is crazy.

My third yawn in as many minutes hits just as Griffin's photo pops up on my phone, and I grin as I hit the green answer button. "Hey there, hotshot. Good game tonight."

"You watched?" Griffin's hazel eyes light up. I watch their games whenever I can, so I don't know why he's surprised, but the pleasure that's written all over his features makes my heart do a little arrhythmic thump.

"Course I did, Griffy. You were on fire tonight."

A goofy grin splits his face as he flops backward onto

his hotel bed and tucks an arm behind his head. "I was thinking about my gorgeous wife, and it spurred me on."

"Griffin…" There's less heat and hesitation behind the warning than there has been, but despite my changing feelings for Griffin Wright—or maybe because of them—I'm still uncomfortable with him calling me his wife. I mean, I know that's what I am legally, but I always thought that word would hold weight and intimate meaning when I had someone in my life who would call me that. Younger Mira never would have thought I'd end up married after partying in Vegas, and she certainly never would have imagined staying in said marriage for six months because she was basically blackmailed into it.

Is blackmail really the right word? It feels wrong when I consider how Griffin has treated me so far, but when it comes right down to it, there's really no other term that would be accurate.

"I'm serious, baby. I've been on top of my game since I woke up married to you. Even Coach has noticed. I want to make you proud."

There's an earnestness in his voice and expression that hits me right in the heart. Not sure there's a woman alive who wouldn't feel some kind of way about a man as sweet, talented, and sexy as Griffin Wright telling them he wants to make her proud. If he was here, I'd be pulling his dick out and gagging on it.

"I am proud of you," I tell him softly. Because I know he needs to hear it, but also because it's true. Ever since the whole Quinoa story debacle, it's become clear that Griffin hides his insecurities behind smiles and his goofy persona, but they're there. And they're loud.

How often do people tell him they're proud or that they

admire him? I hate that I've been guilty of overlooking him myself. The man took me in and asked nothing in return, and I took it for granted.

No more.

"You're amazing, Griffin. I hope you know that. And I know we're on different pages about this whole marriage thing, but it's important to me that you understand how much I admire and value you. Not only because you're great at hockey. But because you're kind and thoughtful, you're loyal, selfless, and you care so much about the people in your life. I'm lucky to have you. So is my brother and everyone else."

Griffin stares at me through the phone for a few beats, a hesitant smile twitching at the corners of his lips. "You think I'm amazing?"

"Of course I do." Rolling my eyes, I level him with a look that says he's being ridiculous. "You know I do."

As that smile blooms into something beautiful, my heart skips a beat. "My wife thinks I'm amazing." He says it more to himself than me, and it sparks warmth throughout my body. It's a heady sensation, and I change the subject so I don't have time to ruminate on it.

"Have you heard anything from the mechanic about my car?"

Unfortunately, that question makes Griffin's smile falter. He runs a hand through his golden hair and winces. "Uh, yeah, I have, actually."

Well, that doesn't sound like good news. Not that I'm surprised. Bracing myself, I force the next question out of my mouth. "What's the damage?"

"My guy told me he can get it back up and running, but that if it was someone he cared about driving the thing, he'd never sleep at night." Griffin's lips twist into a displeased grimace. "I know you love that car, but it belongs in a junkyard."

It does, but I can't afford to replace it, so I ignore his last statement altogether. "How much will it cost to get it running?"

"Sunshine, it's not safe."

I wave a hand in front of the phone. "It's fine. I've driven the thing for years. I know how to handle his temperamental bullshit. Now, just tell me how much I need to pay him."

Griffin shakes his head, grumbling something about stubborn Graveses and spankings. The latter part has my libido waking up and stretching like a sleepy jungle cat.

"I didn't get a final figure from him. I'll find out." He doesn't make direct eye contact with me.

"Don't forget, I want to pay for it, okay? You've done enough for me."

My accidental husband rolls his eyes and grumbles something else before saying, "I'll have your car brought to the parking garage as soon as it's ready. Ed will have the keys behind the security desk for you, okay? In the meantime, just keep driving my car."

My eyes track Griffin's hand as he starts to unbutton his dress shirt. Distracted, I say, "Kay. Don't worry, I'm taking great care of Gertie."

Griffin's long fingers still, his eyes twinkling as one eyebrow lifts. "Gertie?"

Cheeks heating, I try to act like it's no big deal that I named his car, even though it's kind of embarrassing. "Gertie the G-Wagon. It has a nice ring to it, don't you think? Besides, the poor thing has been nameless for so long."

Rich, honeyed laughter spills from Griffin's lips, and god, do I love that sound. His head tips back and his chest shakes, but he never takes his eyes off me. "Oh, sunshine. You're too fucking cute for words. You know that, right?"

Blushing furiously, I purse my lips as he continues.

"But the G-Wagon already has a name."

That has me peeking up at him. "It does?"

"Mm-hmm." The corners of his lips twitch as he fights a smile that does funny things to my tummy. "I call her the G-Spot."

Silence stretches between us as I blink, owlishly, at the ridiculous name. He can't be serious, right? Nobody names their car the G-Spot. That's... That's absolutely something Griffin would do to make his friends laugh. "You're joking, right?"

His smile blooms into something so bright, I blink a few times more. "Nope. Totally serious. I can always find the G-Spot."

I groan, trying not to giggle, because that is so lame, but it's also the tiniest bit funny. "You're the worst."

"You love me," he says. The words are nonchalant as they spill from his full lips, and I know he doesn't mean anything by them, but I can't help noticing the flutter they elicit in my belly and the way they ping around like a pinball in my brain.

I do not love Griffin Wright. I don't. But I sort of do. Because after all these months of living together, and the way he's been pursuing me since we got married, Griffin has become my best friend.

The smile slips off my face as the reality of our situation hits me square in the tit.

If things get messy because of this marriage—well, messier than they already are—I could lose my best friend. The person who makes me laugh, who supports my dreams and cheers me on, the person who just *gets* me.

I don't want to lose Griffin.

"Sunshine?" Griffin's concern bleeds through in his tone, which has become soft and careful. "What's wrong? What happened?"

Do I tell him? Pretend that everything is fine? These are uncharted waters, and I'm worried we'll drown.

"You're my best friend," I blurt out, dropping my chin and letting my hair fall like a curtain around the sides of my face. I don't know why it feels so vulnerable to admit that to him, but it does, and that makes me want to hide.

"Mira." Griffin's voice is soft and my name catches in his throat. "Baby, you're my best friend too."

I look up at him through the fringe of my lashes. "I thought my brother is your best friend."

"He was. Is, I guess. But you're my best friend too. They're just... different. The way I feel about you is so much—" Griffin scrubs a hand through his golden hair, messing it up so the long strands stick up at all angles. Hazel eyes pin me in place. "How I feel about you is something else. Something more. Does that make sense?"

Does it?

Yeah, it does. And that scares the shit out of me, because, once again, it reinforces that if this marriage implodes, like I'm sure it will, losing him will hurt.

Badly.

Still, I can't leave him hanging when he's looking at me so earnestly. So I nod. "Yeah. That makes sense."

"I want to tell everyone about us," he says after a moment's pause. "I hate lying to your brother."

Panic hits me hard, making my stomach flip. But this is a different kind of panic. This isn't the theoretical panic of loss; this is the sure knowledge that my brother will kick his friend's ass and look at me with those disappointed eyes only an older, protective brother can manage. The kind of look that makes you feel ten inches tall because you know you could have done better. *Should* have done better.

I don't want him to be disappointed in me. And I really don't want to be the reason his friendship with Griffin is ruined.

"I don't think..." My words trail off as I shift in our bed, my lower lip rolling between my teeth. "It's just that Maddox will..."

The sigh that puffs out between Griffin's lips cuts me to my core, but I don't finish my thought or take the words back.

"It's okay, sunshine. Forget I said anything. We'll give it some more time." He sounds so disappointed, but he doesn't press me further. We're both quiet for a minute before he changes the subject and says, "Oh, I almost forgot. I ran into someone today. My former college coach was at the game. We got to talking, and he was telling me all about how the team's doing. How they've been winning up a storm, and he got the go-ahead to revamp their website and marketing material so they could recruit better players to their program."

My heart does a little pitter-patter as Griffin's multi-hued eyes connect with mine.

"I told him about you. Showed him the work you've done for me and some of the other guys. Told him about the site you're building for that baseball team. He asked for your contact information and if I thought you'd be interested in flying out to Michigan for a meeting to discuss their needs."

Speechless. I'm stunned speechless. I gape at Griffin, thinking I must have misheard him. "Are you serious?"

"As a heart attack. I thought maybe I could go with you, show you around, introduce you to the coach, and we could make a fun weekend of it." The man staring out at me through my phone screen is full of vulnerability as he waits for my response. He searches my eyes, as if he may be able to discern my thoughts and see into my soul. Maybe he can, at least a little.

"Griffin, I don't know what to say. That's incredible. It would be huge to redo a college team's online presence like that."

"Maybe the football team too," he says with a smile.

"Oh my god." I fan my face, suddenly feeling hot and more than a little overwhelmed. "Yes, I would love to go with you. It would be fun, and having you there would help me not be nervous. The last thing I want to do is ramble and screw up this opportunity. Although people may talk if we take a trip together."

"You could never screw this up. You're Mira fucking Wright. You're a badass. And we'll find something to tell people so they don't think twice about us going together."

I roll my eyes. "For the hundredth time, I'm not changing my last name to Wright."

My accidental husband shrugs, unbothered. "That's fine. I've been looking into what it would take to change my last name to Graves. It would be a lot of work, but I'm up for it."

Unable to hold it in, I giggle. "You're an idiot."

Griffin smiles brightly. "You don't really think that. You think I'm awesome."

I do, he's right.

I really do.

twenty-two

MIRA

"Hey, Ed." I give the security guard a friendly little wave as I stop in front of his desk. He called up to the apartment, letting me know the shop delivered my car.

Delivered. Griffin spent extra money just to have someone bring the hunk of rust back when I could have gone and gotten it. Now I'm going to owe him more money, even though I know he'll try to get out of letting me pay him back. He keeps acting dodgy when I ask how much everything cost.

"Miss Mira, how are you today?" The older man smiles brightly at me with what I imagine is a fatherly expression. Not that I'd really know, because my sperm donor is an absent piece of shit.

"I'm good, Ed. How are you?"

"Oh, you know, trying to keep busy. It can be pretty quiet here." He scans the lobby before leaning closer, one hand covering the side of his face like he's worried someone will read his lips. He gives me a conspiratorial look and whispers, "I'm reading a fairy romance book that my daughter keeps going on about. Got all the boys into it. We have a book club planned for the end of the month."

With wide eyes, I try to suppress a giggle. "Fairy romance, huh? Sounds good to me."

"You're welcome to join our book club." Ed winks.

Honestly? Joining a book club with a bunch of middle-aged security guards where they talk about romantasy sounds like a good time. "Email me the details. Maybe I could get Griffin to join with me."

That makes Ed's eyes light up. "Do you think he would?"

"He has a whole shelf full of romance books," I say with my own conspiratorial tone. "I'd say there's a pretty solid chance he'll go for it."

Ed's eyes twinkle with excitement. "Thanks, Miss Mira. Here, I have your car keys for you." He reaches under his desk and grabs my keys, making a clacking sound as he hands them over.

"Please, just Mira. None of this *miss* stuff, okay?" Grinning, I take the keys from Ed as he hems and haws about calling me only by my name. After we say our goodbyes, I head toward the parking garage and twirl my keys in my hand.

Except, they're not my keys.

I was so distracted by my conversation with Ed that I didn't notice. I frown when I see two brand-spanking-new fobs with flip keys on the ring instead of my beat-up and cracked single key.

Great. They left the wrong keys. So much for taking him grocery shopping before Griffin gets home.

Grumbling under my breath, I stalk out to my parking spot to check on Artax, even though I won't be able to start him and stop dead in my tracks. "What. The actual. Fuck?"

Artax isn't in my spot. My familiar, formerly trusty rust bucket is nowhere to be seen. In its place is a gleaming yellow Camry with a sunroof and black rims. The damn thing is Rogues yellow. And maybe I could tell myself that was a coincidence if there wasn't a massive red bow on the roof and a small white vinyl decal with the number 16 on the driver's side window.

Griffin's number. The one on his jersey, which he keeps trying to get me to wear. My whole body goes hot and my chest tightens as I circle the car. It's a strange mix of panic, excitement, and burgeoning rage. Then I see the license plate. It reads *sunshne*.

The crazy bastard didn't fix my car. He bought me a brand-new one. One that he clearly had customized. One I could never afford.

I start to shake, and steam may very well be pouring from my ears because this is too much. It's completely out of line. How could he do something like this without even asking me? All the money I've worked so hard to save— gone. And then some.

Fire scorches my veins as I pull my phone out of my pocket and tap on Griffin's contact. The thing goes straight to voicemail, but I try again anyway and let out a little screech. They're probably in the air or getting ready to land, because today's the day they get home from their away series. Figures I can't even call and shout at him the way I want to. But that's fine. I can be patient.

Leaning against the door of the pretty yellow car

Griffin will most definitely be returning, I settle in and wait.

My accidental husband will get home soon. And when he does, I'm going to murder him.

GRIFFIN

I have two missed calls from Mira by the time we land at the airstrip and I can finally turn my phone back on. No messages, though. She's probably so excited about her new car that she can't even form complete sentences.

Sebastian notices my goofy grin and playfully elbows me. "What are you so happy about? Does it involve a certain dark-haired roommate?"

"Shh," I hiss, looking around to make sure no one heard the idiot. When I'm certain no one is paying attention to us, I grin. "But maybe. My mechanic told me her car was a death trap. So I bought her a new one and had it delivered today."

Bash goes utterly silent and still. He stands there, staring at me, not even blinking. Which is kinda freaky, if I'm being honest. When he finally does blink, the motion is slow and exaggerated. "I'm sorry. I could have sworn you just said that you bought Mira a car."

His body shakes when I clap him hard on the shoulder. "Dude, you need to get your ears checked out or something?" I guess I could drive him to the doctor if he needs me to, but I really want to get home to my wife. I can't wait to see her reaction to the car.

"Did she agree to letting you buy her a car?" Bash asks

very slowly, speaking to me the way a parent addresses a toddler who's just learning to speak.

I roll my eyes. "Nah, man. It was a surprise."

More slow blinks. "A surprise." Sebastian's eyebrows rise all the way up his forehead until they're fist-bumping his hairline. "You bought your roommate a brand-new car without her knowledge because you wanted to surprise her?"

Am I missing something? Why is Bash looking at me like I've lost my mind? All I wanted to do was take care of my wife. Not that he knows she's my wife, but still. "Yeah, man. She needed a new car but couldn't afford it, and she wouldn't let Madds buy her one. So I took care of it." Bash doesn't need to know that I wouldn't let Madds buy her one, anyway. That's my job now.

"Griffin, what's really going on with you two? Because buying a car for your roommate isn't normal."

I squirm as my friend's dark brown eyes bore a hole in my head. The dude is trying to see into my soul and learn all my secrets, and as much as I want to be honest about my relationship with Mira, she's not ready for that. So I shrug and try to play it off.

"She's become my best friend. Can't best friends look out for each other? Especially if one has more money than he knows what to do with? I worry she's going to break down somewhere dangerous in the middle of the night with a dead phone and be stuck, you know? Like, it's actually kept me up at night a few times. And I surprised her because you know how stubborn the Graves siblings are. She never would have agreed to let me buy it. Better to ask for forgiveness, and all that."

"Holy shit," Bash says on an exhalation. "You're in love with her."

"What?" The word comes out in a high-pitched squeak that sounds more like the sound a ten-year-old girl would make than a guy in his thirties. "I'm n— No, I... Psh." I wave my hand wildly. "Don't be ridiculous."

"Oh my god. You are. I knew there was something going on with you two." Our goalie takes a step closer to me, so there's only a couple of inches of space between us and looks me dead in the eyes. "Are you two dating?"

I snort. "No."

We're married.

Bash's thick eyebrows pull together and his eyes go all squinty as he studies me. "Are you fucking?"

"What? Dude, no. I have never fucked Mira." *With my dick*, I add in my head. Because I've definitely fucked her with my fingers and my tongue. And I've woken up to her grinding against my thigh once when she was having a sexy dream, but I'm not sure that counts. Still, I know I must be doing a shit job of keeping a smirk off my face, because Bash groans.

"Wright, do you have a death wish? Because I truly believe he'd get over it if you two are serious about each other, but Madds will kill you if he finds out you're messing around with his sister." There's genuine concern written into every frown line on my friend's face, so I drop the stupid act with a sigh.

"I'm not messing around with her," I say seriously. "Things between us are...complicated. I can't really tell you more than that without breaking her trust, and that's one thing I will never do. But I'm fucking crazy about her, man. Like, totally gone for her. I would *never* do anything to hurt Mira, and that includes messing up her relationship with Maddox."

It's why, despite hating every second of keeping our marriage a secret, I've complied with her wishes. I know she's worried about how this will affect her relationship with her brother, and I know she's worried about how it will affect my friendship with him. The problem is, I'm unsure if she's worried that he'll be mad at her for marrying someone who's not good enough for her, or if she's worried he'll be mad that she married his best friend.

My concern lies with the former. I'm not good enough for her, and I know it. There's no chance her brother won't know it too. The guy has been around for all my one-night stands, my flirtations, and what I now realize he sees as my general instability. If he didn't believe I was unstable, wouldn't he have considered me as a possibility for his sister and not some asshole marketing bro he's never even met?

Sebastian watches me. He takes in the frown lines between my eyebrows, the thin set of my lips, and even though he's not actually a mind reader, some ridiculous part of me worries he'll figure it out. "Then, are things serious with you two?"

"I..." There's no point in trying to deny that *something* is going on between Mira and me. He already suspects. I just can't tell him the extent of what's going on. Scrubbing a hand through my hair, I nod slowly. "Yeah, man. They kind of are."

I expect Bash to punch me in the arm or tell me I'm an idiot with a death wish again, but he doesn't. He simply nods a few times as a smile twitches at the corners of his lips.

"Then you need to tell Maddox."

Blowing out a breath, I try to tamp down the growing unease churning in my gut. "It's not my call, man, it's hers. I promised her I'd let her take the lead about when we tell people we're—" I cut myself off with a shake of my head. Almost let it slip. "When we tell people about us. If it was up to me, everyone would already know."

Sebastian settles a hand on my shoulder and gives it a squeeze. "All right, man. Just be careful, okay? I don't want to see you get hurt."

The words surprise me, and I jolt back. "You're not going to threaten me and tell me not to hurt Mira or screw things up with Madds?"

My friend offers me a patient smile. "Wright, you'd never hurt her if you could help it. And Madds has been your best friend since college. Whatever this is, you'll work things out with him if you have to. But I know you. You don't do things by halves. And if things with Mira are serious, then I'm sure your heart is already on the line. Just... Just make sure she's as invested as you are, okay? Because you deserve to have someone who's all in for you."

My chest feels tight, and there's a lump in my throat I can't seem to dislodge, even after clearing it a few times. "Thanks, bro. I really appreciate that."

Sebastian grins. "Of course. Now, let's get you home so Mira can kick your ass for buying her a new car."

She won't kick my ass. She'll be thrilled.

twenty-three

GRIFFIN

Mira is not thrilled.

When Bash drops me off, she's leaning against her new car, arms crossed over her chest—which makes her tits look amazing—and a furious scowl on her face. Bash just laughs, the bastard, gives Mira a little wave, which she returns with a sharp nod and a fake smile, and tells me to quit being a pussy when it's clear I'm taking my sweet time getting out of the car and retrieving my gear from his trunk.

My wife keeps a scary-looking fake smile on her face until Sebastian drives away, then she whirls around, throws her hands out to her sides, and shouts, "What the hell, Wright?"

Ignoring the death glare she's aiming my way, I drop my bags and close the distance between us. In less than two heartbeats, she's in my arms and I'm crushing her against me in a tight hug. "Goddamn, I missed you. So fucking much."

Some of the rigid tension bleeds out of Mira's body with those words, and she sighs, bringing her arms around my waist to hug me back. "Missed you, too, you big, stupid idiot," she grumbles into my chest.

I can't help it. I laugh.

"This isn't funny," Mira growls. Or at least, she tries to growl. She sounds more like a pissed-off kitten than a scary lion, but hell if I'm going to tell her that when she looks ready to murder me or chop off my balls.

"It's kind of funny," I reply before tilting Mira's chin up and kissing her. It's soft at first, my lips feathering over hers, teasing, testing. But the moment she goes up on her toes and the softest whimper escapes her throat, the kiss turns bruising. I can't get enough of my wife's taste, the feel of her soft lips against mine, the warmth of her tongue as she opens for me and sweeps it inside my mouth.

God, I missed her.

Being apart this long was really wearing on me. I didn't realize just how much I've come to rely on being able to kiss her whenever I want, to hold her as she falls asleep, to watch her beautiful, peaceful face for a few minutes before one of our alarms wakes her and she blinks those gorgeous green eyes at me.

After another minute of making out, Mira pushes me away, albeit reluctantly if her expression is anything to go by. She stares at me for a beat, sighs, and says, "You have to take it back."

Like hell I'm taking her car back. It's not happening. I wasn't kidding when I told Bash I've stayed up worried a few nights. "I'm not taking it back, baby. The car is yours.

Artax is gone. He finally succumbed to the swamp of sadness."

"Not funny," Mira says with a scowl as my lips twitch against the smile I'm fighting. "I'm serious, Griffin. I need my car back."

Cocking my head to the side, I ask, "Why? It barely ran. My mechanic told me he'd never let someone he loves drive that thing. It's not safe, sunshine." She jolts a little at my use of the word *love*, but I barrel on. "This one is safe, has all the bells and whistles you could want, and it matches your sunny disposition."

She doesn't love that line of logic. I watch, entranced, as Mira's eyes flutter closed, her hands clench into fists, and she takes several deep breaths in, holds them, then lets them out slowly. *Oh, she's pissed.*

"Griffin, while it's sweet that you want to take care of me and make sure I'm safe, this is too much. I can't afford a brand-new car like this." She pinches the bridge of her nose as her gaze bounces between me and the yellow car.

Ah, stubborn, self-sufficient woman. I should have known this would be a point of contention with her. I should have anticipated this. Running my hands up and down her arms and enjoying the warmth of her, I bend down to look my wife in the eye. "Sweetheart, you really can. You're my wife. I'm serious when I tell you that what's mine is yours now. You can afford a way nicer car than this, but I knew you wouldn't want something super expensive or flashy. Trust me, if it was up to me, you'd be driving around in a yellow G-Wagon, not a Camry."

Those big, green eyes of hers meet mine, and I see the flash of hope and longing there before she can hide it. My wife is so used to taking care of herself, so used to that fierce independence being a point of pride and a cornerstone of her personality, but deep down, she's no different from anyone else. She wants to be loved and taken care of. Hell, I doubt there's a human alive—male or female—who doesn't. She opens her mouth, probably to protest again, but I beat her to it.

"Mira, I don't want to sound like an asshole here, but believe me when I tell you that this is nothing for me. This is a drop in the bucket. And I know all of this is a lot for you. Being married to me is a lot…"

Her eyes soften at that, and she reaches up to cup my face. "No, Griffin. Being married to you is not a lot. It's…" She blows out a breath that ruffles her hair. "It's amazing, actually. A little baffling at times, and I still think we should have annulled this right away, but even with all that, being married to you is…"

My chest is tight from holding my breath. My body screams at me to suck in a lungful of oxygen, but my head refuses to miss a single thing this gorgeous woman before me is saying. Everything hangs on the words she speaks next.

"Being apart from you this last week made me realize that being married to you may not have been planned, but it also may be one of the best things that's ever happened to me."

Releasing the breath I've been holding in a whoosh, I tangle my hand in the hair at the nape of Mira's neck and tilt her head back to look at me. My heart is thundering like I've just completed a brutal shift on the ice, my throat is tight with emotion, and my body thrums with energy. "Do you mean that?"

Mira's soft fingers stroke my cheek, and her eyes soften even further as she gazes up at me. "Yeah, Griffy, I do."

I gulp. "Does that mean you're ready to give this marriage a real shot?"

Please say yes. Please say yes.

I can see the war in her. It plays out vividly over those perfect features I've spent so many silent mornings memorizing. Whatever answer she gives me, she's not without doubts. That's okay, though. I can work with doubts. What I can't work with is a steady refusal to continue this marriage. If this is the moment Mira tells me she's done, I'll respect that and let her go, six months be damned. It would break me, but it's better than breaking her by forcing her to stay.

"Look, I'm still not sure about all of this. We did everything backward. But yes, Griffin, I think I'm ready to give this a real shot."

The moment the words leave her mouth, I'm lifting my wife in my arms, swinging her around, and cheering like we've just won the cup. I still have work to do, but this is progress. Real progress.

Burying my face in her hair, I exhale deeply. "You have no idea how happy that makes me."

Mira runs a hand through my hair. "I'm still pissed about the car."

That makes me laugh. "Why? Mad I didn't get you a yellow G-Wagon?"

Her lips purse, and she shakes her head as I finally put her down. "No, hotshot, I'm mad that you didn't talk to me about it first. You took the decision away from me."

Well, shit. Sufficiently humbled by that little nugget of truth, I press my forehead to Mira's and try to show I hear her. "I'm sorry, baby. Really, I am. I was just trying to do something nice for you and got excited by the prospect of being able to spoil you and take care of you." Guilt spears through me as I realize this isn't the first time I've taken her choice away, and it makes me feel like a huge piece of shit. "I'm an asshole."

She laughs at that. A full, head-thrown-back, chest-shaking laugh that reverberates off the concrete walls of the parking garage until it sounds like there's at least five people cracking up. "You're not an asshole, Griffin. A little high-handed maybe, but not an asshole." She leans forward and presses a warm, slow kiss to the scruff of my jaw. "Now let's go. I'm hungry."

God, this woman. I'm so fucking gone for her. "All right, baby. Let's go order something and have it delivered."

Mira looks at me like I'm an idiot. "Uh, no, we're not having something delivered." She presses a button on her new car key and the trunk pops open. "Throw your gear in. I want to take Princess Buttercup for a spin." She turns around, rips the massive bow off the car, and shoves it in the trunk.

"Princess Buttercup? What is it with you and '80s movies?"

She offers me a blinding smile as I stow my gear, slam the trunk, and make my way to the passenger side. "Our mom made us watch all of them. She'd pop popcorn, give us sodas, which were a rare treat, and buy candy from the store. She'd sit in between Maddox and me, and we'd all snuggle up together." Her smile grows wistful and her eyes take on a faraway quality that tells me she's reliving those memories. "They were some of my favorite nights."

"Makes sense to me, sunshine."

Her eyes flash with mischief and all of that wistfulness melts away into something louder. "Get in and hold on to your ass. Let's see what Princess Buttercup can do."

I don't know whether I should be scared or amused. Doesn't really matter. My wife is happy and, more importantly, she's finally giving in to this thing between us.

I'm seeing this through to the finish line.

twenty-four

MIRA

"So," I say as I pull my new car out of the parking garage and turn onto the street. It rides like a dream, and even though I want to stay mad at Griffin, it's proving more difficult each block I drive without my car shaking or making unsettling noises. "You've been dressing a little differently lately."

Out of the corner of my eye, I see Griffin shrug. When he's not dressing for a game day, Griffin's usually pretty casual. Jeans, athletic gear, tees, flannels, and sneakers are his go-to wardrobe. But not lately. Lately, he's been wearing a lot of khakis and polos and brown leather loafers. Essentially, he looks as though he's ready to go to the country club, and it's weirding me out. Not that I've ever been to a country club, but I imagine all the stuffy rich guys dress like this.

"Oh, d'you like it?" He runs a hand down the front of his navy polo. He looks handsome—he always does—but something about it just isn't *him*. It's like he's wearing a costume for a role I don't understand.

"Uh, yeah, it's nice. It's definitely a change."

When Griffin glances at me, my stomach does a little flip at the look in his eyes. It's a strange cocktail of hope, worry, and insecurity? "I've decided it's time to be more serious and responsible. No more fuckboy shit, you know?"

My heart squeezes. Oh, Griffin. He really took that night at dinner to heart. I knew he had, but since he hadn't brought it up again, I assumed he was over it. I can see now that he isn't. "Griffin, you are serious and responsible. You don't have to change how you dress."

My accidental husband shifts in his seat and stares out the window. "You don't have to pacify me, sunshine. I know how people see me. If I want them to see me as smart or serious or responsible, I have to change, and updating my wardrobe is the easiest place to start." When he glances at me, I make a decision to change our lunch destination.

"Griffy, you don't need to change for anyone. Not the way you dress or the way you act. The people in your life love you for who you are. You're funny, intelligent, loyal, insightful, and you're always there for everyone. You see the best in people, and you refuse to let them do stupid things because they're scared or being shortsighted. My brother and Isla wouldn't be engaged right now if it wasn't for you." Reaching across the center armrest, I grab Griffin's hand and intertwine our fingers. "People see all that. They see that you're a leader. That you're selfless."

When he scoffs, it hurts my heart. "If that was true,

why would your brother want to set you up with some complete stranger and not me?"

Ah. So that's what this is all about. I should have realized after Lexi mentioned my brother's plans that Griffin had been there to hear them. My stupid, overbearing brother. "Babe, you're his best friend. You know he loves you, right? I'm sure he didn't think of you because, in his mind, you're his teammate and best friend. I'm just his annoying little sister."

Wide hazel eyes sparkle, and Griffin's lips turn up in a dazzling smile. "Babe?"

I shrug. Calling him babe wasn't a conscious decision, but I can't deny how right it feels. Nothing about this relationship has been conventional, but I can't lie and say it's not starting to feel... right. Inevitable, even. "What? I can't call my husband *babe*?"

The husband in question sucks in a sharp breath. "What did you say?"

"Um, I said shouldn't I be able to call my husband babe? Are you okay?" I glance at him as I pull into the parking lot of the arcade-slash-restaurant I decided would be the perfect place to go to help Griffin have fun and let go of this *I have to be serious* shit. He stares at me as I park, and as soon as I've turned the car off, he acts.

Lunging forward, Griffin grabs hold of my face with a ferocious tenderness that turns my insides into Jell-O and makes my cheeks heat. His hazel eyes search mine as his tongue sweeps over his lower lip.

"Griffin?"

His voice is rough when he speaks. "You called me your husband."

Oh. *Oh.*

Swallowing hard, I nod. Honestly, I didn't mean to say it. The words just slipped out of my mouth. I can't take them back now, and I'm not sure I would. It's what he is, right? Legally speaking, he's my husband, even though it goes much deeper than that by now. "Well, you are, aren't you?"

"Fuck yeah, baby girl." His eyes blaze as he brings his face closer to mine, the tip of his nose skimming along mine. The warmth of his breath has my skin erupting in goose bumps. "I'm your husband. I'm yours, Mira, all yours. You fucking own me."

Oh, shit. My panties are not going to survive this moment. They're already soaked. *I own him?* Who says shit like that? And why do I like it so much? "Griffin..."

"If we weren't in a parking lot full of families right now, I'd rip those clothes off your body, pull your ass into the air, and fuck your pretty little cunt until every inch of you is branded with my cum. I'd show you just how fully you own me, and how I intend to own you." One of his hands lets go of my face and slips down my body to cup my throbbing sex over my jeans. The gesture is rough and possessive, and fuck if I don't whimper against his lips, which hover a hairsbreadth away from mine. "You have no idea how long I've been waiting to hear you call me that."

"Husband?" I ask, my voice breathless and needy. I want to push him over the edge. I want him to slip those long, strong fingers of his inside the waistband of my pants and plunge them into my pussy.

Griffin lets out a growl—the kind all the heroes in my romance books do when they're turned on and nearly feral for the woman they love—and nips at my bottom lip. Heat suffuses my body, and I gasp against his mouth. "Yes, wife.

Since the moment I woke up next to your perfect naked body with that ring on my finger, I've been waiting to hear you call me husband."

When his fingers stroke along the seam of my jeans at my core, I whimper, and Griffin's eyes flare with lust. He presses a hard, demanding kiss to my lips, but when I open for him, he pulls away rather than deepening it, and I whimper again.

A self-satisfied smile overtakes Griffin's lips as his hand leaves my sex. "Good thing I'm a pro at waiting now, or it would be really hard to tear myself away from you so we could get lunch." He winks at me. The bastard winks at me. "But I know you're hungry, so I'd hate to make *you* wait."

My mouth is open like a fish, my whole body is on fire, and Griffin Wright, clit-tease extraordinaire, kisses me on the nose, opens his door, and gets out of the car. When I don't immediately follow, because I'm trying to get over the physical whiplash of the moment, he leans in with a deliberately concerned look on his face.

"You coming, sunshine?"

"Apparently not," I growl as I unbuckle myself and shove open my door.

Griffin's laughter follows me all the way inside the restaurant.

"Can I get you anything else?" our server, Eisley, asks. She can't be older than seventeen, and she's a million times cooler than I ever hoped to be at her age. She recognized Griffin immediately when we sat down, but instead of fawning over him, she's been giving him shit the entire lunch. He's had a blast.

"I think we're good," Griffin says, patting his stomach. "Everything was perfect. Thanks, Eisley."

The girl grins. "Anytime. We make sure all our customers feel like the most important people in the world. Even if they're only a hockey player."

I bark out a laugh as Griffin grips his chest and pretends to be wounded. "Oh, we're definitely requesting you the next time we come back here," I tell her as Griffin hands her his card. He's laughing, too, and I'm so glad to see him having fun. Even if I do want to kick his ass because my panties are still damp, and it's uncomfortable.

Once she returns with Griffin's card and he leaves her a more than generous tip, we head into the arcade portion of the building. It's noisy, chaotic, and full of neon signs and flashing lights. There's everything from basketball hoops to pinball machines, virtual reality to billiards. And Griffin looks like a kid in—well, like a kid in an arcade.

"Oh, air hockey," he says with a boyish grin, pointing to an empty table.

I raise one eyebrow. "Really? You just got home from an away series, and you want to play air hockey?"

"Hell yeah, sunshine, let's go. Unless you're afraid I'll kick your ass?" Griffin waggles his eyebrows at me tauntingly.

Never one to back down when faced with a challenge, I shrug. "Oh, you're definitely going to kick my ass, but let's go." I scan the arcade when he grabs my hand and tugs me toward the game, but no one is paying us any attention. It seems that none of the patrons have realized there's a pro hockey player in their midst, so I don't need to worry about some nosy stranger taking a photo of us holding hands and posting it on the internet for all the world—and my brother—to see.

I know we'll have to tell Maddox and everyone else about this marriage soon if things keep going the way they're going, but I'm still not ready. Maybe that makes me a coward, but I don't care. My feelings for Griffin are growing, and they're growing quickly, but I'm well aware that, no matter how I feel, there's going to be a whole lot of drama surrounding our announcement. So I need to be sure this is what I want before we tell anyone. If I'm not dead set on staying married to Griffin, there's no point in potentially blowing up his friendship with my brother or annihilating my brother's trust in me.

Griffin wins the air hockey game—because of course he does—and the Skee-Ball game we play afterward. But then I kick his ass when he challenges me to a racing game, and soon all my worries about our secret coming out dissipate like fog on a sunny day amid our laughter and cheeky banter.

A few hours later, Griffin leads me out of the building, his fingers laced in mine, a huge stuffed animal tucked under my arm. My cheeks hurt from smiling, and I'm ready to go home and cuddle up on the couch. Even though I drove my new car here, it still takes me by surprise to see it sitting in the parking lot, instead of my clunky old junker, and I smile like a fool.

"You're so fucking beautiful when you smile," Griffin says, leaning his elbows on the roof of the car. "Then again, you're always beautiful. The most beautiful woman I've ever seen. And you're mine." He shakes his head as though he simply can't believe it.

Heat floods my face, and my heart gives a happy thump. "You're not so bad yourself," I tease. "And you're mine." The way his salacious grin melts my insides and makes me clench my thighs has my voice coming out breathy and laced with innuendo. "Ready to head home?"

"Oh, wifey, my head is more than ready to be home." He winks, and I laugh as we get in the car.

"That was a terrible line." Not that my vagina seems to have gotten the memo. She's pretty excited about all of this.

Griffin chuckles. "I'll make it up to you. Now let's go, baby. All those games made me work up an appetite. I'm hungry for something sweet."

I shiver when he drags his knuckles along my inner thigh and pray I don't get a ticket as I peel out of the parking lot and speed all the way home.

twenty-five

GRIFFIN

Finally. She finally said it. Mira called me her husband.

I can't keep my hands to myself as she drives us home, looking cute as fuck in her new Rogues-yellow car with my number on it. Not sure how I'm going to explain that to her brother, but I can't worry about that now. Right now, all I can think about is making love to my wife for the first time. I vowed she wouldn't get my cock until she called me her husband, but now that she has?

I'm going to live in her tight, wet pussy.

"What are you smiling about?" Mira says, a little gasp punctuating the question as I run the pads of my fingers along the seam of her jeans and over her hot center. "Fuck, babe, you're gonna make me crash my brand-new car."

"Sorry." I'm not. I can buy her another one. "I'm smiling about all the dirty, filthy things I'm going to do to you once we get home."

My wife wiggles in her seat, knuckles white as she strangles the steering wheel. Oh, she's thinking dirty thoughts, too, isn't she? I bet if I petted her pretty, pink pussy, I'd find it dripping for me. My dick has been hard since the moment she called me her husband, but somehow the thought of her dripping with need for me has me even harder.

Damn, I wish I was wearing something more comfortable than these stupid chinos. The fabric has zero give, and my dick is trying to bust out of the damn things.

"Do you want to hear about my plans for you, wifey?" My voice is a low rumble as we get closer to home. Mira shifts in her seat again, her cheeks flushing a rosy red. "How I'm going to strip you naked the minute we get inside, throw you onto our bed, and make you scream my name when I bury myself inside that perfect pussy of yours? How I'm going to make you come over and over again until you're a shaking, sobbing mess, begging for mercy?"

"Oh, fuck," Mira whispers, clenching her knees together as she pulls into the parking garage.

"Fuck is right, baby girl. I've been waiting to fill you with my cock. You gonna let me paint your insides with my cum? I want to mark you as mine. Write my name on you with every drop."

"Jesus, Wright." Mira's chest heaves as she pulls into her spot and parks the car. Her breath comes out in shaky little puffs, and when I meet her beautiful eyes, my whole body tingles with the desire reflected in those emerald pools.

Smirking, I reach over and turn off the car, taking her keys before stepping out and walking around it. I open her door to find her sitting there, staring at me, and lean in to unbuckle her. As I pull back, I graze her jaw with my teeth and my lips before whispering in her ear. "I'm going to ruin you, baby girl. Just like you've ruined me. Now, get your beautiful round ass out of this car, or I'll carry you, caveman style, up to our place and I won't give a damn who sees it."

Breath shaking, Mira licks her lips as I pull away and offer her my hand. Her big, lust-filled eyes flick up to meet mine as she places her palm on mine. "Don't you dare carry me."

The command lacks any real heat, and I'm tempted to do just that, but I won't do anything to jeopardize this moment. I'm going to make love to my wife for the very first time. If everything goes well, I'll have years to throw her over my shoulder, bite that luscious ass, and manhandle her whenever I please. Linking our fingers, I don't bother grabbing my gear out of her trunk. I'll have to buy an air freshener for it later, but that's a problem for Future Griffin. My hard, aching cock is a problem for Right Now Griffin. A problem I intend to remedy.

"God, I can't wait to lick your pussy," I whisper against her ear as we step inside the building. Mira's steps falter, and I try not to chuckle. She's so confident and unflappable. It gives me an undeniable thrill knowing that I can make my wife lose her composure with nothing more than a whispered promise. One that makes her hurry to the elevator once she's gotten over the shock of my words.

As soon as the elevator doors close, I'm on her. Our lips crash together, my hand fisting the hair at her nape as I tilt her head back and angle it the way I need so I can sweep my tongue inside her mouth. My dick strains against my pants and I grind it against her lower belly. Mira moans, soft and breathy, into my mouth. I want to push my hand beneath the hem of her shirt and cup her breasts, but the last thing I need is the security guys getting an eyeful of my wife's tits, because there's no way they're not sitting in a dark office somewhere enjoying this little show.

The elevator dings and opens on our floor, then we're stumbling out of it in a tangle of limbs and tongues and searching hands. It takes me three tries to get the goddamn door unlocked, then we're crashing through and there's nothing holding me back from stripping Mira bare.

"I want you naked." As I tug the shirt over her head, she lifts her arms to help. Once it's gone, my eyes zero in on her heaving tits covered in simple gray cotton. It's just as sexy as any little scrap of lace, and I almost come in my pants like a teenage boy. "You're fucking beautiful."

Mira gasps and hums her pleasure as I trail nips and kisses down her neck, over her shoulders, and across the swell of her breasts. Her back arches, inviting me to take my fill, and I do, quickly reaching around her and unclasping the bra. My hands are on her the moment her breasts break free.

"Oh, shit," she hisses as I pinch one nipple and lean down to suck the other into my mouth. "Oh, god, you're good with that mouth."

Grinning around her nipple, I lave my tongue around the tight, peaked tip. "Just wait, baby. You think I'm good with my mouth, but you've never ridden my dick."

I release her other nipple from my hand and make quick work of her jeans. With the button undone, I push them down her legs, and Mira kicks them off. "How wet are you for me, wife?"

"Soaked," she says breathlessly as I push my hand beneath the waistband of her panties and drag two fingers through her slick slit.

Soaked is right. Fuck, I can't wait to sheath myself in that tight cunt. It's going to be a battle of wills with myself to keep from pushing inside of her in one brutal thrust, because I'm determined to make love to this woman, to show her what she means to me, but my dick just wants to rut her.

My dick is not the boss of me.

Giving myself a minute to calm down, I pump my fingers in and out of her a few times with torturous slowness. Mira's hands grip my shoulders to the point of pain. Like clinging to me is the only thing keeping her upright. She watches with wide, sparkling eyes as I withdraw my fingers from her dripping pussy and lick them clean.

"Damn, you taste good, sunshine. And I promise I'm gonna eat you out, but if I don't get inside you first, I may lose my mind."

Mira sucks in a breath, her eyes heavy-lidded as she nods her agreement. In seconds, her panties and socks are off, and I'm carrying my naked wife, bridal style, to our bed. I set her down gently, reverently. There'll be plenty of time for throwing her down and watching her tits bounce and her eyes light up with humor later. For now, I want her to feel worshipped. I want her to feel loved and cherished. After living with Mira for a few months, she'd become one of my best friends. But since we woke up in that bed, naked in Vegas with rings on our fingers, she's become so much more.

Surveying her gorgeous body, fingers fisted around the

comforter, I realize what this moment is missing and turn around, heading for the closet.

"Griffin?" Mira sounds confused. "Where are you going?"

"Just grabbing something. Give me a second." I rifle around in my sock drawer until my fingers close around my prize. Grinning, I stalk back to the bed where Mira watches me with hungry eyes. Reaching for her left hand, I hold eye contact while slipping her simple wedding band over her finger.

Breath catching, Mira bounces her gaze between the gold band and me. Neither of us have worn the rings since that morning in Vegas, but I've kept them safe. Sometimes, when she's not home, I wear mine. Hell, I want to wear it everywhere every day, but she's not ready for that. But this, right now? If we're making love, we're wearing these rings.

"Griffin..." Those emerald eyes of hers are soft, but I don't miss the flicker of something that looks a lot like fear that darkens them for a split second. Then she glances at the larger band still clutched in my palm and takes it, sliding it over my ring finger.

My breath hitches. This moment is huge. It's everything. I'm not stupid enough to believe that Mira is one hundred percent on board with this marriage, but between her calling me *husband* and this? Maybe she's finally starting to admit what I already know.

Mira and I are end game. We're forever. Inevitable.

I hold her gaze as I rip off my polo, followed by the rest of my clothes. Pre-cum already beads at the tip of my dick as I drag my boxer briefs down my legs, and I grin when Mira sucks in a sharp breath and licks her lips.

"Baby," I croon as I crawl across the bed to her, "please

tell me I can take you bare. I got tested a few weeks after you moved in, and I haven't been with anyone since then." She looks surprised at that, but I don't know why. I've never brought a woman home or even talked about one since she moved in with me. "And I've never been with anyone bare. Ever."

"I-I have an IUD and I'm all clear too," she says, a little breathless.

A grin curves my lips. "Is that a yes, wifey? Are you gonna let me take you bare and fill your pussy with my cum?"

"Fuck," Mira moans, squeezing her thighs together. "Yes. Please, Griffin, yes."

That's all it takes for me to lose the last tenuous grip on my control. Hauling Mira up, I pull her onto my lap, my knees bent beneath me, her wet, bare pussy sliding along my shaft as she straddles me. I kiss her like I'll die if I don't. I kiss her like I've been poisoned and, with only moments to live, her lips are the antidote. Our tongues tangling, I gently grip the back of her neck, reveling in the feel of all her soft skin pressed against mine. Her peaked nipples drag across my chest and I moan into her mouth, my hips flexing involuntarily at the sensation, and the head of my cock bumps against her clit before sliding through her slick folds.

"Oh, oh *fuck*," she gasps, rolling her hips against my length.

"Soon, baby," I promise, thrusting up again, coating my dick in her arousal. She's dripping for me, soaking my cock with her desire. "I'm going to fuck you hard and fast, and in every position I can think of before the day is over. Your pussy is going to be swollen and sore by the time I'm done with you. My cum will drip down your thighs and paint these pretty tits, and I'm going to rub it into your skin so I become as much a part of you as you are of me."

Mira whimpers and rolls her hips against me. Her breathing is shallow and erratic, and I suspect that if she keeps grinding against my cock like this, she's going to come.

Gripping her hips, I push her center down as I thrust up. The choked sound of pleasure she makes as she slides along the length of me makes me practically feral. If she thinks this feels good, just wait until I'm inside of her. "I'm going to fuck you until you can't remember your name or what day it is, and you'll still beg for more," I promise as her body shakes and quivers, so close to her impending orgasm. And then I hold her still.

"What?" Those beautiful, previously half-lidded eyes fly open as Mira's nose wrinkles in indignation. "Griffin, what the hell?" She tries to roll her hips, but I don't let her. Frustration pinches her brow, and her lips drop into a pout.

My chest squeezes. Fuck. I'm so gone for this woman.

I kiss her jaw. "If you keep grinding on my dick like that, I'm going to explode. And I already told you, sunshine, I've been dying to fill you up with my cum. Not gonna waste a drop."

Pulling back so our eyes are locked, I grip Mira's hips, encouraging her to lift onto her knees. She does, shuddering breaths puffing from her lips, and I grip my rock-hard dick and drag the head through her slick folds. It's a struggle to keep my eyes from rolling back in my head, but I'm glad I manage it because if I hadn't, I would have missed the way Mira's lashes flutter and her breath catches.

"Griffin…"

"Mira. My beautiful, amazing wife." I notch the head of my dick at her entrance and lift my hips slightly. "Do you know what you do to me?"

She gasps and shakes her head.

"Do you know how much I care about you?" Using my grip on her hip, I urge her down my length another few centimeters. "You fucking own me, sunshine." I pull her down farther. "I'm yours." And with that, I surge up, filling her completely. I've never felt anything like it. She's so tight, so warm, so wet. The sensation of her pussy gripping my cock is everything. "Shit, baby, you feel so good. This pussy was made for me. So tight. So perfect."

"Oh, god," she cries, her head falling back as I hold her still, filled with me, owned by me. *Owning me.*

I lean forward, nipping at the exposed column of her throat. "What god? All I can see is a goddess. My wife." Slowly, with more restraint than I thought myself capable of, I roll my hips, making sure to drag her clit along my pubic bone.

"Griffin…"

My hands roam across her body, touching, tracing every silky inch of skin. I whisper my devotion as I move in her, reveling in her little moans and gasps. Mira's fingers clutch my shoulders, and our bodies grow slicker with sweat with every languid thrust. "My beautiful wife," I murmur, pressing my forehead to hers.

"Please, Griffin, *please.*" Mira rolls her hips as a whine slips past her lips. "I need to come. Please fuck me."

"Don't worry, baby. I'm going to fuck you so hard. But

you have to be patient. We have all day to fuck. Right now? Right now, I'm making love to my wife for the first time."

As Mira's eyes glisten with unshed tears, warmth spreads through my body. My chest tightens with emotions, and my balls tighten with my impending release.

I brush a sweat-soak strand of hair away from her face. "Are you close, sweetheart?"

She only nods, her breath ragged and choppy, a beautiful flush working its way across her chest and up her neck. When I slip my hand between our bodies and rub her clit as I surge up into her, she gasps and I lose my tenuous grip on my control.

Our lips crash together in time with our bodies, my heart pounding in my chest as all thoughts of anything outside of Mira evaporate like fog from my mind. She's the sun, chasing everything else away. Her breasts bounce against my bare chest, and the erotic slap of skin against skin has my muscles tightening. Tingles work up from my thighs, over my groin, and through my abs.

"You're so perfect," I praise as needy whines and mewls flow from my wife's mouth. She's close. So am I. My fingers circle her clit faster and faster as Mira's stomach hollows out. She cries out against my mouth, her eyes falling closed as she throws her head back. Her inner walls ripple and contract against my dick, and pleasure rips through me as everything tightens. And then I'm burying my face in her neck and biting down on her shoulder as I shatter, coming inside my wife with a long, low moan.

She swivels her hips, riding me through our orgasms, and I chuckle when she tenses her inner muscles and squeezes my dick. She's perfect. Absolutely perfect for me.

"Griffin," she whispers, smiling shyly at me, "that was…"

"Only the first of many," I promise, sealing it with an intense kiss.

It's a promise I deliver on. Again and again and again. By the time it's dark outside and the world is quiet, Mira is a sweat-soaked, sated mess. Despite having cleaned up after each round, if I pressed a finger to her slit, I'd feel my cum dripping out of her. The thought gives me no small amount of satisfaction, but even that doesn't hold a candle to the sheer intensity of my joy. Because, while this marriage may still be an uphill climb, I'm no longer dragging my wife up the mountain with me, kicking and screaming. She's climbing with me, side by side.

All those failed relationships. All those years feeling cursed to watch the people around me fall in love while I was sitting on the bench, jealously hoping for my turn. Now, here I am, holding my sleeping wife. And sure, we still have to find a way to tell her brother and my teammates, and yeah, I could still screw this all up, but for now?

For now, I'm going to hold my exhausted wife as she breathes deeply and rhythmically in her sleep beside me and soak up every single second. Because she's everything to me.

"I love you," I whisper, wishing I had the courage to say it when she was awake, but knowing I'll get another chance.

She called me her husband, after all.

twenty-six

MIRA

"I forgot to tell you," I say as I stretch beside Griffin in the early morning sun, his glorious naked body wrapped around me. "Ed invited us to join his book club."

A shiver works through my body as Griffin's low chuckle makes his chest vibrate against mine. "Oh yeah? What do they like to read, thrillers or something?"

"Nope." I try to suppress my giggle. "Fairy smut."

I squeal when Griffin sits up in bed, causing me to roll off his chest. His hazel eyes glitter when he turns to look at me. "Shut up. Ed does not read fairy smut."

"Oh, but he does. He *and* his friends, who, by the sound of it, are all older gentlemen." I giggle at Griffin's wide-eyed expression of pure excitement. "I told him you read romance, so he invited both of us to join."

"Fuck yeah! I've been trying to get the guys to start a smutty book club with me, but the only one who even considered it was Ryder. Killjoys." Griffin shakes his head.

His eyes are still squinty from sleep, and his shaggy golden hair is sticking up in every direction, but *god* is he sexy.

I must make a small sound, because a moment later, Griffin leans over and nips at my neck. "Like what you see, wife?"

"Mm-hmm." I do, I really do. Between the perfection of Griffin's naked form beside me and the memories of all the ways he owned my body yesterday, I basically woke up horny. Which is why I was trying to distract myself with thoughts of old-guy book clubs, something that clearly backfired.

As Griffin's long fingers cup one of my breasts, I instinctively reach for him. When my hand wraps around his hard shaft, he groans, and his grip on my breast tightens. "My husband is so sexy," I murmur, more to myself than Griffin, but it makes his face light up in a luminescent smile.

"Say it again."

I chuckle, stroking up and down his length. "You're sexy."

"Not that part," he says with a choked voice. "The other part."

Confused, I pinch my eyebrows together. "What other part?"

"The part where you called me your husband."

Oh. *Oh.* Sweet, sweet man. I lean in and press a soft kiss to the scruff of his jaw. "My husband." I kiss his cheek. "My husband." His eyes flutter closed and I kiss him there. "My husband. Mine."

The world spins, and I let out a squeak as Griffin flips me over onto my back. His eyes are blazing, multi-hued orbs of pure desire.

"Fuck, baby, hearing you call me that makes me so hard." He presses his length against my lower belly to illustrate his point as he hovers over me, eyes locked on mine. "Are you sore, wifey?"

Am I sore? The man fucked me so hard and so thoroughly, I'm not actually sure I'm capable of standing. So yeah, I'm sore, but in the best way. "I'm not sore," I lie.

Of course, Griffin notices my moment of hesitation. "Don't lie to me, sunshine. The last thing I want to do is hurt you."

"What if I want to be hurt?" I ask, voice saccharine sweet.

Griffin groans and fists his cock. "Shit. My wife is such a perfect, needy little slut, aren't you?"

I nod, moisture pooling between my thighs at the way he makes the word *slut* sound like the highest praise. If anyone else tried to call me that, I'd punch them in the balls. With Griffin, though? I know he's not trying to make me feel small or dirty. Well, maybe a little dirty, but in the best way.

"Baby, there are so many ways I can please you and take you without making you more sore." His fingers pluck and play with one of my nipples as his hips roll against mine.

"Oh, yeah?" I ask breathlessly. "Like what?"

"Well..." Griffin grins, and then I'm being flipped again, this time onto my belly. Strong fingers grip my hips and pull my ass into the air. I stare at my accidental husband over my shoulder while he palms my ass cheeks and rubs his shaft between them. "Has anyone ever taken this perfect, round ass, sunshine?"

Oh, fuck. My core clenches. "No."

"Mmm." Griffin hums appreciatively, his palms smoothing over the globes of my ass before he spreads me and presses a thumb against the tight ring of muscles. "Never?"

I can't even form words as he circles my asshole with his thumb. All I can manage is to shake my head. The men I've been with before Griffin were…vanilla. Lots of missionary, grunting, and quick fucks that didn't always get me off. Even if one of them had suggested we try something different, I'm not sure I would have trusted them to do something like take my ass. But Griffin? I trust him.

Griffin watches my reactions as he plays, notes the slight tensing of my body when his thumb starts to breach that tight ring of muscles, and leans forward to plant a kiss between my shoulder blades. "One day, I'm going to fuck this pretty ass."

I whine as he pushes his thumb deeper. The sensation is different, but not bad.

"Relax, sunshine. We'll have to work up to that. But only if you want to." He starts to pump his thumb slowly in and out of me, and I'm surprised by how good it feels once I allow myself to relax into it. He grins when I gasp and tighten around him. "The things I'm going to do to you…"

"Yes," I whine. I think I'd let him do just about anything to me and love it. With his thumb still in my ass, he runs his fingers through my dripping slit, and my stomach hollows out as I arch into him. "Oh, fuck."

"Not this morning. Maybe tonight, if you're not as sore. This morning, I'm going to eat my wife for breakfast."

My eyes are screwed shut with pleasure as he presses a finger inside me, dragging it along my inner walls, both of my holes filled. It's heady, and he's not even using his dick. When he lowers his mouth to my pussy and starts to fuck me with his tongue, it feels like I'm floating.

Griffin presses my shoulders down with his free hand, arching my back even more while he devours me and fucks my ass with his thumb. Pleasure zips through my body like electrical currents, and already, my orgasm is building.

"Oh, god, babe. Oh, fuck." I barely recognize my voice, it's so breathless and needy.

"That's it, sunshine, let me have it," he coaxes, his voice muffled against my pussy. "Flood my mouth with your cum, baby."

Then he eats me with abandon, his thumb still pumping in and out of me, and his other hand wraps around my hips and presses on my clit. And I explode.

Screaming into the mattress, I writhe and buck against Griffin's mouth. He's relentless. The way he draws my orgasm out until I'm shaking, tears streaming down my face, my body overwhelmed with pleasure, is everything. This man plays my body like a world-class musician, and I know he's just getting started.

He finally pulls away when I beg him to stop, so sensitive that every new flick of his tongue has me shaking. Slowly, he pulls his thumb from my ass and gently flips me over onto my back.

Griffin's mouth and chin are covered with my arousal, his eyes are heavy-lidded, and his dick is hard and leaking pre-cum. He licks his lips and levels me with a salacious grin. "Delicious."

"Holy shit," I murmur to myself. The man is a sex god. I married a sex god. This could be how things are for the rest of my life if I let myself fall for him and give in to this crazy chemistry between us.

Leaning forward, Griffin kisses me. "Come on, sunshine. Let's get cleaned up, then I'll take you out for breakfast. I want to spend as much time with you as I can before practice."

"Okay," I say, still a bit dazed. It makes Griffin chuckle. Then he's standing and pulling me into his arms. I squeak, grabbing hold of his neck, and enjoy the way his laughter vibrates through me as he carries me to the bathroom. He sets me down, so I'm sitting on the cold countertop of the sink, and laughs harder when I let out another startled squeal.

"Sorry, baby. I'll warm your ass up in a second." He winks at me before turning on the shower and checking the water temperature.

"Not sure my ass can handle anything else this morning." Heat floods my body at the look he gives me.

"Oh, I think your ass could handle plenty more with the right prep."

When my thighs clench together, he totally notices. With an ever-wider grin, and satisfied that the water temperature is perfect, Griffin lifts me off the sink, cradles me to his body, and pulls me under the spray. Between the heat of his chest and the warmth of the water, my chilly ass is quickly forgotten.

"Don't want to put you down," he murmurs with his forehead resting against mine. "But I can't wash my hair while I'm holding you."

We wash quickly, trading heated kisses and teasing touches. It's...everything. This is what I always dreamed marriage could be like when I was a girl. Okay, so I didn't imagine butt stuff and smoking-hot sex, but the tenderness, the closeness, the undeniable feeling of safety? Those, I imagined. The other stuff is merely a bonus.

It has my mind wandering to what the future with Griffin could look like. I've been finding myself daydreaming about it a lot lately, and it still freaks me out a bit, but not nearly the way it did when we first woke up married. I know Griffin doesn't like that I've asked him to keep this a secret, and I hate that we're lying to my brother and Isla, but I'm still not ready to let the world in. I need to know my own mind before I invite the opinions of others.

The crazy thing is, I'm realizing that my mind, and heart, are softening to my accidental husband more and more each day. That, when I picture being married, Jared's stupid face isn't even a shadow in my mind's eye any longer. No, when I picture waking up each morning next to someone, he's blond with shaggy hair, an impeccable jawline, hazel eyes, and a scruffy jaw. I think I did love Jared, in my own way, but those feelings have been so easily eclipsed by my feelings for Griffin that it's clear Jared and I never would have had a lasting love.

But could Griffin and I? Is that what I want? Can I let myself hope for that? He's every woman's dream, isn't he? Handsome, funny, so very kind, tall, muscular, supportive, smart...the list goes on. But he was my brother's best friend, so I never let myself picture him any other way. Never thought he'd want me. I know Griffin believes he's cursed, but I think he just dated shallow women who didn't try to see past his easy smiles to the incredible depth beneath. Some part of me is worried he has latched on to me because I *have* seen past the surface. But I'm not the only woman who will. What happens when he meets someone prettier or richer or more interesting? Will I be enough?

I wasn't for my dad.

"Hey." Griffin palms my cheek. His voice is gentle as his hazel eyes search my face. "You're thinking awfully hard right now. Want to talk about it?"

Shaking my head to clear it, I force a smile. What would I even say?

I think maybe I'm developing feelings for you, and I'm scared you'll realize you settled for me, then leave like my dad did?

It sounds pathetic, even in my head.

"Nah," I say instead. "There's nothing to talk about."

Griffin frowns as his eyes bounce over my features. Hesitantly, he asks, "Do you regret it?"

My body jolts at the worry in his tone. "What?"

His cheeks flush pink and his shoulders tense. "Do you regret sleeping with me?"

Shit. "No, not even a little. Not for a second." I press my palms to his chest and my heart twinges when I feel how fast his is racing. "I'm sorry. I got in my own head for a minute, but I swear I don't regret anything. I'm really happy." *And that's what worries me.* "You make me happy."

"You make me happy too," he murmurs, eyes softening. My stomach decides this is the perfect moment to growl. He grins. "Really fucking happy, sunshine. Now, let's dry off and get dressed so we can feed you. We don't want a hangry Mira."

"No," I agree. "We really don't."

twenty-seven

MIRA

A FEW DAYS LATER, THE INCESSANT BEEPING OF Griffin's alarm clock has me groaning and pulling my pillow over my head. It's early—the guys have practice at six a.m., so Griffin sets his alarm for five—and it's not like him to hit the snooze, let alone ignore it altogether.

Reaching out blindly, I push Griffin's naked chest, shaking him. He's uncharacteristically far away from me in bed. And warm. Normally, he's wrapped around me like a koala. "Griffin? Your alarm is going off. Get your sexy ass up."

He simply groans, so I shake him again, then blindly feel for his face so I can poke his cheeks. When my fingers touch his skin, my eyes open, and I push the pillow off my face.

He's burning up.

"Griffin?" Sitting up in bed, I find my husband sprawled out, arms and legs akimbo, in nothing but his boxer briefs. He's pushed the blankets to the side so I'm still wrapped in them, but he's completely uncovered. Sweat beads along Griffin's furrowed brow, and his face is flushed. "Babe?"

He groans, stirring, but not opening his eyes. I grab his phone and turn off the alarm, relieved to end the squawking. Griffin must be relieved, too, because his brow smooths ever so slightly. "Baby?"

"Hey," I murmur, running my palm over his forehead. He's hot to the touch. "Can you open your eyes for me, big guy?" I need to get him some water and Tylenol, but first I need to see those hazel irises and make sure he's with me.

Thick, dark blond lashes flutter before I'm finally met with bloodshot hazel eyes. "Mir?" He grimaces. "I don't feel so good."

Running my fingers through his sweat-slicked hair, I hum my understanding. "I bet. You have a fever. I'm going to get you some water and meds. Can you sit up?"

Griffin groans, his usually graceful movements replaced by a jerky shakiness that makes my stomach twist with worry. It takes him too long—and my eventual help —to leverage himself into a sitting position. "What time is it?"

I glance at his phone. "Almost five-thirty."

"Shit," he mumbles, twisting onto his hands and knees. "I'm gonna be late for practice."

"Babe." His skin practically sizzles when I grab his shoulders and force him back into a seated position. "You're not going to practice today. You can barely sit up, let alone lift weights or skate."

"I'm fine," he says unconvincingly. The man winces as he says it, his eyes falling closed.

"Sure. You're totally fine. That's why you can't even keep your eyes open." I grab my cell after I pull the blankets up over Griffin's legs and kiss his forehead. "Stay right here. I'll be back."

I can't help glancing back at Griffin as I hurry from our bedroom and into the kitchen, where he keeps first aid supplies in the pantry. After grabbing the Tylenol and filling up a glass with cold water, I call my brother.

"Mi-Mi?" Maddox's gruff voice is low, like he's trying not to wake Isla. "Are you okay? What's wrong?"

I huff out a soft chuckle. "Why would you assume something's wrong?"

"Because it's not even six yet, and I know what a grumpy ass you are this early in the morning. What's wrong?"

"Fine," I say with a sigh. "Something is wrong."

"Do you need me to get you? Are you safe?" I want to be annoyed at Maddox's protective schtick, but honestly, it makes me feel all warm and fuzzy inside.

"Chill, Maddy, I'm fine."

My big brother lets out a sigh of relief.

"It's Griffin."

There's a beat of silence. "What about him?"

"He's burning up, Maddy. I think he's really sick. There's no way he'll be able to drive to practice, let alone skate, or whatever you're supposed to do today." More silence stretches out between us, and I fidget, my feet cold against the kitchen tile.

"So why are you calling and not him?"

Does he sound suspicious? "Because he can't even keep his eyes open. I had to wake him up. His alarm must have been going off for almost half an hour." It's not a lie, but it's definitely only half the truth. I know I made it sound like Griffin's alarm woke me up all the way in my own room and not because I was sleeping next to him in our bed, so hopefully that's how my brother takes it. "You need to tell your coach he won't be there today."

Maddox grunts. "Yeah, all right. Do you need me to bring him anything?"

"No, I'll take care of him. You go to practice. Besides, the last thing the team needs is another player down with the flu or whatever this is."

"Thanks, Mi-Mi. Call me if you need reinforcements. He can be a big baby when he's sick."

I chuckle at that. "Aren't all guys?"

"Touché, Mira. Touché. All right. I gotta get going. I'll check in later. Love you."

"Love you too, Maddy. Have a good practice." Balancing my phone, the glass of water, and the Tylenol, I pad back into our bedroom to find Griffin still sitting, but his eyes are closed and his head lolls to the side. Soft little snores puff out of his slightly open mouth.

Damn, he's cute. Yes, he's sick, and I'm worried about him, but there's something so innocent about him like this. I switch the water and Tylenol to my left hand and quickly snap a few photos with my phone before softly calling his name to wake him up.

"Griffy? Wake up, babe. I have medicine for you to help bring your fever down. And water. You need to stay hydrated."

My husband stirs, blinking owlishly at me, his gaze unfocused. "Hmm?"

Holding the glass to his lips, I encourage him to take a few slow sips before giving him the medicine. He grimaces when he swallows it, but he manages to paste a small smile on his face.

"Thanks, sunshine."

"Of course, babe." I set the glass down on the bedside table and feel his forehead. I need to make sure he's not dangerously feverish. "Where's your thermometer?"

"Bathroom vanity," he says, eyes slipping closed.

I find it easily and scowl when it reads 102.1 "Shit. We need to keep you hydrated and cool. It's not dangerously high, but I can't imagine you feel good right now."

Griffin shakes his head. Or at least he attempts to. "Nope. Feel like shit."

"Don't worry, I'll take care of you." A rush of something warm and pure rises in my chest when my accidental husband grins at me through his discomfort. Emotions shine out of his bloodshot, glassy eyes, emotions I'm not quite ready to name, and I'm not sure he is, either.

"You don't have to do that, baby. I'm a grown-ass man. I can take care of myself." As if to illustrate my point, he swings his feet off the bed before rising on shaky legs.

"What are you doing?"

"Gotta pee, sunshine," he says with a grin. "I'll be fine."

Except, he's not. This feverish, muscular giant of a man must feel absolutely terrible, because he can barely stand. I quickly rush to his side and position myself under his arm, my own wrapped around his waist so I can act as a crutch. He tries to protest, but it quickly becomes apparent that he really does need my help and finally relents.

"Thanks, baby. I don't know what I'd do without you."

I grin. "Probably pee your pants."

That has him laughing and even more unsteady on his feet.

The morning goes by in a blur, and once I've made sure Griffin is hydrated and has eaten something, I help him get comfortable in bed. He snuggles in to watch a movie on his laptop while I sit next to him on mine. I'm not sure I'll get a full day's work done, but I can't completely neglect it, either. I have deadlines to meet, and I'm putting the finishing touches on the baseball team's website. They aren't expecting a finished product for another week, but I'm excited to show them the final result before the deadline.

"That looks amazing," Griffin says, looking over my shoulder. "Seriously, Mira, I knew you were talented, but that's something else."

I can feel the blush warming my cheeks and creeping up my chest. "Thank you."

Everyone has been supportive of me and my business, but I've never sat down with someone and shown them what I'm working on. It makes me feel vulnerable in a way I can't quite explain. Maybe it's because this is my dream, my baby, and I care about Griffin's opinions. I value what he thinks of me and what I do—more than I thought I would.

"Oh"—he grins—"I almost forgot. I heard from my contact at the University of Michigan, and they want to meet with you soon."

Nerves do a tap dance in my stomach. I've been working on my pitch for the university's hockey team, and I think I have some great ideas. I want to highlight their current program, as well as their alumni success stories. Griffin isn't the only player who's gone on to the NHL, AHL, or ECHL.

"Really?"

He nods, smiling brightly despite feeling sick. "Yep. I've been working on an endorsement deal with a company based in Michigan. They're also in Ann Arbor, so I figure we can schedule our meetings for the same weekend."

"That would be... That would be amazing, babe." I lean over and press a kiss on his fevered forehead. "You're amazing. How did I get so lucky?"

"I'm the lucky one." He sighs contentedly, letting his head rest on my shoulder.

Outwardly, we settle back into a companionable quiet. Inwardly, I'm a riot of excitement, worry, hope, and affection that grows stronger with each passing day. Griffin Wright is everything I have ever wanted and more than I could have hoped for, and I'm falling hard for my accidental husband.

twenty-eight

GRIFFIN

"WRIGHT, YOU'RE ON FIRE OUT THERE." COACH FRY slaps me on the back, his face lit up with a pleased smile. "Whatever has you amped up tonight, keep that momentum going through the third period."

"Thanks, Coach," I say before downing some water and resting my sweaty head against the locker behind me. We only have five more minutes before we have to be back on the ice for the last period of the game, and I'm exhausted, but I'm also hyped. Because we're at home, and my wife is in the family box with Isla and Lexi. *My wife.* My gorgeous, sexy-as-sin wife, who spent the last week fussing over my sick ass because she *cares.*

"Doing all right?" Maddox flops his ass down beside me, bumping me with his shoulder.

"Yep. Doing good, man. You?" Graves is having just as good of a game as I am. Hell, we all are. The kind of synergy we have going on tonight is the shit of legends. If we can keep this up for the rest of the season, we have a real chance of going all the way.

"I'm feeling good. Want to hit Chasers after the game? It's been too long since we all went out."

I chuckle. "That's what happens when you're engaged, bro. You end up going home to your lady, and you don't spend as much time with your boys."

"From what I've heard, you haven't been going out as much lately, either. Byrne won't stop bitching about it."

Shit.

"What am I bitching about?" Logan stands in front of us with a scowl.

"Wright's antisocial tendencies," Maddox replies.

I shrug. "I'm just done with the whole scene, you know? It feels shallow. I'm too old to be going out and hooking up with random women every night."

"Since when?" Logan says, one brow raised. "Seriously, you don't have a brain tumor or something, right?"

"That's not even funny," Bash says, shaking his head.

Logan shrugs. "He's being weird."

"Who's being weird?" Ryder asks.

"No one," I say as Coach claps his hands and shouts at us to get geared back up and out on the ice. Saved by the bell, or whatever. "But yeah, I'll go out tonight, as long as everyone's there."

"Isla's already asking the girls," Maddox says with a clap on my shoulder.

"Then, let's go win this thing so we can celebrate."

The guys all roar their agreement as we get back on the ice.

THE WHOLE BAR CHEERS AS WE SAUNTER IN, HIGH off a shutout. The crush of people chanting our names and crowding around us would have given me a thrill before, but now all it does is make me worry about Mira and the girls' safety.

Maddox has Isla tucked into his side, a scowl on his grumpy face for anyone who gets too close. Ryder's hand clutches Lexi's, and even though he doesn't look as menacing as my best friend, it's clear that if anyone messes with his girlfriend, he won't hesitate to fuck them up.

Then there's me.

My fingers itch to wrap around Mira's waist. I want to lay claim to her in front of every single man in this bar, so they know not to touch her. Hell, I want them to know they shouldn't so much as look at her. But I can't. I can't, because Mira isn't ready to tell everyone that she's my wife. So I do the only thing I really can do and glare at any dumb fucker who gets too close.

Sebastian chuckles next to me, but I ignore him.

We make it to the massive booth in the back that Chasers reserves for us on nights we're playing at home, and I let out the breath I've been holding. Everyone slides into the booth, and I can't keep my fingers from skimming my wife's lower back as I encourage her to slip in next to Bash. I'm the last one in, leaving me on the outside seat. I don't want Mira fending off the fans. No way would I let her take the outside seat.

We order several pitchers of beer and enough appetizers for everyone. The atmosphere is celebratory, and we're garnering plenty of attention due to how loud and rowdy everyone is. A few fans make their way over to congratulate Bash on the shutout and gush over the win, but for the most part, they leave us alone. It's one of the reasons we love this place. The patrons are fans, but there's an unspoken understanding that when we're here, we're largely off-limits.

And that's the way it stays for the first hour. We laugh and goof around. Mira smiles brightly beside me, just as much a part of the Rogues family as Isla and Lexi, even though none of them know she and I are together. She's Maddox's little sister—not to mention, she's cool as shit—but she's also my roommate, and she's not afraid to give the guys shit.

She's laughing at something Sebastian says when I feel a tap on my shoulder. Turning, I prepare myself to smile at a middle-aged fan with a beer belly and glassy eyes. Except, that's not who I see.

"Hi," a bubbly blonde with curly hair and a low-cut top chirps. Her lips curve in what I imagine she believes is a sultry smile, but it doesn't do a thing for me. There's not a woman on this earth who can affect me the way my wife does, and I realize with total clarity that I don't even notice women anymore. Not the way I used to. Sure, I notice them as human beings, but that's the extent of it. There's no hint of attraction, no bolt of lust, nothing.

I have eyes for one woman, and it's the beautiful brunette sitting beside me, laughing her gorgeous ass off, uncaring of how loud she is or who may be watching her.

"Uh, hey," I say, polite but dismissive. I immediately turn my attention back to the table, but the blonde is undeterred. She taps my shoulder again and flips her hair. "You're that hockey player, right?"

My smile is tight. "Yes?"

The woman smiles brightly. "Ohmygod, I told my

friends it was you." She turns to a group of three women watching her intently and waves them over. They talk excitedly to each other as they stand from their table and saunter over. The blonde eyes Logan and Bash. "We are such big fans."

"Thanks," I say with a tight smile as I feel Mira stiffen beside me. I press my knee to hers, hoping she takes it as the reassurance I mean it to be. I want to ignore this woman and her friends, but everything we do has the potential to end up online, and each member of the team has had it hammered into our heads that we always treat our fans well. The last thing the team wants is bad press because one of us was an asshole to some random man or woman on the street with a huge social media following.

Normally, that doesn't bother me. But with my wife beside me—the wife no one knows is mine—and a gaggle of women with predatory expressions and way too much cleavage in front of me, I want nothing more than to tell them to fuck right off.

"You're Griffin, right?" a short brunette asks.

I nod.

"And you're Sebastian?" She looks at Bash, who pastes a fake-ass smile on his face and also nods.

Logan, never one to ignore pretty women who are obviously looking to hook up with a hockey player, perks up and sticks his hand out across the table with a salacious smile. "I'm Logan. What are your names, ladies?"

The women rattle off their names, but I'm not paying attention. Not to them. All my focus is on the woman beside me. The one who owns me, body and soul. The one bristling as the brunette rests a hand on my shoulder.

"We were at the game tonight. You played so well."

"Thanks," I grind out. Nothing about my tone says I want to continue this conversation, but the woman either doesn't notice or doesn't care.

"I have to say, though, my favorite part is the warm-ups." Her cheeks flush.

Before Mira, I probably would have found it attractive, but now? I'm annoyed because I have a feeling I know what's coming.

"It's so hot when you guys stretch out your hips." She giggles.

Jesus Christ.

If I thought Mira was stiff before, it's got nothing on the absolute rigidity of her body now. She's practically vibrating with annoyance. It shouldn't make me happy, but I can't help the pleasure I get from knowing she's feeling territorial. With my left hand beneath the table, I discreetly run my pinkie over her thigh. I need her to know that she's the only one I care about. The only one I want to touch.

A second blonde pops a hip out and offers up a sultry smile. Her gaze skips from me, to Sebastian, then to Logan. She's after a night with a Rogue, and I get the impression she doesn't care who takes her up on it. "You guys are so tall. You can't really tell just how *big* you are from the seats."

The woman's eyes flick down my body when she says the word *big*, and Mira snorts beside me. It has my lips twitching, which is unfortunate, because the woman seems to take it as a sign that I'm interested.

"And you're all so strong. You must have so much stamina to play professional hockey."

"Oh my god," Mira mutters under her breath. It's low

enough that only Navarro and I hear it. Bash chuckles, and I lightly pinch my wife's leg.

"We were wondering if any of you guys would like to join us? The next round is on us." The brunette flutters her false eyelashes at me, and not only do I not feel even the tiniest hint of attraction, but I'm actually disgusted. It's a struggle to keep my face from screwing up in a look of blatant distaste.

"Sure," Logan says, running his eyes over the woman's body. "We'd love to join you, wouldn't we, Wright?"

I look at Mira, eyes wide, silently asking her to pipe up and say she's tired and wants to go home, then ask me to take her. I want her to claim me. To tell these women to fuck off because I'm hers. But she doesn't. She frowns, obviously unhappy, but she doesn't say a thing.

Clearing my throat, I shake my head. "I don't think so."

"Come on, Wright, quit being such a stick in the mud. These gorgeous women want to buy us some drinks. Are you really going to deny them the pleasure of your company?"

I see Lexi roll her eyes, and Isla glances surreptitiously at Mira. Sebastian shakes his head.

"I'm good, man." I turn to the women. "Thanks for the invite, ladies, but I'm going to pass."

"Oh, come on," the blonde with curly hair says. She runs her finger up my arm to my shoulder, and I shift away from her toward Mira. "I promise we'll make it worth your while."

Isla chokes on her beer, and Madds pats her back. She mutters something about *brazen bunnies* to her fiancé and shakes her head. Isla has dealt with her fair share of bull-shit from female fans since she started dating Maddox, and so has Lexi. Unfortunately, it seems to come with the territory when you're dating a professional athlete. It's bullshit, plain and simple. Some people don't understand boundaries or simply don't respect them.

I clear my throat, increasingly uncomfortable, and shoot Mira another pleading look. This time when I catch her eye, she frowns before peering down at the table. I want to shake her. She's finally claimed me in private, called me her husband, and we've had mind-blowing, intimate sex every day since, but she's just sitting here silently, letting these women proposition me? I want her to get mad, to tell them to get lost. I want her to be *bothered*.

A sharp pang of hurt spears through me, and I suck in a sharp breath.

Even after the last week, she still isn't ready to admit who I am to her. Would she let me get up and walk away with one of these women without a single protest? Would she just let it happen? I thought we were making progress, but maybe I was wrong. Maybe she'll always be embarrassed of me.

"Mira?" I say her name so quietly, I know she and Bash are the only ones who catch it. My friend frowns when she remains silent, and my stomach drops.

I guess we haven't made as much progress as I thought, and it calls to mind all my previous girlfriends who were more than happy to give me their bodies but were never willing to give me their hearts.

The pain of that parallel is like a physical blow.

"You know what?" I press my palms on the table and move to stand. "I'm actually beat. I'm heading out."

The blonde's face lights up. "Oh, do you want some company?"

"Yeah," I say, my voice tight, "I do. But not from you."

And with that, I shoulder past our little fan club, ignoring the calls of my boys, ignoring Mira's sharp inhalation, and walk out into the cold Minneapolis night.

I'm sure that little interaction will end up all over social media, but I can't find it in me to give a single flying fuck.

twenty-nine

MIRA

HE DOESN'T COME HOME. AFTER THE SHIT SHOW AT the bar and those stupid fucking girls—*no*, stupid fucking me for sitting there and letting them hit on Griffin while he was clearly looking for me to step in—I sat at that damn booth for another fifteen minutes before I couldn't take it anymore. I made my excuses, ordered a rideshare, and ran home to talk to him. My heart felt like it was trying to beat its way out of my chest, and nausea made every pothole dangerous.

I hurt him. I hurt the man who's done nothing but be sweet and patient and supportive of me.

I'm such an asshole.

Now here I am, alone in our bed, five ignored calls, twenty unanswered texts, and a solitary night of tossing and turning later, and it feels like my stomach is eating itself. A quick glance at my phone tells me it's still early—

six a.m.—and still dark out. There's no way I'll fall back asleep. Not with how worried I am about Griffin. Is he safe somewhere? Is he with someone? Is he done with me?

"Fuck," I mutter, dragging my exhausted ass out of our bed. I quickly use the bathroom and brush my teeth, then walk out of our room through the door I never closed and into the main part of the apartment. Will he be home? What will I say to him?

When I see Griffin's broad shoulders and back in front of the kitchen island, the rush of relief that floods me almost knocks my knees out from under me. He's slumped on a stool, his blond hair greasy and sticking up, as if he spent hours running his hands through it. His shoulders curve inward, and his head hangs so his chin almost touches his chest.

He's here. He's safe. But he's so obviously not himself that my steps falter and I go still, just watching him.

"There's coffee in the pot." His voice is flat, and I hate it.

Clearing my throat to dislodge the lump choking me, I take a tentative step toward him. My hand lifts from my side like it has a mind of its own, and my fingers twitch as I reach for him. "Griffin..."

"I have practice this afternoon," he says, shifting to avoid my touch and rising from the stool. He shuffles to the sink, where he rinses out his mug before placing it into the dishwasher. "I'm going to shower and grab my gear, then I'm meeting Bash for breakfast. Do you need anything?"

Look at me, I silently command. *Look at me, Griffin.*

He doesn't.

"No." My voice cracks. "I don't need anything."

I need you to look at me. I need you to let me make this right. I need you to be patient with me.

"Kay. Text if you do."

Griffin walks toward our bedroom, and each step he takes away from me feels like the lash of a whip or the slice of a knife. I'm bleeding, but I deserve it.

"Will you... Will you be home tonight?"

His steps falter at the doorway. Does he hear how desperate I am for him to look at me? Does he hear all the words I should say but can't seem to force out? "Yeah. Yeah, I'll be home tonight."

And with that, he walks into the bathroom and shuts the door. The soft *click* of the lock reverberates through my very bones, and the first tear I've ever cried over Griffin Wright slips down my cheeks, followed closely by more than I can count.

I'M WAITING FOR GRIFFIN ON THE COUCH WHEN HE walks out of our bedroom with damp hair and his duffel bag slung over his shoulder. He doesn't look up at me, so I take a moment to study him.

There are dark circles under his hazel eyes, the line of his jaw is tight, and the muscle there tics. It brings to mind that night when Isla's friends were making jokes about his relationships, or lack thereof. I hated seeing him like that, but this is so much worse because I put this expression on his face. This time, it's my fault.

Rising from the couch, and with more than a little trep- idation, I step in front of Griffin before he can make it to the door. My heart is a whole flock of birds trying to fly right out of my chest. He has to stop short, our chests almost touching. Only then does he lift those eyes I've become so intimately familiar with, and when they connect with mine, I suck in a breath.

"I'm sorry," I whisper. "I'm so sorry."

Griffin swallows thickly. He cants his head to the side, searching my face with a solemnity so at odds with his normal jovial nature. "Sorry for what?"

So many things. I'm sorry I didn't react how you wanted last night. I'm sorry I didn't chase after you and wrap my arms around you. I'm sorry that I'm not sure about us the way you seem to be. That my stupid, scared heart keeps making me balk. I'm sorry that I'm not ready to tell Maddox and everyone else about us.

I'm just so fucking sorry.

"I... I'm sorry I didn't say anything to those girls last night. I wanted to, Griffin, I really did, but I froze because I was scared."

He continues to study me, and I can't stop myself from squirming under his scrutiny. "What were you scared of?"

Everything. The way I feel about you, the way you feel about me, how my brother will react...that if we say what's happening out loud, it will somehow ruin everything we're building here.

I clear my throat. "I didn't want to make a scene."

The excuse is weak, even to my ears, and I know Griffin feels the same when he shakes his head. "Some things are worth making a scene over."

"You're right," I say, my hands gripping his face when he moves to turn away from me. "Please be patient with me. All of this is terrifying, Griffin. We both have so much to lose."

It's the wrong thing to say, but I don't realize it until his eyes close and his shoulders slump. "Yeah, sunshine, we do. But I don't think we mean the same thing when we say that."

Sweat slicks my palms as my heart begins to race. "We do, babe. We do. I don't want to lose you. You're my best friend. Living with you has been the best thing that's ever happened to me, and maybe I didn't plan to marry you, but I wouldn't change it. Well, maybe I'd change a little of it, because waking up married is a lot more complicated than being proposed to, planning a wedding, and saying *I do* in front of family and friends, rather than sidelining them with the news. But being with you makes me happy. So happy."

The words tumble out of me, panicked and wavering, but I need to fix this. I need him to know that I'm falling for him a little more each day. So maybe I'm not ready to say those three little words or tell my brother and mom that we're married, but I'm getting there. Six months ago, when I imagined my future, Griffin wasn't in it.

Now, he's at the heart of every single dream.

"I'm sorry I'm not on the same page as you yet. I wish I was. Trust me, I do. But I'll get there, Griffin. I care about you so much, and I can't imagine my life without you."

Hearing my panic and seeing my wide-eyed expression, Griffin sighs and rests his forehead against mine. "I can't imagine my life without you either, sunshine."

"I just need time," I beg. "Please, babe. I just need time."

"I guess I did give you six months and we're not there

yet," he says, his voice low and gravelly. "It's not really fair of me to change the terms."

Latching on to his thought process, I loop my arms around his neck and pull him closer. "Right. Six months. This is all so fast, and I'm not... I'm not as brave as you are."

"You're braver than you give yourself credit for."

"I don't know about that, but thank you." Lifting my chin, I press a soft, tentative kiss to the corner of Griffin's lips. "I wish I had been brave enough to go after you last night."

Griffin's lashes flutter as I press a kiss to the other corner of his lips.

"Where..." My stomach churns, afraid of the answer to a question I have to ask. "Where were you last night?"

Strong arms wrap around my midsection, and Griffin pulls me close. "I stayed at Bash's, baby. I drove around for half an hour, then went to his place when he called to check on me."

My relief is tempered by the guilt over worrying, even for a moment, that Griffin might have sought comfort in another woman's arms. "Does he know about us?"

"No. Well, sort of. He doesn't know we're married, but he's perceptive. He sees how I am with you."

"Oh. I'm glad you have him."

The corners of Griffin's lips twitch infinitesimally. "He's a good friend."

"I'm sorry, Griffin. I'm really sorry." A tear slips down my cheek, and he's right there to catch it and wipe it away.

"Hey. None of that now." Slowly, he leans in, lips parted. He gives me time to pull away if I want, but I would never. If he doesn't kiss me, I may scream.

In the end, I'm the one to close the last few centimeters of distance between us, pressing my lips to Griffin's with a need that makes my body buzz. I don't want him to pull away from me.

He groans when my tongue swipes along the inside of his lips, his grip on me growing tighter. My breasts press against his chest, and the heat of him finally chases away the cold my fears had wrapped me in. We're still kissing several minutes later when his phone buzzes in his pocket.

"Fuck, Mir," he says with a sigh as he pulls away from me. His dark blond lashes fan over his high cheekbones before they open on me. "I gotta go. I'll be back for dinner, okay?"

"Do you have to go?"

One large hand cups my cheek, and I lean into it. "Yeah, baby, I do. I need…" He blows out a breath. "I need a little time today, okay?"

Whatever expression I'm making has his eyes softening and his voice gentles. "We're okay, sunshine, I promise. I just need to get my head on straight, and since I can't exactly talk to your brother about this, Bash is the best option. He won't pry, but he'll listen."

"I get that," I say, wishing I hadn't ditched my closest friends because of Jared. I wish I could talk all of this out with Isla, but I would never ask her to keep such a huge secret from my brother. Even if I think she suspects something is going on between us. Maybe I could talk to Lexi?

Griffin presses another kiss to my lips, then my forehead. "I gotta go, baby. Bash is waiting. Call if you need me, okay? I'll drop everything for you."

"I know," I say. And I do. Griffin Wright would absolutely drop everything for me if I asked him to. But what kind of wife would I be if I took advantage of that fact? Especially when he so clearly needs some time. "I'll be okay."

Lifting onto my toes, I slant my mouth over my husband's. "Don't give up on me. Please."

"Never," he whispers against my lips.

I only hope that's a promise he can keep.

thirty

GRIFFIN

"You good, brother?" Bash looks me over as I slip into the booth situated in the back of the little diner that makes the best protein pancakes I've ever had.

The concern in his eyes warms the cockles of my heart and shit. I'm lucky, I know I am. How many guys have such a solid group of friends that would have their back in any situation, even brawls on the ice involving massive dudes and sharp blades? Not many, that's for sure. It's probably why there are so many butthurt assholes out there. Either get some friends that you can talk about your feelings with or go to counseling.

Actually, I should probably do some counseling. Maybe it's time I get a professional to help me work through this curse crap. But something I do have in abundance are friends that will let me bare my soul and will never judge me for how I'm feeling.

"I'm good," I tell Bash. It's mostly the truth. I feel better after talking with Mira this morning, even if things didn't get resolved the way I wish they had. I know it's going to take her longer to warm up to all of this, and, yes, I know I asked her for six months, but I wasn't anticipating how much the secrecy would grate on me.

Bash isn't fooled. I'm not surprised. He's a goalie, after all, and those guys don't miss a thing. They can't. "Are you ready to tell me what's really going on with you two?"

Damn, I wish I could. I'd love nothing more than to get this off my chest. "I can't, yet. I want to, man, but I can't betray her trust."

My friend nods. "Fair enough. Did you get a chance to talk to her this morning?"

"A little. I just…"

"Was hurt when she acted like she didn't care that those women were coming onto you?" His words sting, but the expression on Bash's face is soft and brotherly. Of course, he saw all of that.

No sense denying it.

"Yeah. Yeah, I was hurt. She's got her reasons for keeping us a secret, but I can't help it—I still hate it."

Bash opens his mouth but holds his tongue when our server stops by to take our orders. After he sets two coffees on the table and promises to return quickly with our breakfast, Sebastian turns back to me. "You hate it because you've been burned before by women who weren't all in when you were."

Damn. Not pulling his punches, is he?

"Mira's not like that," I say, defensive, even as an uncomfortable seed of doubt sprouts in my chest.

Hands held in front of him, Bash nods. "I'm not saying she is, just that I get why it was triggering for you."

Huh. I suppose triggering is an accurate way to look at it. "Yeah, I guess. I just need to be patient with her and show her I'm all in and I'm not going anywhere. Be the man she needs, you know?"

"I think that's great, as long as she's also the woman you need." My friend studies me, watching as my face crumples into a frown.

"Of course she's the woman I need." She's perfect. I've fallen for women before, but none of them have also been my best friend. What I have with Mira is everything.

"I'm not suggesting she isn't, but I am saying that love needs to go both ways. It should never be all on one person to bend for the other. She has to be willing to bend for you, too, Griffin. I've seen the way she looks at you. Mira cares about you, and I think she cares a lot. But at some point, if she's not willing to show you she's all in, you'll have to make some hard decisions."

I don't realize I'm rubbing my chest until the server places our plates in front of us and I have to stop to pick up my fork. "I don't want to lose her."

My friend's brown eyes soften at the corners. "I know, man, and I hope things work out between the two of you. I really do. All I'm saying is that you deserve to be loved just as much as she does, and if this becomes more painful than life-giving, I hope you choose yourself."

I don't want to choose myself. I want someone else to choose me, for once, dammit.

Still, there's wisdom in what he's saying, so I nod. "I will. And if I don't, you can call me on it."

With a mouth full of eggs, Bash nods his promise, and I can only hope he never has to make good on it.

I THROW MYSELF INTO PRACTICE WITH A vengeance. Not only do I want to make it to the cup this year, but the burn of my muscles helps take my mind off Mira. If I push myself hard enough, I won't have the energy to overthink things.

"Good, Wright," Coach Fry calls out as I snap the puck past Navarro's mitt.

Feet crossing over one another, I swing around the back of the net and speed toward the stack of pucks at the blue line.

"You're focused today," Maddox observes as we wait our turn to charge the net again.

I grunt an acknowledgement. His eyes burn a hole in the side of my head, but I don't look his way. Part of me is worried that if I do, he'll see right through my bullshit and realize I'm fucking his sister. That's not a revelation I want to have happen on the ice while he's wearing blades on his feet.

I don't have a death wish.

"Isla wanted me to ask if you could come over for dinner when we get back from our next away series. She's been doing some wedding planning and wants to have the best man and maid of honor over to discuss stuff." He puts an emphasis on the word *stuff* that tells me he's not as excited as his fiancée is about the planning.

Me? I always thought it would be fun to plan a wedding. And someday, if Mira agrees, I want to have a big one. I want to see her in a fluffy white dress, pick out fun suits, and celebrate our love with a huge-ass party filled with everyone we love. Maddox is lucky as shit.

"Yeah, man, of course. You know I'm excited for you, and I'll help however you need me to."

He places a gloved hand on my shoulder and gives me the carefree grin he's been sporting more and more often since meeting Isla. "I know you will. You're a good friend, Wright, and a good man. Isla and I wouldn't be where we are without you."

"You'd have found your way back to each other, eventually," I say with a shrug.

He shakes his head. "I'm not so sure about that."

It's our turn to run the puck down the ice again, and this time, Bash manages to block both shots.

"Oh, I meant to ask you, did everything get settled with Mira's car?"

Well, shit. I should have seen this question coming. Should have been prepared with an answer, but I'm not. "Uh, yeah."

Madds eyes me with a raised eyebrow. "And? What was the damage? Do I need to call the shop and pay it for her?"

"No..." I clear my throat. "Uh, her car wasn't safe to repair. The owner advised she junk it."

My best friend's eyes widen. "Shit. I knew that thing wasn't in great shape, but I didn't realize it was a death trap. I'll talk her into letting me buy her a car. Hell, I've been trying to talk her into letting me help her since I got my signing bonus, but she's so stubborn. Determined to make her own way. And I know her business is doing well so far, but I doubt she has enough saved to buy a car."

"Actually, I already helped her out."

Maddox stills, turning his whole body to face me. "What do you mean, you already helped her out?"

"Uh, I did some promotional work for a Toyota dealership a couple of years ago, so when I contacted them, I got a really good deal on a new Camry." I shrug like it's not a big deal. It is a big deal, and I know that, but I don't want Maddox to look too closely at this, because I'm worried he'll see right through me.

"Can she afford the monthly payments?" He's in big brother mode, and I'm trying not to shit myself.

So I tell a half truth. "Yep."

She can afford the monthly payments because they're zero dollars. But he doesn't need to know that.

Madds stares at me for another few seconds before he grins and claps me on the shoulder. "Thanks, Wright. I appreciate you helping her out when she won't let me. I don't know how you got her to agree, but I'm glad you did."

"Of course, bro. I've got her back."

"I know you do. I wouldn't trust anyone else around my sister."

Well, shit.

"Yeah. Totally."

thirty-one

GRIFFIN

THE NEXT FEW WEEKS FLY BY IN A BLUR OF practice, games, and quiet moments with Mira. Things with her are mostly back to the way they were prior to that night at the bar, but I wish I felt that euphoria I had when Mir called me her husband for the first time.

Even though it's what she calls me when we're alone, now, and I love it, I can't help feeling like I'm still waiting for the other shoe to drop. Maybe it's self-sabotaging, but whenever we have really great moments, my mind keeps wondering if it's the last time.

We have epic sex that ends with us wrapped tightly around each other, Mira's face flushed and glowing with sweat, and I wonder if this is the last time I'll get to make love to her. She laughs, so free and beautiful, and I wonder if one day she'll look at me with the same cold disdain so many of my exes wore in the end. It's not healthy, and I know it, but my confidence is shaken, and I can't help comparing this marriage with all my failed relationships.

Mira has picked up on the shift in my moods, and she's been trying so hard to reassure me. Whenever we're alone, she's touching me, kissing me, telling me all the things she loves about me. Still, she doesn't come right out and say that she loves *me*, and I can't shake my fears enough to tell her I love her.

And I do, I've realized. I fucking love the woman with every terrified fiber of my being.

"Hey, babe?" Mira's voice pulls me out of my thoughts as I stare at my clothes, contemplating what to pack for our next away series. We leave in two days, and I've been dreading it and looking forward to it in almost equal measure. I don't want to be away from my wife, but I'm also looking forward to four days of quality time with my boys. We're playing New York in their barn, and I'm excited to explore the city. We've got a list of places we want to go, with each of us contributing our New York bucket list ideas.

Looking over my shoulder at my wife, I drink her in and smile. She looks beautiful. Her hair is curled and loose around her shoulders, the deep purple sweater she's wearing makes her green eyes appear even more vibrant than normal, and her jeans hug her ass perfectly. "Hey, sunshine. What's up?"

"I was just thinking that we haven't really gone out anywhere this week. Want to walk around the North Loop? I've been wanting to visit that cute little bookshop down there, and then I thought we could get some lunch?" She pulls her bottom lip between her teeth, looking almost shy.

Maybe I'm not the only one feeling insecure.

Turning, I close the distance between us and pull my wife into my arms, enjoying the way she sighs and presses into my chest like there's nowhere else she'd rather be. "That romance bookstore? What's it called again?"

"It's a Love Story," she says, her words muffled against my chest.

Right. "I've heard that place is awesome, and I could use something to read on the plane. Let's do it."

The smile Mira gifts me with when she looks up at me is blinding. "Really?"

"Hell, yeah, babe. You know I love a good romance."

"I do. Maybe we..." Mira chews on her bottom lip again, and I tug it free with my thumb.

"Maybe we what?"

"Maybe we could read the same book while you're in New York?"

I love that idea. Especially since I think I can make it even better. "That sounds fun. Can I pick the book? I got a few recommendations from one of the Facebook groups I'm in that I think would be perfect. We can read our favorite passages to each other."

I'm going to read her straight smut. The books I have in mind are apparently absolutely filthy in the best way. My smile grows as I imagine how pink Mira's cheeks will get when I read sex scenes to her. Hopefully, I can convince her to act some of them out with me. Swear to god, some of these authors have the dirtiest fucking minds. And maybe I'll pick one where the dude does that growly thing women seem to go wild for. I'll have to practice my growling if I do that, though. There's a right way and a wrong way to do the romance growl. I want to make Mira wet, not keel over with laughter.

"You'd really do that?" she asks.

Why is she surprised? She's seen my bookshelves. They're like twenty percent hockey related, ten percent biographies, a few sci-fi books, then the rest are romance.

"I'd do anything for you, sunshine. You should know that by now." Leaning down, I take her mouth in a kiss that's anything but chaste. My tongue sweeps across hers, earning a moan that has me hard as a fucking rock. I'm tempted to strip her naked right here in our closet, but she got dressed all cute and did her makeup, so as much as I'd love to ruin it in the best way, I force myself to pull away.

Our physical chemistry has never been an issue. But Mira is right—we don't spend enough time with each other out and about—and I don't want our relationship to suffer for it.

"Let me change out of these sweats and we can go, okay?"

Breathing hard, Mira looks up at me with flushed cheeks and blown pupils, nodding. "Okay. But Griffin?"

"Yeah, babe?"

"Maybe wear your normal stuff instead of the polos and khakis you've been wearing lately?"

I bark out a laugh. "You don't like the polos?" Here I thought I was dressing like the kind of guy Mira was looking for. Someone serious and staid.

"They're fine, if that's what you really want to wear, but they don't feel like *you,* you know?" She rests her palm on my chest and blinks up at me with those pretty green eyes. "I just want you to be you. So, if that's polos and khakis, cool. But if not, wear what you're comfortable in, okay?"

Damn. My chest warms. It's stupid, because it's such a small thing, but I guess I needed the reassurance that my girl doesn't want me to be someone I'm not. Grinning like an idiot, I nod. "Got it. Give me a minute and I'll be ready to go."

AN HOUR LATER, I'M WALKING DOWN THE SIDEWALK in jeans and a hoodie, a baseball cap pulled low to hide my face from as many curious fans as possible, my wife's hand in mine. It's probably a risk to be openly affectionate in public like this, but Mira hasn't tried to pull away, and I'm at the point where I don't care if Madds beats the shit out of me if someone publishes a photo of me and his sister. I just need to hold her hand, kiss her, claim her.

Mira sips her coffee, laughing at a stupid story about the trouble her brother and I got into our first couple of years on the Rogues. It feels good. Right. Like this is what I want to do for the next fifty years and beyond. We don't have to do anything exciting or earth-shattering. As long as I've got my wife at my side, we could spend the rest of our days in the Twin Cities, walking hand in hand, eating at the same three restaurants, sitting in the same coffee shop, and I'd be happy as a goddamn clam.

"I didn't know my brother was such a troublemaker," Mira says between giggles.

"He wasn't, not really. I just dragged him along with me."

"You're a bad influence." She looks up at me, eyes shining and smile bright.

I chuckle. "Yeah, probably."

"But he needs that, sometimes. He's always been so serious and responsible. I think he felt like he had to be after our dad left."

Glancing down at the beautiful woman who lights up my life, I'm struck by a deep sense of anger and disbelief that her deadbeat dad could have walked away from her and never looked back. Madds and I don't talk about it much, but there were a few times in college when he got drunk and told me the whole story. It was one of the things that motivated him to be the best. If he was the best, he'd be able to make sure his mom and sister were always taken care of.

"You're probably right. Even in college, it was hard to get him to let go. I dragged him to parties and events as often as I could, but he was adamant that he couldn't do anything that would jeopardize his scholarship."

Mira nods. "It was also so he could lecture me."

I bark out a laugh at that. "What?"

She grins, her eyes crinkling at the corners. "Yeah. One weekend during my junior year of high school, I got drunk enough at a party that my best friend had to call my mom to come pick me up. She was not happy. Especially since it was at one of the football player's houses, and he had a bit of a reputation. Plus, I kinda puked in her car."

"Oh shit," I say, laughing. "Your mom is sweet as hell, but I know she can be scary." You can't be a single mom and not develop some fire.

"Yeah. She didn't yell at me that night, but the next day, she let me have it, made me clean out the car, grounded me for a month, and told Maddox what I'd done." She says it all with this wistful tone that speaks to how close the three of them are. "Maddy lectured me for an hour and told me that if he could keep from going out and getting drunk in college, surrounded by parties every weekend and teammates who were always going out to bars, that I had no excuse. Then he lectured me for another hour about never taking a drink from anyone, never setting a cup down, and about how it was normal at my age to be curious about sex and how to be safe about it."

I can picture that awkward conversation in perfect clarity, and I'm laughing my ass off as we get closer to the bookstore. "Oh man, he didn't."

She nods. "He did. It was mortifying. And maybe it makes no sense, but I was almost more scared to disappoint Maddy than I was to disappoint my mom. We've always been so close, and he's always been my protector."

Her words don't diminish the tightness that's wrapped itself around my chest like a boa constrictor ever since that night at the bar, but it puts things in perspective for me. For as long as Mira can remember, she's looked up to her big brother. He's been her friend and protector, and even though they're not far apart in age, in lots of ways, he was the father figure she never had. I've always known this to a degree, but I guess I didn't realize how deep it runs for her. But with that perspective comes the unwelcome worry I've been fighting off since the morning we woke up in bed together in Vegas.

Does she think Maddox will be disappointed in her for marrying me?

"It's also one of the reasons I decided to go to school in

Chicago," she continues. "Because I love my brother to pieces, but do you know how much it sucks to be a teenager living in the shadow of your perfect brother? Not only was he this hockey phenomenon, but he was serious and studious and never did anything irresponsible." She rolls her eyes, even though there's no real annoyance behind it.

"I don't have any siblings, so I don't totally get it, but I do have an older cousin who is literally a rocket scientist. It doesn't matter that I'm one of the best wingers in the league. When we have family reunions, she's still the scientist, and I'm the guy who plays with sticks for a living." My cousin Erica is cool as hell, but I get how it may suck to feel you're constantly living in the shadow of a family member.

Her little giggle is bright, and I need her closer. Dropping her hand, I wrap my arm around her shoulder, and when she reaches up and links her fingers with mine, my heart feels like it's a ball of light. "You do more than play with sticks for a living, babe. But yeah. I guess sometimes it seems like he has all these expectations for me, and I've worked so hard to make something of myself, but he's this famous hockey player, and I just make websites."

"You're incredibly talented. It's more than just making websites, and you know it. You take photos and information and create something that pulls people in and lets them feel like they're a part of something. Don't sell yourself short." As we pause in front of the bookstore, I make sure my wife meets my gaze so she can see how serious I am.

"Your brother is proud as hell of you, sunshine. I get

that you feel like you have something to prove, but he just wants you to be happy."

Mira hums, and I can tell she's not convinced.

"He'd probably be your biggest fan if it wasn't for me."

"Oh yeah?"

"Yeah, babe. I wish you could believe in yourself the way I believe in you. But that's okay, you'll get there. I'll make sure of it." And I will. As we stand there on the sidewalk, people flowing around us like living water, resolve fills me. "You're fucking amazing, Mir. So talented and driven. And you aren't in your brother's shadow, because you're pure light and sunshine."

Mira's cheeks are pink, and not just from the chilly late-February wind stinging her face. Her voice is a quiet caress as she stares up at me. "You have to say that because you're my husband."

Leaning down so our noses touch, I hold her gaze. "I have to say that because I'm not a liar and it's the truth. Now, Mrs. Wright, let's go into this bookstore and pick out some smutty books to keep you all hot and bothered while I'm away in New York. I want you primed and ready for me when I get home."

"Still not changing my last name," she says, chuckling as I open the door to It's a Love Story and lead her in.

We stop in front of a wall full of sports romance books and I shrug. "Still willing to change mine."

"You're ridiculous." She rests her head on my chest, her eyes scanning the colorful spines in front of us.

She still thinks I'm kidding. "Just wait, wifey. Now, how many books do you think you can carry back to the car?"

Her eyes widen, sparkling like emeralds. She sucks in a breath. "Are you serious?"

"As a heart attack. I'll buy you as many books as you can hold." I drop her hand and give her ass a little smack. "Now get to shopping, sunshine. I'm going to find us two copies of that book I was talking about."

My wife squeals and does a happy little wiggle, and before I'm even three feet away, she has four books in her arms and holds a fifth, reading the blurb on the back. Every trace of her previous insecurity has been wiped off her face and replaced with the kind of joy I'm determined to inspire again and again.

I'll spend my entire salary on books if it makes her happy.

thirty-two

MIRA

"Hell yeah, Handsome!" Lexi shouts at her boyfriend through the TV.

I giggle, because you'd never know just by looking at the blonde-haired, blue-eyed woman that she's absolutely bloodthirsty when she cheers for her boyfriend on the ice. Ryder is a defenseman, so he spends a lot of time checking the opposing team's players into the boards when they get too close to Sebastian and the Rogues' goal. I'm pretty sure it turns Lexi on when he does.

"I wish we could have traveled with them," Isla says wistfully from her spot next to me on the couch. "I hate being away from Maddox."

"You and my brother are disgustingly cute." I gently nudge her shoulder, smirking. "Pretty sure I just vomited in my mouth a little."

My soon-to-be sister-in-law smacks my arm. "Oh shut it, missy."

Lexi laughs, agreeing with her. "One day you're going to find a man that you can't live without, and then you'll understand. And god forbid he plays hockey, because watching your man get slammed into the boards by some asshole with blades on his feet is so freaking scary sometimes."

As if to illustrate her point, one of the New York Warriors checks Griffin into the glass. Hard. I can't stifle my little gasp, and Lexi nods.

"See? It's bad even watching your roommate get checked. Imagine if he was your boyfriend."

I don't have to imagine. I know intimately. But Griffin isn't just my boyfriend; he's my husband. Not that I can say that to Lexi. So all I can do is offer her a little grimace. "Yeah. I can imagine."

Isla watches me, her blue eyes slightly narrowed. I doubt she has any idea that Griffin and I are *married*, but I'm worried she's putting the pieces together. To be honest, I thought Lexi would be the one figuring this out after I showed up in a car with Griffin's number on it, but she's a little wrapped up in her own relationship. It's been a whirlwind since her dad was fired and her relationship with Ryder became something of a viral sensation.

Would it be so bad if Isla figured it out? Keeping this secret is wearing on me, and I could really use someone to talk it all out with. But if she knows, it's only a matter of time before my brother will, too, and then it'll make its way to my mom. And that is something I'm not ready for. Not yet.

"Go, go, go!" Isla shouts at the big screen as Maddox breaks away from the pack and flies down the ice. He passes to Logan, who passes to Griffin, and all my worries about her perceptiveness disappear.

Griffin slides the puck back to Maddox before two New York players surround my brother. They block his access to the net and give New York's defensemen time to form a human wall. Cool as a cucumber, Madds scans the ice, noting that Logan is busy trying to create an opening before finding Griffin. My husband skates around the back of the net, cutting between the defensemen and shoving one toward the boards. It's the opening Madds needs, and he taps the puck toward Griffin, who tips the puck up onto his stick before slapping it over the goalie's shoulder and into the top left corner of the net.

The horns blare, the commentators go wild, and the camera focuses on the face I've woken up to almost every morning since that night in Las Vegas. Leaping up off the couch, I shout, "Hell yeah, ba—" Then I clamp my lips shut, realizing what I was about to say.

Lexi doesn't notice, but Isla does. She lifts one eyebrow and cocks her head to the side in a silent question. I give her the most clueless expression I can muster in response as I sink back onto the couch, but it feels like my cheeks are on fire, so I doubt I'm fooling her.

Shit. I have to be more careful. With every week I'm married to Griffin Wright, this all feels more and more normal. More right. But I can't forget that our marriage was a drunken decision, that Griffin is my brother's best friend, and that staying married to him is the furthest thing from proving myself and emerging from Maddox's shadow.

The problem is, I'm not so sure I care anymore.

I'M IN BED WEARING NOTHING BUT A LACE camisole and matching thong when Griffin calls. These post-game video calls have become our routine when he's on the road. And they always lead to ridiculously hot video sex.

But tonight, we're talking about the book we've been reading. Griffin texted me this morning to tell me he has several scenes picked out to read to me. I can't wait, because the book is hot. It's enemies to lovers, and the buildup to the characters falling for each other is so good. And the sex scenes?

Let's just say, I've had to take some breaks after the spicy chapters to—ahem—let off some steam.

"Fuck, baby. Look at you." Griffin's hazel eyes drink me in when I answer the call. I can't see all of him, but I see enough to know he's shirtless. Griffin shirtless is a work of art. I wish he was here so I could run my hands all over him.

Letting the camera dip lower so he can see all of me, I grin when he mutters another low, "Fuck."

"Good game tonight," I say, my voice husky as I pan the phone back up. "That goal was a thing of beauty."

"It has nothing on you, sunshine. Nothing does."

Now my heart *and* my lady parts are squeezing.

"Man, I wish you were here."

I sigh, snuggling into the pillow. "Me too. Are you having fun, though? You have some free time to explore tomorrow, right?"

"Yeah. We have some things planned. But I don't want to talk about New York or the guys or our plans. I want to talk about you and the chapters we were supposed to read. Then I want you to take off that sexy little scrap of lace, spread your legs for me, and let me watch you fuck yourself while I pretend my hand is your warm, wet pussy."

As a moan drips from my lips, Griffin smirks.

"You're such a good little slut for me, wife, and damn, I love it."

"Your mouth," I rasp, shaking my head.

"I'm going to use this mouth to eat your pussy when I get home, but for now, I'll have to settle for reading you some spicy scenes in this book. Then I'll use it to tell you how to fuck yourself."

My thighs squeeze together, my body flushing with heat. What is he doing to me? I've never been as needy as I have been since we got married. I've never been a prude, but I've also never been a wanton sex goddess. But that's how he makes me feel. Free and sexy and *hungry*.

"Now, have you gotten to chapter fifteen yet, baby?" Griffin's dark blond brows waggle, and I giggle.

"Yes."

"Good. Then lie back and let me read it to you."

And he does. The chapter is spicy, the author leaving nothing out. I get more and more wound up as Griffin reads about cocks thrusting into pussies, heaving breasts, and fingertips digging into full hips. My body grows warmer, between my thighs slicker, and when Griffin reads the part where the hero growls *mine* while fucking the heroine, I can't help it, I let my fingers roam down to where I'm aching and slip them beneath the waistband of my thong.

"Is my wife wet and needy?" Griffin rumbles. He sets

the book down and leans forward so his face fills the screen. "Is your pussy begging to be filled?"

I suck in a breath, my back arching at his words. "Yes."

"Open my bedside table drawer," Griffin says. His voice is gruff and filled with dark promise. I arch one eyebrow at him but set the phone on my bedside table before leaning over to do as he says. He groans when my movements expose my ass to him.

Smirking, I pull his drawer open. Inside is a long box wrapped in butcher paper and a golden ribbon bow. "What is this?"

"Open it."

Glancing between my husband and the box in my hands, I make quick work of unwrapping the package. He's grinning when I look up at him. "A thrusting dildo?"

"The best one money could buy," he confirms smugly. "It's already washed and charged, so get your beautiful ass naked, coat it with lube, and let me watch as you stuff your pussy full and fuck yourself."

Goddamn. He doesn't have to tell me twice. I do as he says, stripping for him, before positioning myself so he has a front-row seat for the show. He moans when I spread my legs, putting his phone down so I can see him fisting his cock. Pre-cum glistens as it beads at the tip, and I wish he was here so I could wrap my lips around him.

"Show me what that thing can do, baby girl," Griffin says, his eyes on the toy in my hand.

I suck in a breath as I turn it on. The head of the silicone toy thrusts forward before withdrawing and thrusting again. Testing out the settings, I click the power button again, and the mechanical dick moves faster. Another click has the whole thing vibrating as it moves.

"Damn. This is going to be so hot," my husband murmurs as he strokes his dick. "Now, lube that dick up and fuck yourself hard, Mira. I want you to fill yourself with one hard thrust like I would if I were with you."

His eyes glitter with lust as I generously lube the toy and position it at my entrance.

"That's right, sweetheart, just like that. Now stretch that tight little hole and turn on your toy. I want to hear you scream my name."

With my gaze on his through the phone, I obey, pushing the toy into my pussy with one slow movement. The silky lube helps it glide inside, but the toy is thick, and I throw my head back and curse as I fill myself. It feels so good already, but not nearly as good as Griffin's cock.

"Turn it on."

As soon as I press the button, the toy begins to thrust inside of me. I gasp when I push it deeper, my pussy clenching around it as it drags along my inner walls. "Oh, god, Griffin."

"Look at you," he says. His voice is low and hungry, and when I watch him through the phone, his arm moves faster, the muscles flexing as he fists his dick. "You're so pretty. So perfect. The way you take that toy like such a greedy girl." His words trail off in a moan as he continues to stroke himself. The sound fills my lower belly with fire.

"Griffin..."

"I know, baby. You wish it was my cock stuffing your tight little pussy, don't you? You wish my fingers were digging into your hips while I fuck you hard and fast."

"Yes," I gasp as the toy drags along my inner walls again and again.

"If I were there, it would be my dick you were cream-ing, not some fake cock. You'd be begging me to let you come, but I'd make you taste yourself first. I'd pull out, tell you to open your pretty mouth, then fill it with my cock and make you lick off every drop of your cream."

"Oh, fuck." I moan, and Griffin chuckles darkly.

"You know what, baby girl? Take that toy out of your pussy. Right now."

My eyes widen at his command, and I hesitate.

"Now, Mira. Be my good little girl and suck every drop of your arousal off that toy. And don't you dare turn it off. I want to hear you gag when it fucks your throat."

Oh my god. I hesitate for another few seconds before doing as he asked. His eyes grow even more hooded as I pull the toy free and let him see my thick arousal coating the length of it. This is so dirty. Wrong. But damn it all, I'm desperate to please him, so I open my mouth wide and take it into my mouth. The smoky flavor of my slick mixes with the light fruity taste of the lube as I close my lips around it.

"That's it, sunshine. Suck your cum off the toy. Every inch of it. Take it all the way, baby."

I gag as the toy thrusts once I have the full length of it in my mouth, and Griffin moans again in response. Bobbing my head, I make a show of it for my husband, gagging again when it hits the back of my throat. Griffin is fucking his hand faster now, and I'm aching. My clit throbs, begging for attention.

"Such a good girl. So perfect. Now, put the toy down, spread those creamy thighs, and play with your clit. I'm gonna come, and I want to watch your pussy pulse as I do."

The first touch of my fingers on my swollen clit has me

crying out. I circle the throbbing bundle of nerves, speeding up to match the rhythm of Griffin stroking himself. It's so damn hot. I won't last long.

"Look at you." Griffin grunts, his abs twitching. His voice is strained, and I know he's close. "You're so wet. Your pussy is glistening, begging me to fill it."

"Yes," I say, gasping as pressure builds low in my stomach. Fingers circle my clit faster and faster to the sound of Griffin's pants and groans and the slick sound of his hand sliding up and down his lubed cock.

"I'm going to fuck you so hard when I get home, baby. Gonna tie you to our bed and have my way with you over and over and over until you beg me to stop."

That pressure in me hits a tipping point, and I gasp as the first tingles start to build. I cry out. "I'm gonna come."

"Yes, baby," Griffin growls. "Let go. Let me see you come. I want you crying out my name as your pussy pulses. And don't you dare close those thighs."

I force my legs wider and rub furiously at my clit to the sounds of Griffin fucking his hand, then my eyes roll back in my head, pleasure detonates inside me, and I'm screaming my husband's name as I writhe and whimper in front of the phone, so he has a front-row seat.

"Oh, fuck," he groans. "Fuck, baby, I wish I was coming inside that tight pussy." And then his abs contract, his jaw clenches, and hot ropes of cum paint his hand and stomach. Little aftershocks of pleasure roll through me as I continue to circle my clit until Griffin's body stops spasming and his hazel eyes meet mine. He appears as dazed and satisfied as I feel. And just as disappointed that we're states away from each other.

"You're everything," he says, still languidly stroking his softening cock. "Everything."

I don't have to wonder if he actually means it. I know he does. And I'm realizing that I feel the same way about him.

If I'm honest with myself, I've felt that way for a while.

Griffin yawns. "Let's get cleaned up and ready for bed. I want to fall asleep with you next to me."

And we do. I lie in bed, still on the video call, the rhythmic sound of Griffin's breathing lulling me to sleep.

thirty-three

MIRA

My stomach is about to eat itself.

"You need to calm down, sunshine." Griffin reaches over and gives my hand a squeeze as he pulls into a guest spot at Maddox and Isla's building. "Everything will be fine."

I'm not sure that's true. So far, all our interactions with my brother and his fiancée have been in group settings with plenty of distractions to keep him from looking too closely at the evolving dynamic between me and his best friend. But tonight? Tonight, we're having dinner. Just the four of us. To say I'm nervous is an understatement.

I'm so scared, I may throw up. What if we do something or say something that outs our secret? What if Maddox beats the shit out of Griffin, gets arrested, kicked off the team, then disowns me? Coming here tonight was a mistake.

"Mira." Griffin's voice is low and reassuring, and as

soon as he parks the G-Wagon, he turns and takes my face in his hands. "Baby, take a deep breath." He sucks in a deep lungful of air, and I mirror him. "Good. Again."

"I'm fine," I tell him after exhaling deeply. "Sorry. I'm just worried."

Griffin searches my face, a little divot forming between his eyebrows. "You're worried your brother will find out about us."

It's not a question. He knows that's what has me panicking. "Yes."

"Would it really be so bad?" His frown deepens and my stomach lurches at the undertones of hurt coloring the question. "What if we use tonight as an opportunity to tell them we're married? There won't be anyone else around. We're not out in public, and we're coming off a win, so your brother will be in a good mood. Plus, I'm sure he spent all last night getting laid by Teach, so really, I'm not sure there could be a more perfect chance."

Despite my anxiety, that makes me chuckle. It's tempting. I hate keeping secrets, and this is a big one. The biggest. But I'm not as optimistic as Griffin about my brother's reaction. The last thing I want to do is screw things up between them, let alone do anything to hurt the team's unity and chance to take the season to the Cup. Not when they're doing so well.

"I think we should wait." When Griffin's expression crumples, I hurry to add, "I don't want to take away from Madds and Isla's engagement, you know? And I don't want to mess things up for you and my brother."

Griffin's hazel eyes bounce between mine as he studies me. Whatever he sees makes him sigh deeply. "Mira, I've been friends with your brother for a long time. We've been through lots of shit together. I love him like a brother, and I know he feels the same way about me. If he can't see that we're perfect for each other and learn to be happy for us, that would suck, but ultimately it's a risk I'm willing to take."

He is? My traitorous heart skips a beat before it races. While I don't want Griffin risking anything for me, I also can't deny that primal longing to have someone fight for me, to claim me against all odds and say *fuck it* despite all the things they stand to lose. What person doesn't want that? I think you'd be hard pressed to find a red-blooded woman alive who doesn't dream of being the most important thing in her partner's life. I'm no different.

But I'm also a coward.

"I don't want you to risk your friendship or your career for me."

Griffin sighs, leaning forward and pressing his forehead to mine. "Mira, I love your brother, and I love hockey. They're two of my favorite things in life. Maybe the top two until you came along. But now? I'd give them both up in order to keep you, and I wouldn't even blink."

Why does he have to be so perfect? And why am I such a scaredy cat? All of this should be a no-brainer. I should say *Yes, of course you're right. Let's tell my brother we're married. Let's tell the world.* But the words won't come out of my mouth. They're stuck in my throat, and no self-pep talks or internal guilt trips can dislodge them.

"Griffin..." My voice is weak and so am I. I'm incapable of finishing the thought.

My husband sighs, his eyes closing as his hands tighten slightly on my face. "Right. Let's go, then."

I miss the warmth of his touch the moment he pulls

away, and it makes me want to shout that I'm ready. It makes me want to find my courage and tell him he's worth all the risks, too.

Instead, I climb out of the G-Wagon and take Griffin's offered hand. He leads me to the elevator in silence, and when it opens on Maddy's floor, he gives my fingers a squeeze before dropping them.

It's what I wanted. What I asked for. But I hate it, all the same.

"Hey, you two!" Isla beams when she opens the door for us. She waves us in, then tackles us with hugs. "I'm so glad we're able to do this. I swear, all the wedding stuff has me so crazy. I hope you don't feel like I'm neglecting you."

Grinning, I shake my head. "No, I don't feel that way."

"Neither do I, Teach." Griffin ruffles Isla's red hair, which earns him a comical scowl from my future sister-in-law. "Man, something smells good."

"Maddox is finishing up some steaks. Can I get either of you a glass of wine or a beer or something?"

"I'd love a glass of wine," I say, following Isla into the kitchen where my brother is at the stove. "Hey, Madddy."

"Hey, Mir. Missed you." My brother pulls me to his side for a hug. "Thanks for coming over. Wright. How's it going, man?"

"Hey, bro. It's going. I'm glad to be home. New York was fun, but way too crowded for my taste." He and Maddox do the bro-hug thing where it starts as a cross-body high-five and turns into a one-armed hug.

My brother nods in agreement. "Logan was the only one not excited to go home."

"Yeah, because he hooked up with a bunch of models." Griffin chuckles and rolls his eyes. I fight back the little twinge of insecurity that gnaws on my insides. I trust Griffin. I know he wouldn't do anything with anyone else, and he spent every night calling me. Still, the reminder of his past exploits with Logan makes my stomach feel funny.

Maddox grins. "I'm still surprised you didn't join him. That used to be your scene."

I hate the way my stomach rolls at that, and I lower my eyes to the floor, not wanting to give away my discomfort. But Griffin notices. Of course he does. He gently nudges me with his shoulder.

"Nah, I told you, man, I'm done with all that. I'm a one-woman guy from now on."

My cheeks flush with warmth, and the uncomfortable knot in my stomach loosens. I only hope my brother doesn't notice. Luckily, when I look up, I see that Maddox's attention is back on the steaks. Unfortunately, Isla is peering at me with a curious glint in her eyes I don't like.

"And is there someone you want to tell us about?" she asks him.

His smooth chuckle rolls over my body, leaving goose bumps in its wake. "Trust me, Teach. When I can tell you I've found *the one*, I'll be screaming it from the rooftops."

Isla studies Griffin, weighing his carefully chosen words, and I almost think we've already blown it when her gaze shifts quickly to me. But if my intelligent friend has her suspicions, she thankfully doesn't voice them. Instead, she smiles and rests a hand on Griffin's arm. "Well, hopefully that will happen for you soon. You're a great guy, Griffin. You deserve that."

"Thanks." He clears his throat, his voice rough. "That means a lot."

"All right, enough of this mushy shit," Maddox says, rolling his eyes. "The food is done, so let's eat."

Dinner passes quickly with easy conversation, lots of talk about the upcoming wedding, and so much laughter. Being here with Griffin, Maddox, and Isla feels so natural that I wonder if Griffin was right. Maybe this would be the perfect time to tell them we got married. Because, outside of my mom, these three people are my family. They're the closest humans in the world to me, and they mean everything. How could Maddox and Isla not be happy for me if I tell them I married the man who's become my best friend? Sure, I may not have made the decision when I was fully in my right mind, but Griffin makes me happy. He supports me, believes in me, and cheers me on. He's the first person I want to tell good news to, the first person I turn to when I'm upset, the person I want to spend all my time with.

He's my person.

Surely, Maddox would see that, right?

I'm lost in my thoughts, wrestling with this growing urge to spill it all right here and now, when my brother kicks my shin under the table.

"Ow, Maddy, what the hell?"

Rolling his eyes, he arches an eyebrow. "I said your name like five times. I was trying to get your attention."

"Okay, well, you have it now."

Griffin and Isla chuckle when I huff out a breath, sounding like a petulant teenager, but that's the effect siblings can have on you. They bring you right back to those angsty years when all you did was piss each other off. I shoot my husband a dark look, and the jerk just laughs louder.

"I was going to say that I know you don't want to talk

about what happened with your shithead ex-boyfriend, but I wanted to check on you and make sure you're good now. You over him?"

It's been *months*. Even if I didn't have Griffin to help me move on from that asshole, I'd still be over him by now. I frown. "Of course I'm over him. I'm good, Maddy. Promise."

Apparently, that was the reassurance he needed, because his shoulders lose some of their tension as he runs a hand through his dark hair. "Good. I'm glad to hear that because I think I have something to tell you that you're really going to like."

Confusion muddies my already distracted thoughts. Does he have more wedding news or something to tell me? I arch an eyebrow and make a face at my brother, which makes him chuckle. "Okay?"

"I've been talking with my agent, and we had an idea."

Griffin stiffens beside me, his knee pressing against mine. I glance at him and notice how tight his jaw is, but I don't have time to wonder about it further, because that's when my brother drops a bomb at the dinner table.

"He has a nephew your age. The guy's super smart, really driven, and when my agent showed him a photo of you, he said he'd be happy to go on a date with you. His name is Rhett, and I gave him your number. He's going to text you this week to set something up." My brother smiles so wide, he clearly thinks this is something I'll be excited about. "Isn't that great?"

My head is a chaotic mess. I was just considering telling my brother that I married his best friend and have been happier than I've been in...well, maybe ever, and now I have to switch gears to process the fact that he gave some guy my number without asking my permission and is trying to set me up on a date. It's like I'm in one of those carnival rides that spins so fast, it pins you to the wall before the floor drops out. It's impossible to get my bearings, and I'm not sure if I'm going to puke or pass out.

"You gave my number to a guy named Rhett?"

Completely unaware of the way my mind is spinning out of control, my brother grins. "He's perfect for you, Mir. I told Mom about him, and even she agreed he sounds like he could be exactly what you need. Plus, he's in marketing, so he can help you with your business."

"She doesn't need help with her business," Griffin says, his voice low and dangerous. "She's built it up from nothing all on her own."

Maddox waves a hand dismissively. "I know, I'm not saying she hasn't, just that dating someone else who's business minded and experienced is perfect for her. They can bounce ideas off one another, and he can help her level up her branding."

I get that he's trying to be sweet, but my brother is way out of line with all of this. *Way* out of line. To give a stranger my phone number and set this all up without talking to me is one thing, but to insinuate that I'm not capable and creative enough to succeed on my own is such *bullshit*. I've worked so hard to prove myself. I've done everything I can to step out of his shadow, and now he wants me to step into some random guy's because he's good at marketing?

What the hell?

It makes my brain stall out.

"She doesn't want you to set her up, do you, Mira?"

Griffin presses his leg against mine, and I can practically feel him vibrating with barely restrained fury.

"I..." They're all staring at me. Maddox with this expectant look on his face, Isla with concern, and Griffin —Griffin's expression is a potent cocktail of rage, need, and worry. My throat going dry, all I can do is splutter like an idiot. "I..."

"Maybe this isn't a good time to talk about this," Isla says, her attention bouncing between me and Griffin. "In fact, maybe bringing this up at all was a mistake."

Blissfully unaware of the minefield he just threw me into, Maddox scoffs. "It's not a mistake. He's perfect for Mira, and come on, let's be real here. My sister doesn't have the best track record with choosing men."

Oh. His words are an arrow, and boy, do they find their target.

"Maddox!" Isla's eyes flash with anger and a warning, but I barely notice. I'm stuck in an echo chamber where his words bounce around and around, leaving bruises and doubt in their wake.

"Oh, come on, Short-Stack, you know what I mean. Mira's a hopeless romantic like our mom. It's not a bad thing, it just means she's prone to giving men who don't deserve it a chance. I don't want to see her make the same mistake our mom did and give some flaky asshole chances he doesn't deserve. You know she's too good for every guy she's ever dated." Maddox rolls his eyes like all of this is obvious. Like he didn't just inadvertently insult his best friend in the whole world by implying that, yes, my picker is, in fact, completely broken and that I must be incapable of choosing a good man for myself.

"Are you serious right now?" Griffin snarls. "Mira, you can't possibly believe this shit, right?"

My brother likely doesn't hear the worry in Griffin's voice, but I do. I do, and I hate it. But my mind is reeling, my heart is hurting, and I'm so caught off guard by this entire situation that I can't think straight.

"I…"

"Maddox," Isla warns, her cheeks red with anger as she glances between me and Griffin. Does she see the rift growing between us right now? Does she have any idea what my brother just did?

"Mira?" Griffin's voice grows ragged.

"That's really what you think of me?" I ask my brother. The words waver as they leave my lips. "You think I need you to pick someone for me because I can't?"

Finally, Maddox scowls, confusion skittering across his face. "That's not what I said, Mir. I just think this guy would be perfect for you, that's all. You deserve better than the man-children you usually go for. I don't want to see you waste any more time on guys who don't take life as seriously as you do."

Griffin's spine straightens at that, and I want to rage at my brother. I want to tell him to shut the fuck up. I want to tell him I don't need him to choose for me, because I've chosen for myself, and the man I've picked is perfect. He doesn't have to be serious all the time. He doesn't have to be someone who works in a similar field as me. He just has to *see* me and *choose* me, which Griffin does. Every day.

But how can I say any of that to my brother now that he's made it crystal clear he'll never take anyone I choose seriously? Not only that, but he hit Griffin right in a soft spot, and he doesn't even know.

All Griffin wants is to be taken seriously, but everyone treats him like he's a joke or some guy stuck in a perpetual state of arrested development. A man-child. The same word my brother used to describe every man I've ever dated, apparently.

"You know what? I want to leave. Griffin, can you take me home?"

Isla's face blanches. She reaches across the table to grab my hand, but I can't even look her in the eye. "Mira, please don't go. I'm sorry. Give me a chance to talk to your brother and educate him on what a colossal ass he is."

"Hey!" Maddox rears back like his fiancée slapped him. "I did nothing wrong. I was just trying to set my sister up with a good guy for once."

Reaching beneath the dining room table, I find Griffin's hand and give it a pleading squeeze. "Please, can we go?"

My husband doesn't meet my eyes when he nods. He doesn't meet anyone's eyes as he stands silently and grabs my coat and purse for me while Maddox splutters and stammers about how he doesn't understand what just happened and how everyone is blowing things out of proportion.

When we're at the door, I turn to Maddox, my blood somehow simultaneously molten with rage and icing over with fear that my slow reaction time to everything that happened will cost me Griffin. "You know what, Maddy? I expected better from you. When did you turn into such a judgmental asshat? Yeah, maybe the guys I dated before sucked, but that doesn't give you the right to judge me. All it takes is getting it right once. And seeing as though some of your teammates are both free spirits and the most loyal, best men you could ask to watch your back, I'd think you'd realize that being *serious* doesn't have to look like wearing a suit to the office and helping me with a career I didn't ask for help with. Tell *Rhett* to lose my number. And butt the fuck out of my love life."

My brother's face slackens as I blast him with the full force of my growing anger and panic. I'd stay and continue to rip him a new asshole, but my husband is stepping into the elevator, his hazel eyes pinned on the floor and shoulders slumped. My heart races when Griffin doesn't look up at me or hold the door. The metal slides shut, hiding my husband from my view as it descends to the ground floor, taking my heart with it.

Maddox reaches for my wrist, trying to apologize and get me to talk to him, but I pull away, racing for the elevators.

He has no idea how much damage he's just done.

And how much I did by not finally coming clean.

thirty-four

MIRA

I keep fucking up. Every time Griffin and I make progress, every time I start to feel like I know what I want or what I need to do, shit hits the fan. There's no one to blame but myself. I should have claimed Griffin the other week at the bar. Should have told my brother to shove his meddling up his ass because I've already found the man who's right for me. But I'm a fucking coward, and for some reason, I've been so worried about what my big brother might think, I haven't stopped to consider what it's making my husband think.

And fuck. *Fuck.* Because as much as I love my brother, I love Griffin more.

I love Griffin more.

Waiting for the elevator to open, my chest is a yawning chasm of viscous, dark fear. Because I love Griffin Wright, and I let him walk away. Somehow, in the months of living together, in the months of being married, the man has worked his way into my heart and made himself at home there.

He's my best friend, my confidant, my fiercest supporter. He's the first one to tell me he believes in me, the first one to upend his life to help me. When no one else has ever really fought for me, he has. Even from that first terrifying morning when we woke up naked, hungover, and married. My first instinct was to run, and his was to hold on to me and fight for this.

Finally, *finally*, the elevator doors open and I step inside, smash my finger on the button for the ground floor, and mutter, "Hurry up, hurry up," under my breath until it comes to a stop and the doors open again. Griffin isn't there waiting for me. My heart pounds, and my mouth goes dry. What if he left me here? No, he wouldn't do that.

I'm practically running as I push through the doors into the parking garage. Everything in me screams to get to him. I need to tell him how I feel. To show him. And most importantly, I need to apologize again for hurting him by staying silent. The doubts have been my own, and if I'm honest with myself, they have everything to do with me and my own insecurities, and almost nothing to do with Griffin himself. But I know he won't see it that way. I can't let him drive away without making it clear how I feel about him.

A huge, relieved breath gusts out of me when I find Griffin's SUV still parked where we left it. It's not running, but he's sitting in the driver's seat, white-knuckle gripping the steering wheel with this heartbreaking, faraway look on his face. A look that I put there.

Fuck.

"Griffin," I whisper when I climb in the passenger seat and close the door.

He doesn't respond. Doesn't look at me. Hell, he barely even blinks.

"I'm sorry. I'm so sorry. Maddox took me by surprise with that whole thing. I'd been lost in my head thinking about us... About telling him about us, and then he started spouting all of that bullshit, and my brain short-circuited. I couldn't think straight. If I'd been able to, I would have told Maddy to fuck off sooner. Would have told him that he was out of line."

"You would have told him you're mine?"

I hate how flat the words are when they leave his lips. He doesn't look my way, and nothing about his tone says he believes a word I'm saying. Fair enough, I guess. I haven't really given him a reason to believe me, have I? Which is why I need him to look at me when I say what I'm about to say. Reaching up, I gently coax Griffin to look at me by cupping his face.

"Yes. I would have told him you're mine. That's what I was thinking about when he couldn't get my attention. Because I've realized that I'm tired of hiding this. You are everything I didn't know I needed, babe. You're my best friend, the most supportive partner I've ever had, and you make me laugh harder than anyone else. You have such a huge heart, and you're so fiercely loyal, and you never hesitate to protect the people you consider your own."

My thumbs brush along his cheekbones, making his dark-blond eyelashes flutter and his breath catch. I lean in and press a gentle kiss to one eyelid and then the other.

"I don't know how I got so lucky to have you consider me yours, but I'm tired of fighting this. If you want me to,

I'll march right back up to Maddy's apartment and tell him we're married and that if he can't accept it, he can go fuck himself." That earns a watery chuckle from Griffin, so I grin, press another kiss to the tip of his nose, and continue. "But I've been thinking that it might be fun to plan some big announcement where we can get all the important people in our lives together and tell them at the same time."

Glittering hazel eyes rise to meet mine for the first time since I got in the car, and some of the gnawing ache in my chest eases. "You want to tell everyone?"

I nod. "I want to tell everyone. Maybe we could have a party at our place? Pull out the *Mr.* and *Mrs.* towels, pop a bunch of champagne, and tell everyone that we're married."

One of those smiles I love so much spreads across Griffin's face. It tugs on his cheeks and crinkles the corners of his eyes. He's beautiful like this. A golden angel who outshines the sun. "I finally get to tell everyone that you're Mira Wright?"

"I never agreed to change my name, husband. Let's not push it."

Griffin chuckles. The raspy quality of it sends a pleasant shiver skittering down my spine. "I think I can convince you, baby girl."

"Oh yeah? And how do you plan to do that?"

Smirking, Griffin opens the car door, climbs out, and rounds the hood to my side. He opens my door and yanks me out, chuckling when I let out a squeal. Then he's opening the back door and tossing me onto the bench seat before following me in. "Like this."

The tinted windows and shadows of the parking garage

shroud us in velvety darkness as Griffin looms over me. His eyes rake over my body, taking in my heaving chest and dilated pupils before his long fingers move to the fly of my jeans. Before I can ask him what he's doing, he has my jeans and panties down my thighs and over my feet. Then those fingers deftly unbutton his jeans and shove the fabric down his hips. The denim puddles around his ankles, and his glorious cock springs free.

"Come here, wife."

I let out a squeak as Griffin's strong hands grip my naked hips and pull me into his lap. He settles on the middle of the bench seat, dragging my soaking core down onto his thighs with my knees on either side of him. My eyes roll back in my head as my bare pussy drags against the silky hardness of his shaft. When I gasp, he chuckles darkly, his fingers tightening hard enough on my hips to dimple my skin, then he drags my slit over the length of him again and again.

"Oh," I moan, my eyes darting to the windows and the empty parking garage. Anyone could see us. Hear us. Sure, the windows are tinted and we're covered in shadows, but the windshield isn't dark enough to hide what we're doing. "We shouldn't do this here."

"Beg to differ, wife. This is exactly where we should be doing this. I'm hard as a fucking rock, and you just told me you want to claim me in front of the world. Now I'm going to claim you. I don't give a fuck if someone hears. And if they see us? Good. Let them see how perfectly you take my cock. How you fall apart when I stuff your greedy cunt full. Let them see and be jealous that you're all mine."

Groaning, I move my hips, desperate to relieve some of this growing need. I don't want anyone seeing us, but I can't deny the way my blood roars from the threat of being caught. Well, caught by anyone except my brother.

"Oh, wife, you like that idea, don't you? Your sweet little pussy is drenching my dick, and I'm not even inside you yet." As Griffin leans in and nips at the juncture of my shoulder and neck, I gasp. "You better be quiet, unless you want the world to know just how good I fuck my wife."

"Stop talking and put your dick in me."

Griffin barks out a laugh. "Impatient, aren't we?" He tries to grab his jeans but can't quite reach. "Be a good girl and grab a condom out of my wallet."

"Fuck the condoms. I want you in me now. Unless you're worried about making a mess of your back seat."

He flashes me a wicked grin as he fists the base of his dick. "Oh, sunshine, you should know better than that. I'd like nothing more than to carry the scent of your hot little pussy everywhere I go. Now, lift up for me and let me in."

Nearly quivering with anticipation, I lift onto my knees and watch as Griffin guides the head of his dick to my entrance. He glides it through the slick wetness of my slit, then pushes me down his length with one firm hand on my hip. The sound of his moan hollows my stomach, and I arch my back and sink the rest of the way down his rock-hard cock.

"That's it, baby. Such a perfect girl, taking my cock so well. Fuck."

I'm so turned on by the possibility of being caught and the raw, unfiltered need in my husband's voice that it won't take me long at all to find my release. Hips rocking, I begin to ride him. Each drag of his cock along my insides has me writhing. My need for him is all-consuming. Now that I've finally decided to embrace this, it's like

Griffin's touch is even more potent and drugging than before.

"Need more. Need you."

Griffin tightens his grip on my hips. The small bite of pain is the most delicious contrast to the pleasure building in me. I gasp when he lifts me up and slams me back down as his hips rise to meet me. He controls my movements like it's nothing, and it's scorching hot. "I'll give you more, sunshine. Give you fucking everything. My cock, my heart, my soul, my name. It all belongs to you, baby. You fucking own me."

"Oh." I sigh, throwing my head back as the car rocks, our gasps and moans filling the cab, along with the growing scent of sex. The windows fog, and it'll be very obvious what's happening in here to anyone who walks by, but I can't seem to care. Not when my husband, who I'm in love with, is filling me up and commanding my body so perfectly. A needy whine builds in my throat as pleasure burns hot in my lower belly.

"Griffin..."

"I know, baby. I've got you." Letting go of one of my hips, Griffin tugs my sweater down, revealing one side of my bra. Then he pulls the cup down, freeing my breast. He groans when my nipple pebbles in the cool air before leaning down and taking the aching bud in his mouth. He licks and sucks and nips at my breast, stoking the fire in me higher until it spreads from my lower belly to my chest, my arms, my legs.

"Need more. Please."

"I'll always give you what you need."

I believe him. He's proven his devotion again and again. Proven his loyalty and his feelings. And when I stare deep into those multi-hued hazel eyes I can't get enough of, I swear I see love shining back at me. And more than the head of his cock dragging along that perfect place inside of me, more than the thumb he moves to my clit or the drag of his teeth over my nipple, it's that love that throws gasoline on the bonfire in my body and heart, setting me ablaze.

"Griffin." I gasp and cry out his name as his movements grow faster and more erratic. He pounds into me with such force that my tits bounce and the car rocks violently.

"That's it, sunshine. Strangle my cock with that perfect pussy. Milk me fucking dry. I want my cum dripping out of you the whole ride home. I want your panties soaked. Want the scent of you to saturate the fabric of your seat so it always smells like your cunt and my cum. Then I'm going to fill you up again."

And with that, I burst into flames, my orgasm so intense, I have to bury my face in the crook of Griffin's neck to muffle my screams. He hugs me tighter as he slams into me again and again, catching fire and burning with me, moaning my name. Warmth floods me as his cock twitches and pulses inside of me. He fills me. Brands me. Claims me.

We cling to each other, a sweaty tangle of limbs and hearts that have been forged into something beautiful and terrifying and life changing, and I know, without a shadow of a doubt, that whatever happens now, there's no turning back.

thirty-five

GRIFFIN

With my naked wife curled up against my chest, our bedroom filled with the scent of sex and my balls utterly empty, I couldn't be happier. Well, I guess I could be happier if everyone already knew we're married, but we'll get there. She's done fighting this, thank the hockey gods. Now all we need to do is figure out when we can host a party to tell everyone and what last name we're going to use.

She thinks I'm kidding about taking her last name, but I'm not. If that's what would make my wife happy, that's what we'll do. Or maybe we could hyphenate them. Griffin Graves-Wright doesn't have quite the same ring to it as Griffin Wright, but it's not terrible.

"What are you thinking about?" Mira draws little hearts and circles on my bare, sweaty chest while she rests her head on my shoulder.

"A couple of things."

"Oh yeah? Like what?"

I kiss her forehead. "Like when we can plan the party to tell everyone we're married. Think we could pull that off next weekend? The weekend after that, we have an away series, then we'll be in Michigan for your meeting with the University of Michigan."

As Mira's soft chuckle vibrates through my body, my tired dick stirs. Relentless fucker. I ignore him, because as much as I'd love to sink into my wife again, this is more important. This is our future we're talking about, and the sooner we can get this figured out, the sooner I can tell the world that Mira Graves is all mine and I am hers.

"I think next weekend is a little too quick. We'll have to figure out food..."

"I'll find a caterer." With enough money, I'm sure I could find someone willing to work on a quick turnaround.

"We need to put together a guest list. I don't want it to be some huge thing, but we need to make sure all the important people are free and able to come. I need a cute dress, and I was thinking..." Mira nibbles on her lower lip as her words taper off.

"You were thinking what, sunshine?"

"Well, if we're going to tell everyone we're married, maybe we should get some nicer wedding bands?"

Ah, shit. I should have already thought of that. Of course, she'll want to wear something nicer than a gold-plated ring that looks like it came from a toy dispenser at the mall where you put in a dollar and it pops out a jewelry-filled egg. She'll want something pretty. She deserves something pretty. And expensive.

She deserves a huge-ass diamond that can be seen from

space, so every thirsty fucker on the planet knows her heart belongs to me.

Grinning, my heart feeling like it may explode right out of my chest in a spray of blood and gooey love, I pull Mira's lips to mine in a searing kiss. "Let's go right now."

"It's one in the morning," she says, giggling. "They'll all be closed."

"That's stupid."

She giggles again. "Yep."

"Fine. We'll go tomorrow morning. I don't have to be at the arena until three." I grab her hand and bring it to my lips. Kissing each slender digit, I let my lips linger on her ring finger.

"Okay. What else were you thinking about?"

"Just trying to figure out what would sound best if you didn't want to change your last name to Wright. Griffin Graves sounds cool, I guess. Alliteration is fun. Might get a little confusing on the ice, but that's okay. Graves-Wright sounds better than Wright-Graves, because that sounds like you're trying to find the plot where your grandma's buried or some shit and you finally found the right grave."

She laughs at that, and I tighten my hold on her. She's soft and warm, and I love how loose she is when she's happy and at ease. Like sexy Jell-O.

"You're ridiculous."

"No, for now, I'm Wright. Not sure Ridiculous would make a great last name. Though I suppose we don't have to stick with either of our last names. We could make one up."

"What?" Her voice shakes with laughter.

"We could combine them. Gright. Or Wraves."

It's my turn to laugh when her cute little nose wrinkles. "Those are horrible names. Definitely not."

"Okay, okay, you're right. We could just pick something cool, I guess. What about something badass, like a Greek god's name or something? Like Poseidon. Griffin and Mira Poseidon." I don't actually want to change our last names to something stupid like Poseidon, but I do want to make my wife laugh more. And I definitely succeed. She stares at me with wide eyes for a beat, and then her head tips back and she laughs so loud, it almost hurts my ear.

"No. Absolutely not."

I shrug. "Yeah, it's not quite right. But you know what *is*?"

"Let me guess. Wright?"

"Bingo." I lean in and kiss the tip of her nose. She yawns. "But we can figure that all out in the morning. Time for sleep, baby. It's been a long day, and we're ring shopping tomorrow. Gonna need our energy."

"Yeah. Good idea." My beautiful wife yawns again, and I tug her close enough that she can nestle her face in the crook of my neck, exactly where she belongs. "Night, husband."

The word lights up every single pleasure center in my brain. "Night, wife."

Somehow, I untangled myself from Mira's clinging arms and legs without waking her and, despite the salty scent of bacon mingling with fresh coffee in the kitchen, I'm pretty sure she's still asleep.

Good. I want to pamper my wife this morning. Breakfast in bed, maybe an orgasm or two, then I'm taking her to the nicest jewelry store I could find. I called, and they were able to fit us in for an appointment later this morning.

It's surreal. After Maddox said all that shit last night, I never thought this would be how I'd spend the day. But Mira surprised me. Surprised me with semi-public sex in a parking garage—that was definitely a bucket list item—and by telling me she's ready to reveal our marriage to our friends and family.

In between frying eggs and bacon, I've been looking at photos of engagement rings online. I had no idea there were so many styles and cuts. Mira doesn't know I'm planning to get her a diamond, and I'm not going to tell her, but I'm planning to watch her like a hawk while we're there. Women love looking at sparkly jewelry, right? She's bound to make googly eyes at something, and when she does, I'll go back another day and buy it.

The thought makes me giddy. Maybe we went about all of this backward, but I'm going to propose to my wife, and I'm going to do it sooner than later.

I want to give her everything. Just spoil her absolutely rotten. Because I've never been as happy as I am with Mira.

After piling two plates, silverware, and coffees on a tray, I carefully carry everything into our room where Mira still sleeps, curled up and naked, in our bed. Everything about her is perfect. From the dark tangles of hair that fan out around her head in a messy halo, to the way her lips are always parted—just barely open—when she sleeps. There's a cluster of freckles on her left shoulder, a few silvery stretch marks adorn her hips and upper thighs from when she must have hit a growth spurt as a teenager, and she's got the cutest little dimples above her ass cheeks. She's perfectly imperfect, and I'm going to spend my life learning every single one of those imperfections.

Unable to keep my hands off her any longer, I set the tray of food on my bedside table and crawl toward her on the bed. Her eyelids flutter, but she doesn't wake, so I lean over her, pressing gentle kisses to her shoulders, her arms, her breasts. Soft little moans slip from her mouth before she's fully awake and aware, and I decide to ask my wife how she would feel about being awakened by my fingers or my cock in her sweet little pussy one day.

"Rise and shine, baby." I press a kiss to her belly, then drag my lips to just below her belly button.

Mira sucks in a sharp breath when I drag my tongue down to the top of her mound. "Am I dreaming?"

"I don't know. Were you dreaming about me kissing all over your perfect body?"

"Mm, no, but I wish I had been." Green eyes flutter open and focus on me. "Then again, real life kisses are better."

Her sleepy smile slays me. It's better than a hit of caffeine, sweeter than the strawberries waiting for us on our plates, and it warms me better than all the coffee in the world ever could. I'm so gone for this woman.

She sniffs as her brain comes back online, and her smile grows when she sees the food and coffee. "Griffin, did you make me breakfast in bed?"

There's so much pleasure in the question that I vow to make my wife breakfast in bed at least once a month. If something so simple can make her so happy, I'd do it every day just to make her smile.

"Sure did." I lean two pillows against the headboard for her and give them a pat. "Now, sit your cute, naked ass up so I can feed you."

"I can't believe you did this for me." She pushes herself into a seated position and reclines against the pillows. I hand her a plate and some silverware and decide I'll need to buy some lap trays if this is going to be a regular occurrence. But Mira doesn't seem to mind eating with the plate in her lap, so I won't worry about it this time. "It smells amazing."

"Good. Eat up."

I don't start eating until Mira brings the first forkful of fluffy eggs to her lips. Her eyes flutter closed as she chews and she hums her approval.

"So good."

Not as good as those sexy little sounds she makes when she's happy. Damn.

"Are we really going wedding ring shopping this morning?" she asks as we eat.

"Hell yeah. And I can't wait. Do you know how much I've wanted to see you walking around with my ring on your finger, wifey? To know that, even when I'm on the road, any man who sees you will know you're mine?" Whether Mira wears my ring is inconsequential in the grand scheme of things. It's a little piece of metal. What matters is that she's mine. Heart, body, and soul. But I'm a possessive bastard, not to mention hopelessly romantic about shit like this, and it's killed me having her walk around the Twin Cities with a bare ring finger. I want her to *want* to show the world that she's taken.

And now she does.

"I have to admit, I hated seeing those women throw

themselves at you that night at the bar. Maybe if you'd been wearing your wedding band, they would have backed off." Mira's cheeks flush as she admits her jealousy, and I grin like an idiot.

"Why do you look embarrassed about that, sunshine? I want you to stake your claim. It's fucking hot that you were all jealous and possessive. If you had told those women to back off, I may have bent you over that table and taken you right there in front of everyone."

Mira's nose wrinkles. "Ew. My brother was there."

Oops. Yeah, I guess he was. "Okay, well, then I would have thrown you over my shoulder and taken you to a supply closet and fucked you so good that you'd be screaming my name, and every woman in the bar would have known who I belong to."

"My brother can never hear us have sex, Griffin. I cannot stress enough how much I do not want that ever to happen."

She looks so utterly disgusted by the idea. It's hilarious.

She doesn't think so, though, and when I chuckle, she narrows those pretty green eyes at me. "I'm serious, babe."

I hold my hands up, palms out, in surrender. "Okay, okay. I won't bang you when your brother is around. Duly noted. Can I finger you under the table?"

"Griffin," she shrieks. I laugh and duck when she grabs a pillow and swings it at my head.

Yeah. This right here is everything I've been missing. Everything I always hoped for. Breakfast in bed and naked pillow fights with the most beautiful woman on the planet?

Someone pinch me.

thirty-six

GRIFFIN

I'M RING SHOPPING WITH MY WIFE.

This is such a surreal moment, and I can't calm my mind or body down. Mira grips my hand and rests her head on my arm to get me to stop bouncing on the balls of my feet. But how can I stay calm? This is fucking everything.

"I like that one." Mira points at a sparkly band covered in tiny diamonds.

"Let's get it." I pull out my wallet as my wife giggles.

"Babe, we can't just buy the first rings we see. We have to try them on first." She rolls her eyes like I'm being silly. Maybe I am. I don't know what in the hell I'm doing right now. This is a first for me.

The saleswoman tries to stifle her grin, but she loses the battle when I give her a helpless shrug. Can she tell how keyed up I am? It's this potent combination of nerves and fucking bliss.

My wife is going to wear my ring. She's going to claim me in public and let me claim her. And there are so many ways I want to claim her. I wonder if she'd kick my ass if I climbed into the announcer's booth at a game and told the whole arena that she's my wife?

Probably.

It would be worth it, though.

"Now, what a lot of people like to do is match their band to their engagement ring," the saleswoman says helpfully.

Mira's face scrunches in this little grimace. "Oh, um, that's okay. We're just looking for bands on their own. No engagement rings." Mira smiles at the girl before lowering her eyes to the rings on display in the glass case.

I get the saleswoman's attention and discreetly motion to the cases filled with engagement rings, then at Mira. I give the girl a wink before clearing my throat and playfully poking Mira's side. "All that coffee really ran through me this morning. I gotta take a shit." Mira's nose scrunches up, and I punch myself in the metaphorical dick for not coming up with a less disgusting excuse, but it's too late to change course now. "You look around. I'll be back in a few minutes."

The saleswoman tries not to laugh when I ask her where the bathroom is. Then I tell her to let Mira look at whatever catches her eye, motioning with my head at the engagement rings. To her credit, the saleswoman's eyes widen and she nods. As I walk away, she says, "Why don't we look at these engagement rings first? It may help me suggest the right band for you if I get a better idea of your style."

"Oh, that's not necessary," Mira says as I hide around the corner, watching.

The saleswoman leans in conspiratorially. "Come on, it'll be fun. Sometimes, when everyone else is at lunch and the shop is empty, I open the cases and try all the rings on. No one has to know."

My beautiful wife giggles, and I have to duck behind the wall when she glances over her shoulder to make sure no one is around. Then she says, "Sure, why not?"

I watch as Mira leans over cases filled with glittering diamonds and my heart swells in my chest. She points out a few rings she likes and listens as the saleswoman tells her about each one. She says something to Mira about how she seems to favor the less traditional styles. The ones that look a bit more artistic and bohemian, and Mira agrees. She tries on a few that catch her eye, and when she slips the fourth ring onto her finger, her whole body stills. Standing there, green eyes glued to a ring I can't see from my hiding spot, Mira sucks in a deep breath.

"Oh," she says just loud enough for me to catch it. "This one is so beautiful."

"Mm, yes. One of my favorites," the saleswoman agrees. "The way the emerald cut gives it that sense of vintage charm, but the surrounding diamonds add sparkle, is magical. And I love that the setting makes them look like leaves."

"It's like a fairy princess ring." Mira holds her hand out, twisting her wrist this way and that to catch the light. I can't see her expression from here, but the woman behind the counter catches my eye and gives me the slightest nod.

That's the one. Now I'll just have to find a way to get the saleswoman to add it to my bill without Mira noticing.

I wait until she's taken the ring off before clearing my throat and walking back into the showroom. My wife turns to watch me with a soft smile that almost makes my steps falter. Because the look she's giving me? That soft, tender expression looks a hell of a lot like love, and I've been waiting my whole life to see that expression on the right woman's face.

And Mira Graves is the right woman. There's not a single fucking doubt in my mind.

"Sorry," I say, wrapping her in my arms and pressing a lingering kiss to her forehead. "Where were we?"

"I think I have the perfect band for your wife, Mr. Wright." The saleswoman gives me a knowing smile when Mira briefly presses her face into my chest. "It's beautiful on its own, but if you ever did pair it with another ring, it would complement Mrs. Wright's style just wonderfully."

She called Mira Mrs. Wright. I wait for my feisty wife to correct her, but Mira never does. And that feels like the biggest win. More exciting than a shutout. Maybe better than winning the Cup. Because Mira has never once let me call her Mrs. Wright. Things have changed with us. Between last night and this morning, something has shifted.

I can practically feel my curse shattering.

Floating. I'm floating when the woman pulls a delicate white gold band out of the display case. It's encrusted in tiny diamonds, and it sparkles as they each catch the light.

"Why don't you do the honors?"

Anything I may want to say gets lodged in my throat as I carefully accept the ring from the woman behind the counter and take my wife's left hand. My eyes never leave hers as I slip it onto her trembling finger. We're both breathing hard. Like the gravity in the room has increased and is pressing down on us. The enormity of the moment makes it feel like we're alone in the world. Just me and Mira. The way it should be.

"It's perfect," she whispers, finally looking down at her finger.

"Yeah. Perfect." But I'm not talking about the ring.

After a few seconds, the saleswoman clears her throat. "It looks like the jeweler won't need to do much to size this for you. It's maybe half a size too big right now."

"And how long will it take for them to size it?" I ask, still staring at my bride.

"We can typically have that done within seventy-two hours."

"Is this the one?" I ask Mira. I'm still holding her hand, and my fingers trail across hers, causing a little shiver to work its way through my wife's body.

She nods. "I think so."

The woman behind the counter beams at us. "Fantastic. Shall we look at the men's bands?"

We follow her to the next case. There aren't as many options, but I find a thick, carbon fiber ring that's black on the outside and silver on the inside. It's simple, but stylish, and it sort of reminds me of a hockey puck. When Mira gives me her approval, the associate figures out my ring size and tells me she will have to special order mine. I pay extra to rush it, not wanting to wait even a day more than necessary before I can wear Mira's ring.

I can't keep my hands off my wife as I pay. With my left hand tangled in the hair at her nape, I sign the receipt with my right and try to focus as the saleswoman rattles off a list of information and takes my number down so the store can call me when our bands are ready. Whatever I missed while distracted by Mira, they'll remind me when they call.

I need to get her out of here. Need to get her home, throw her onto our bed, and fuck her senseless before practice. Now that she's agreed to let me publicly claim her, I'm even more determined to claim her at home. Every last inch of her perfect body. Again and again.

thirty-seven

MIRA

WEDDING PLANNING CONSUMES MY DAYS WHILE Griffin is on the road for their latest away series, and I hardly have time to miss him. After a serious heart-to-heart where Isla apologized repeatedly for Maddy's meddling and her not stopping him, I've helped Isla pick out flowers, centerpieces, a photographer... Hell, I even went cake taste testing with her because she and Maddox couldn't seem to make it work between their schedules. Today, we're shopping for bridesmaids' dresses.

"Okay." Isla claps her hands, silencing the group of women around her. Lexi and I share a grin, while Isla's best friends, Jess and Nevaeh, beam at my future sister-in-law. And they deserve to beam at her. After all, the two of them are the reason she met my brother. Isla puts her hands on her hips and smiles. "The wedding colors are cream and sage, so your dresses will be sage. They've pulled a handful of different style options for you to choose from by the same designer. Pick whichever one you like the best."

A consultant wheels a rack of satin, sage-green dresses out. They're all floor length, but some have spaghetti straps while others have draped bodices or sweetheart necklines. The color will perfectly offset Isla's pretty red hair, and I love it. The employee waves Nev over first, and we all sip champagne and enjoy the mini fashion show.

One by one, each of the bridesmaids tries on dresses until only I remain. It's been fun, spending the day with these women. I'm so happy I'll be able to call Isla my sister-in-law in a couple of short months.

"Hey," the woman in question says softly. She places a palm on my hand to get my attention and leans in. "I just wanted to say sorry again."

"You have nothing to be sorry about. I know my brother's heart was in the right place. But I'm an adult, and I don't need him to butt into my life anymore. He doesn't have to save the day or fight my battles for me. It was sweet when we were younger, but now I need him to trust that I know what's best for me."

My sweet, soon-to-be sister-in-law nods. She studies me a little too intently. "He does. Whenever you have someone important to introduce to him, I hope you know he'll support you. As long as you're happy, he'll be happy."

"I sure as hell hope so," I mutter.

Isla cocks her head to the side and the faintest smile twitches at her lips. "He will be. Even if it requires some adjustments on his part." That smile of hers finally slips free and grows.

I'm opening my mouth to ask her what she means by that—because that's an oddly specific thing to say—when the consultant calls my name and waves me toward the dressing room. "Right. We can finish chatting about this later."

"I'm all ears whenever you want to *chat*," she says. "About anything."

Right. That feels... Does she suspect something?

Not allowing myself to go down that rabbit hole, I follow the employee back to the dressing room, where she has my top three choices hanging and ready for me. As I change into the first one, I can't help thinking about Griffin. All this wedding planning makes me a little sad that he and I skipped right over this part. I was never the girl who spent time actively dreaming about her wedding, but I did always assume I'd have one.

Getting married by a young Elvis in Vegas was never a thought that crossed my mind.

The first two dresses are okay, but the third is perfect. It's got a simple, classic design that makes me look tall and curvy in all the right places. The neckline has a drape to it, the straps are thin, and there's a slit that goes halfway up my left thigh. When I leave the dressing room to show Isla and the girls, they all cheer and clap.

Isla's eyes tear up, and she clasps her hands in front of her chest. "You look so beautiful. I can't believe I'm going to have a sister, let alone one so hot!"

I laugh at that, even though I'm tearing up too. I couldn't have asked for a better sister-in-law, and I'm so glad my brother got his head out of his ass. Part of me was worried he'd never find someone after the way a couple of his exes treated him, but I'm happy to be wrong.

We all pay for our dresses and make appointments for alterations. It's a quick timeline, but with Maddy's career and the time the Rogues spend out of town, they only have a small window where they can get married and go on a honeymoon without having to plan around hockey.

After we settle everything at the dress shop, we go out for mimosas and brunch. Conversation flows so easily, and not for the first time, I'm filled with gratitude that things with Jared didn't work out. If he and I had stayed together, I never would have left Chicago. I would have missed out on this time with Isla and my brother, I never would have become friends with Lexi, and I never would have wound up married to the sweetest man in the entire world.

When talk turns to men, and Isla grills Jess and Nev about their dating lives, I am so close to spilling the beans and blurting out that Griffin and I are in a relationship. That we're married, and the sex is earth-shatteringly amazing. But I don't. I can wait for another week. I can.

I wonder what would have happened if we'd come clean about everything that first morning in Vegas? How different would things have been?

But it's pointless to consider what-ifs, because I can't go back in time and change anything. And I'm not sure I would. The months we've spent married in secret have given us time to grow closer and let our relationship evolve without any pressure or outside input. And I think we needed that, even though I know Griffin has hated keeping this a secret.

Just another week. I can wait another week.

"I MISS THE HELL OUT OF YOU." GRIFFIN SIGHS AS

he flops down onto a hotel bed, his hair still wet from a post-game shower.

"I miss you too. You look tired."

"I am. It was an intense game. I swear they had the refs on the payroll for this one."

The Rogues won tonight, but barely. It was an intensely physical game, and I shouted at the television more times than I could count. Especially when one of the opposing players checked Griffin so hard into the boards that he looked slightly dazed afterward.

"I'll give you a massage when you get home."

Griffin perks up at that. "A naked massage? Because that would definitely help me feel better."

"Yeah," I say, chuckling. "A naked massage."

"Hell yeah. You can oil up your tits and rub them all over me." His expression goes dreamy. "I miss your tits."

Rolling my eyes, I arch an eyebrow at my husband. "Only my tits?"

"Yep." Griffin's eyes sparkle with mischief. It's such an achingly familiar expression, and one I love so much.

Shit. I love him. I've fought it, but there's no point in denying it any longer. I love Griffin Wright.

"Well, my tits miss you too."

"They should come out and say hi, then."

I lose the fight with my laughter, and it comes spilling out of me as I tug my shirt up and flash Griffin my boobs.

"Ladies," he drawls, "so lovely to see you." He blows my tits a kiss before turning his attention back to my face with a huge smile. "How was your day, baby? Did you have fun with Isla and the girls?"

"I did. You'll love the dress I picked out. And lunch was great. It was hard not to tell them about you, though."

He nods. "I know. I've had to stop myself from blurting it out to Bash at least half a dozen times since we got on the plane."

"I swear, Isla suspects something. Has Maddox been acting weird? You don't think she's said anything to him, do you?"

Griffin's head tilts to the side and his eyes narrow as he considers it. He's so handsome, it makes my heart beat wildly in my chest. I miss him. I wish he was here so I could curl up in his arms and surround myself with the rich scent of his cologne and the light musk that's all him. "I don't think so. He hasn't tried to kill me, so seems unlikely."

He says the words lightly, coated in his typical humor, but his eyes tighten enough that I know there's some real hurt there. Griffin is truly worried my brother won't accept our relationship, and that he'll lose his best friend. I wish I could say I didn't share at least some of that worry, but I have to believe Maddox will pull his head out of his ass and see how happy Griffin makes me.

"He'll be happy for us," I say, keeping my voice soft. "He loves you, and he knows that you're one of the best men in the world. Just wait. I think he'll surprise you."

I hate the doubt I see flickering in Griffin's eyes as he forces a smile. I hate that we're hours away from each other. There's nothing I want more in this moment than to wrap my husband in my arms and reassure him.

"Yeah, I'm sure you're right."

"I'm always right."

He chuckles. "You could be. We'd just have to file the paperwork."

"You're incorrigible."

"No, babe, I'm Griffin. You should know my name by now. I mean, shit, we're married."

I bark out a laugh. "I miss you."

"I miss you too. Can't wait for our trip. You're going to kill that meeting with U of M."

"And you're going to lock that sponsorship deal down."

"I'm just excited to spend time alone with you. The sponsorship is just a bonus."

I feel exactly the same. My heart settles in my chest, content and hopeful. Maybe we didn't have a conventional start to our relationship, but it's real, and amazing, and so much more than I could have hoped for.

I've never been happier.

thirty-eight

MIRA

"So you're meeting with the heads of the hockey program, and Griffin is meeting with that gear company?" Isla glances at me out of the corner of her eye as we stand in line to order coffee.

"Mm-hmm. I'm super nervous, but it's Griffin and Maddy's old coach, so hopefully it will be okay and I won't make a fool of myself." I shouldn't. I've spent days working up what I think is the perfect proposal for the hockey program, along with some mock-ups so I can show them my vision. At the same time, this is the biggest pitch I've ever made, and I can't deny my nerves.

"And it's only you and Griffin going?"

There's an undertone to that question that, once again, leads me to wonder if Isla suspects something is going on between Griffin and me. It's so tempting to spill my guts, but we're planning on announcing our marriage to everyone the week after we get back. I can wait a little longer. Besides, seeing everyone's expressions will make all this subterfuge worth it.

"We won't be there long enough to make it some big thing, so it didn't make sense to invite anyone else. It's just work meetings, nothing fun."

"Of course," Isla says as we make it to the front of the line. "Two roommates traveling together for work meetings."

"Exactly."

She grins as she orders but thankfully drops it. As soon as we have our coffees, we settle at a circular table in the corner of the café, where Isla sets her wedding binder. The date is coming up fast, and it's crunch time. If everything is going to be done on time, it's all hands on deck whenever possible. So of course, I help as much as I can. Isla has become one of my best friends, and she's about to be my sister.

After we get through all the boring, important details, talk turns to parties.

"Jess and Nev are planning your bachelorette party, right?" Isla's best friends have been keeping their plans pretty tight-lipped, so I don't know what to expect, but I'm sure it will be fun.

"Yeah. I told them nothing crazy, but things have a way of getting out of hand with those two." Isla chuckles, her blue eyes taking on the faraway look of someone lost in a memory.

She's probably right. When they decided Isla had spent too much time moping after her jerk of an ex-fiancé, their plan to push her back into the dating pool went a little off the rails. Though that was as much my brother's fault as anything they did.

"I'm sure they'll plan something fun. I can always do some recon if you're worried."

Isla giggles but shakes her head. "That's okay. I trust them. Mostly."

"Speaking of parties…" I clear my throat and shift in my seat. "Griffin and I were thinking it would be fun to have everyone over the week after we get back from Michigan. It's been too long, and he's itching to host something."

My future sister-in-law arches one red eyebrow. "Oh yeah?"

I nod.

"That sounds fun. Do you want us to bring anything?"

"No, we'll have it all covered. I'll text you and Maddy the details in the next couple of days. I just wanted to make sure you didn't have anything coming up that would conflict. Obviously, we'll plan it around the Rogues' schedule."

"I don't have any scheduling conflicts," she says, studying me curiously. "Let me know if you need any help planning it."

I roll my eyes playfully at her. "No way. You have a much more important party to plan. Just make sure you keep the date open."

"Of course we will."

"Great. Now, let's figure out these floral centerpieces. I found a few inspiration photos I think would be perfect with your vibe." Pulling out my phone, I ignore the staccato beat of my heart, and the nerves that fill me from the announcement party talk, and refocus on Isla and Maddy's wedding. Because once we're done here, I'll be heading home to our empty apartment, packing my bags for our trip, and waiting for Griffin to get home from New York so we can head to the airport and fly to Michigan.

Since the next two weeks will be full of nerve-racking moments for me, I'll have plenty of time to freak out about everything. Which is why I throw myself into helping Isla. Because I can't think about my own worries if I'm busy planning her dreams.

"BABY, I'M HOME!"

My stomach does an excited little flip as Griffin's voice precedes him. He strides into our bedroom with a huge smile on his face, even though I can see hints of exhaustion in the lines around his eyes. Setting my book down on our bed, I launch myself into his arms, giggling when he lets out a soft *oomph*.

"Miss me, sunshine?"

"So much," I say before attacking his lips with mine. "I don't like being apart for that long."

Griffin's arms tighten around me, and he sways us while kissing me back with as much hunger as I feel. "Me neither, wifey. Fuck, I missed holding you."

We sway like that for a few minutes, all the tension of the morning fading away as I relax into Griffin's strong, lean body. Neither one of us makes any move to let go until the alarm I set on my phone goes off.

"We should head to the airport."

My sweet, formerly accidental, husband groans. "I feel like I never left."

"I know, and I'm sorry. But just think—once we're there, it's only you and me in a hotel room and two days of exploring where we don't know anyone." Our first day in Michigan is a free day. We're going to explore Ann Arbor, enjoy each other's company, and let loose. The second day, we both have our meetings. Griffin's sponsorship meeting is in the morning, while mine will be right after lunch. His is far enough away from the college that we'll arrive separately, but he's promised to be there, right by my side, while I make my pitch.

It means more to me than he knows.

"I can't wait, baby. Let me grab my other suitcase, then we can head out. Do you have everything you need?"

"Yeah, I'm good."

"Yeah, you are." He smiles affectionately at me, the corners of his eyes crinkling despite his exhaustion. Before heading to our room to grab his suitcase, Griffin leans down and presses a lingering kiss to my forehead. It's a gesture he does often, and one I've come to love. It's so sweet and tender, much like the man himself.

I can't wait to spend the next two days alone with Griffin. No matter what happens at this meeting with the university, I know everything will be okay. My future is looking brighter than ever, and I can't wait to step into it.

thirty-nine

GRIFFIN

Today's the day I propose to my wife.

The jewelry shop called while I was in New York, and I rushed to pick up Mira's engagement ring and our bands as soon as the team's plane touched down. I left the bands at home, but the little black velvet box containing her giant, sparkly diamond is burning a hole in my pocket as we wander around downtown Ann Arbor, trying to decide where to eat breakfast.

I'm not sure where or when or how I'm going to pop the question, but I'll know when the time is right. The stars will align, a chorus of fat little angel babies will sing, and a ray of sunlight will hit my sunshine, illuminating her beautiful face. I'll drop down onto one knee, tell her I love the shit out of her, and ask her to be my wife. On purpose, this time.

"That place looks cute," Mira says, her teeth chattering as she points to a little cafe with a cinnamon bun painted on the window. Pulling her in close to my side to keep her warm in the frigid late-winter morning, I nod.

"Let's do it." It does look cute, but I also just want to get my girl out of the cold. Her adorable little nose is pink, and I can't have her getting sick right before I propose. Or before her pitch to the university bigwigs tomorrow.

Not a single soul gives us more than a cursory glance when we enter the cafe, and I'm reminded of one of the reasons I enjoy traveling so much. Outside of the Twin Cities, it's unlikely anyone will recognize me. It's not like I get mobbed at home, but I get recognized enough that it feels like I can never fully relax. Gotta be on at all times in case some random fan is taking a video or asks for an autograph. It's exhausting. Thank fuck I didn't decide to be a movie star or something. If it's annoying to be recognized occasionally, I can only imagine how much it sucks to be bombarded constantly.

"Here you go," the hostess says with a kind smile, motioning to a booth beside the window. It gives us the perfect view of Main Street's storefronts and the fast-walking patrons trying to hustle so they can get out of the cold. "Your server will be with you shortly."

Mira grins as she opens the menu. Her attention bounces between the laminated booklet in front of her and me. She's fucking beautiful. I have to tell myself not to get down on one knee right here and now, because that's just bacon sizzling on the grill in the kitchen, not angels singing.

"Everything looks so good. How am I supposed to choose?"

Who the hell says she has to choose? I'll order everything on the menu, if that's what she wants. "What are you torn between?"

"The lemon poppyseed pancakes with icing drizzle look amazing. But so does the cinnamon roll French toast." She hums as she scans the menu, and I don't think she realizes she's doing it, but she keeps doing this excited little shimmy in her seat that has me grinning like a lovesick idiot. "Oh, they have spicy biscuits and gravy. Yum."

She's still muttering to herself when the server stops at our table, introduces himself, and asks if we'd like coffee. He fills our mugs, and, noticing Mira is still studying the options, asks if we'd like another minute to decide.

"Nah," I say, smiling. "We'll take the lemon poppyseed pancakes, the cinnamon roll French toast, the biscuits and gravy, a spinach and mushroom omelet, and an order of bacon."

The guy's eyes go wide, and so do Mira's. I get it. It's a lot of food. But I'm determined to make this the best day ever for my wife, which means she doesn't have to choose between breakfast foods. She can take two bites of each and ask for something different for all I care. I have the money to order the whole menu, and I will if that makes her smile.

"Griffin, we don't need all that."

"We'll take whatever we don't finish to go," I tell her. Then, looking at the server, I give him a little nod. "I think that's it, man."

He chuckles, promising it will be ready soon, and leaves me with my bride, who is staring at me with this soft expression that makes me go all gooey and shit.

"You didn't have to order all of that. I would have decided, eventually."

I chuckle at that, and her eyes dance with an answering mirth I love to see. "Maybe, but you're cute when you're indecisive. Plus, I'm totally planning on stealing bites from all of your food. My omelet doesn't sound nearly as good as cinnamon roll French toast."

When the food arrives, it fills the table until there's barely any surface area left, and our server has to have a buddy help him carry an extra tray. Mira giggles as they arrange it all, and I soak up the sound, memorizing the way her eyes crinkle in the corners, the way they sparkle, and the soft flush of her cheeks. Every moment with her like this gets stored away in the part of my brain labeled *never forget*, so I can pull them up whenever we're on the road and I can't be with her.

"Oh my god," she moans after taking a bite of the poppyseed pancakes. "This is so good. You have to try it."

Before I can reach over and spear a forkful for myself, Mira holds out hers and offers me a bite. Leaning over the table, I meet her eyes and take the offered bite. She watches me expectantly, and I can't help it—I close my eyes and groan, because holy shit, that's good.

"Save those noises for the bedroom, hot stuff. All the ladies in the place are looking at you like you're on the menu."

I have to cover my mouth when I laugh, because she's right. There are quite a few women staring at me with expressions ranging from curiosity to hunger to disgust. The disgust is coming from a little old lady with white hair and a kid sitting across from her who must be a granddaughter.

"Oops." I widen my eyes at my wife, and soon we're both laughing. Definitely not dropping to one knee now. Not with Nana over there throwing me the evil eye. That's okay. I have all day.

"WAIT, WE'RE GOING WHERE?"

Mira's eyes are wide as she turns her body to face me from the passenger seat of the rental car.

"The Creature Conservancy. It's like a little zoo with a bunch of exotic animals. I scheduled a private tour, and guess what?"

"What?"

"We even get to pet some of the animals."

My beautiful wife lets out a happy little squeal and does a shimmy in her seat. The jewelry box in my pocket digs into my hip, begging to be pulled out. Maybe this place will give me the right opportunity to propose. I wonder if there are any monkeys that are trained? Maybe one could bring the ring out to her?

Nah, that seems risky.

Mira has her phone out, telling me all about the animals we can expect to see when we park. She's particularly excited that they have several sloths. Those weird little fuckers *are* pretty adorable. I'm excited to see the reindeer.

"Welcome to The Creature Conservancy," a young guy, who appears to be in his early twenties, says when we step inside the large building. He pushes his thick-framed glasses up the bridge of his nose, his gaze skimming right over me and landing squarely on my wife. He offers her a lopsided smile and sticks out a hand. "I'm Matt. I'll be leading your tour today."

"Thanks, Matt." I grab his hand and give it a firm shake, which makes Mira giggle. Her body vibrates against mine as I wrap an arm around her and pull her close. "I'm Griffin, and this is my wife, Mira."

Mira sucks in a sharp little breath at being publicly introduced as my wife. And I get it. Saying it out loud was like a jolt of electricity zinging through my body. Holy shit, that felt good. And so does knowing I made my girl blush. She doesn't shake Matt's hand but offers him a little wave.

Poor Matt looks disappointed that Mira is married. Not that I blame him. Hell, I'd be disappointed, too, if I was him. But I'm not, thank god, and I get to make love to this goddess whenever I want. Sucks to suck.

"Right, well, if you'll both follow me, we'll start in our reptiles room."

We follow our guide through the conservancy, stopping often so Mira can coo over some scaled, feathered, and furry creature or other. We take tons of photos. She focuses on the animals, but I focus on her. My camera roll is going to be filled with my wife by the time this trip is over. We take selfies, and Matt takes several of us together in front of different enclosures.

I think one of my favorite moments is when we're introduced to Scooter the warthog. The expression on Mira's face is absolutely priceless.

"Oh my god, he's so ugly he's cute!" she cries when she sees the thing. He's got little tufts of wild hair that stick out all over his head, long, curved tusks that jut from his mouth, and a body that's covered in sparse, coarse hair, except for the dark mane along his back.

Ugly isn't a strong enough word.

"You think that thing is cute?" How is it cute? Women are weird.

"Of course he is. Look at his lil' snout." She leans forward and coos at the thing like he's some adorable little baby she wants to cuddle and kiss.

"He needs to trim his ear hair." I wrinkle my nose at him. "A little manscaping could go a long way, dude."

Cracking up, we barely hear anything our guide says about Scooter, too lost in each other. Just when I'm considering pulling the ring from my pocket, Scooter lifts his whip-like tail and lets one rip. I swear to god, it's the longest, loudest fart I've ever heard.

Fucking warthog.

Okay, so that wasn't the perfect moment. That's fine. The next thing we're going to do is feed a few macaws. That'll be romantic. I'll propose then.

The macaws are much larger than I thought they'd be. They're beautiful—a feathery rainbow of colors with long tails and sharp beaks—but they also freak me out a bit. Their little clawed feet are creepy, and their talons pinch when they perch on my arm.

"You're so beautiful," Mira coos to the gentle bird she holds. The creature preens under her praise and leans into each soft touch she gives as she runs the side of her fingers down its neck and chest. I can relate. There's really nothing better than being stroked by Mira someday-she'll-agree-to-change-her-last-name Graves.

The rainbow dinosaur gently plucks a blueberry out of Mira's palm, eating it as daintily as a bird can.

Mine pecks at my watch, ignoring the berries in my

palm entirely. The damn thing manages to catch an arm hair in its sharp beak. "Motherfucker. You little shit!"

Matt, the guide, snickers behind his hand. The dude's lucky I'm a nice guy, because if I wasn't, he wouldn't be getting a tip for that shit. "Looks like Spike is feeling a bit feisty today. Sorry about that."

"It's fine," I grumble, tucking my watch beneath my shirt sleeve. Turning my attention to the feathered fiend, I glare at him. "Do you want these berries or not? I guarantee they taste better than my watch."

Spike side-eyes me but seems to listen. He bends down to snatch a berry from my palm, keeping one beady little eye on me the whole time.

"You have to pet him," Mira says. "Look at mine. She likes it."

"Right. Just pet the mini raptor with rainbow feathers. Whose idea was this, anyway?"

The bright, tinkling laugh I get in response makes dealing with this rude bird worthwhile. As long as Mira's happy, I'm happy. And judging by the massive smile she's sporting and the sparkle in her eyes, Mira is very happy.

"All right, buddy. Time to shoo. I think this is the moment." I drop the last two blueberries from my hand and flap my arm, trying to get the bird to fly away while I reach for the ring in my right pocket.

Spike, the little shit, squawks with displeasure as he flaps his wings and launches off my arm. Indignant at my treatment, Spike grabs at my hair with his beak before flying above my head, circling me. I ignore him, my fingers clutched around the little velvet box, and take a step toward my wife.

Spike circles again, and just as I'm about to get down

on one knee, the feathered bastard squawks again, then shits on my head.

On. My. Head.

"Sonofabitch," I growl, letting go of the ring box in my pocket. I'm not proposing to my wife with a glop of parrot shit dripping down the side of my face. No way in hell. That is a story that would never die, and I'd never live it down.

"Oh!" Mira covers her mouth, her wide green eyes tracking the slow drip of the bird shit as it streaks down my temple and onto my cheek. "Oh, no."

Matt chuckles, unable to contain it this time, but to his credit, he hurries over to a table off to the side of the room and grabs a package of wet wipes. Holding them out to me, he winces when he sees my expression. "You know, they say it's good luck to be pooped on by a bird?"

Yeah. It's great fucking luck, Matt. Great fucking luck.

Taking the wipes from him, Mira hurries over to me and wipes the slop off my face. She cleans my skin with another wipe before grabbing a third and cleaning the mess out of my hair. Her sassy lips twitch with suppressed laughter the entire time.

"Think this is funny, wife?"

She shakes her head. Little liar. She can't even say the word no because she has her lips pressed so tightly together to keep the laughter at bay. It's a battle she finally loses with a little giggle snort that turns into full-bellied laughter.

"I'm sorry," she says, gasping between bouts of laughter. "It's just, you should have seen your face." She makes her eyes go wide, her jaw drops open, and her top lip curls as she imitates what I must have looked like when I got shat on.

"Keep laughing, baby, and I'll spank that luscious ass later."

It doesn't make her laughter stop, but it does make a pretty pink flush work up from her chest, all the way to the tips of her ears.

So I didn't find the perfect moment to propose today. But I did learn that my wife seems turned on by the idea of being spanked, so it's not a total loss.

I keep that little tidbit of information locked away for later while our guide leads us out of the bird enclosure and toward the sloths, Mira's fingers intertwined with mine, a massive smile on her beautiful face.

The ring continues to burn a hole in my pocket.

forty

GRIFFIN

Our day together was amazing, but every time I considered proposing, something would ruin the moment. Whatever, it's fine. I'll propose tomorrow after Mira kills her pitch. She'll be riding a high from booking a huge job, and I'll take her somewhere romantic to celebrate. I have time.

Right now? Now I'm going to spank my wife's sweet ass for laughing at me when the damn bird shat on my head, and then I'm going to kiss it better.

The moment we're in our hotel suite, I shut the door behind us, turn to my wife with a wicked grin, and back her up against the door. Caging her in with my body, need thrumming through my veins like electricity in a live wire, I lower my head to meet her eyes.

"Alone at last."

Mira gasps when I press my hips into her and nip at her jaw. She looks up at me with those big, green eyes, pupils dilated with instant desire, and I'm gone. Deceased. Absolutely fucking done for this woman.

"Do you know how many times today I almost pushed you into a bathroom and fucked you silly against the door? How much restraint it took not to slip my hand beneath the waistband of your jeans and dip my fingers into your pussy while we were at dinner?" My fingers go to the button of her pants and flick them open. Mira shifts, rubbing her thighs together as I drag the zipper down. "Do you think you could have kept quiet if I finger-fucked you in a crowded restaurant?"

"I-I..." She stammers, breathing picking up, dark lashes fluttering with every kiss I drag along her jaw and every brush of my thumb along her stomach.

"You what, baby?" I tug her jeans down her hips, dropping to my knees so I can pull them the rest of the way off. Mira toes off her shoes but lets me do the rest. Her panties fall to the floor in a puddle with the denim, leaving her pussy bare for me. Fuck. This will never get old. Seeing her naked and needy, thighs shifting against each other, the scent of her arousal blooming in the air like a decadent flower. "Tell me. Do you think you could stay quiet?"

Glassy eyes hooded with raw, undiluted need stare down at me. She nods.

"Words, sunshine."

"Y-yes."

A wicked grin slowly morphs my face into something primal. "Oh, you think so? How about we put that to the test? And every time you fail and make a noise, I'll bend you over my knee and spank that pretty ass of yours."

Mira lets out a little squeak when my fingers dig into the soft globes of her ass, kneading and spreading her.

There's no fucking way she's staying silent. She's never silent when I fuck her.

"You want to spank me?"

"If the idea turns you on as much as it does me, then yes. Fuck yes, baby." I study her face, because as much as I believe she'll enjoy a spanking, it's only sexy if she's into it. If she wants it as much as I do. "What do you think?"

Mira shifts, her thighs squeezing again, and her hands move unconsciously to play with her breasts. "Yes. Fuck, the idea of it shouldn't turn me on as much as it does, but the answer is yes."

Grinning, I lean forward and press a kiss to her lower belly above her mound. "Never feel bad for exploring what makes you feel good, baby. I'll try anything with you. Everything. Now, take your shirt and bra off so I can play with those perfect tits."

My wife hurries to do as I ask, and in moments, she's standing in front of me, naked and beautiful, with her back pressed against the door. Perfect.

"Spread your legs," I demand. "Use the doorframe to brace yourself. I'm going to eat your perfect pussy right here against the door, so you'd better be quiet, or anyone walking by in the hallway will hear you."

Mira sucks her bottom lip between her teeth, a brief flicker of hesitation puckering her brow before it once again smooths out and lust overtakes every other emotion. When she doesn't immediately spread her creamy thighs, I arch an eyebrow and give one leg a tap. She sucks in a deep breath, then does as I ask.

"That's my good girl," I rasp as I inch forward and lift one of her legs, letting it rest over my shoulder with her foot against my back. "Shit, baby. Look at you, so wet and ready for me."

Mira braces herself against the doorframe as I press on her belly with one hand to keep her steady and drag my thumb through her soaking folds with the other. She lets out a whine that shoots straight to my dick when I apply gentle pressure to her clit.

"Quiet," I warn her before leaning forward and slowly licking her pussy. I can't hold back my grin when she gasps and her head flops back against the door with a soft *thud*. There's no fucking way she's keeping quiet. Not by the time I'm done with her.

With one hand keeping Mira pinned to the door, I use the other to grab her ass and angle her hips up so I have better access to what I want. With her knee over my shoulder and the more exaggerated tilt of her hips, she's open wide for me. I take full advantage, alternating between nipping at her inner thigh and lapping at her wet slit. Her soft little gasps become quiet little moans as each lick of my tongue brings her closer to the edge.

I can do better.

Letting go of Mira's ass, I press two fingers into her warmth as my tongue lashes her clit. The moan she gives me is far louder than the stifled noises she's been making until this point, and I grin up at her wickedly, her arousal covering my mouth.

"Oh, baby, they definitely heard that in the hall. This is your last warning to be quiet, or I'm going to bend that perfect ass over my knee and make it red."

"Shit," she whimpers, covering her mouth with both hands.

It won't be enough.

Determined to make her scream, I push a third finger inside of her, curling them to find that magical spot, while my lips latch on to her clit and I suck. Hard.

"Oh, Griffin, fuck!" There's nothing quiet about my girl's garbled scream. She's close to the edge, and I know just how I want to get her there.

Pushing her knee off my shoulder, I rise to my feet and pick Mira up, throwing her stomach over my shoulder, her ass close enough to bite and her breasts pressed against my back.

"Griffin," she shrieks, only to yelp louder when I turn my head and sink my teeth into the soft flesh that's been tempting me all night. She moans when I lick it to make it better.

When I get to the sofa in the middle of the large suite, I let her slide down my fully clothed body. She watches me with dazed, glassy eyes as I sit at the edge of the couch, my knees spread. I crook my finger at her. "Come here, wife."

Hesitantly, she takes a step closer. She's obviously turned on but unsure of what I want from her.

I pat my knees. "You didn't do what I told you, baby. You were a very bad girl, and now I have to punish you. Face down, ass up. Now."

Fuck, the way her eyes widen with the most fleeting expression of hesitation before melting into a raw need that makes my dick twitch. I watch her to make sure all that hesitation is gone before grabbing her hand and tugging her down until her upper body is supported by my knees. Her head and shoulders hang off one side, her ass hangs off the other.

It's one of the hottest things I've ever seen. My wife is completely naked and willingly at my mercy while I'm fully dressed and eliciting gasps and whines from her with each soft drag of my fingers up and down her spine, over the sides of her breasts, and down the curve of her butt. She stiffens slightly when I let my palm rest open on the fullest part of it.

"You told me you could be quiet, baby." I drag my palm in a circular motion over the curve of her, letting my fingers dip into the gap between her legs and dragging them through her dripping slit. She sucks in a breath and her hips buck, looking for the release I withheld from her when she made too much noise. I dip my middle finger into her wetness and drag it up to her clit, circling, working her back up. "I told you there'd be consequences if you didn't listen."

"I'm sorry," she whines, her voice breathy and petulant. My sexy little brat.

"I don't think you are." I stop playing with her clit, grinning when she whines again. "But you will be."

With an open palm, I smack Mira's ass. Not hard enough to hurt, but enough to make her soft skin flush with color. She jolts against my lap and lets out a startled squeak that turns into a whimper when I rub her pink skin.

"Good girls get fucked. Good girls get orgasms."

"I can be a good girl," she pleads, wiggling in my lap.

"Can you?"

"Yes." Her tone is still petulant. Still bratty.

We can fix that. "See, I don't think you've learned your lesson yet, baby girl. I think you're playing me right now. You're not sorry at all, you just want my tongue back in your needy little cunt."

"Griffin..."

The smack I give her ass is harder this time. It leaves a faint pink outline of my hand, and Mira moans loudly, letting me know she's as into this as I am. Thank fuck, because I'm not ready for this game to end. I raise my hand and spank her other cheek, then do it again.

"Oh. Griffin, I... Please, I need..."

"I know what you need," I say, dipping my fingers between her thighs. She's even wetter now. Dripping for me.

With one last, stinging smack to her ass, I lift Mira up and carry her to the back of the couch. Once her feet hit the floor, I press on the center of her back between her shoulder blades and bend her over the back of the sofa. She moves willingly, turning her face so one cheek rests on the cushion as she looks up at me.

Using my foot, I nudge her stance wider, groaning at the sight of her swollen pink pussy. Never able to completely let go of her sass—which I love—Mira wiggles her pink ass.

"Please, husband. Please, I need your cock."

There's a wild animal prowling beneath my skin, desperate to claim her, mark her, own her. The same way she owns me. With a growl, I unzip my jeans and pull out my dick. I don't even bother pulling the pants all the way off, only tugging them far enough down to fuck my wife.

"You need my cock, baby?" I palm her ass before spanking it once more. Mira gasps and groans. She nods, unintelligible words flowing from her lips. "Then, beg. Tell me how sorry you are that you didn't do what you were told."

"I'm sorry," she says, her voice cracking with frustration and need. "I tried to be good, I swear. I tried to be quiet. But you made me feel so good, babe, and I couldn't hold it in. I'm sorry."

"Apology accepted," I say as I grip her hips and slam inside of her with one brutal thrust.

Mira cries out, the sound muffled as she screams into the cushion, her pussy tightening around me once I'm balls deep. I don't give her time to adjust to the intrusion. Not this time. Not when I'm so far gone. I'm feral with need for her. My fingers dig into her hips and ass as I pound into her again and again, and I know it'll leave a mark, but I can't seem to feel anything but pleased by the thought.

"Look at you," I praise. "You're taking my cock like such a good girl. Keeping yourself quiet as I fuck you hard and deep. My perfect wife."

With her face turned to the side, I watch, enthralled, as Mira's eyes roll back into her head at the praise and the slamming of my hips against her ass. Reaching around her hips, I use two fingers to circle her clit. I'm so close to the edge. I need her to come, because I'm not going to last. The muscles in my thighs and back tense with the pleasure I'm trying to hold at bay.

"Come on my cock, baby. I want to feel you clamp down on me as I fill your pussy up."

Mira's muffled curses and pleas only add to my pleasure. Her fingers scrabble to grip the couch cushions as I fuck her hard and fast and play with her clit. When she begins to flutter around me, I have to grit my teeth so I don't blow.

"Griffin, I'm gonna... Oh, god. Oh, fuck."

When my wife screams into the cushions, her pussy clamping down on me in her own primal claiming, I lose the battle with my control and come with a roar. I thrust into her once, twice, then still, spilling in her fluttering heat with a guttural moan.

Leaning over Mira, I press open-mouthed kisses along her spine while I rock into her gently with my softening cock. "You're amazing."

She's so spent, she only manages to mumble something incoherent.

"Come on, sunshine. Let's get you cleaned up, then I'll feed you. I'm sure you're hungry after all of that. Let me take care of you."

Her smile is soft and trusting, and I can't hold the words in any longer. Not for another second. So I let them out as I scoop her up into my arms.

"I love you, Mira. So fucking much."

Wide green eyes blink up at me, colored with something that looks like shock. "You love me?"

"Yeah, baby. For a while now."

Mira's breath catches, then she wraps her arms around my neck and presses her face into the space between my head and shoulders. "I love you, too, Griffin. I love you too."

I'm not sure how we make it into the bathroom, or how I manage to turn the shower on with my wife cradled in my arms, both of us stealing desperate kisses from the other, but we do. Maybe we float there. Who the hell knows? All I know for sure is that I've never felt happier. Nothing has ever felt so right. And we stay up far later than we should as we show our love for each other over and over before falling into the most peaceful sleep I've ever experienced.

Tonight, I told my wife I love her. Tomorrow, I propose.

forty-one

MIRA

Despite yesterday being the most fun I've had in ages—not to mention some of the best sex I've ever had—it does nothing to calm my current nerves. Because today is my first big pitch to an organization that could change the course of my business.

Yes, I've worked with some relatively high-profile athletes from the Rogues, and yes, I finally completed the job for the baseball team in Georgia, but this is next level. This is a NCAA Division 1 hockey team at a major university, and it could lead to working with their football team and possibly other teams in their athletic program. And if I do a good job? Who knows what it could lead to? This is a potentially life-changing meeting, and I can't seem to stop overthinking it.

"Hey." Griffin grabs my hand as he drives to the university. "You're going to kill it, sunshine. You have no reason to be nervous."

I know he believes that, which is the sweetest thing ever, but I'm not so convinced. "It's a big deal. What if I mess it up?"

My husband rolls his eyes. "Baby, you won't mess it up. You're smart, talented, and insanely creative. These guys will be lucky to bring you on for this project. Just remember that. Plus, I'll be there for moral support. Not that you need me."

He's wrong, though. I *do* need him. More and more each day. And knowing he'll be there, sitting beside me as strong, silent support, is everything. I just wish his own meeting wasn't before mine. He offered to bring me with him, but I've decided to have him drop me off on the campus. I'll grab a coffee and walk around for an hour or so. I want to get a better feel for the vibes and culture of the place so I can make last-minute tweaks to my proposal if necessary.

"I wish I didn't have to leave you for my meeting."

That makes me smile because I know he means it. Griffin has been almost more excited about this opportunity than I have been. He's so supportive and sweet. I'm not sure how I got this lucky. He really is everything I could want or need in a partner. And he's mine.

"I know, but this deal is important for you too. I'll be fine on my own for a bit, and you'll be back in time for my meeting."

"Of course I will. I wouldn't miss it." Eyes still on the road, Griffin lifts my hand to his lips and kisses it. "I'm so fucking proud of you, sunshine."

His praise makes me light up. I'm practically glowing from within. "I'm proud of you too. And thanks for believing in me."

"I'll always believe in you. I'm your biggest fan. I hope you know that by now." Griffin gifts me a radiant smile that I want to lose myself in. And I probably would, if not for the buzzing of his phone in the center console of the car we've rented. "Can you see who that is and what they want?"

I tap on the text that popped up on the screen and see that it's from my brother. "It's Maddy. He wants to do a guys' night when we get back. And he wants to know if you'll plan his bachelor party."

Griffin chuckles. The sound rolls through my body and lights me up. "Tell him to name the time and place for guys' night and I'll be there, and of course I'm gonna plan his bachelor party. Who the hell does he think I am?"

Sniggering, I type out a response to my brother and hit send. As I do, Griffin's phone flashes a warning that it only has twenty percent battery life left.

"I think you're a guy who didn't charge his phone last night."

With a wince, Griffin glances at his phone in my hand. "Ah, shit. I got distracted by your pretty cunt and forgot to plug it in."

"At least you have a good excuse. I guess we'll have to refrain from texting each other all morning so you don't end up with a dead phone."

"Probably shouldn't be texting while I'm in that meeting, anyway. Though, for my wife, I'd leave any meeting to respond to a text."

The sincerity in Griffin's tone makes my heart skip a beat or two, and I have to restrain myself from grabbing him in a hug. Probably not the best idea when he's driving. So I do something better.

"I love you," I tell him softly.

"I love you, too, baby girl. I love you more than anything."

"Anything?" Though my tone is teasing, there's a scared little girl, deep inside me, who was abandoned by the man who was supposed to love her more than anything once before, and she needs to hear this. I wish she didn't, but she does.

Griffin is serious when he grabs my hand and strokes his thumb along mine. He alternates between watching me and the road.

"I love you more than sunrises or dreary fall days. I love you more than my favorite ice cream during a heat wave, that moment a couple gets together in romance novels, or the quiet pleasure of taping up a new stick. I love you more than stepping out onto fresh ice or winning with a full arena at home. More than hockey. More than *anything*. You're it for me, Mira, and I'll do whatever it takes to prove that to you."

I can't seem to swallow past the lump in my throat as my eyes well up with tears. He sounds so earnest.

"And today, I'm going to show you just how much I love you by showing up for your pitch, sitting beside you for moral support, and cheering you on." His thumb circles my hand slowly, gently, causing goose bumps to rise on my flesh. "Then I'm going to keep showing up, keep cheering you on, keep being there for you. Every single day."

"Griffin..." A single tear falls from my lashes, and I quickly wipe it away. I don't want to have to redo my makeup.

My sweet, no-longer-accidental husband lifts my hand and kisses it, his eyes serious and filled with understanding. "We're here, love. Should I drop you off at my favorite coffee shop?"

I nod, words failing me.

"Wish I could come with you," he says quietly.

"You'll be back with me soon."

"I will," Griffin says. "I promise."

MY SAPPY MOOD DOESN'T LEAVE ME AS I WANDER the campus my husband and brother met on. Griffin gave me a list of his favorite places, and I've visited almost all of them. It's a busy campus. Students walk around, laughing and mingling, even in the cold winter temperatures.

When it gets closer to the meeting time, I grab coffees for Griffin and me and begin my walk to the Yost Ice Arena. Griffin set everything up so that the coach and administrators I'll be meeting with will give me a tour of the facility before he arrives and meets us in one of the office areas.

When I push through the doors of the arena, I'm greeted by a large, jovial looking man with brown hair peppered with strands of gray. He notes the laptop bag slung over my shoulders, the coffees in my hand, and the nervous look on my face, and smiles brightly.

"Mira?"

I nod, returning his smile. "Hi, yes. I'm Mira."

The man extends a hand to shake but chuckles when he realizes mine are full. "I'm Troy Roberts, the head coach for the Wolverines. Why don't we put your stuff in the office, and I'll give you a tour?"

"That sounds great."

Troy smiles again and motions for me to follow him. He leads me to a small conference room where I leave my things on the table, then we walk through the arena. While telling me about the history of the building—how it started out as a field house and has been renovated several times—he points out areas of interest. He's a fantastic tour guide, and his kind demeanor puts me at ease.

"Griffin said that you're Maddox Graves's sister?"

I nod.

Troy smiles. "He was always such a serious kid. Has that changed?"

"He's engaged to the sweetest woman ever," I reply. "So he's still serious, but he's less of a grump."

That has the coach chuckling. "Yeah, I suppose he could be a little grumpy. And Griffin said you and he are…"

I try not to laugh at the way Troy is assessing me out of the corner of his eye. Not sure what Griffin told him, but since we're coming clean to everyone we love next week, what's the harm in telling the truth now? "We're married. It's kind of a secret."

Troy's eyes widen, as does the smile on his face. "You're married? I knew that boy was being cagey with me. Hell, that's fantastic news. Congratulations."

"Thank you."

"If I'd have known, I would have insisted my wife and I take the two of you out for a celebratory dinner."

I'm blushing now. I can feel the heat creeping up my cheeks. "Oh, that isn't necessary, but thank you so much. We're only here for such a short time, we wouldn't want to put you out."

Troy shakes his head as we make our way back up to

the conference room. "It wouldn't have been any trouble. Next time you're here, we'll schedule something. I have a good feeling about this meeting and suspect we'll be working with each other moving forward."

His easy confidence soothes some of my nerves, but not for long. They ramp up again as we walk into the conference room to see two other large men and an elegant woman already seated around the table.

No Griffin, yet. But the meeting doesn't officially start for another ten minutes. He'll be here. He promised.

***

"THANK YOU SO MUCH FOR YOUR TIME," I SAY TO Troy, trying to keep my lower lip from trembling.

"We're looking forward to working with you." The older man gives me a friendly, encouraging pat on the shoulder. As he walks away, I look at my phone for the hundredth time and wince when the coach looks back at me and catches me doing it.

Griffin never showed.

I won't say I bombed the pitch, because I didn't, but it could have gone better. I must have checked my phone and the clock every thirty seconds as it got closer and closer to the official start of the meeting, and I hated the sympathetic looks Troy kept shooting my way. I texted Griffin several times, only to have them go unread.

I was so distracted by wondering where he was, so out of sorts because he'd promised he'd be there, that I fumbled my words for the first five minutes and nearly knocked my laptop on the floor with an ill-timed swing of my arm.

And now, here I am, hurrying out of the arena, trying not to cry like a little baby because my husband missed the meeting he promised he'd show up for. I don't know if I'm more worried, upset with him, or angry at myself.

What if Griffin is dead in a ditch somewhere? He'd never stand me up for something this important. And if, god forbid, he is, what kind of person does that make me that I'm upset about a missed meeting and angry at him for not calling?

You can't make phone calls if you're bleeding out on the side of the road.

Get it together, Mira. This is not helping.

With shaking fingers, I unlock my phone and call Griffin. It goes straight to voicemail. I know his battery was low, but he promised not to use it so he could get in contact with me. It hasn't been long enough for the thing to die. So why isn't he answering? When his voicemail message plays in my ear, I let out a frustrated little growl, hang up, and try again.

Straight to voicemail. Again.

This time, I leave a message. I hate the way my voice shakes. Hate the way it feels like everything inside of me shakes as I push through the arena doors and stumble outside into the cold.

"Griffin? Where are you? I'm done with my meeting. I... You weren't here. Are you okay? Did something happen? How am I supposed to know where you are or if you're okay if you don't answer your phone?" Glancing up at the darkening sky, I shiver as wind whips through my hair and bites my skin through my coat. The weather is taking a turn for the cold and gloomy, matching my mood.

And making my worry increase. "Just... Call me when you get this. Please be okay."

Unable to sit still, I pace the area outside of the arena while I stare at my phone. Five minutes go by, then ten, then twenty. It's freezing, and I can't stand out in this cold anymore. I order a ride back to the hotel because I don't know what else to do. Maybe they'll have a message from him?

By the time I get back to the hotel, I'm practically vibrating with worry, and it only increases when the front desk tells me they don't have any messages from my husband. Hurrying to our room, I throw the door open but find the suite empty. Griffin's bags are still here, so I know he hasn't left, but he's not here.

"What if he's hurt?" I tug at my hair, pacing the room. "What if he's hurt and I'm not there?"

My phone vibrates in my hand, and all the air leaves my chest in a *whoosh*. It has to be Griffin.

Except, it's not.

LEXI

I thought Griffin was done with the hookup stuff? He better not be ditching you for random women while you're on this trip together.

Bile rises in my throat. *What?* Why would she say something like that?

LEXI

The stupid Rogues' fan sites are all
speculating because he hasn't been
pictured with a woman like this in

months.

What is she talking about? My pulse roars in my ears
and my hands shake as I type out a response.

ME

What do you mean he's been pictured
with a woman?

LEXI

Is he with you?

No. I don't know where he is. He was
supposed to be at that meeting with me,
but he never showed. IDK if he's hurt or if
something happened… What photo are
you talking about, Lexi?

Shit. I wasn't trying to upset you. I just
thought he was done with the random
hookups and wondered what the
deal was.

The photo, Lexi. Show me the damn
photo.

My heart plummets to the ugly carpet floor a moment
later when the photo comes through. It's a shot of Griffin
and some pretty blonde woman. His arm is around her
shoulders, and she's looking up at him like he's her knight
in shining armor. He's staring down at her with a look of
genuine concern. Neither seems aware that they're being

photographed.

This can't be happening.

It can't be what it looks like.

ME

Where did you see that photo, Lex?

LEXI

...

It popped up on social media. On one of
the Rogues' fan sites I follow to make
sure the women don't get all gross about
Ryder.

When?

Five minutes ago.

Five minutes ago. This photo was posted five minutes ago, which means it can't have been taken too long before that. Which means Griffin was more than likely with this woman when he promised he'd be with me at my pitch. The one he secured for me. The one with his old coach.

My throat feels like it's closing. My eyes tear up. And my heart squeezes painfully in my chest. Then my mouth waters and bile rises up my throat. I barely make it into the bathroom in time to puke my guts up. All the while, my phone buzzes with incoming messages from Lexi.

LEXI

I'm sorry. I shouldn't have said anything.
I'm sure there's a reasonable explanation.
Griffin cares about you. He would never
miss something important if he promised
to be there. Not without a good excuse. I
just thought it was weird after the stuff
he's said lately.

Are you okay?

Am I okay?

Not even close.

Even though I'm terrified of what he'll say if he answers, I call Griffin one more time. I'm not sure if I'm relieved or furious when it goes straight to voicemail.

He ditched me. He made a promise that he'd be there, and he broke it. For some blonde woman with legs for days. He set this whole thing up, then couldn't even be bothered to show. After telling me he loves me.

What a fucking joke.

I should have known all of this was too good to be true. Should have known he'd disappoint me. Just like my dad. Just like every other man in my life, outside of my brother.

Tears blur my vision as I pull up the airline app. I'm not thinking straight, I know I'm not, but my mind and body are telling me to flee, to run away, to get as far away from Griffin Wright as I can so he can't hurt me anymore today. In minutes, I've changed my flight to the first available out of Michigan, and then I make the call I'm dreading more than anything in the world.

He picks up on the third ring.

"Hey, Mi-Mi. How's it going, squirt?"

"Maddy?" There's no hiding the tremor in my voice, or

the thick, sticky quality of my words. And if all that isn't bad enough, I hiccup a sob at the end of his name.

Instantly in full protector mode, Maddox asks, "Mira? What's wrong? Are you okay? Where are you?" His concern for me nearly rips me in half.

"Can I stay with you and Isla for a while?"

Heavy silence falls over the line, and then my brother's voice takes on a brutal quality that would be terrifying if it wasn't in defense of me. "What the fuck did Wright do?"

"I can't—I don't… Just, can you pick me up from the airport in three hours? Please?"

"Of course, Mi-Mi. Of course I can. Are you okay?"

Maddox growls when I sob through the phone.

"No, I don't think I am. But I will be."

Somehow, I will be.

I just need to hold it together long enough to get out of here and home to Maddox. Then I can let myself break. Then I can figure out what in the hell happened. Then I can tell my brother about my stupid, drunken marriage to his best friend.

And once I've done all that, I'll file for divorce and never, *ever* let myself do something so life-alteringly stupid. Ever again.

forty-two

GRIFFIN

SHIT. SHIT, SHIT, SHIT!

Breakaway Hockey's head of marketing lets out a shriek as the elevator lurches, the lights inside flicker, then the whole thing shudders to a stop and goes dark. Silence fills the dark car, broken only by Serena's increasingly fast breaths.

"You okay, Miss Kent?"

Her laugh is breathy and a little wild. "Serena. Seriously, please call me Serena."

"Right. You doing okay, Serena? You sound like you're freaking out a little." She's not the only one. The meeting with Breakaway went longer than expected, and I have to bust ass if I'm going to make it to Mira's pitch on time.

And I *will* make it there on time. I promised my wife, and I keep my promises.

Serena sounds a little wheezy this time when she says, "I'm uh, I'm a little claustrophobic. Especially if it's dark."

Well, shit.

"Why don't you turn your phone's flashlight on? I'm sure that would help, right?"

She does another one of those borderline-crazy laughs. "I'm sure it would, but I left my phone up on my desk since I thought I'd just be walking you out and going right back up. I'm sure the elevator will start working again any minute."

I sure as hell hope so. I take out my phone to text Mira and let her know I'm running late and why, typing out a quick message telling my girl I'm stuck in an elevator with the head of marketing, that I'm sorry, and I'll get there as soon as possible.

Except, the message fails to send.

"Shit."

Serena looks my way, and even in the dim light of my cell phone screen, I can see the sweat beading on her brow. She looks tense. I'm down to seventeen percent battery life, and I need to conserve it, but what kind of asshole would I be if I turned it off and put it in my pocket when it could help this poor woman stop panicking?

"This whole building sucks for cell service, but the elevator is a straight-up black hole," she tells me with a commiserating wince. "I don't think you'll be able to text or call anyone for help."

As if saying that made her realize something, she reaches over and pushes the red emergency button. A ringing sound fills the car, and soon a man is answering, his voice filtering out of the speaker on the wall panel and filling the space. He asks if there's an emergency, and after Serena explains that we're stuck and the power is out, promises help is on the way.

"How long do you think it will take for them to get us out of here?" the poor woman to my left asks, hugging herself like a scared child. She's shaking now, slight tremors racking her body.

"I'm sure it won't take long at all. Here, I'll put my phone's flashlight on." Mira will understand. She won't be happy if I miss her pitch, but once I explain, she'll understand. And I know if she was here, she'd tell me to use my phone's flashlight. Even if it does drain the battery. "Why don't you sit down, Miss Kent?"

"Serena." She huffs out a shaky laugh, but she does as I suggest and starts to lower herself to the floor. When her knees shake and she almost falls on her ass, I reach out and help her. "I hope to hell someone has cleaned this floor recently."

It's my turn to chuckle at that. "Something to talk to maintenance about after they get us out, I guess."

"Yeah."

We fall silent, and I rock on my heels to burn up some of the nervous energy coursing through my body. I want to get out of here. I can't let Mira down.

Even though it's probably pointless, I try texting her again. This time, I warn her that I may run out of battery life and that if I don't make it to her pitch, to head to the coffee shop and meet me there. Of course, the message fails to send.

"Crap."

"You okay?" Serena looks up at me. "Please don't tell me you're also claustrophobic."

"No, it's not that. I'm supposed to be meeting my wife in like fifteen minutes at the university campus, and I'm worried I won't make it." Restless energy has me running my hand through my hair.

"Your wife, huh? I didn't realize you were married." Serena sounds curious, and I kick myself for saying anything before we've gone public with our friends and family, but this is a marketing exec I'm talking to. They've just signed me on to represent their company. They won't do anything to mess with my image or the relationship we just forged.

"Uh yeah, it's not public knowledge yet, so I'd appreciate it if that didn't leave this elevator." I give her a smile that probably looks more like a grimace.

"Of course. Breakaway would never overstep like that." The lights in the elevator flicker twice, then plunge us back into darkness. Serena shudders and closes her eyes. "Tell me about her. I need a distraction."

So I do. For the next hour, I tell Breakaway Hockey's head of marketing all about my wife. I tell her about her work, her sense of humor, the way she makes me feel like I can do anything. I pull the little black velvet box out of my pocket and show her the engagement ring I'm going to give to Mira today. Tell her about getting married in Vegas—leaving out the part about how we were drunk and I basically blackmailed my wife to stay married to me—and how I want to give Mira a real engagement and wedding. I talk until my phone dies and we're encased in darkness, then I keep talking to keep both of us distracted and only stop when, finally, the lights turn back on and the elevator jolts to life.

When the doors open on the ground floor, I help Serena to her feet, and when she almost crumples to the ground after spending over an hour fighting off a panic attack, I wrap my arm around her shoulder and grip her elbow with my other hand and walk her to her toward the crowd of waiting people. A man with jet black hair and a furrowed brow shouts her name when he sees us, and then he sweeps her out of my arms and holds her close.

"Are you okay?" he asks her.

Serena nods. "Yeah, I'm good. Griffin here helped me fight off a panic attack."

The dark-haired main turns my way and extends a hand, which I shake. "Thank you. Thank you so much. I was so worried. She is deathly afraid of being stuck in small spaces."

Serena nods. "I'd rather walk up thirty flights of stairs than take an elevator ever again. You're never getting me back in one of those things."

When I chuckle, she turns to me with a scowl, but it quickly turns into a smile.

"Thank you, Griffin, really. I'm looking forward to working with you, and we'll be in touch. Now, go find your wife."

Shit. My wife. With a nod of my head and a grateful smile, I say my goodbyes and run to my rental car. My stomach sinks when I see the time.

Mira's pitch started over an hour ago. By the time I make it to the campus, I'll be more than an hour and a half late. I wish I had a charging cord with me so I could call her.

I drive as fast as I safely can to the campus. I check the arena first, but she's not there. Then I check the coffee shop. No Mira. I drive around looking for her for another twenty minutes before the twisting feeling in my stomach starts to make me sick.

"Maybe she went back to the hotel."

It's the only other place she can be. She doesn't have a car, but she could have ordered a ride. The need to find her is a prowling beast inside of me, scratching up my insides. What if something happened to her? I need to know that she's okay. All I can think about is my sweet wife stuck outside in this weather, wondering where I am, scared, upset, alone. How did this day go so fucking wrong?

The ring box in my pocket urges me to drive faster, to get to her sooner. And when I finally pull up to the hotel and park, I run to the door, bypassing the elevators because there's no way I'm risking being stuck in another one of those today, and race up to our room on the fourth floor.

Pushing through the door, I call for her. "Mira? Baby, are you here?"

I'm met with silence.

Shit.

My body feels hot and my skin too tight. I look for her in the bathroom, on the balcony, hell, I even look in the closet like a total idiot. And then I notice it.

Her things are gone. Mira's white carry-on is gone. There's no straightener in the bathroom. Her toothbrush isn't lying next to the sink.

Where is she? Why would she take her stuff and leave the hotel room?

Now I'm really freaking out. My hands shake as I plug my phone into the charger. It takes forever to boot up.

"Come on, come on."

When the cursed thing finally turns on, it buzzes with several notifications. Missed calls and texts from Mira. A lot of them.

"Fuck!"

There are texts from before the meeting started, asking where I was. They start off calm and get progressively more worried in tone. Then the texts stop, and forty minutes later, there are two missed calls and a voicemail.

My stomach twists when I hear the tremble in my wife's voice. "Griffin? Where are you? I'm done with my meeting. I... You weren't here. Are you okay? Did something happen? How am I supposed to know where you are or if you're okay if you don't answer your phone? Just... Call me when you get this. Please be okay."

Dammit. *Dammit.*

I'm tapping her name on my favorites list, without even consciously thinking about it, and curse when it goes straight to voicemail. Holding the phone between my cheek and my shoulder, I start to throw everything in my suitcase. Wherever Mira is, I have to find her.

"Baby, hey. I'm so fucking sorry I missed your pitch. I tried to call and text you, but I didn't have any phone service. It was the craziest thing, sunshine. I got trapped in an elevator for almost an hour.

"I'm at the hotel and all your stuff is gone. Where are you? Please call me back. I'm so so sorry, baby. I swear I did everything I could to get to you. Did the meeting go well, I hope?" I run a hand through my hair, agitated. "Please call me back. I love you."

Hanging up, I text her, telling her the same thing I did in my voicemail. That I'm sorry I missed her meeting. That I was stuck in an elevator. That I love her and want to know where she is and if she's okay.

Then I suck in a deep breath and make a call I really don't want to make.

Maddox picks up on the first ring. I don't even give him a chance to say anything before I ask, "Have you heard from your sister?"

Silence stretches down the line, and a prickle of unease makes the hair on my neck rise.

"Yeah, Wright. I've heard from my sister." My best friend's voice is colder than the ice we skate on when he says, "The fuck did you do?"

I have no idea what she told him, and right now I don't care. Let him hate me, let him beat the shit out of me; it doesn't matter. I need to know that my wife is okay. "Where is she, Madds? All her stuff is gone from the hotel. I just need to know where she is and if she's safe."

Maybe it's the sheer panic in my voice, maybe he doesn't know anything, or maybe he's merely lulling me into a false sense of security before he buries a skate in my throat, but he doesn't bullshit me. "She's safe. Changed her flight to an earlier one. She's on her way home."

"Oh, thank god."

"She was crying, Wright. Wouldn't tell me what happened, but my little sister, who you were supposed to take care of, called me crying."

My momentary relief burns away, and that panic claws at my chest once again. "I can't get ahold of her. Please have her call me, man. I fucked up, but I couldn't help it. I need to tell her what happened."

Maddox scoffs. "You couldn't help fucking up? I love you, man, but you need to do better than that. You own your mistakes when you make them. Whatever the hell you did—which I will find out when I pick my sister up— was a big enough screwup that she asked to stay with me and Isla."

"No." The word is a broken plea. I need to talk to her. Explain what happened.

All of this is a stupid misunderstanding. I won't let Mira do the same thing her brother did when he overheard his future wife having a tense discussion with her ex, assumed the worst, and blew up his relationship without ever asking for Isla's side of the story. I won't let her walk away without talking to me.

"Please, man, you can't let her do that. I need to talk to her first. She needs to hear what happened."

Maddox, my best friend in the world, outside of Mira, scoffs. He fucking scoffs like what I'm saying is stupid. Like I'm stupid. "I'm not telling my sister that she can't move in with me. She's my sister, Wright. It's my job to protect her and be there for her, and if you did something that made her want to move out, I'm sure as shit not telling her she has to stay with you."

"I didn't do anything," I say, pleading with him to believe me. "Seriously, Madds, this is all a misunderstanding."

My friend sighs. "All I can do is tell her you want to talk to her. But I swear to god, Wright, if I don't like what I hear when I pick her up from the airport, I'm going to kick your ass, best friend or not."

My lungs seize up. I can't breathe, can't respond, can't do anything but freak the hell out that everything I was planning, everything I had finally let myself hope for, is falling apart, and there's nothing I can do about it. Mira's engagement ring feels like a thousand pounds in my pocket. The lack of her belongings in the hotel room is a noose around my neck.

"I'll be there as soon as I can. Please, whatever she tells you, just know I'm going to make it right."

I don't give my best friend a chance to reply before hanging up. Frantic, I try to find an earlier flight out, but nothing will get me back to Minneapolis sooner than our original flight. I drive to the airport, anyway. Just in case.

I refuse to lose my wife because of a stuck elevator and horrible timing.

I told Mira that I would never give up on her or let her go. That I'd fight for her. For us. And that's exactly what I'm going to do.

Whatever it takes, Mira will wear my rings and never want to take them off again.

forty-three

MIRA

My phone burns a hole in my pocket as I deboard the plane, dodging impatient travelers and harried flight attendants. I'll have to turn off airplane mode to let Maddy know I've arrived, but the thought has me breaking out in hives.

Did Griffin text or call me while I was in the air, or was he too busy doing *other* things to notice I'm gone? Which would be worse? I'm so consumed by my worries that I don't even notice the dark-haired, hulking figure until his hands grip my shoulders and he says my name. Twice.

"Maddy?" I didn't expect him to park the car and meet me at the gate. And I certainly didn't expect to be pulled into a tight, protective hug in front of hundreds of passengers. It's all I can do to hold in a sob as I bury my face in my brother's broad chest.

I may not have a dad, but I have an older brother who

loves the hell out of me, and sometimes I wonder if that's almost better. And then I wonder if telling him the truth will ruin everything.

"Hey, Mi-Mi." His voice is gruff, almost as clogged with emotion as mine, and it's nearly my undoing. "Come on. Let's get you home."

Maddox doesn't ask me what happened; he just grabs my suitcase from me and leads me out of the airport with a brotherly arm slung over my shoulder. His silent support gives me the strength to walk out with my head held high, even as a few tears slip past my defenses and down my cheeks.

Once we're situated in his car, he turns to me, his face set in a protective-brother scowl I know is *for* me and not *because* of me, and asks, "Do you want to talk about it now or at home?"

"When we get to your place. I don't think I have it in me to tell this story twice." My voice wavers but doesn't break. Small victories.

With a nod, Maddox pulls out of the parking lot, silently maneuvering through airport traffic as he gets us onto the highway. His eyes dart to me every so often, but he never gives in to his curiosity to push for information. I'm grateful. I have no clue what I'm going to tell him and Isla. How in the hell do you break it to your brother that you got drunkenly married to his best friend, kept it a secret for months, and now you think said husband may be cheating on you?

It's going to destroy Maddy. And probably his friendship with Griffin.

That makes me feel like shit. Even though, if Griffin is

cheating, it shouldn't. But I know how much his friendship means to Maddox. They've been close since college, they play on the same pro team, hell, they're on the same line. Not only could my admission blow up years of friendship, but it could have a devastating effect on the team itself.

All too soon, we're parking and making our way up to Maddox and Isla's apartment, and my worry turns to acid in my gut. I hold on to my purse strap like it's a lifeline because it's the only thing keeping my hands from trembling. Sweat beads along my back, and I have a flash of worry that I may puke again.

But then I'm walking into their place, and Isla pulls me into a tight, sisterly hug. I don't puke, but I lose the battle with my tears. Great, heaving sobs shake my body as I break apart right there in the entryway.

"Oh, Mira." Isla's voice bleeds concern as she hugs me. I catch her exchanging a worried glance with my brother before he herds us both into the living room, where I collapse into the embrace of their very comfortable couch.

"I need you to tell me what happened," Maddox says roughly.

Swallowing, I give myself a few moments to calm down before I look up at my brother and attempt to extract a promise I know he won't want to give. "First, I need you to promise that you won't do anything stupid."

He grunts, eyes narrowing and lips pursing.

"I'm serious, Maddy. You can't go off and start a fight with Griffin. I know you'll want to, but I'm telling you right now, you can't. Promise me."

My brother's brown eyes flare. "I'm not promising shit

like that, Mi-Mi. If he hurt you, he's going to pay. Whether that's with fists or something else, that's between me and him."

"It's not, though. It's between *me* and him."

That has Maddox's eyes narrowing on me. "What, exactly, is between you and him?"

When Isla gives my hand a squeeze, I shoot her a grateful, tremulous smile before sucking in a fortifying breath and saying the words I thought I'd be sharing under very different circumstances in a few short days. "I didn't plan any of this."

"Plan what, Mira?"

Tears slip down my cheeks, hot and fast. "It started out as a stupid, drunken mistake. I didn't expect it to turn into something real."

Maddox growls at that, and I can practically see his hackles rising. "*What* was a drunken mistake? I'm going to need you to stop being cryptic and fucking explain, because the conclusions I'm jumping to are all going to result in my best friend getting his face broken in."

Pretty sure the truth is worse than whatever my brother is thinking, but I can't hide this from him or Isla any longer. Especially if I'm asking to stay with them. They deserve to know why. Even as resolve fills me, my body shakes and my lower lip trembles.

"Our marriage."

Silence. Dead fucking silence meets those two words, and I swear the air grows thick and charged as my brother struggles to digest what I said.

"I must have misheard you," Maddox says with a slow, measured cadence that belies his internal struggle to remain calm. "I could have sworn I just heard you say the thing that was your drunken mistake was your marriage."

Swallowing over the lump in my throat isn't easy, but I manage it and look my brother in the eye as I nod. "You didn't mishear me. It—it happened in Vegas. We were drunk, which was mostly my fault, and then we were walking around the Strip, and there was a young Elvis and a Dolly Parton, and then I woke up with a ring on my finger and Griffin next to me, and the next thing I know, he's convinced me to give our marriage a shot, and I didn't think it would work, but then I fell in love with the stupid idiot, and then he went and fucked it all up today, and I don't know what I'm supposed to do now."

Once I start speaking, the words come out in a rush. It's all one big run-on sentence of my truth, pain, and fears, and by the end, I break down into a sobbing, snotty mess. As Isla gathers me into a hug, I close my eyes while my brother's form seems to grow and expand beside me.

He pushes up off the couch and shouts, "That mother-fucker! I'm going to kick his fucking ass. I warned him to keep his hands off you. I *warned* him." Maddy paces in front of the couch. "Married. You're *married?*"

"We were going to tell you all at dinner this week."

"Vegas was like three and a half months ago, Mira. You've kept this from me for three and a half months, which means my best friend—no, my *former* best friend—has been lying to me for almost four months. Four months!"

My chest tightens at the look of absolute betrayal etched into every line of my brother's face. This is bad. This is so bad.

"I trusted him. I trusted him, and this is how he repays that? And you"—Maddox turns his ire on me—"you know what he's like. I thought you were more mature than this. To get so sloppy drunk that you marry the one guy on my team who has never grown up... I don't fuckin' get it, Mira."

Despite Griffin not showing up for me today, despite that damn photo that ripped my heart to shreds, I can't stop myself from standing up, going chest to chest with my brother, and letting him have it. "Don't. Don't you dare, Maddox. You claim he's your best friend, but you don't know him at all, do you? If you did, you'd never say something like that about him. Never grown up..." I scoff, enraged for my husband, even now.

"You don't even realize he's the glue that holds your stupid hockey team together, do you? Hell, he's the glue that kept you and Isla together. He's always there for everyone without having to be asked. He shows up, day after day after day, and encourages you morons, pushes you to be better on and off the ice, and does it all with a smile on his face.

"The minute I said I needed a place to stay, Griffin was there with an offer to help. He never let me pay rent, never asked me for a thing. Hell, he never even lets me pay for groceries. Do you know he had someone remodel the guest room for me? And it's perfect. It's cozy and beautiful and exactly what I would have chosen for myself, and he did all of it without being asked or asking for a *thank you* in return.

"No one has been a bigger supporter of my business than Griffin. Not only did he set up the meeting with the

University of Michigan this weekend, but do you know what I found out a while back? He's been telling all his hockey buddies about me and sending them my way when they want to rebrand or set up websites. Never told me he was doing it, either. The only reason I know is because one of the guys spilled the beans.

"And when my stupid, ancient car broke down, he bought me a brand-new one. Did he tell you that? I tried to make him take it back, but he wouldn't hear of it. All he cared about was that I was safe.

"And what about what he did for you? You almost lost the woman you love because you were too hurt to go after her, so he did that for you. He made sure you didn't blow up your life because of some dumb understanding. You're marrying her because your best friend cared too much about both of you to let you blow it all up."

I'm sobbing now. Each word is a knife that slices off a little piece of my heart and the anger I've been feeling toward Griffin. Each truth I recount makes me question the photo and the events of the day. Because with every word I speak, it becomes clearer and clearer that Griffin Wright isn't just a good man—he's a great one.

And I am exactly like my brother.

When Maddox overheard Isla talking to her stupid asshole ex, he assumed the worst and walked away without letting her explain. Because we grew up with a dad who walked away. It's something that, on some level, we must both expect the people we love to do. Abandon us and walk away.

Except, the people you love can't walk away if you beat them to it.

And at the first test of my love for Griffin—even if it

looked bad—I did the same thing. I got on a plane, turned my phone off so he couldn't reach me, and walked away.

The truth of it all slams into me like a runaway bus, and with a sob, I run to the guestroom and lock myself in. I'm falling apart and don't want an audience.

What if there was a very logical explanation for what happened today, and I not only didn't give my husband a chance to explain, but jumped to the most nuclear option? Griffin is one of the most selfless men I know. He's always rooting for the underdog, always a hopeless romantic. He sees the good in people, and he steps in and steps up for them over and over again. Here I am, assuming the worst about him, when all he ever does is see the best in everyone else. In all our time together, he's never done a single thing that would make me believe he'd cheat on me.

Not one.

Yet, that's exactly where my mind went when I saw that photo with the blonde.

Ignoring my brother's voice through the door, I pull my phone out with shaking hands and turn off airplane mode.

It only takes seconds for notifications to flood my screen, and I suck in a breath as I tap on the texts and scroll to the earliest one.

GRIFFIN

> Hey, baby, I am so sorry, but I'm running late. This is going to sound like a crazy excuse, but I swear it's not. I'm stuck in an elevator with the head of marketing for Breakaway. The power cut out, and the elevator stopped moving. I'm going to do whatever I can to get to you, but don't wait for me, okay? I'm so sorry I'm not there already, but you're going to kill this pitch. I believe in you, sunshine. You don't need me. You've got this. I love you.

> It's not looking like I'm going to make the meeting. I'm sorry, baby. I'm also kicking myself because my battery is almost dead, but the woman in the elevator with me—the head of marketing—is severely claustrophobic, and she left her phone in her office. She was only supposed to be walking me out. I'm using my flashlight app so she doesn't have a full-blown panic attack. If you can't reach me after you get out of your meeting, that's why.

Now I'm sobbing again, but this time it's not because of what Griffin has done; it's because of what I've done. Scared to hear it, I press play on the voicemail and hold the phone to my ear. When Griffin's panicked voice hits me, I stifle my sob with my hand.

"Baby, hey. I'm so fucking sorry I missed your pitch. I tried to call and text you, but I didn't have any phone service. It was the craziest thing, sunshine. I got trapped in an elevator for almost an hour.

"I'm at the hotel and all your stuff is gone. Where are you? Please call me back. I'm so so sorry, baby. I swear I did

everything I could to get to you. Did the meeting go well, I hope? Please call me back. I love you."

He didn't ditch me. He was literally trapped in an elevator. And that blonde woman in the photo? I'd bet a million bucks she was the marketing exec who was having a panic attack. Because *of course* my husband would do everything he could to help her. He's good like that. So genuinely good. And I immediately believed the worst.

It hits me then.

My brother is worried about Griffin not being good enough for me, but the fact of the matter is that I'm not good enough for Griffin. Not even close.

And that's the realization that finally, truly breaks me.

forty-four

GRIFFIN

It's late by the time I get to Maddox's place, and even though pounding on the door at one a.m. is probably a dick move that will have someone calling the cops on me, I don't care. I need to see my wife.

After the fourth knock, my best friend wrenches the door open, a hockey stick in his hand, ready to use it as a weapon. Some of the tension in his shoulders eases when he sees me, but that only lasts for a moment. Then he's using his stick and his palm to push me out into the hallway.

The way he's looking at me, I know our friendship might be over, and I fucking hate it, but I can't focus on that now. Not when my wife is just through that door and upset with me. She's the only thing that matters.

"I need to talk to her. Let me in."

"Like hell." He shoves me again. "How the fuck could you do this? You lied to me for months. Looked me right in the eye and acted like you weren't fucking my sister, you piece of shit."

I growl and shove him back. "Don't. It's not like that, and it never was. She's my wife, Madds. I fucking love her."

"You love her." His chuckle is low and sardonic. "You love her, but you tried to force her into staying married to you, asked her to lie to her family and friends, and then you fucking ditch her when you promised to be there for her?"

"I didn't ask her to lie to you! Yeah, okay, I talked her into staying married—that part is true—but I didn't want to keep this a secret. I wanted to tell everyone. She's the one who wanted to keep it a secret, and because I love her, I agreed. Doesn't mean I liked it. And I didn't ditch her. I was stuck in a goddamn elevator with a panicking woman from Breakaway. It was a freak thing, and there was nothing I could have done about it. I would never, ever intentionally ditch your sister. Ever."

Running a hand through my hair, which is probably a greasy mess by now because I can't seem to stop tugging on it, I glower at my best friend. "I get that you're pissed at me, man, I do, but this isn't about you and me. This is about my wife, and I need to talk to her." And with that, I push past my best friend, and before he can grab me, I shove the door to his place open and call my wife's name.

"Mira! Mira, I need to talk to you." I know she's in the guest bedroom, so that's where I'm headed when I'm yanked backward. Maddox grabs me by the collar of my shirt and swings me around, slamming me into the wall.

I push him, ready to fight to get to her, if that's what it

takes. "Let me go, man. I need to talk to her. I need to explain."

"Tough shit, asshole. She cried herself to sleep hours ago. Now, get the fuck out before I break your goddamn jaw."

"Do what you have to," I say, pushing him again. "But I'm going to do what I have to do."

"What's going on?" Isla squints at us as she comes rushing down the hall and into the living room where I'm tussling with her fiancé. Her eyes widen when she sees us. "Griffin?"

"Isla." If anyone will be on my side, it's the redhead standing before me. Maddox walked away from her and almost ruined everything. She knows how important it is to talk things out when shit hits the fan in your relationship. She knows how stupid it is to let a misunderstanding fester until it breaks the most important thing in your life.

"I need to talk to Mira. Please. I have to explain. You, of all people, should understand that." My voice cracks as desperation rides me hard, making my insides buzz and vibrate.

Isla opens her mouth to respond when the soft sound of shuffling footsteps makes my heart seize. And when my wife stumbles into the room, her eyes red and puffy, hair a tangled mess, I can't help it. I crack. A strangled sound claws its way out of my throat, drawing her eyes to me.

"Fuck, sunshine, I was so worried."

Mira's green eyes take me in, her chin wobbles, then tears start dripping down her cheeks. Maddox growls, and I barely notice his arm drawing back before pain sparks across my jaw, momentarily blinding me. He's shouting about me hurting his sister, calling me a piece of shit, telling me I'm dead, but all I can see is my wife as she rushes toward us, those emerald eyes of hers wide with worry. For me?

"Maddy, stop. Stop it! Let him go." And then she's right there, pushing her brother away from me. "You need to back off. It's fine, I'm fine. Go back to your room. I need to talk to Griffin."

"Like hell am I going back to my room and leaving you alone with him. I never should have left you alone with him in the first place. That's why you're in this mess."

Isla places a hand on Maddox's arm, her eyes looking me over with concern. I give her a half smile and nod, letting her know I'm okay.

"Come on, big guy. Let's let these two talk." She tries to drag him back to their room, but he levels me with a hard glare.

"If you try anything, you're dead. Hurt her, and it'll be the last thing you do."

Not backing down, I hold my best friend's gaze, making sure he sees the truth in my words when I say, "I would never intentionally hurt her. She's my wife. She's everything."

After staring me down for another few seconds, Maddox grunts and lets Isla drag him down the hall to their room. The moment their door snicks shut, I move, closing the distance between Mira and me and pulling her into my arms.

"Fuck, baby, I was so scared when I couldn't find you. I'm sorry. So damn sorry that I missed your pitch. You have to know I wanted to be there. If there was anything I could have done to get to you, I would have."

Mira's lip wobbles while I cup her face in my hands, brushing tears away with my thumbs.

"Why did you leave? I get that you were upset with me for missing the meeting, but why did you fly home without telling me? And Maddox said you asked him to stay here?"

Something unreadable flickers over Mira's face before her eyebrows pinch and she rolls her lips between her teeth. "I didn't leave because you missed the meeting."

"Okay... I don't understand, sunshine. Why'd you leave? What happened?"

My beautiful wife searches my face before she sighs. "Wait here a second. I need to grab my phone."

Confused, I can only nod. Whatever she's about to show me, I have a feeling I'm not going to like it. But whatever it is, we'll work through it. Together. Because that's what married people do. They work through their issues.

Mira twists the phone in her hands as she returns, and I can tell she's hesitant to show me whatever is on there that pushed her to walk away from me.

"What is it, baby?"

"I'm scared to show you," she whispers. Her eyes drop to the floor and her shoulders hunch. I hate it.

"Why are you scared?" I nudge her chin up with the side of my finger.

"Because there are two ways this could go. In one, you hurt me. The other, I hurt you."

Her words have my heart speeding up, and my chest gives a lurch. Steadying my voice, I ask, "What do you mean?"

There is so much sadness in my wife's face when she unlocks her phone, taps on the screen a few times, then turns it around to show me a photo. A photo of me with my arm around Serena Kent as I walked her to her husband. Except, her husband isn't in the shot, and she's looking up at me with what I know to be gratitude, but what could very easily appear to be affection if you didn't know any better.

So this is why Mira left. She saw a picture of me with my arm around another woman when I was supposed to be by her side, supporting her. It's very clear what she thought was happening, and it's a kick to the balls.

My wife thought I was cheating on her.

I let my hand fall away from her face and stagger back a step. The walls are closing in on me and my chest feels tight. Like I can't breathe. "You think I…" I bark out a laugh, but there's nothing humorous in the sound. It's harsh and broken. "That's not what it looks like. She was having a panic attack. I was helping her get to her husband because she was so freaked out she could barely walk. But you thought…"

Closing my eyes, I cover my face with both hands, so I don't see Mira when she lets out a strangled cry. I don't see her close the distance between us or cover my hands with hers.

"Griffin."

"I would never choose another woman over you." The words are muffled through my hands, but I can't bring myself to look at my wife right now. Not while I'm strug-gling to hold myself together. "I would *never* hurt you like that."

"I know," Mira sobs. "I know that now, but in the moment, I was so hurt that you didn't show up, and then I saw that photo and I had already been spiraling, so I freaked out even more. All I could think about was how hurt I was, you know? I wasn't working on logic. I'm sorry. I'm so sorry for doubting you, even for a moment. I'm sorry for leaving without talking to you. It was shitty and awful of me, and you deserved so much better than that."

There's nothing worse than hearing your wife break down into heart-wrenching sobs. Not even the pain of knowing she doubted me can touch it. Does it hurt? Absolutely. But not as much as almost losing her did. Not as much as seeing her beat herself up over it.

Wrapping her in my arms, I let her cry. I hold her, stroke her hair, and whisper that it will all be okay. I vow that we'll work this out. That I don't blame her for freaking out. And I don't. It hurts like hell, but I spent years being photographed with different women on my arm. I earned my reputation, and I can't really blame Mira for thinking about it when faced with a photo that looks damning.

I'll have to prove to her that there's no other woman for me. She's it.

And I know just how to do that.

"I was waiting for the perfect moment all weekend," I murmur into her hair, dropping my right hand and reaching into my pocket. "There must have been five different times I almost did it, but then the damn warthog farted and the bird took a shit in my hair…"

Mira's forehead crinkles with confusion as she stares up at me. Dragging the knuckles of my left hand across her cheek, I take a step back and drop to one knee.

"Then I was gonna do it after your meeting, but well, you know what happened then. And I realize this isn't exactly the perfect moment, but maybe it's better this way.

Because I want you to know, all the way to your bones, that I choose you, even in the imperfect moments. That my love for you doesn't require everything to go according to plan."

Mira's eyes are wide as she looks down at me on one knee, and when I flip open the lid of the little black box and she sees her dream ring from the jewelry store sparkling up at her, she gasps and covers her mouth with both hands. "Griffin..."

"I was waiting for the perfect moment, but if today has made me realize anything, it's that you can't wait to show the depth of your love. Something will always be less than perfect, but love isn't about perfection. It's about choice and commitment. It's about putting someone else before yourself. And, sunshine, I'll always try to put you first.

"You're the most important person in my life. I have never loved anyone the way I love you, and I know we're already married, but will you marry me again? On purpose this time. No alcohol or Elvises involved?"

Mira's eyes flutter, tears streak her cheeks, and her hair is a tangled mess, but to me, she's never looked more beautiful. I'm slipping the ring out of the box as she drops her hands and opens her mouth to answer me. Today was awful, but this right here makes it all worth it.

"No."

I swear to god, the world stops spinning. My ears ring. My chest lurches. I shake my head, sure I heard her wrong.

"No?"

Devastation. It's painted on her face in salty tears and carved into my heart in the searing sting of rejection.

Mira shakes her head, a sob leaving her lips before she

repeats the word that rips my whole fucking world to shreds. "No."

I'm still on one knee when I try to blink through the confusion. Still on one knee when Mira starts to speak through her tears.

"I realized tonight that I've been treating this marriage like a test or an audition. You asked me for six months to prove you're right for me, and I agreed. I held myself back while you went out of your way to prove that you are good enough, loyal enough, dependable enough…"

Mira's eyes flutter closed, and she wraps her arms around her middle. Like it's taking every ounce of strength to hold herself together. My instincts scream at me to hold her, to comfort her, but I'm paralyzed. Frozen to the floor as my wife rips my heart out, one choked word at a time.

"But do you know what you never asked me?" She looks so fucking sad. "You never asked me to prove the same. You never once asked me to prove that I am good enough for you, loyal enough, dependable enough. And what I've realized is that I'm not. I'm not good enough for you."

"What?" I choke on the word. "What are you talking about? Of course, you're good enough for me. You're perfect for me, baby."

Mira shakes her head, little hiccuping sobs punctuating the movement.

"I'm not. I've been so selfish, Griffin. You deserve better than me. You're so good. So kind and loving and selfless. You deserve someone who is all of those things too. Someone who will believe in you the way you believe in me. Someone who won't let her stupid daddy issues cause her to believe the worst in a man who has only ever given his best."

Standing, I tug Mira into my chest, wrapping my arms around her, the ring box still in my hand. "Baby, no. You're not selfish. And you don't have daddy issues. For fuck's sake. You're a human being who has wounds and insecurities, just like everyone else. That doesn't mean you're not right for me. It doesn't mean you're not worthy of being loved."

"See?" she says through her tears. "You're proving my point. You're amazing, Griffin. You're so good. I wish like hell things with us had started differently. But all of this came out of a drunken night. You never would have been with me if not for that. And I'm the one who pushed you to drink more and stay out later. This is my fault. All of this is my fault. Which means it's my responsibility to fix it."

My arms tighten around Mira. "Don't you fucking say it. Don't you do this."

"I think it's time we admit this was a mistake. I won't be the reason you twist yourself into a pretzel. Because, let's be real, I didn't make you feel like you could be yourself or that who you are is good enough. You felt like you had to change your clothes, your house, your interests... You don't deserve that. You deserve so much more."

"You never asked me to change," I growl. "Don't you fucking dare use that as an excuse to pull away from me. You never asked me to do any of those things. That was because of my own insecurities."

"Yeah, but I'm the one who made you feel insecure."

"No. That was my best friend." I shake my head. "No, I can't even blame him. That's all on me. My issues are my responsibility. And, baby, the people you love most are always the people you hurt most. It's just a shitty fact of life. But I'm telling you right now, there is no one in this world I would rather be hurt by. I love you. So fucking much, it feels like I might burst. And I'm not letting you walk away from this, because I think you love me the same way. We're meant to be, baby. But that doesn't mean it's going to be easy. Nothing worthwhile ever is."

"I'm not worth all of this," she cries, burying her face in my chest, her hands fisted in my shirt. "Maybe my dad had the right idea when he walked away."

"Don't you dare," I growl. Shoving the ring box back into my pocket, I grab Mira's face with both hands. "Don't you fucking dare say shit like that about the woman I love. That's bullshit, baby. Anyone with half a brain can see the truth, same as I do. That it's impossible to walk away from you. That you're worth all the effort, all the time, all the patience and pain, and I'll prove it to you. All I ask is that you don't shut me out. That you give this thing between us a chance."

When she won't meet my gaze, I lean down and claim her mouth, pouring every ounce of love, fear, and pain into the kiss until we're both breathless and gasping. Pulling away, I rest my forehead against hers.

"Don't shut me out. Please, give this a real chance. You promised me six months, and I still have two and a half left. Please, come home."

"I can't come home."

Her words are a punch to my gut.

"I'm going to stay with Maddy for now. But I won't shut you out, Griffin. I can't. You're my best friend and I love you. But because I love you, I'm going to do the right thing and take a step back."

No. Unacceptable.

"Stepping back isn't the right thing. Fighting for us is."

Her smile is so devastatingly sad when she looks up at me from beneath her long lashes. "It is. Someday you'll see that, even if it's not anytime soon."

She's wrong. I know it, and I think she knows it too. She's scared, and outside of her brother, every man in her life has walked away, so I get it. I understand.

What Mira doesn't understand is that I'm not like the other men in her life. I won't walk away, no matter how hard she pushes. I've meant every word I've ever said about fighting for Mira Graves, and I'm not a man who gives up. I fight for what I want. I work hard. And I win.

Mira may have convinced herself that this thing between us is a mistake, but I know better. I'll prove her wrong. In the meantime, I'll do everything in my power to be the mistake she craves.

"You're wrong, baby girl, and I'll prove it. You can stay with your brother for now, but when you're ready to come home, I'll be waiting with open arms. I don't care if that's one hour from now, a week from now, a year from now... Your home is with me."

Leaning down, I press one more lingering kiss to Mira's swollen lips before forcing myself to take a step back.

"You should get some sleep. I'll see you in the morning."

Before she can protest or utter another word, I turn around and walk out the door.

I have plans to make and a wife to win back.

This isn't over between us. It's just begun.

forty-five

GRIFFIN

ISLA OPENS THE DOOR THE NEXT MORNING WHEN I knock. She doesn't look all that surprised to see me standing there, holding a tray of four coffees.

"Hey."

Her eyes, soft and sympathetic, sweep my face, lingering on the bruise her fiancé gave me the night before. "Hey. What are you doing here?"

"Bringing coffee to my wife. And my brother- and sister-in-law."

She grins at that. "Not sure that's how it works."

"I guess I don't really care how it works. I consider you family, Teach. That's all that matters to me." The smile I give her is genuine, but it fades when my thoughts turn to Mira. "How is she?"

Isla sighs. "I don't know. She hasn't come out of her room yet this morning. You two have really been married these past three and a half months?"

"We have. Best three and a half months of my life."

Heavy footsteps sound from inside the apartment, then Maddox is there at his fiancée's back. My best friend of over a decade greets me with a fierce scowl. "The fuck you doing here, Wright?"

I knew it would hurt if Maddox decided to hate me rather than accept my marriage to Mira, but I didn't expect to feel such a sharp pang of loss. She's his sister, and I'm glad his loyalty is to her—I am—but that doesn't mean I'm not hurt by the distance he's putting between us. Maybe for the first time, I realize that not only could I lose my wife, but I could lose my best friend too. Losing either one would wreck me, but losing both? How the hell am I supposed to move on from that?

I can't let it happen.

"Can we talk?"

Maddox's scowl grows deeper, the lines between his eyebrows becoming canyons. "There's nothing to talk about."

"Nothing to talk about? There's everything to talk about, Madds. I'm married to your sister. I'm in love with her. And I get that you're pissed at me, but you're my best friend. We're teammates. We play on the same line, for fuck's sake. We can't just ignore this." I'm sure he'd like to. I'm starting to see that the Graves siblings would choose to ignore a lot of things if people let them.

"You *were* my best friend," he says, voice cold. But beneath the icy exterior, he's hurt. In his mind, I lied to him for months. Betrayed him. I try to remember that when my chest squeezes and aches.

Isla puts her hand on Maddox's chest. "You don't mean that."

Though his face softens when he looks down at his fiancée, his tone is steel. "I do."

"Look, man, I know you think I'm the bad guy here, and I'd probably feel the same way in your shoes. But I won't apologize for loving your sister, and I'm not sorry we're married. I wish we would have told you right away, but Mira asked me not to, and you, of all people, should understand that when the woman you love asks you to do something, you do it. Because you want to make her happy. To make sure she knows that she's the most important person in the world and her comfort is your top priority. So I'm sorry if you're hurt, but I'm not sorry for putting Mira's needs and wishes above yours."

Maddox's eyes blaze, and his mouth opens, a retort on his lips. But whatever he's going to say is cut short by a soft voice.

"Griffin?"

The door swings fully open, and the sight of her settles the beast in my chest that's been pacing since I left her last night. My wife.

She looks tired. Dark circles make her green eyes look haunted. Her skin is paler than normal, and her dark hair struggles to escape the confines of two messy braids. One of my shirts hangs down to her knees, which are covered in a pair of leggings. If she was waking up at home with me, she'd only wear the shirt. Or nothing.

I clear my throat, telling myself that this is not the time to be thinking about my wife naked. Not when she's looking at me with those big, sad eyes. She looks as lost as I feel without her.

"Sunshine. Hi." I hold out the coffees. "Brought you your favorite."

Maddox scowls, Isla smiles, but I only have eyes for the woman I love as she fights an internal battle. She wants to run into my arms. I can see it, clear as day. But she holds herself back. That's fine. I can be patient. I can wait her out, prove I'm not going anywhere. I can show up every day for as long as it takes until she's ready to admit what I already know.

Mira and I are as inevitable as the tides. She's the moon and I'm the waves. She calls, I answer.

"Can I take you out for breakfast, baby?"

My best friend doesn't like that, and I have to fight a grin when he grumbles his displeasure. Tough shit. He's gonna have to get used to me calling his sister all sorts of sickening pet names.

Mira sucks her lower lip between her teeth, considering me. "I have a lot of work to do…"

I nod, having expected this. I'm not happy, but I expected it. Snagging my coffee from the carrier, I hand her the rest. Then I grab the bag I'd set to the side and hand her that too. "Okay. Tomorrow, then. I brought you some clothes and things I thought you might need. Obviously, you can come home whenever you want. To pick things up or to stay. But this way, you have the essentials."

Tears pool in Mira's eyes, and I hate it. I want to shove my way through the door and wrap her in my arms, kiss her senseless, and promise that everything will work out. But I won't. Because I pushed her to accept this in the beginning. I pushed her to accept me.

This time, the choice has to be all hers.

So I'll show her all the reasons she should choose me.

"Call me if you need anything, sunshine. I don't care

where I am or what I'm doing, I'll drop everything for you. I love you."

"Griffin, I…" Mira's mouth moves, the words I know she wants to say trapped in her throat.

I smile sadly at her. "I know, baby. I'll see you later."

Isla reaches out and gives my hand a squeeze before Maddox shoves me back. His eyes are hard as he glares at me. Then he shuts the door in my face.

Practice today should be interesting.

"WHAT HAPPENED TO YOUR FACE?" RYDER REACHES out and grabs my chin, studying the love mark my best friend gave me. He pulls back when I wince.

"Long story."

"Did you sleep with someone's wife?" Logan asks, teasing me. I know he's just being a little shit, but the comment pisses me off.

"Yeah, my own," I mutter. I think it's quiet enough that no one will hear, but Ryder's mouth drops open.

"Dude. What?"

Well, they're bound to find out, eventually. Especially with what I have planned. And there won't be any hiding the rift between Maddox and me. I clear my throat and find Ryder, Logan, and Sebastian looking at me like some sideshow animal with two heads.

Right. Here goes nothing.

"Yeah. So, I'm married."

Total. Fucking. Silence falls over the locker room. The whole team is staring at me now.

Logan is the first one to speak, his voice high and pitchy. "You're what, now?"

"Hitched. Off the market. Married." I run a hand through my hair, agitated by this whole situation.

"When?" Logan gapes at me.

"Uh, for almost four months."

"Four months? The fuck? To who?"

"To whom," I mutter. Logan is not amused.

"Wait, almost four months ago, we played that away series in Vegas." Ryder is squinting at me like that'll help him figure this all out. Maybe he's hoping he'll suddenly develop X-ray vision or telepathy or some shit.

Logan frowns. "Wait, you're married? What does your roommate think about that? She's just what, been staying in the spare room, with you and your wife across the hall? That's weird, dude."

Jesus fucking Christ. Pinching the bridge of my nose, my eyes fall closed.

"Seriously?" I hear Bash mutter incredulously at Logan.

"What the fuck are you all doing, standing around?" Maddox's voice booms like a cannon in the locker room, and my eyes fly open. He slams his bag down on the bench and glares at all of us, his angry eyes lingering on me.

"Dude, did you know Griffin is married?" Logan asks.

Pretty sure steam is about to pour out of Maddox's ears. His face gets all red, and his eyes practically glow with the fires of hell. "Stop standing around gossiping like a bunch of old ladies, get your gear on, and get your asses on the ice," he shouts before shooting daggers at everyone and storming into the bathroom.

Ryder looks between Maddox's retreating form and me. His mouth drops open. "You didn't."

My silence is answer enough, and the rookie gapes at me.

"You married his sister in Vegas? Do you have a death wish?"

"I knew it," Bash says.

"Wait. Wait, you and Mira?" Logan runs a hand over the scruff of his jaw. His eyes narrow on me. "That's why you stopped going out with me? You married Maddox's sister? What the hell?"

"How many times are you assholes going to ask me the same questions?" Turning my back on them, I tug off my hoodie and start changing into my practice gear. "Yes, I married Mira. No, Maddox didn't know until yesterday. He's obviously pissed about it, and yes, he's the one who punched me in the face. No, I don't regret it, no, I don't care what any of you think, and yes, it's complicated right now, but it won't be forever, because I fucking love my wife and I'm going to do whatever it takes to prove it to her. Any more questions?"

"Yeah," Maddox says. He's standing behind me with his arms crossed over his chest and a deep frown marring his face. "Are you ready to drop down to the second line? Because I sure as shit can't trust you to have my back on the ice when you just stabbed me in it."

Right.

Lifting my chin, I stare my best friend down, ignoring the sting of his distrust and rejection. "Do whatever you have to do, man. I plan to."

$$forty\text{-}six$$

MIRA

EVERY DAY FOR THE FIRST TWO WEEKS POST Michigan, Griffin shows up to Maddy's door with coffee, pastries, or flowers. Every day, he asks me to breakfast, and despite desperately wanting to say yes, I decline. He sends me lunch deliveries, texts me every few hours to tell me he loves me and always will, and sends me random GIFs and links to things he thinks are funny. Every night, he shows back up, hazel eyes full of hope, to tell me goodnight before he hands me a love note or a new romance novel with his favorite passages highlighted and annotated.

It's killing me. I miss him so fucking much it hurts, I'm not sleeping well, and I can't seem to eat anything. I've lost enough weight that Isla noticed and has started to worry. To her credit, she hasn't pushed me to talk about more than I'm ready to discuss, even though I know she's dying to hear what happened.

The thing is, I'm worried that if I tell her everything,

I'll lose my nerve and what little resolve I have left. Because two weeks without Griffin has made a few things painfully clear.

One, he's my best friend. And I don't just mean he's one of them—I mean he's the best friend I've ever had in my entire life. He gets me in a way no one else ever has, sees me more clearly than even my mom and my brother, and has always been one hundred percent in my corner.

Two, I'm hopelessly in love with him. Although our marriage and romantic relationship started from a drunken night, I'd been fighting my attraction to him way before Vegas. And, yes, I know I told him that our marriage was a mistake and that one day he'd see the truth of it, but how can he believe that's the truth when I don't even believe it?

And three, I've been really fucking selfish. I meant what I said when I told Griffin he should have asked more of me. I've spent every single torturous night in bed thinking back on all the things he did to try to prove he was right for me while I, what? Marked off little tic-marks on some imagined list of requirements for a perfect partner? What did I do to prove my worth to him? What did I sacrifice for him?

I'm the reason he and Maddox have barely been speaking. I'm the reason he's playing on the second line. Because I'm the one who demanded we keep this relationship a secret, and look at how that ended up? I goaded him into drinking more that night. I brought up chapels and marriage.

Griffin has every right to be pissed at me. He'd have every right to blame me for the rift between him and his best friend, and the fact that he's not playing on the first line in the last weeks of the regular season like he deserves to.

I almost wish he was mad. Maybe it would distract me from the absolute misery I'm wallowing in.

Maddox and Isla are both gone and I'm alone in their apartment when the doorbell rings. Looking down at myself, I cringe when I realize I haven't changed out of my pajamas or brushed my hair yet today. At least I've brushed my teeth, so I won't knock out whoever's at the door. That is, if I answer it.

Tiptoeing through the apartment, I look through the peephole to find Griffin standing there, a book in his hand. Since he can't see me, I allow myself a moment to study him. He's still as golden and gorgeous as ever, but there are signs of stress on his face that weren't there before. The little crease between his eyebrows seems deeper, and his jaw is tighter. His hair is messy, and not in that artful way it normally is.

After a few moments, he looks directly at the peephole, a slow grin curving his lips as he says, "You gonna stand there and stare at me, or are you gonna let me in, sunshine?"

"Shit."

His chuckle floats through the door and embeds itself in my heart, like fuel for my soul. I hurry to open it and step aside, allowing him to come in.

It's the first time we've been alone in weeks, and I have to fight my body's urge to throw myself in his arms, bury my face in his neck, and refuse to let him go. A similar urge plays across Griffin's face, but to my dismay, he doesn't act on it. I wish he would. If he made the first move, I could let myself sink into him and still tell myself I held my ground.

"Hey, baby." Griffin openly drinks me in, those hazel eyes I know so well—every striation and fleck of color mapped over our months together—scanning me from head to sock-covered toe. "How are you?"

Miserable, I want to say. *Missing you. I don't want to do this anymore. Please ask me to come home. Please tell me you hate this as much as me.*

"Good," I lie.

His lips twitch, forming into a frown before he catches himself. Like he knows I'm lying but has the grace not to call me on it. "Good. That's good."

We stare at each other for a moment. "What are you doing here?"

My words snap him out of whatever trance he's in, and he shakes his head, handing me the book.

"Brought this for you. I thought maybe we could read it together while I'm out of town for this away series like we did before. I've heard nothing but good things."

God, I hate the tentative way he asks. I want my confident, cocky husband back. This is my fault.

"I'd like that." I take a step toward him, my lower lip between my teeth. "Maybe we can FaceTime and share our favorite parts?"

Griffin's lips curve again, this time into a smile, as he moves a step toward me. There are mere inches between us now. "Yeah?"

"Yeah." My voice is breathy as I respond, and my breathing grows shallow when he reaches out and tucks a lock of hair behind my ear, his fingers skimming along my cheekbone before dragging along my lips.

"It's a date."

Leaning into his touch, I close my eyes as a pained sound tears from my lips. "Griffin."

"Yeah, baby?" Hot breath ghosts over my lips, and they part without a conscious thought.

"I…"

"I know, sunshine. I know."

Then, for the first time in two weeks, he kisses me. It's soft, tentative, *hopeful*. As he pulls away, my lips chase his, seeking his warmth, needing his breath, needing *him*. He gives me what I need, but only briefly, before he pulls back and rests his forehead on mine.

"Fuck, baby. I miss you so fucking much."

I want to tell him I miss him too. But my head is still a mess, and if I give voice to how much I miss him and how broken I've felt without him, he'll take that as me giving in to this thing between us, and I'm not there yet. Though I've done some real soul searching, and I've been meeting with a therapist twice a week since moving in with Maddy, I need more time.

Griffin deserves to have someone be as all in as he is, and I want that person to be me. But I've realized that, despite living for twenty years without my dad in my life and thinking I was over his abandonment, that's not completely true. I don't expect therapy to heal me. I know that's not how this works. But I want to make sure I can give the man I love the love and commitment he so desperately wants and deserves. And that's going to take longer than two weeks.

He doesn't wait for me to say it back, which breaks my heart but is also a relief. He just kisses my forehead and steps back before saying, "I wanted to stop by before the series to give you the book, but I also wanted to give you this." He reaches into the inside pocket of his coat and withdraws an envelope. There's an address on it, along with a name that sounds an awful lot like a law firm.

"What is this?"

He runs a hand through his sandy blond hair and won't meet my eyes. "It's the deed to my place."

"What?" I'm so confused. Slipping my finger into the envelope, I pull out a packet of papers. The first is on official letterhead, and my heart picks up speed as I read the words there. He didn't...

"I'm not giving up on us, baby, so don't for a second think that's what this is. But I want you to know that whatever happens, you're taken care of. I moved my clothes and stuff out yesterday. Everything else is exactly where you left it. Bash is letting me stay with him for as long as I need to. I figured you won't want to live with your brother and Isla once they're married, and you deserve to have your own space and a place to do your work. The apartment's yours. It's completely paid for, and so are the next two years of property taxes and insurance."

My throat is so tight, I can barely force words out, and when I do, they come out in a croak. "Why would you do this?"

There's not a trace of hesitation or doubt in his eyes when he smiles at me. Only so much love that I have to fight back tears. "Because I love you, Mira. Because you're my wife, and I promised to take care of you. I told you I wouldn't walk away, and I won't. But I realized that when you walk back into my arms, I want to know that you're doing it with no hesitation. I don't want you coming back because you don't have a place to stay or because you feel you don't have any other options. I want you to run back into my arms because there's no other place you'd rather be."

He trails his fingers over my cheek one last time before stepping away. I feel cold without him.

"Will you come to our home games next week? There are seats for you, Isla, and Lexi."

It's the first game of the conference quarterfinals. Despite the tension between Maddox and Griffin, the Rogues have played their way into the playoffs. It's a huge deal, and to say that everyone is excited would be an understatement.

"Of course I'll be there. I wouldn't miss it."

For the first time in weeks, Griffin gives me a wide, uninhibited smile, and my insides go squishy. "Good. That's good. Well, I should go before your brother shows up and gives me a black eye. Start on that book, baby girl, and I'll talk to you later. I love you."

He's out the door, the mechanism clicking shut before my brain catches up with my heart, and I whisper, "I love you too."

"WE NEED TO TALK," I SAY TO MADDOX THAT evening when he walks through the door. Stalks through the door is more accurate. He's been in a foul mood for weeks, responding to me mostly in grunts and nods, and I'm sick of it.

Enough is enough.

My brother scowls. "I need to pack my shit and get to the airport, Mi-Mi. Can it wait?"

"Nope." Crossing my arms over my chest, I glower right back at him. Two can play this game, and I'm just as much a Graves as my grumpy brother. "Sit your big ass down before I have to kick it."

The asshole has the audacity to almost grin. We'll see if he's still smiling when we're done with this conversation. At least he does as I say, flopping down onto the couch with a groan. I stay standing. I'm determined to have the upper hand, which means I need all the height advantage I can get.

"You need to stop this shit."

One dark eyebrow rises. "Stop what shit?"

"Stop punishing Griffin. You're being a dick."

Mirroring my pose, my brother crosses his arms. "I'm not punishing him. He fucked around, and now he's finding out."

"Stop it. Seriously, just stop. You're such a hypocritical asshole, Maddox! Like a month ago you were trying to set me up with someone, and now you're mad because I'm with someone good and kind and selfless because he's not the guy you picked? Do you realize how ridiculous that is?"

Maddox pushes up from the couch. So much for the height advantage.

"Good and kind and selfless? Yeah, sure, Mir. He went behind my back, seduced my sister, tricked her into marrying him, then lied to me about it. Tell me how any of that is good or kind? And don't even get me started on selfless. Everything he's done is selfish. He fucking deserves to be knocked off the first line. Hell, if I had my way, he'd be benched."

"He didn't do anything behind your back, Maddox! I'm the one who asked him to keep this a secret. I'm the one who got him drunk. I'm the one who asked him to lie. All the shit you're mad about is my fault, but you're blaming him."

I'm pissed now, and I shove Maddy's chest.

"He hated keeping us a secret, especially from you. He wouldn't even sleep with me until I was sure about our marriage, and believe me, I tried to seduce *him* multiple times so he'd go back on that decision, but he never did."

My brother growls. "I don't want to hear this."

"Tough shit," I shout. "You're going to hear it. Griffin is better than good, Maddy. He's the best man I know. He's done nothing but protect me and take care of me and love me. And you want to talk about selfless? Do you know what he did today?" I pull the envelope with the deed to his apartment, as well as a bank statement that shows an account in my name with more money in it than I can comprehend. I didn't find that little gem until after Griffin left. Probably because he knew I'd never accept it. I shove the papers against my brother's chest.

"What is this?"

"Read them."

Maddy frowns as he takes the envelope from my hand, and it deepens as he reads before the muscles in his face go lax, then his mouth is hanging open like a fish. His brown eyes scan the words faster and faster until he's at the end of the last page.

When he looks at me, I see the same shock I felt reflected back at me. "He gave you his apartment?"

I nod.

"He loves that place."

My chest fills with tingling warmth and light. "It would seem he loves me even more. He gave me a home and the means to take care of myself because he's good and kind and selfless. Do you know he didn't ask anything of me in return? Just that if I do come back to him, it's because I can't live without him, not because I can't live without his house or the things he could do for me."

"I..." Maddox looks between me and the papers, his jaw working.

"You owe him an apology. A big one. Don't throw your friendship away because of your stupid pride or a misplaced need to protect me from the only other man besides you who's gone above and beyond to protect me." I sigh, suddenly completely drained. "And put him back on the first line. He doesn't deserve to be on the second, and you know you need him with you and Logan going into the playoffs. Don't be an idiot."

"He gave you his house."

We're still stuck on that?

"He bought me a car, gave me his house and way too much money. He loves the shit out of me, Maddy. If anything, I've been the selfish one." I'm going to do everything I can to work on myself and deserve him. "So pull your giant head out of your ass, make up with your best friend, and win some hockey games."

"Shit." Maddox hands me the envelope and rubs his temples. "Shit."

"I know the feeling."

"I need to get to the airfield."

I nod. "Hurry up and pack. Then talk to your best friend." A wicked grin curls my lips. "Go talk to your brother-in-law."

That stops my brother dead in his tracks. "Shit."

All I can do is laugh.

forty-seven

MIRA

The arena buzzes with anticipation as Isla, Lexi, and I walk in. Eyes turn our way when they notice our playoff jackets, and I squirm. Everyone knows Lexi and Isla are with Rogues players, but me? That wasn't public knowledge. Until now.

Hell, I tried to fight the girls on giving me a jacket, but once the other WAGS heard through the locker room grapevine and their significant others that Griffin and I are married, they wouldn't hear it. It didn't matter to them that things between Griffin and me are still up in the air. I'm his wife, and that's all they needed to know.

The black faux leather jackets are emblazoned with the bejeweled names and numbers of our partners. Isla wears an 84 with Graves on the back, Lexi wears a 13 with Hanson on the back, and I'm wearing 16 with Wright on the back. I try to ignore the whispers and speculation, but it has my hackles up. I'd probably enjoy showing off his name on my back if things had gone according to plan before everything went down in Michigan. If we'd announced our marriage to excited family and friends, instead of having to explain to them why we're... Well, I'm not even sure what we are. We're not broken up, but we're not entirely together, either.

It's all way too complicated, and I feel the weight of that tonight more than ever.

"Come on. Let's get to the box and order some drinks. I'm going to need at least two." Isla grabs my hand and drags me behind her. "This is so stressful, and I'm not even the one playing."

Lexi nods. "Seriously. This is almost as bad as when everything went down with my dad." Lexi's dad had been the head coach of the Rogues for years before finding out she was secretly dating the rookie, Ryder Hanson. He almost started a fight with Ryder in the middle of the game, and when Lexi ran through the seats to get to the bench, she heard her dad say some incredibly hurtful things no woman should have to hear from her father. Needless to say, he's not the coach anymore.

"I just want everyone to stop looking at me," I mutter. Both women chuckle at that.

"You'll get used to it." Isla squeezes my hand. "Sort of."

I don't think so. I'm used to being mostly invisible as Maddox's little sister. This—walking around with Griffin's last name sparkling like a beacon for all to see on my back in a playoff jacket that makes it very clear I'm with him— is not something I can imagine getting used to. I feel exposed and vulnerable. And the weight of his last name, knowing how much he wants me to take it for my own, is doubly heavy.

At least the box is full of family, so I can relax. We're still visible up here, but there are walls between us and the rest of the fans. Walls I need right now.

We say our hellos to the other wives and girlfriends, as well as a few cute kids and a handful of parents, order some drinks, and settle into our seats. We arrived early enough that the warm-ups haven't started yet, and the televisions in the box are tuned into a sports channel where analysts offer commentary, speculation, and banter back and forth.

I can't stop bouncing my knee.

Griffin and I spent every night during their final away series of the regular season talking and video chatting. We didn't have any sexy times over the phone, but we did fall asleep together. Every morning, I'd wake up to the sound of his soft breathing or a sleepy hello.

I'm still doing therapy twice a week, and even though I have a long way to go, I do feel like I'm getting a handle on my issues. Talking to someone who can help me analyze why I react to certain things the way I do has already brought me a deeper level of self-understanding. Griffin was so proud of me when I told him I've been going.

Staying away from him is getting harder and harder, and I'm not sure how much longer I'll be able to last, even though I'm determined to be in a better place before telling him I'm ready to give this thing between us a real shot. Because the only thing I know with absolute certainty after my time away from Griffin is that I don't want to be apart from him for much longer.

"Hey." Lexi bumps her shoulder against mine. "You okay? You seem a little lost in your head."

"I'm good," I tell her. "Just a lot on my mind."

Isla squeezes my hand from my other side. "We know. How have things been between the two of you since they got back from Colorado?"

"Well, it's not like we've had much time together. They spent all week going over film and practicing." This week leading up to the first quarterfinal game has been busy for the players. "But we went out to dinner together."

It was the first time we've been on a date since everything went south. We went to a quiet little restaurant and sat next to each other. He held my hand or stroked my knee the entire time before kissing me gently and taking me home. Part of me—the very lonely, very horny part of me—wanted to yell at him when he didn't try to take things further. But another part of me knew he was holding back because it's what I wanted.

He's still protecting me and putting me first.

"He really loves you," Isla says softly.

"I know. And I really love him, but I need to make sure I'm in a place where I can love him the way he deserves." Staring at the ice, I sag into my chair. "I just hope he doesn't give up on me in the meantime."

Both women smile and Lexi says, "No chance of that happening. You'll see."

Before I can respond with how much I hope that's true, the voice of the announcer rings out over the music playing in the arena, and my eyes go to the ice.

"Good evening, Rogues fans!" the voice booms through the cavernous space, vibrating through my chest. "Welcome to game one of the Western Conference Quarterfinals. Get ready to make some noise and welcome your Minnesota Rogues as they go up against the St. Louis Steam."

The crowd boos as the announcer names the head and assistant coaches of the opposing team and their players skate onto the ice for pregame warm-ups in a flurry of red and blue.

"And now, please welcome your Minnesota Rogues!"

If the volume level during the *boos* was loud, it has nothing on the cheers of the fans as they welcome the third and second lines, the players in their yellow and gray flying over the ice like conquering heroes. My heart begins to roar as the announcer's voice grows louder, winding up to introduce the individual names of the starting line.

"From the Rogues, starting on right wing, number twenty-seven, Logan Byrne!" The crowd cheers as Logan steps onto the ice, stick raised in his hand. He heads for the Rogues' goal and the pile of pucks waiting there for them.

I'm leaning forward in my seat, because the announcements always follow the same pattern. The offensive wingers, defense, the center, then the goalie. Which Means Griffin is next.

"Starting on left wing, we have an interesting change tonight."

I glance at Lexi and Isla, confused. There was a lineup change? Where's Griffin?

"Just breathe," Isla says, smiling. She pats my hand like she's not worried. Like the announcer calling out an *interesting change* during such a vital game isn't terrifying. Maddox swore he and Griffin had worked things out. He promised he would put him back on the first line.

"With the same number and tenacious playing as always, on left wing, number sixteen, Griffin Graves. That's right, folks, don't be confused when you see two jerseys with Graves stitched on their backs tonight. I'm told it's not a mistake." The announcer chuckles, but I don't even hear it. I don't hear anything else the man says, nor do I notice the roars and confused shouts of the crowd.

All these months, Griffin has been saying he'd change his name if I didn't want to. I thought he was kidding, that it was a silly flirtation.

"He changed the name on his jersey," I say to no one in particular. "He's wearing my last name."

Lexi clasps her hands over her heart and squeals. "Oh my god, I can't believe he did that. Iconic."

That's one word for it. Insane is another. So is romantic and touching and utterly, undeniably Griffin.

"He loves you so much," Isla says, leaning close. We both watch as Griffin takes a lap before stopping directly in the family box's line of sight with his back to us. He looks at me over his shoulder with sparkling eyes and a grin that transforms his face into something so beautiful it hurts to look at. He does a little shimmy with his ass, turns to stare right at me, and makes a heart with his hands.

"Oh my god." I'm pretty sure my mouth is hanging open, which is just great, because I swear every person in the arena cranes their neck to look at me. I'm about to combust into flames right here in the box. But it's not only the embarrassment of being the center of attention; it's the way this public declaration of his love has melted away any last vestiges of the worry that Griffin could one day leave me the way my dad did.

Intellectually, I've always known Griffin is nothing like my dad. But fear and decades-old trauma aren't things that exist in an intellectual space. They're roots of decay and deeply ingrained protective instincts that can be self-destructive, but they spread so deep, become so pervasive, that it takes an act of god to root them out and burn them away.

Or an act of love so loud and powerful, so selfless and pointed, that it pulses light and life through every deep vein of rot until there's nothing left of the beliefs that had been so omnipresent and damaging for so long.

This isn't the first time Griffin has shown his love in a public way, and I doubt it will be the last. But the fact that he did this when things are up in the air between us and I could still reject him? This is Griffin making himself vulnerable in front of thousands, if not millions of people. This is his way of telling me I'm more important than his reputation or pride, that he'll fight for me even when the outcome isn't assured.

Griffin's gesture has decimated one of my fears and shed a glaring light on the other. Because now, more than ever, I worry that I'm not good enough for Griffin Wright. I'm no longer worried that he'll hurt me, but I'm doubly worried I'll end up hurting him.

I've been retreating ever since our trip, letting my fears and insecurities dictate my future, when Griffin has been out here fighting for me with no promise of success. He's fought against my doubts, my brother's doubts, and his own deep-seated fear that no one will ever love him and choose him the way he longs to be chosen and loved.

It's time I stopped retreating. I'm not sure I will ever completely banish the whispering worry that I'll be left alone one day. But I'd guess Griffin feels the same, and he still shows up, day after day, to fight for me.

Griffin Wright deserves someone to go to battle for him. He deserves someone to put him first, push past their insecurities, and be a warm, safe place for him to rest. I'm determined to be that person. No matter what it takes, I'm going to fight like hell to be good enough for Griffin. Maybe I'm not there yet, but I will never stop striving to become the woman he deserves. I'm going to fight for him every bit as hard as he's been fighting for me.

I wish I could run to him right now. I wish I could tell him how much I love him. That I may need a bit more time to work through some of my issues, but I'm all in. I just hope that, on some level, he can feel my love from here.

I can't take my eyes off him as the rest of the team skates onto the ice and they begin their warm-ups. My eyes ping between his face and the name stitched in gray on the back of his jersey. My name. I'm up here wearing his, he's down there wearing mine, and my heart is forever branded *Griffin's*.

forty-eight

GRIFFIN

My blood is pounding like a drum in my veins.

Not only is it game one of the playoffs, but I just made an undeniable declaration of love in front of the whole fucking country. More importantly, I made it in front of my wife.

"She can't take her eyes off you," Ryder says, chuckling as he looks up at the box to blow a kiss to his girlfriend, Lexi.

"Do you think she liked it?" I kept telling Mira I'd change my name to hers if she wanted. I'm not stupid, I know she never took me seriously. I hope she can finally see that I am. Because when it comes to making promises to my wife, I mean every word I say. The guys will still call me Wright on the ice—because let's face it, it would be confusing as hell if they called Maddox and I both Graves —but the whole arena, and every hockey fan in the US and

Canada just saw how far I'm willing to go for the woman I love.

"Of course she liked it," Bash says as he stops the puck I send sailing toward the net as we warm up. "I know things are still a little up in the air with you two, but she loves you, man. You'd have to be blind not to see it."

Logan chuckles and elbows Maddox, who scowls. "Yeah. Blind like her brother."

"Shut the fuck up," Madds growls. There's no real heat behind the words. We've spent hours talking and working our shit out, so we're good. He knows now, beyond any shadow of a doubt, that I will do whatever it takes to love and take care of his sister. I've made it clear that she's it for me, and he's finally accepted it.

"Don't hassle my brother-in-law." I grin, hip checking Byrne.

"Still weird," Maddox grumbles. But even he's smiling. He can claim it's weird all he wants, and I guess on some level it is, but he likes it. So do I. It doesn't get much better than having your best friend for a brother-in-law.

I allow myself to feel all the nerves and excitement about everything with Mira during warm-ups, but the moment we head back into the locker room so the crew can prepare the ice, I push all that back. She's who I'm playing for—the reason I want to have the best game of my life—but I'm also playing for the men around me who have become my family.

Through all of this, they've stood by me, listened to me, encouraged me, and yeah, punched me in the face. But family isn't always sunshine and roses. It's hard and gritty and sometimes it hurts more than you think it should. Then you band together, work your shit out, and have each other's backs.

"You guys ready to kick the Steam's ass?" Maddox shouts in the locker room, his brown eyes blazing with the fire of upcoming battle. He surveys each of us, locking eyes with the men who call him captain, as our anticipation and determination to win grows and thickens like smoke until we're all breathing it in with deep gulps.

"Fuck, yeah," I shout. It's a response echoed by the men around me, growing louder and louder.

"This is our barn, boys. This is our ice. Our time. Our moment. Let's get out there and show St. Louis how dangerous it is when Rogues band together and fight like one. I want Bash to be bored because we're doing such a good job of keeping the puck out of the defensive zone. I want the fans to be tired because they have to jump to their feet to cheer so often, their legs ache." Maddox surveys us all like a general preparing his troops for war.

"We've been through a lot this year, and we've exceeded the expectations of the fans and commentators. We overcame a coaching shake-up halfway through the season, injuries, long weeks on the road. There were so many times this year when we could have grown weary or given up, but we didn't. And it's all come to this. Tonight, we show the world what the Rogues are made of. Tonight, we get one step closer to the cup. Are you ready?"

The answering roar is so loud, I feel it in my chest. It settles in right beside my love for Mira, filling me with the kind of determination that strengthens your bones and elongates your spine.

We skate out to the thunderous cheers of a packed barn, but I swear I can pick hers out above it all.

Time to win this. For my boys and for my wife.

We head into the third period down by one. It's been an intensely physical game, and both teams are feeling the strain.

"We've got this, boys," I shout as we retake the ice. "St. Louis is starting to lose their *steam*." Waggling my eyebrows, I make my teammates chuckle at the play on the other team's name. "But we aren't. We could do this all night. Let's fucking go."

Bumping gloves, we take our positions at center ice. Maddox offers a feral grin to the opposing captain, dropping his stick in preparation for the puck drop.

"I hope you boys have enjoyed your momentary lead. We'll be taking that away now," I say conversationally to one of St. Louis's wingers.

"The same way you took a woman's name?" The asshole scoffs, rolling his eyes. "Fucking pussy."

The second the puck drops, the chirpy little shit goes for possession, and I smile wickedly. Can't really hit an opponent if they're not going for the puck, but if he is? Well, then it's game on.

He lets out a grunt of pain as I slam him hard into the boards. Music to my ears. He staggers and struggles to stay on his feet.

"You know," I say to the guy as I pass the puck to Byrne, "pussies can take quite the pounding. Unlike you, you pansy-ass little bitch. No matter what name I'm wearing on my jersey, I can still kick your ass."

The winger lets out a strangled cry and speeds my way,

trying to check me. I spin out of the way with a grin, and the dumbass goes careening into the boards. If we weren't behind, I'd drop my gloves and blow off some steam on the guy's face, but there's no way in hell I'm getting sent to the penalty box in the third while we're down a point.

As I race down the ice, everything fades away, except for my teammates, the puck, and the driving need to win this one for my girl. The guys and I pick up speed while St. Louis flags. The cheers and chants of our hometown crowd are a shot of adrenaline as we outmaneuver and out-finesse our opponents.

Two minutes into the third, Maddox passes to Byrne, who fakes out a defenseman before tapping the puck to me. Glancing at Madds, I act like I'm about to set him up for a shot. The Steam's goalie tracks my attention and shifts in the goal, leaving the upper right corner open. Without shifting my full attention to the crease, I tip the puck onto my stick and send it sailing up over the goalie's shoulder and into the net.

The sirens sound, the red lights flash, and just like that, the game is tied. My teammates crowd around me, hugging and fist-bumping, but as soon as I can, I look up at my wife, who's jumping up and down in the box, and make a heart with my hands. I expect her to blush or maybe cover her face with her hands, because I know she doesn't love the public attention she's getting tonight, but she doesn't. She holds her hands up and returns the gesture.

And man, does that feel good.

With the game now tied, both sides up the intensity, and the already physical game ratchets up a notch. I'm panting when I hit the bench after a line change, but the adrenaline rushing through my system doesn't slow.

We're going to win this game.

Coach Fry talks us through strategies for the remaining fifteen minutes of play, then the guys and I are hopping the boards and back on the ice. We drive hard toward the Steam's crease and do our best to keep the assholes away from Bash. It's a constant game of back and forth, and the minutes tick down too quickly.

We need to lock this up without going into overtime. I want to see my wife.

Eighteen minutes into the third period, our mascot leads the crowd in a chant of *let's go, Rogues*, and the atmosphere crackles with expectation. Ryder and the other d-man have the Steam held up at the boards, chipping away at a stuck puck, when Hanson gets a piece of it and sends the biscuit my way. With enough of the Steam still occupied by our guys, Logan, Maddox, and I streak down the ice on a breakaway.

The crowd cheers as I pass the puck to Byrne, who taps a blind pass to Graves when the Steam's center gets too close. Graves sees an opening and slaps the puck hard at the net. It glances off the pipe on the long side of the goal, rebounding and heading straight for Byrne. Intercepting the Steam player heading for Logan, I buy him time to tap the puck back at the net. The arena falls silent for a beat, waiting to see if the shot is good, then the puck hits the net, the siren blares, and with a minute and a half left in play, we've taken the lead.

With the clock ticking down, we don't let our intensity slip because a lot can happen in a minute and a half on the ice. It's a brutal battle down to the last second, but when the buzzer sounds, we celebrate, along with the fans.

Game one of the quarterfinals is in the bag. Our first win of the postseason, and I scored a goal wearing my wife's last name. Perfection.

All I can think about is showering, answering the questions I know the press will ask about my little display tonight, then holding Mira in my arms. Because as much as I love this game and my team, as hungry as I am to take this all the way to the Cup, what I'm most worried about winning is my wife back.

Everything else is icing on the cake.

forty-nine

MIRA

THE ENERGY IN THE ARENA IS ELECTRIC AS THE guys celebrate their win on the ice. Fans cheer, lights flash, and music blares over the sound system.

"Oh my god," Isla shouts. She and Lexi have their arms around me, jumping up and down as we hug, much like the guys are doing below us on the ice. "That was amazing! My man is going to get laid tonight!"

That makes me groan. "Ew. That's my brother you're talking about."

She giggles. "Sorry, not sorry. The way he set up that last goal was…" She mimes a chef's kiss.

"I'm sure Logan won't have any trouble finding someone to celebrate with, either," Lexi says, giggling right along with Isla.

"One day, he's going to find some woman who knocks him off his feet, and he's going to regret sleeping around." I know Griffin does, and he wasn't nearly as bad as Logan.

"I don't know." Lexi watches the guys file off the ice and down the tunnel. "From what Ryder's said, it sounds like Logan is very anti-relationship. I could see Bash ending up in a relationship and Logan being the lone single guy in their group."

Isla does a little head wobble. "I think he's got a softer center than he lets on."

"Only time will tell. All I know is that, right now, I couldn't care less about Logan Byrne's slutty ways. I just want to see my husband. I still can't believe he wore my name on his back."

"That was seriously romantic." Lexi clutches her hands over her heart. "Who knew so many of these guys were secret softies?"

"Me," Isla replies with a shrug before turning my way. "I won't say I *knew* something would happen between you two when you moved in, but I'm also not surprised. Griffin's always been a romantic. Just look at what he did for me and Maddox."

"So, are you two officially back together?" Lexi asks. "Were you ever really not together?"

"Both great questions. And I'm not sure how to answer them," I tell her honestly. "I guess we never really broke up, but I asked him for some time to figure things out. After the thing in Michigan, I freaked out a little. When we woke up married in Vegas, I never believed he could be my forever. Then when I started to fall for him, it was amazing but terrifying, you know?

"I don't have a good framework for forever. And I know I'm not doomed to live my mom's life or anything, but I let the fear that maybe he'd leave fester, and I was pulling Griffin toward me with one hand while pushing him away with the other. Then, when I pulled a Maddox and assumed things were over without ever talking to Griffin, I realized I have some work to do if I want to be the wife he deserves."

"No one is perfect," Isla says, a gentle look in her eyes. "Everyone has work they need to do, right, Lexi?"

My blonde friend nods. "Absolutely. You're not the only woman in the room with daddy issues." She says it with a smile, but I know how hurtful the whole situation with her dad was. That kind of pain leaves a mark. I'm glad she has Ryder by her side to support her as she heals.

Just like I have Griffin.

"I've been seeing a counselor, and I plan to continue. She's been really helpful. I need to talk to Griffin tonight, but I think I need a little more time to focus on healing while he focuses on the postseason. After that, I'm all in. No more holding back."

"Because you're in love with him." Isla says what I haven't, and even though hearing her speak the words out loud makes my heart beat faster in my chest and a lump form in my throat, I can say with absolute certainty that they're good responses. Not because I'm scared—and okay, I'm still a little scared, but who wouldn't be?—but because I'm excited.

"Yeah. I'm really in love with him."

My future sister-in-law and the woman I'm certain will end up being one of my best friends squeal and wrap me in a hug.

Lexi beams at me. "Then, let's get you down to him. The rest of your life awaits."

Hell yeah, it does. And I'm ready.

———

THE MOMENT GRIFFIN STRIDES OUT OF THE LOCKER room, I'm throwing myself into his arms.

"Oh my god, babe. You played so well. I'm so proud of you." Pulling my face away from his neck, I peer up at the man I'm hopelessly in love with and lick my lips.

He groans, holding me tighter. "Fuck, baby. Keep looking at me like that, and I won't be able to control myself. I'll take you in a janitor's closet or something, and that is not how I want to reconnect with you for the first time."

I chuckle, but I know exactly how he feels. It's taking every ounce of my self-control not to grind against him with my legs wrapped around his waist the way they are.

Griffin's expression goes soft and he whispers, "Can I kiss you, sunshine?"

Without bothering to answer, I press my lips to his. He's kissed my cheeks and my forehead since everything went down in Michigan, but we haven't *kissed* in the weeks that followed. He's been so sweet and good, following my lead and never pushing me. But I've missed kissing him. So much.

He groans against me as his tongue sweeps against my lips, and I allow him entry, deepening the kiss. It stokes the rising flame in my belly, and I sigh into him. Until someone jostles us.

"Get a fuckin' room," my brother grumbles, elbowing Griffin. "I don't need to see this shit."

Chuckling, Griffin turns to Maddy with one raised eyebrow. "You want me to get a room with your sister?

Damn. You were always a solid wingman, but I never thought you'd be encouraging me to fuck your sister."

My cheeks are hot and no doubt bright pink as the people around us laugh, having heard all of that. Luckily, Isla is there to put a hand on my brother's chest and softly remind him that he can't start a fight with his brother-in-law in the locker room. Especially not with the press outside.

"Speaking of press," Maddox says with a sigh, "we need to go answer a few questions." He levels Griffin with a pointed look. "And you know they're going to want to talk to you. Let's go get this over with so we can celebrate."

The guys grumble but move toward the press room. None of them love giving post-game interviews, but they just won the first game of the playoffs. There's no getting out of it.

"Drive with me to the bar after?" Griffin asks me softly. His eyes are full of hope and vulnerability.

"Of course. I wouldn't want to be anywhere else."

Watching Griffin walk out of the friends and family room with the rest of the guys makes my chest physically ache. He's not wearing his jersey anymore, but I can still see the phantom *Graves* stitched there. A very public declaration that he will do whatever it takes to make me happy, including taking my name.

Suddenly, all the excuses I've been making about needing more time to get myself in a better place feel flimsy and hollow. What was it that Griffin said when he proposed to me that night after flying back to the Twin Cities alone because I'd left without him? Something about how he'd been waiting for the perfect time to propose, but love isn't about perfection. That it's about choice and commitment and putting someone else before yourself?

I'm an idiot.

While working on my issues is important and necessary, it could take me *years* to feel like I've really gotten a handle on them. I may never feel that way. So what, I'm just supposed to lock myself away and live a half-life without love or commitment or risk in the meantime? I'm supposed to look my husband—my best friend in the world—in the eye and tell him I'm not perfect enough yet to love him?

Griffin has never once asked for my perfection. Not once. So why would I think he'd ask for it in this?

No, all these barriers between us have been laid, brick by brick, entirely by me. And it's time I tear them down.

Heart hammering in my chest, I turn to Lexi and ask, "Do you know someone who can get me into the press room? It's important."

My friend grins. "My dad may not be the coach anymore, but I still have some connections. Come on."

"No way are you leaving me behind," Isla says, grabbing my hand. "I have a feeling I won't want to miss this."

We trail behind Lexi, who taps a man wearing a Rogues polo on the shoulder and leans in to whisper in his ear. My heartbeat picks up speed.

Isla's right. She definitely won't want to miss this.

GRIFFIN

THE PRESS ROOM IS FULL TO BURSTING.

"What are you going to tell them when they ask about the name change?" Bash asks me under his breath so none of the reporters can hear.

I shrug. "I'm gonna tell them the truth."

"You're going to tell them you and Mira are married? Is she cool with that?" My friend's dark brows dip and furrow. He's been nothing but supportive, letting me stay with him, listening to me talk about Mira every second of the day, and doing his best to help me come up with ways to win my wife back.

When I told him I was going to change the name on the back of my jersey to hers, he worried it could backfire spectacularly. All along, Mira has been the one who wanted to keep our marriage a secret, and if I made such a public gesture—one that would be real damn hard to misconstrue—I could make her feel backed into a corner in a big way and undo all the progress I've made. I told him he wasn't wrong, but once the idea popped into my head, there was no ignoring it.

"I'm going to tell them the truth."

Bash's smile is grim. "I hope this works."

"Me too, man. Me too." If it doesn't? If he's right and this backfires? Well, fuck, I don't know what I'll do. But as the last of the Rogues players and staff take their seats behind the microphones at the long table and the noise in the room grows, I don't have time to dwell on my worry.

These sharks can scent fear and weakness, so I won't show them any.

"Good evening, everyone," our coach, Mike Fry, says in his honeyed tenor. The room quiets, all eyes focusing on him. "Thanks for coming. We're going to make this brief tonight because these guys have played their asses off, and I know they're looking forward to celebrating their win with family and friends."

A murmur of agreement fills the room.

"Now, who wants to start us off?"

Ten hands shoot up in the air, and Coach Fry points to a middle-aged man with jet black hair. He asks Coach how he feels about the win, how we could improve in game two, and if there are any lessons we'd take away from tonight's matchup going into the rest of the series.

The next few questions are more of the same, and I zone out as the coaching staff and Maddox field them like the pros they are. Then Coach calls on a young reporter for an online publication, and the guy's attention snaps to me.

"Griffin, you had an interesting modification to your uniform tonight. Can you tell us what made you change the name on your jersey to Graves?"

My heart does a little flip. Here we go. "Well, it's no secret that Madds here is my best friend. We've often called ourselves brothers."

Chuckles flood the room, especially when Maddox rolls his eyes and shakes his head beside me.

The young reporter grins. "So you just thought it would be fun to use his name?"

I shrug, not answering.

"Were you trying to confuse St. Louis?" another reporter asks. "Was it all some weird mind game?"

That makes me laugh. "That would be a pretty elaborate mind game."

"It would," the young guy says, cutting back in. "And I doubt the league would be okay with something like that. So why don't you tell us the real reason behind the change?"

This is it. I'm about to put it all out there, and if Mira rejects me, the whole fuckin' world will know. I should be terrified, but all I feel is a deep, unshakeable peace.

"The real reason?" I offer the kid a genuine smile. "It's something I should have done months ago. D'you know that almost eighty percent of women in the U.S. take their husband's last name when they get married? Eighty percent." I shake my head, still smiling, as the reporters begin to murmur.

"I guess if the woman has a weird last name, and she wants to change it to something cooler, I can understand. But we treat it like a given that she should have to give up her identity for her husband's. What if she doesn't want to change it? I mean, let's be real, man. We still have some archaic views on shit in this country, and I personally think women get the short end of the stick way too often."

"What exactly are you saying?" the reporter asks, one brow cocked.

"I'm saying that society views a name change as a sign of ownership, and we can deny that until we're all blue in the face, but it's true, whether we like it or not. The thing is, I'd never try to own my wife." A slow grin curves my lips. "But she sure as shit owns me. What better way to show her, and the rest of the world, that I'm proud as hell to be hers than by taking her last name?"

Thick silence blankets the room for one beat, then two, then the whole place erupts into shouts and blinding light as reporters yell over one another and cameras flash.

"Holy shit," Bash mutters on my left.

"She's going to kill you," Maddox grumbles on my right.

She might. It was a gamble, putting it all out there like this. But Mira is worth every risk. Whatever the consequences are, I'll deal with them.

"Are you telling us that you married your captain's sister?" a female reporter shouts over the din.

"Sounds that way, doesn't it?" I reply, chuckling.

The woman laughs. "But there haven't been any reports of you two being together, let alone married."

I run a hand through my hair, not sure how much I should say, but knowing I'll have to say something. "Our story is long, and it didn't have the most traditional start. But it's still our story, and unless I get the go-ahead from her to share more, that's all I'm going to say."

My answer doesn't appease the circling sharks now that there's blood in the water, and the next five questions are all about my personal life. Coach tries to redirect them to the game the Quarterfinals, and the impressive effort my teammates and I put in, but everyone is more interested in trying to figure out how Mira and I ended up together.

"All right, all right." Coach makes a *settle down* motion with his palms. "I think we've about hit our time limit tonight. Let's take one more question. Does anyone else have something new to ask?"

Hands shoot up all over the room and reporters clamor to be chosen, but above the din, a clear, familiar voice rings out louder than the rest.

"I have a question."

Coach grins at the dark-haired woman as she steps forward, the number 16 glittering on her jacket in clear and yellow gems. Reporters part around her, cameras flash, and people call out to her for comments. It's chaos, but it doesn't touch me. The moment my eyes lock on her fathomless green irises, everything else fades away. It may as well be me and Mira alone in this room. Nothing and no one else matters.

"Go ahead, miss."

"My question is for Griffin," Mira says, a soft, secret smile on her face that makes my heart race.

"And what question might that be, Mrs. Graves?" I return her smile.

Reporters look at each other, sharing wide-eyed stares. But I'm only looking at her.

"Well, I was wondering if you'd marry me. For real this time. With a white dress and a tux and invitations. With our families and friends there instead of Dolly Parton." Those pretty lips of hers twitch into the most bewitching smile. "Though I suppose we could still invite her and Elvis, if you really want to."

Tears make my vision waver as I laugh at that and push out of my seat. Mira takes a few more steps toward me, and it's clear I'm not the only one trying not to cry.

"What do you say? Will you marry me?"

The whole room holds its breath.

I smile wider than I ever thought possible.

"Thought you'd never ask, sunshine."

Then I vault over the table like I'm taking to the ice, close the distance between us, wrap my wife up in my arms, and spin her around right there in the middle of a sea of reporters. I notice Isla and Lexi beaming and jumping up and down in the corner of the room, my teammates and closest friends cheering, and the flashes that come so fast and often that they look like strobe lights. But mostly, I notice the way Mira's tears spill down her cheeks, the way her hair tickles my neck, and the cherry flavor of her lip gloss as I take her mouth in a kiss that will no doubt be plastered all over the internet within minutes.

"I thought you needed time," I whisper against her lips.

Soulful green eyes pierce my heart as she whispers her reply. "A wise man once told me that love isn't about perfection, and I realized he was right. That you don't need me to be perfect, you just need me to be present. To love you to the best of my ability. A few more weeks or months won't change that, and I really, *really* hate being apart from you."

"Fuck, baby, I hate it, too. So much." I press my forehead against hers before stealing another kiss.

"Come home? We can figure the rest out later."

"You're sure?"

She nods. "More sure than I've ever been. I love you."

The deep-seated part of me that's always waiting to be

rejected unclenches and sighs. She's here. She's choosing me. *Claiming* me. Publicly. And it hasn't even been six months.

"I love you too. More than you'll ever know."

Mira grins. "I think I have a pretty good idea after tonight."

"Baby, this is just the beginning."

Sweeping her into my arms, we ignore the shouts and chaos around us as I carry my wife, bridal style, out of the room. We have a win to celebrate. And a wedding to plan.

fifty-one

GRIFFIN

MY WIFE JUST PROPOSED TO ME IN FRONT OF A room full of reporters and press. Holy shit.

She giggles and burrows her face in my neck as I carry her to my car, letting Maddox and Isla know we'll meet them at Chasers to celebrate. For a little while. Then I have some celebratory plans that would get us arrested for indecent exposure. We'll have to go home for those.

Home. She wants me to come home. She wants to stay married.

She wants me.

When we get to the G-Wagon, I set Mira's feet on the ground, only to push her back against the car. Caging her body in, I press my forehead to hers, closing my eyes and savoring her softness and warmth against me, the sound of her shallow breathing, and the floral scent of her hair. She's my safe place. My home. And even though I was determined not to let her go, I can't deny the fear that crept in like shadowy vines at the edge of my mind. Every other woman I'd been with had decided I wasn't forever material. What if Mira had come to the same decision?

"I'm sorry," she whispers. Her soft hands cup my face, chasing the last remnants of fear away with their warmth. "I'm so fucking sorry."

"No, baby. You have nothing to be sorry for."

"I do, though. I hurt you. I made you question my love for you and I pulled away. It's stupid, but I really thought I was doing the right thing. That I had to fix myself to be worthy of your love or something, but you have never asked me to be perfect or to prove my worth. You've loved me exactly as I am. I was just too scared of being hurt to see it." Tears drip from Mira's lower lashes and her lip trembles.

Reaching up, I dry her eyes with my thumbs. "Oh, sunshine, you don't have to apologize for being scared and trying to protect yourself. I did the same thing for years, remember? It's why I never tried to date anyone or put myself out there. Until you. You got me drunk, and when we woke up married, it was like you handed my chance to me on a silver platter." I kiss her teary eyelids before tilting her chin up and running my thumb over her lower lip. "Not sure I would have had the courage to go after what I wanted if you hadn't."

"And what did you want?"

I grin and nuzzle her nose with mine. "You. Some part of me has always wanted you. But I couldn't let myself acknowledge the attraction I felt, because you were my best friend's little sister. You were beautiful and fiery and hilarious, but you were off-limits.

"Then you moved in and I realized what I felt for you

was so much more than physical attraction. Spending time with you made it easier to breathe. You're sunshine and fresh air and everything good, baby." Reaching into my pocket, my fingers close around the little black velvet box I've carried every day since that first day in Michigan. Not even her *no* when I proposed before made me stop.

Mira's green eyes widen as I pull the box from my pocket and hold it up between us. She clasps her hands over her heart, and they tremble. So do mine.

Flipping the lid of the ring box open, I memorize her soft little inhalation and etch it into my heart. "I know you said no when I asked you to marry me a few weeks ago, but I figure now that you've asked me and I said yes, well…" I take the massive diamond out and slip it onto her ring finger. "I thought you may want to wear it now."

"Yeah," she says with a watery laugh, "I want to wear it now."

Once the ring is on her slender finger, she holds it out between us and admires it. I'm only admiring her. "You're beautiful."

"I love it. I love *you*." Mira leans in and presses a soft kiss to my lips before pulling back with a stunning smile. "I can't wait to show Isla and Lexi."

The way she's looking at me—like I'm everything to her—has me tempted to say *fuck it* to meeting everyone at Chasers so I can take my wife home and make her mine again in every conceivable way. But they'd kick my ass, and I know they'll want to celebrate Mira and me working our shit out as much as they'll want to celebrate the win. So instead of pushing my girl into the car and ravaging her, I settle for slanting my lips over hers and kissing the fuck out of her.

The little gasp she releases in my mouth as she opens for me has my dick painfully hard. I press her against the car, showing her how much I want her, and sweep my tongue inside her mouth. We make out right there in the players' garage until a few of my teammates wolf whistle and shout at us to get a room.

Mira pulls away, the prettiest blush staining her cheeks. She looks up at me, giggles, then leans forward and hides her face in my chest.

"Oh my god."

"Got a little carried away. Sorry, sunshine. Let's go make an appearance at Chasers. The sooner we get there, the sooner we can leave."

She giggles again, and god, I've missed that sound. We don't talk much on the way to the bar, both of us content to soak up the other's company. I don't let her hand go until I'm pulling into the parking lot, then as soon as we're out of the car, it's back in mine.

For the first time in weeks, I feel settled and content. There's no worry eating away at my stomach, no loneliness picking at my heart. I woke up this morning without Mira in my arms, but tonight, I'll fall asleep holding her, and I'll never wake up without her again. Well, without her being mine. Even if there are hundreds of miles between us during away games, I'll still wake up each morning knowing she's mine.

Isla, Lexi, and the guys all cheer as Mira and I walk into Chasers. They stand and clap and shout for us. Even Maddox. Once the other patrons see what the fuss is about, they join in too. And I laugh when I see what's playing on the big screens all over the bar. It's footage of Mira proposing to me after the game.

"This is embarrassing," she mutters, her face turning the brightest shade of red I've ever seen.

Laughing, I grab my wife and dip her low, right there in front of the entire bar, and kiss the hell out of her. When we're standing again, I raise her hand like the winning boxer in a ring and shout, "I said yes!"

Cheers go up again, along with quite a bit of laughter, as we make our way to the table in the back filled with our family and friends. They all crowd around Mira and me, hugging and congratulating us. My wife's smile is blinding, and my heart feels like a helium balloon. If it gets any fuller, it may float out of my chest.

"I'm happy for you," Bash says as he pulls me in for a hug. "You deserve someone to look at you the way your wife does. I'm glad I was wrong about the jersey stunt."

I laugh. "Me too, man, me too."

Ryder hugs me next, then Maddox, then Logan.

"Can't believe my wingman is married," Logan laments. "This is a sad fucking day."

I can't even be annoyed, because his pout is so ridiculous that all I can do is laugh. "Just wait, dude. You'll be next. You have to be, because karma is hilarious like that."

Byrne's nose wrinkles like he smelled something foul. "No. Absolutely not. You won't curse me to a life of misery and disappointment."

"I'm gonna laugh my ass off when you change your tune one day." Shaking my head, I clap my good friend on the shoulder. "Some firecracker of a woman is going to come along and put you in your place, and you'll never live it down."

"Never gonna happen."

I laugh and wrap my arm around Mira when she snuggles into my side. "We'll see, Byrne. We'll see."

MIRA

I can't believe how much my life has changed in less than nine months. Who would have thought back in September, when I agreed to live with Griffin, that this is where we'd be in April? The guys just won their first postseason game, and I proposed to my husband in front of a room full of cameras and reporters.

Life is strange and beautiful.

Snuggled into the large corner booth with Griffin on my left and Isla on my right, I allow myself to get lost in the laughter and conversations. To think, I spent so many years of my adult life trying to separate myself from my big brother's life and shadow, to make something for myself and prove I could do big things, too, and all I was doing was putting distance between myself and the people who love me. It's never been a competition with Maddox, and if I felt like it was, it was all in my head.

Maybe our dad was a giant piece of shit who walked away, but my mom and my brother have always done everything they can to fill the space he left. I've been blessed to have blood family that loves and supports me. I hate thinking about the extra years I could have had with a found family who are just as supportive and loving.

"What are you thinking about?" Isla asks, giving my hand a squeeze. "You look a thousand miles away."

As I scan the overflowing table full of massive men, a

woman who is fast becoming one of my best friends, and one who is now my sister, I smile. "Thinking about family. And how lucky we are to have one this big and amazing. Even if the guys do make everything smell like sweat and hockey funk."

Isla laughs, the sound bright and comforting. "The smell can be awful, but they more than make up for it, don't they?"

I watch as Ryder hugs Lexi to his side and they both laugh at something Sebastian says. Logan shakes his head at them, but it's affectionate and familiar. My brother and my husband are cracking up with a couple of other guys from the team, and Griffin's laughter vibrates through me where he holds me to his side.

Jared isolated me. I let him, but he did. By the time I left Chicago, I didn't have any friends left who would rally around me, celebrate when I had a win, or show up when things were falling apart. On paper, he'd been perfect. Everything I was looking for. In reality, he was just another guy content to take and take until there was nothing left.

Griffin pulled me right into the center of his circle like it was the most natural thing in the world. He's given me so much more than he's taken, and even though he seemed like the opposite of what I should want, he's everything I needed. He's become my safe haven, my home, and my biggest supporter.

"They really do," I finally say to Isla. "They're the best men I know."

"Who's the best man you know?" Griffin asks, breaking away from his conversation with Maddox.

I snuggle into his side and let my hand drop to his leg,

teasing my fingers up the muscles along the inside of his thigh. "You."

Griffin's hand on my hip tightens, the pads of his fingers biting into my flesh. "Sunshine…"

His tone holds a warning, but to me, it sounds like a promise. Isla giggles and I give her a wink.

"Yes, husband?"

"You're playing with fire."

I trail my fingers higher, pleased as fucking punch when his dick hardens and strains against his suit pants. "Am I?"

He stands when I let my fingers just barely graze the head of his cock, bumping the table and making all eyes turn his way. Clearing his throat, he grabs my hand and hauls me to my feet, then says, "Well, it's been fun. I can't wait to celebrate our next win, but my wife is tired, so I'm going to take her home."

"I'm not tired," I say sweetly.

Everyone laughs and Lexi shouts, "Get it, girl!"

Griffin shrugs. "You will be when I'm done with you." Then he bends down, wraps his hand beneath my ass, presses his shoulder into my stomach, and lifts me over his shoulder like a caveman right there at the booth. He salutes our laughing friends with his free hand.

"See you guys tomorrow."

For the second time tonight, he carries me out to the sound of cheers and laughter.

fifty-two

GRIFFIN

I BREAK AT LEAST FOUR TRAFFIC LAWS ON THE WAY home. Honestly, I'm not even remotely sorry.

It's been weeks since I've been with my wife. Slow, agonizing, lonely weeks where I had to wonder if I'd ever get the chance to hold her again, let alone make love to her. And I intend to make love to her. Then I'm going to fuck her brains out.

"Babe, slow down." Mira covers her eyes as I take too sharp a turn into the parking garage, but she's giggling, so I know she's not scared.

"Can't. Pretty sure my dick's gonna fall off if I don't get inside you within the next five minutes."

"You're ridiculous." She laughs, and fuck if it isn't the best sound in the world. I've missed her laughter.

"Ridiculous and horny," I say, agreeing. And then I'm parking the G-Wagon and tugging her out of her seat before she can open the door herself. For the third time tonight, I bend over, lift her into my arms, and carry her bridal style through the lobby and into the elevator while she squeals and demands I put her down.

No fuckin' way am I putting her down until we walk through the door of our bedroom. Then I'll throw her onto the bed. Before that? Nope.

As soon as the elevator doors close and we're alone, I take her mouth in a desperate kiss. I kiss her like I'm going to fuck her—hard, needy, and fast. She moans against my lips as I let the hand under her ass wander. My dick is impossibly hard.

"Why does this elevator take so long?" I complain. But before Mira can answer, our floor number flashes on the LED screen, and the door opens. "Finally."

Mira chuckles, her lips skimming over my jaw and neck while her hands trail over my shoulders and down my arms and back. "So impatient."

"Absolutely, I am. It's been too long since I've had my wife. If I didn't know the security guys would watch like a bunch of pervs, I would have pulled your jeans down and fucked you against the wall of the elevator." I set Mira on her feet so I can unlock the door to our place. "But no one sees your sweet ass but me, sunshine."

She's about to make some snarky retort when the door swings open and I herd her through. As soon as it's shut, I'm ripping at her clothes. Her jacket puddles on the floor, her sweater and bra quickly following. Dusky pink nipples tighten in the cool air, and I don't hesitate to bend down and take one into my mouth.

"Oh, fuck, I've missed your mouth," Mira says, her head falling back against the door.

Grinning against her breast, I suck and lave at those

tight little buds while my fingers work to undo her pants and tug them down her body, along with her panties. When they get stuck on her shoes, I growl, but she giggles.

"Of course, they have laces and you can't just slip them off," I mutter. Bending down, I tug impatiently at the laces of her ankle boots before slipping them off her feet. Then my fingers drag her pants down until she can kick them off. When I look up, I realize what's in front of me.

My wife's cunt glistens with need, and it's been far too long since I've had the taste of her on my tongue. Leaning forward, I grab her hips and tilt her pelvis just enough to let me slide my tongue along her seam.

"Fuck. I almost forgot how delicious you taste."

"Griffin..." Mira's fingers push through my hair before she grabs a handful. "Oh, god."

Grinning against her pussy, I give her another slow lick before forcing myself to stand. There's a bite of pain when Mira tugs my hair before releasing it, but it only heightens my arousal. "Need you, baby. Need to be inside you."

"Yes. Please."

Fisting her hair in one hand, I wrap the other around her waist and guide her backwards to our bedroom while kissing the hell out of her. The little gasps and moans she rewards me with are music to my ears. If the neediness in her tone is any proof, I'm not the only one who's been going out of their mind while we've been apart.

"You're wearing too many clothes," Mira growls as her fingers scrabble to unbutton my shirt. She sounds like an angry kitten, and I'm barely able to hold back my laughter. I want to fuck my wife, not end up castrated.

When her legs bump against the foot of the bed and

she tips backward onto her ass, I grin down at her. "I can fix that."

Grabbing both sides of my shirt, I rip the thing open. Buttons fly across the room and Mira squeals as one barely misses hitting her on the cheek. "Oops?"

My beautiful wife laughs at that and shakes her head. "Just get naked. I need you inside of me. Now."

"Your wish is my command." I swear to god, I've never gotten my pants off faster.

Finally naked, I fall onto my wife with the passion and need of a man coming home after a long and brutal war. I can't get enough of her satiny skin, the way her curves give under my fingers, and the blazing heat of her center.

"Yes," she gasps as my teeth scrape along her collarbone before I soothe the ache with my tongue. "More."

"You want more?" I grind my dick against her core.

"I want everything."

Fuck. I wanted to take this slow. We've been apart, and I need to make sure Mira knows that this need I feel for her isn't merely physical. I've ached for her on a soul-deep level. But how in the hell am I supposed to take it slow when she's undulating her hips against my shaft and coating me in her slick desire? Every circle of her hips brings me closer to slipping inside of her, and I'm not sure I'm capable of holding back much longer.

"Wanted to take this slow," I grit out as the head of my dick bumps against her clit and she sucks in a breath, arching into me.

"Slow is overrated. Need you to fuck me."

Any tenuous grip I had left on my control snaps, and I line myself up at her entrance, pushing inside in one slow, torturous stroke.

"Oh, yes. Oh, god."

I still, my elbows braced on either side of Mira's head, her soft skin beneath me as I cage her in. Lowering my forehead to hers, I let myself savor the heat of her, the floral scent of her hair, the way her breasts brush against my chest with every ragged inhalation.

In the weeks we've been apart, I tried not to let myself think about a life without this. Without her. Optimism isn't something that comes naturally to me regarding relationships, but I did my best to hold on to hope. Because the alternative—a life not shared with the person who means most to me in this world—was too bleak to entertain. Still, when I was lying alone in the guest bedroom at Sebastian's place, it was impossible not to slip into those fears.

Eyes closed, I take in a shuddering breath.

Nimble fingers skate along my cheeks and jaw, followed by a whispered, "I'm here. I'm here and I'm never leaving again."

Fuck.

I'm not ashamed to admit that my eyes fill with tears at that declaration. Mira is here with me. She isn't going anywhere, because she's chosen me the same way I've chosen her.

"Love you." The words are a gruff promise.

"I love you, too, husband. Now, show me who you belong to."

"Oh, Sunshine, I hope you're ready."

Green eyes stare up at me as I begin to move. Green eyes that are more familiar than my own. Mira watches my face as I roll my hips, filling her and withdrawing, then filling her again. She's all softness to my steel, taking what I give with trust in her gaze and sighs on her lips.

"Hated being apart from you," I say with a rasp.

"I know. I hated it too."

"Never again." I thrust harder, punctuating my demand.

Mira makes a keening sound. "Never."

"You fucking own me, baby. I'm yours. And you're mine. If you ever doubt my love and commitment again, I'm going to put you over my knee and paint your ass red."

"Oh," she moans, the word breathy and dripping with sex.

More little gasps spill from her lips, spurring me on. Pushing up onto one palm for better leverage, I grip her hip with my other hand and pick up the pace. Mira's tits bounce with every thrust. Her hips lift to meet mine, and she whines softly when the base of my shaft bumps her clit.

Pleasure builds in my body. It's a static—a buzzing— that grows stronger and stronger with every stroke of my cock along her fluttering inner walls. As much as I want to make this last, it's been too long since I've buried myself in my wife, and I need her to come.

Letting go of Mira's hip, I pull out, grinning when she curses me, and flip her over onto her belly. With her face on the bed, I tug her ass into the air. Before she can demand I touch her, I thrust into her hard. Draping my body over her, I press my sweaty chest against her slick back as I plant a hand on one side of her head and reach around her hips with the other. I have no trouble finding her clit. It's swollen and hard, begging to be touched and teased.

"Shit," Mira yelps as I drag two fingers through the wetness that gathers along the base of my dick before using her arousal to lubricate my fingers. I circle her clit softly at first, savoring the breathy little moans and mewls she rewards me with. But each quiet sound tightens my groin and the muscles in my abdomen.

I'm not going to last much longer.

"Need you to come, baby." I add pressure to her clit. "Strangle my dick. Claim what's yours while I claim what's mine."

"Griffin…"

Her ass bounces against my hips as I fuck her harder and harder, and when she looks over her shoulder at me with glassy, pleasure-drugged eyes, I watch her perfect tits sway with each thrust. She's perfect. A goddess.

"Mine."

Unable to hold back much longer, I pinch Mira's clit and roll it between my fingers as I pound into her from behind. She opens her mouth, a cry on her lips, at the same moment her pussy contracts, squeezing my dick. All sense of rhythm is lost as my need takes over and my body tightens almost to the point of pain before her tight heat grips me like a vise, and I'm gone.

Unintelligible shouts fill our room as lights dance across my vision and pleasure renders me dumb. Mira's body trembles and convulses beneath me, still rippling with pleasure as she rides out her orgasm. I thrust into her twice more before my body goes rigid and I still, cock pulsing as I fill her up.

For precious moments, nothing exists outside of Mira and me. No sounds hit my ears, except for our ragged breathing and gasps. I feel nothing besides the soft, sweat-slicked skin of the woman I love and the wet heat of her center as I begin to soften inside of her. There are no worries, no games to win, no futures to figure out. Just me and Mira, connected in all ways, lost in each other.

It's perfect.

"I love you," I whisper, pressing my face into her hair and kissing her temple.

"I love you too."

Easing out of her, I drag my wife down onto the bed and into my arms. Showers can wait. Right now, I need to hold Mira. And I suspect she needs to be held just as much.

"Thank you," she says. Her tone is gentle and a little reverent.

I shiver when she reaches up to cup my jaw. "For what?"

"For never giving up on me. For fighting for me and refusing to walk away."

"I'll always fight for you," I tell her honestly. "And there's nothing you could do that would make me walk away. You're it for me, sunshine. You're my family. My home. There's no getting rid of me now."

Mira's laughter warms my chest. It burrows in deep, wrapping around my heart and filling me so full I could burst. She's so beautiful like this. Raw, unfiltered, and glowing. And so, so happy.

"I don't know what I did to deserve you, but you're my home too. You're everything I ever wanted and so much more I didn't know I needed."

Light from the bedside lamp refracts off the diamond

on her finger. A promise and a reminder that we're end game.

"Love you always," she whispers.

Tightening my arms around her, I feel the rightness of her vow and offer her one of my own.

"Love you forever."

epilogue

AUGUST

MIRA

"You look so beautiful." My mom, Camila, clasps her hands over her heart as she stares at my reflection in the full-length mirror before me. "I can't believe both of my babies are getting married in one summer."

My mom's brown eyes—almost the same shade as Maddy's—sparkle with unshed tears as I turn to her. She looks lovely and elegant with her dark hair pulled back in a loose chignon, a stylish lilac dress hugging each of her curves.

"Mom, you're going to ruin your makeup," I say. But my chastisement lacks any real conviction since my own voice cracks. I fan my face. I will not ruin the exquisite job the makeup artist did.

"Oh, sweetheart." As Mom pulls me into a hug, I'm

transported back to all the times she's held me just like this. Times of celebration, of pain, uncertainty, and hope. She's always been the constant in my life. She and Maddox.

Now, I have a third constant. My husband. The man I'm marrying again in less than fifteen minutes.

It's not a legally binding ceremony—the wedding in Vegas was very real and very legal—but it's a chance to exchange our vows the way we should have in the first place. Sober, and in front of all the people we love most in the world.

Maddox and Isla were married last month. The Rogues won the Western Conference Quarterfinals and advanced through the playoffs but ultimately fell short of making it to the finals and a bid for the Cup. The guys were obviously disappointed, but not going all the way meant Maddox and Griffin had more time to help Isla and me plan our respective weddings in a very tight timeframe.

A knock on the door has my mom pulling away and dabbing her eyes with a tissue.

I squeeze her hand and call, "Come in!"

A familiar head of dark hair peeks around the door. My brother used to be a perennial grump, but ever since he found Isla, he's been softer. Happier. And now that they're married, the man never stops smiling.

"Mi-Mi. You look..." He steps into the room and runs a hand along his jaw as he takes me in. "You look beautiful."

As soon as Griffin and I decided to throw a wedding, I went back to the bridal shop where Isla tried on dresses and bought the gown that had made my heart flutter. It's somehow both dramatic and elegant with its plunging neckline, beaded lace, delicate straps, and slightly flared skirt.

I do a little twirl, and the modest train sweeps along the floor as I spin. "You like it?"

My brother grins. "It's all right."

Our mom chuckles, no stranger to our antics. But despite my brother's teasing, I don't miss the emotion in his eyes as he takes me in.

"I'm happy for you, Mir. It may have taken me a while to come around to the idea of you being married to my best friend, but you couldn't have chosen better. He loves you."

Smiling, I cross the distance and throw my arms around my big brother. "I know. I love him too."

"That being said, if he ever hurts you, I'll still bury him in a shallow grave in the woods."

"Maddox!" Mom appears scandalized, but I just laugh. "Noted."

My brother grins. "Now, are you ready? Your husband is about to wear a groove in the floor of his room."

I nod, butterflies taking flight in my chest. "Ready."

Bending down, Maddox kisses me on the forehead. "We'll get into position. See you out there in a few. Don't trip."

Mom shakes her head, and as Maddox leaves, Lexi and Isla walk into the room. They look stunning in their lilac chiffon dresses, and even though they were in the room when I got my dress on and had my makeup and hair done, they both still let out little squeals of happiness.

Griffin has Maddox, Sebastian, Logan, and Ryder acting as groomsmen, but I didn't feel the need to find two other women to act as bridesmaids. Lexi and Isla are the best friend and sister-in-law I could ask for, and they're enough. They'll both just get to be escorted by two hulking hockey players after the ceremony.

It should make for some fun photos.

"You're getting married," Lexi cries.

"Again," Isla adds with a snicker.

"I'm getting married." We may have thrown this wedding together quickly, but it's exactly how Griffin and I pictured it. Despite being the height of the summer, we're getting married outside in the Minnesota Landscape Arboretum in front of a beautiful floral arch, surrounded by trees and flowers and so much beauty I can hardly stand it.

"Let's get you to your groom." Isla hands me my bouquet before grabbing hers.

"You ready to walk me down the aisle, Mom?"

"I'm not sure any parent is fully ready to walk their child down the aisle, but I suppose since you're already married..." My mom chuckles, offering me her hand.

I grab hold of her like I did so many times as a little girl, and with Lexi and Isla leading the way, we walk out of the bridal suite and onto the stone path that will lead me to the man I love. The man who is my future.

Music swells as Lexi walks toward the altar, followed by Isla. Then it's my turn.

"I love you, Mom."

"I love you too, sweetheart. I'm so proud of the woman you've become."

I try to hold back the emotions that clog my throat. "It's all thanks to you."

My mom makes a choked, emotional sound just as the music changes. "Ready?"

Always.

"Ready."

It's almost golden hour, and the sun casts a diffused, warm light over the garden, making it look less like we're in the Twin Cities and more like a faerie wonderland. We pass the smiling faces of our friends and family, but I don't even notice them. I'm too busy drinking in the sight of my husband.

Griffin wears a charcoal gray suit with a lilac tie. It fits him perfectly, showing off the lean lines of his muscular body. His dark blond hair is styled away from his face, and he looks so, so handsome.

Tears shimmer in his eyes as I walk toward him, and my own fill in response to the tremble of his lower lip. No one besides Griffin Wright has ever looked at me this way, and I could wear a burlap sack and he'd still make me feel like the most beautiful woman in the room.

As we come to a stop in front of Griffin, our closest friends, and an officiant dressed as young Elvis in a nod to our first wedding, my mom kisses my cheek, places my hand in Griffin's, and pats him affectionately on the cheek.

"Oh, sunshine," he murmurs, eyes full of love. "Look at you."

GRIFFIN

"It's time." Maddox gives me a knowing grin as he enters the room I've been pacing for the last twenty minutes. "You ready to get out there and get married again?"

Am I ready? I almost sprint out the door.

The guys' laughter floats behind me, but I barely hear it. I only have eyes and ears for her.

Things with Mira have been amazing. We spent too much time away from each other during the postseason, but if we weren't together, we were video chatting or texting nonstop. Being without her for those few weeks was more than enough distance for me, and I've become a stage-five clinger. I'm just careful how I show it. So far, she doesn't seem to mind. And every week that goes by makes me feel a little more settled and less worried that she'll change her mind about us.

As I walk the stone pathway leading to the massive floral arch and the officiant dressed like Elvis, I know that exchanging vows here, in front of our friends and family, will settle me even more.

Soft music begins to play, and the crowd shifts in their seats. I can't be the only one who feels this buzzing sense of anticipation. I swear, the whole world is holding its breath with me while we wait for the woman I'll love for the rest of my life to appear.

Maddox, filling the best man role for me, just like I did last month, gives my shoulder a reassuring squeeze. "I don't know how I didn't realize sooner that you're perfect for her." He clears his throat. "There's not another man in the world I'd entrust my baby sister's happiness to. I'd tell you to take care of her, but you already have been. So I'll just say that I love you, man. And I'm glad you found each other, despite my meddling."

"Love you too, bro," I say, pulling my best friend and now brother-in-law in for a hug.

Then the music grows louder as Lexi walks down the

aisle, and all my focus goes to the stone path that will offer the first glimpse of my wife in her wedding dress.

Ryder stares at his girlfriend like she's the most beautiful woman in the world, and when Isla walks down the aisle next, Madds does the same. At least I'm not the only lovesick fool on this team.

When the music changes and swells, so does my heart. I don't even care if it's cheesy to say; it's the truth. That fucker expands like a balloon full of too much helium, and I may just float away. Or I would, if she didn't keep me tethered to the earth.

Mira is a vision in white as she steps onto the pathway, hand in hand with her mom. The way the sun hits her, I'd swear it was waiting for this moment too. Ethereal light washes my bride in a warm glow that makes the beadwork on her dress shine and the light shimmer on her cheekbones gleam.

Her hair is half down in loose curls with a braided crown framing her face. Little pearls are interwoven in the braid, along with small flowers. Her green eyes find me and widen. Those dark lashes that have tickled my body so many times as she kissed me flutter. Her gown accentuates every sexy curve, and I can't wait to peel it off her body later.

She's stunning. I've never seen anything or anyone more beautiful.

And she's mine.

I'm in a daze as Camila places Mira's hands in mine. Completely lost in my wife's eyes as we stand in front of Elvis, our friends, and family and promise to love and support one another, to be faithful and true, and to spend the rest of our lives together.

The tears in Mira's eyes make them glitter as she speaks. "Griffin, I promise to love you and choose you every day for the rest of my life. To cheer you on louder than anyone else. I promise to laugh at your jokes, no matter how bad they are, and hold you when you cry. You are my best friend and my greatest love, and I will spend the rest of our lives feeling so incredibly lucky that you love me back."

"Mira—" I have to clear my throat because her name comes out choked with emotion, and I'm not ashamed to admit that a tear slips down my face when she reaches out to cup my jaw.

"Mira, you are my sunshine, my light. Just like you chase away the darkness for me, I promise to be your shelter in every storm. I vow to love you, encourage you, and be your biggest supporter in everything you do. I promise to be there in good times and bad, and to never, ever leave. You're my person, my everything, and I love you so much more than I thought humanly possible."

Even though we've both been wearing our wedding bands ever since the press conference, my hand still shakes when I slip it onto her ring finger. There's a weight to this moment I didn't feel when we were drunk and impulsive in Vegas. Some part of me must have realized Mira was it for me that night, but all of me knows it now.

Elvis smiles brightly at both of us and holds up his hands. "And now, by the power vested in me by the King himself and the state of Minnesota, you may kiss your bride."

The audience erupts into cheers and applause as I close the distance between Mira and me, cup the back of her neck with one hand and her jaw with the other, and kiss the hell out of her. It's not a chaste kiss, and our friends cheer even louder when my wife's fingers grip the lapels of my suit jacket and our tongues tangle.

We're both breathing hard as we break apart, and I take a moment to memorize her expression in this perfect moment. Eyes bright and glistening, lips parted, her cheeks flush with happiness.

It's everything. She's everything. And now, she's all mine.

"And now, for the *second* time ever," Elvis says with a wink, "I present to you as husband and wife, Mira and Griffin Graves-Wright!"

Our friends and family stand and cheer, filling the evening air with so much love and support. It's everything I ever could have asked for and more.

"Happy?" Mira whispers as I take her hand and soak it all in for a moment.

"So fucking happy."

"I love you, husband."

Lifting her hand, I kiss it reverently. "I love you, wife."

Then I pull her down the aisle toward the sunset, a party that will last late into the night, and the rest of our lives.

I used to believe I was cursed. But now?

Now I know I was waiting for fate to intervene with a drunken night in Vegas, a little bit of blackmail, and a whole lot of love.

acknowledgments

Thank you for reading Griffin and Mira's story!

I intended to have this book done waaaaay sooner than I did, but the world is a bit of a dumpster fire these days, isn't it? Between the stress of everyday garbage and the fact that I wanted to make sure Griffin and Mira's story was exactly right, it took me a hot minute. Thanks for waiting for them, and for being so enthusiastic about your love for these characters. It will always blow my mind that so many of you adore the Rogues as much as I do.

Now for the people who have helped make this book pretty inside and out. Thank you to my awesome beta readers. Kim, Jen, Amanda, Ashley, Andrea, and Jessica—thank you for helping me spit shine these books. Thank you to Andra and Laura for creating the most beautiful covers in the world. You're both so sweet and talented, and I feel privileged to work with you. Finally, thank you, Autumn, for taking away all of my errant commas and adding them back where they belong.

And as always, everything I do is for my amazing kids. Thanks for being my inspiration, my motivation, and my favorite people on the planet.

about the author

Piper Hale is a Midwestern girl who loves golden-retriever heroes, imperfect heroines, and some coffee with her sugar. She lives with her two crazy (but amazing) kids in the middle-of-the-map USA.

Piper grew up listening to her dad's silly stories at bedtime, became a voracious reader as a child, and never forgot her high school creative writing teacher, who told her she had what it took to write romance. Even if she didn't give it a go until the pandemic.

These days, you'll find Piper writing contemporary romance that's sassy, sexy, and chock-full of cinnamon rolls.

For an up-to date list of Piper's books, please click here or visit https://linktr.ee/piperhale

Going Rogue:

The Love You Win

The Christmas You Crash